TH
SH

Lawyer Brandon Rudd had heard about Colt—but never expected to meet him. Especially in a spot like this.

White slaver Willard Lawson had the drop on all of them—Nathan, Elizabeth Macon, and the newcomer who called himself Colt. Grinning, Lawson told Colt, "I'm aiming at this purty little gal here, so's how about you droppin' yer hog-legs?"

Brandon's heart sank as Colt dropped his Peacemakers. Lawson chuckled and swung his rifle toward Colt, but the scout dived forward, while reaching down the back of his shirt. He did a somersault as the rifle boomed and the bullet cracked by his left ear. His hand flipped and spun a large Bowie knife through the air. It buried itself between the collarbone and shoulder blade of Lawson, who bellowed in pain and fired his rifle again. Colt picked up his gun and put five shots into Lawson. He was dead by the second one.

What they said about the Chief of Scouts was true. But all the odds that Colt had fought in the past were nothing compared to what was stacked up against him, and those around him now, in a place called Canon City, where the law had turned lawless, and guns wrote the rules in bullets and blood.

SIGNET

GREAT MILITARY FICTION
BY DON BENDELL

☐ **CHIEF OF SCOUTS** Rich with the passion and adventure of real history, this novel of the U.S. Cavalry brings forth a hero, worthy of the finest military fiction, who had to work above the law to uphold justice. (176901—$4.50)

☐ **COLT** Christopher Columbus Colt, legendary chief of cavalry scouts, was in for the biggest fight of his life—forced to lead an all-black U.S. Cavalry unit on a suicide mission. And even if the Chief of Scouts could conquer his own doubts, he would still have to reckon with two names that struck fear into the hearts of every frontier man: Victorio and Geronimo, renegade Apache chiefs who led their warriors on a bloody trail. (178300—$4.50)

☐ **HORSE SOLDIERS** In the embattled Oregon territory, Christopher Columbus Colt was a wanted man. General O.O. "One-Armed" Howard, commanding the U.S. Cavalry, wanted this legendary scout to guide his forces in his campaign to break the power and take the lands of the proud Nez Perce. The tactical genius, Nez Perce Chief Joseph needed Colt as an ally in this last ditch face-off. And only Colt can decide which side to fight on ... (177207—$4.50)

*Prices slightly higher in Canada

COYOTE RUN

by

Don Bendell

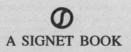

A SIGNET BOOK

SIGNET
Published by the Penguin Group
Penguin Books USA Inc., 375 Hudson Street,
New York, New York 10014, U.S.A.
Penguin Books Ltd, 27 Wrights Lane,
London W8 5TZ, England
Penguin Books Australia Ltd, Ringwood,
Victoria, Australia
Penguin Books Canada Ltd, 10 Alcorn Avenue,
Toronto, Ontario, Canada M4V 3B2
Penguin Books (N.Z.) Ltd, 182-190 Wairau Road,
Auckland 10, New Zealand

Penguin Books Ltd, Registered Offices:
Harmondsworth, Middlesex, England

First published by Signet,
an imprint of Dutton Signet,
a division of Penguin Books USA Inc.

First Printing, November, 1994
10 9 8 7 6 5 4 3 2 1

Copyright © Don Bendell, 1994
All rights reserved
Cover art by Hiram Richardson

Ⓟ   REGISTERED TRADEMARK—MARCA REGISTRADA

Printed in the United States of America

DEDICATION

This book is dedicated to one person: the most important person in my life, the one true stabilizing force when the blizzards have blown across the plains of my existence, the shelter when the gully-washers of pain have crashed into my life, the one who has bandaged my ego when it has been wounded by emotional arrows or business bullets, the one critic who has my best interests only at heart, the one who laughs at my jokes and antics, the one who makes me feel like a protector, the only one in the world who I really want to impress, my soul mate, business partner, best buddy, and sexy mistress, my wife, Shirley Bendell, the one great true love of my life and the best friend that any man could ever have.

Love,
Don Bendell

ACKNOWLEDGMENTS

I wish to thank all the many courageous men and women who were involved in the settling and taming of the Canon City, Colorado, area and added to its colorful history. I also want to thank local historians John Lemons, U. Michael Welch, Byk Banta, Doc Little, Gary Shook and the staff of the Canon City District Library (especially the local history staff), Rosemae Wells Campbell, and Paul Huntley.

Eagles Two

Cock and hen,
  Eagles winging,
    Swirling, circling overhead.
Facing then,
  Black skies bringing,
    Monster storm to wake the dead.

Fighting lightning,
  Cringe at thunder,
    Brave its fury, hearts entwined.
Where is sunshine?
  They both wonder,
    Will it come and ease their mind?

Eagles two,
  Flying, trying,
    Soaring high o'er harvest plains.
Sky so blue,
  Feeling sunlight,
    Climbing up above the rains.

Eagles two,
  They soar together,
    Winging high with iron wills.
Hen dives down
  To catch a rabbit.
    Mate still leads to far-off hills.

Father, mother,
  Friend and lover,
    Eagles two, their hearts shall fly.
Pledging love
  To one another,
    Eagles two, they soar so high.

They will never
  Run from weather,
    Fold their wings and crash below.

Their lives lengthened,
   Love is strengthened
      From the storms and winds that blow.

Eagles two,
   They fly together,
      Struggling towards a distant peak.
Eagles two,
   With tattered feather,
      Climbing high, they brush God's cheek.

—Don Bendell
from *Songs of the Warrior*
(RBF Research Group,
September 1992)

FOREWORD

Although some of the characters in this saga, such as the Colts, are fictional, there were many great families like them who settled the untamed frontier of the American West. Brandon Rudd and Elizabeth Macon are fictional, but the Rudd and Macon families were two of the first pioneer families to settle the Canon City, Colorado, area, and the incidents mentioned in this book about them were true stories and are documented in historical archives, as are most of the anecdotes in this novel.

The author and his family live on a ranch on the side of the mountains overlooking Canon City and surrounding areas and one can walk around the property and pick up arrowheads from the giant encampments of Utes and Cheyennes, mentioned in this book, who used this area as their winter hunting grounds. Bears, elk, mountain lions, and mule deer, which are descendants of those who fed the Utes, Cheyennes, and pioneers in this book, roam all around the author's home.

At night, looking down at the lights of Canon City, Florence, and Penrose, it is very easy to imagine the lights as coming from lanterns and cooking fires. It is easy for the author to ride his horse, Eagle, over the ground that the Colts and the Indian warriors rode on and imagine what went through their minds as they passed through the majestic corridors of granite and marble known as the southern Rockies. The rocks are forever. They have seen many riders pass by them and have many stories to tell.

In the age of computers, rancher-cowboys can still be seen in this area on their horses, pushing cows like their grandfathers and great-grandfathers did. Just like in the time of the Rudds, Macons, and Colts, many modern-day cowboys here still wear chaps, boots, and spurs. Some even still wear guns in holsters on their hips. Occasionally, though, one can be caught wearing a Denver Broncos or Colorado Rockies hat instead of the traditional Stetson. A few can even be caught rounding up cattle with a cellular phone–equipped, all-terrain vehicle, instead of the reliable quarterhorse, but the spirit is still there. The spirit of the American cowboy and pioneer woman. The spirit of the Old West.

If we desire respect for the law,
we must first make the law respectable.

—*Louis D. Brandeis*

Chapter 1

>>>>>>>>>>>>>>>>>>>

The Advocate

Brandon listened to the echoes of the riding heels of his highly polished boots as he strode back and forth on the marble floor. He tried to hit his heels against the floor even harder for a better effect. His eyes went from the stern and puffy face of the judge to the faces of the entranced jurors leaning forward in their chairs.

If the members of the jury were all women instead of all men, maybe his job would have been easier. More than one woman had stopped to admire him as the tall, handsome Brandon Rudd walked by. Although he was a Harvard-educated attorney, his childhood had included many hard hours of work on his father's Missouri farm. He really learned his work ethic at his pa's elbow, following the mule as his father guided the plow straightaway down the cornfield, row after row, over and over again. These lessons were reinforced after his father's sudden and unexpected death at the hands of Porter Wells. Brandon was a lad of only twelve, but he was the oldest child and became the man of the family, taking care of his ma and his six younger sisters and brothers.

It was old Judge Jonathan Stryker who motivated Brandon to take up the study of the law, after the lad appeared before him for shooting his father's assassin.

Porter Wells was a man known for taking a nip or two, or more likely twenty or thirty from a jug of corn squeezings. And he was a man known to have the blackest of hearts when he did so. Riding across the freshly harvested north cornfield of the Rudd farm one crisp autumn day, the drunken killer had been drinking for two days and nights straight and just happened upon the unarmed Jedediah Rudd. The cowardly Wells had pulled out his single-action cap-and-ball and emptied the cylinder in the direction of the hardworking farmer, with two lead balls striking Rudd in the chest. There was no reason for the shooting. It was totally random, and it shocked the countryside. Jedediah Rudd had been one of the those solid men, a man who could be counted on as a friend, as a neighbor.

The young Brandon grabbed his pa's old "meat" gun and went after the cowardly killer. After two days, the boy tracked the drunkard to within sight of the broad brown Mississippi River. Porter Wells decided that a young towheaded pup like Brandon Rudd was certainly no match with any gun for a notorious vicious killer of his repute, so he "grabbed iron."

Porter Wells was wrong. He had no idea how deadly a young man with a lot courage and a lot of principle could be. The killer's blood drained into the Missouri soil as he learned his lesson the hard way.

Brandon Rudd learned a hard lesson that day, too, and in the months to come. He was just a boy, and he had been forced to kill a man. He had to because of a strict moral code his father had raised him by. He had to step in when his father died and grow up in one day. He couldn't tell his ma how the killing bothered him, because that would bother her too much. Brandon would suffer alone with the guilt and the memory of watching the man die.

It would take years of suffering with the pain of taking another's life before Brandon decided that he wished to study the law. He would work hard at school, just the same way he worked hard at anything he did. He would get high marks and would learn the art of advocacy. He came to believe that only by learning and utilizing the laws of civilized man could he help effect a society where men could be free from the fear of being shot down.

It was now some years after making that decision, and the handsome young lawyer strode back and forth on the marble floor. His echoing steps were calculated, as were the pitch of his words. Court was his battlefield. The courtroom was where he now had his showdowns, and he intended to be the "top gun" in the courtrooms of the West.

At this time, he wasn't as far west as he wanted to be. He was in St. Louis, but he was making preparations.

His client sat uneasily in the straight-backed chair behind the mahogany plaintiff's table. The left side of her previously beautiful face puckered by a hideous scar. It was still pink, with traces of a white line starting to run down the middle. Her look was forlorn and the look that Brandon gave her was long, piercing, and full of sympathy and pity. Several of the jurors followed suit.

As Brandon paced back and forth presenting his closing argument, he reached into his right trousers pocket and gave the knife there a reassuring pat.

Brandon Rudd looked over at the defendant's table and grinned. The defendant, Willard Lawson, the president of Lawson Cutlery, was surrounded by three of the highest-priced attorneys that money could buy. He looked confident, even smug, surrounded by his high-priced team of litigators.

"Gentlemen of the jury," Brandon continued, "Willard Lawson, the defendant there, was born with a silver spoon—or I should say a silver knife—in his mouth. His family has made fine knives for years, and he grew up playing with them while other children rolled hoops and played with spinning tops. Knives became such toys to him that, even as a man, he has already tried to impress everyone with his ability to throw, whittle, carve, and handle knives."

He walked over to his client and stood next to her so the jury could get the full effect of looking at his neat appearance and her puckered face.

He went on, "The defendant had a reputation as a bully, braggart, and womanizer, but—"

The chief arbitrator for Lawson, a distinguished gent with a salt-and-pepper mutton-chop mustache, jumped to his feet and yelled, "I object, Your Honor! That's slanderous and preposterous!"

"Sustained."

Brandon continued, "My client only worked for him because she was a poor widow with three children needing the meager earnings badly. We have proven that every day he would slash, cut, chop, and throw knives around her and the other employees to show off. And what happened to her on that one time that he finally slipped up?"

Brandon nodded at two assistants in the back of the courtroom. They came forward with a large square-shaped object covered with a sheet and placed it in front of the jury box. The object was being displayed on an easel, which Brandon now carefully turned so the judge, jury, and rest of the courtroom could all see quite clearly.

With a quick yank of his right hand, the protective sheet was whipped away from the object and there stood a very good quality print of the Mona Lisa. Brandon Rudd froze. He didn't move a muscle, instead letting the jury slowly and carefully study the beautiful piece of artwork. He didn't speak. Didn't move. Instead he waited until several of the jurors began leaning forward slightly, waiting for his next words. The time was right.

"Gentlemen, this is the famous Mona Lisa, or I should actually say a darn good reproduction of same, but what if it were the real Mona Lisa? What would be the value of this painting?"

He turned and smiled at the chief arbitrator for the defense. Several jurors gave each other questioning looks, each wondering how much they actually would charge for such a painting if it were in there possession. He walked over to the other lawyer and stared down at him, then returned to the side of the easel. Except for his heels on the floor, the courtroom was completely silent. The eyes of the jurors finally switched to him, waiting for more words.

Suddenly Brandon's hand came out of his pocket and went high up in the air. As he spun around, several women in the back of the room gasped and the judge, startled, jumped in his seat. His face flushed. The blade in Brandon's grip flashed, and there were several more startled gasps, then screams, as Brandon's powerful arm came down in an arc and the blade tore into the canvas, ripping the cheek out of the face of the Mona Lisa.

The judge rapped his gavel. A woman in the back gasped and fell in a faint, banging her head loudly on the edge of her wooden chair as she fell.

The chief defense counsel again jumped up and shouted, "I object, Your Honor!"

"Overruled!" Came back the judge. "You, sir, and your cronies there have been given quite a bit of latitude in this trial, so sit down and hush that mouth, sir!"

The judge did appreciate good courtroom theatrics, and this young Rudd lad was really becoming talked about in legal circles in the area. The old judge chuckled to himself and even shook his head from side to side.

Brandon continued, "Gentlemen, this was a reproduction of the Mona Lisa, a priceless painting. We couldn't even figure out a cost if the original was slashed, now, could we?"

He walked over to the scarred young woman, gently laid his hand on her shoulder, and went on, "Look at her cheek. Slashed by the defendant's own hand, guided by sheer arrogance and gross negligence. Her cheek is flesh and blood and tissue and can never be repaired. It is not canvas and oil like a painting, even a famous one. What kind of value can you place on her face? Lawson will never be able to say he's sorry enough. He can never pay her enough money for ruining what once was a fresh, innocent, beautiful face."

With this, his scarred client could no longer contain herself and began crying into a hanky. Brandon gave her a reassuring pat on the shoulder.

He added, "How many tear-filled moments will she continue to have like this? You all and I are men. We protect women, not scar them for life. Let that fool pay her for her scars and tears and sleepless nights, Gentlemen. We rest our case, Your Honor."

Brandon Rudd smiled softly at the jury and sat down, pleased by all the angry glances he saw shot in the direction of Lawson. Lawson gave the mutton-chopped attorney a worried glance and received a reassuring pat on the forearm.

It was during the lunch recess, while the sequestered jury deliberated, that Brandon Rudd first saw Elizabeth Macon. She had soft brown hair and eyes that smiled continuously. Brandon and his client were seated in the Bon Ton Café when Elizabeth walked in the door with her fiancé, Linford Crowley, a man who owned a number of barges on the big river.

Elizabeth's eyes met Brandon's, and their gazes held briefly. The young beauty felt a chill ripple up and down her spine, and she quickly looked away. Brandon could barely keep his eyes off her during the meal, but he did pay attention to the conversation with his client. Halfway through the meal a young clerk from the courthouse came in and told Brandon that the jury had already returned with a verdict. Brandon gave the client a smile and pulled her chair out for her. Seeing this, Elizabeth felt a quick flash of jealousy and suddenly felt very foolish. She hoped that Linford didn't notice her even looking in the direction in the man with the nice suit and broad shoulders.

The sum the lady was awarded for her pain and duress would keep her well-heeled the rest of her life. It would even make her quite wealthy and would ruin Willard Lawson. It would also further add to the legendary stature of the handsome young Missouri lawyer.

Leaving the courthouse after the pats on the back, hugs, and handshakes, Brandon Rudd used the back exit. He was quite modest and just wanted to get back to his office to prepare for his next court date. The afternoon was hot and humid and there was no breeze coming across the big river. Brandon really enjoyed that breeze when it blew and wished for it on this day. He whistled and dreamed about traveling to the purple and blue mountains so far, far away. His uncle, Anson Rudd, had been one of the

first settlers of Canon City in Colorado and spoke
about the climate, people, and mountains whenever
he visited on business.

Brandon pictured the rocks, the bighorn sheep, the
elk, and mule deer, the antelope, bison, the angry
churning rapids of the Arkansas River as it dropped
down through the steep-walled canyons and spilled
itself out onto the great prairie with a force that
would send its water all the way to the Gulf of Mexico. In his mind's eye, he saw the clear blue sky his
uncle described that stretched to a distant horizon,
so unlike the sight he was used to in St. Louis.
Anson had told him about standing on various peaks
and seeing across distances that Brandon compared
with so many days of travel in Missouri.

The biggest attraction to Brandon Rudd, however,
was the wildness of the West. It was still an untamed
land: Geronimo was still waging his campaign
against the Army; Custer and Sitting Bull had had
their big fight just a few years earlier; there were
still gunfights and highwaymen and stage robberies.
There had been and were famous gunfighters,
Hickok, John Wesley Hardin, Doc Holliday, the
Earps, Chris Colt, Bat Masterson. It was romantic to
Brandon and a bit unsettling. The law was still not
established in many parts of that untamed land and
Brandon Rudd believed in the law. He wanted to im-
prove the law and the country where it was blos-
soming. He knew and believed strongly that the law,
not the gun, was the real way to tame that wild land.
The dashing young attorney just wanted to be a part
of it.

He was only a few steps from the false-front
building that housed his law office, when he saw her
again. She was walking toward him on the arm of
Linford Crowley. It was the second time in one day,

and Elizabeth Macon was the most beautiful creature he had ever laid eyes on.

Elizabeth was in midsentence and midstride when her eyes drifted up and she again saw the tall, handsome, well-dressed man headed in her direction. Her face flushed and her eyes dropped as she felt a sudden twinge of guilt. After all, she was on the arm of her betrothed, and the sight of this stranger was making her heart pound in her ears and temples. Elizabeth suddenly realized her chest was rising and falling as if she had just run around the perimeter of St. Louis twenty times.

What a gorgeous woman, Brandon thought. They were just a few paces apart now.

Linford saw the way the stranger stared at his woman and was angry inside. He would carefully maintain his facade in front of Elizabeth. However, he thought about how he would love to take this dude down to the waterfront and teach him all about "knuckle and skull" fighting. Elizabeth thought he had inherited his wealth and didn't really know that he had actually won the first of his fleet of barges while fighting for wagers on the river.

Linford had never been beaten by anybody in a rough-and-tumble fight. When he won the first three barges, he had put up all of his savings from previous battles against the title to the three boats. Although he was tough, he wanted to ensure success, so he paid his opponent's corner man to use a towel that was soaked in a powerful solution that caused lethargy and weakness. Many in the crowd could tell that there had been foul play, but Linford's repute for vengeance and violence was such that not a man in the wagering crowd questioned the tactics by Crowley's corner.

The fleet of barges was also a cover for a white slavery operation where pretty young girls were smuggled out of the country and eventually shipped to Linford's partner in Mexico, who peddled the girls off to wealthy businessmen from various countries. It was a very lucrative and secret undertaking, and Elizabeth Macon had no clue. She had been told that Linford Crowley was a very proper and wealthy businessman. He was always a gentleman to her and seemed well-heeled, proper, and educated. He had lavished her with expensive gifts, love poetry, and gifts of anything she even mentioned. It really had been quite overwhelming to Elizabeth, but there was still something about him that made her want to move a little bit slowly with their romance. She could not quite figure it out, but she knew there was something amiss. Now seeing this handsome stranger made her feel even more uncomfortable, and she didn't know why.

Elizabeth was the one classy, beautiful part of Linford's life that he somehow thought would give him respectability. She would not be shipped south. He didn't want to be a white slaver, but it was simply a way to make a lot of money fast, for he wanted to be accepted and respected by people. He never had that respect growing up along the docks of New York, son of a prostitute.

They were only two paces apart now when they heard a sharp *crack,* followed by a soft *whump.* A bullet passed between the three people and Brandon Rudd dove at the young lady, covering her with his body and knocking her backward, landing on top of her. She screamed, and he gently placed his palm over her mouth, looking all around. She understood he was trying to place the source of the gunshot, so she kept quiet. He remained there covering her body with his.

In the meantime, Linford pulled out a hidden Smith & Wesson pocket .32 which had been hidden from view in a shoulder holster under his armpit. His eyes scoured the windows across the street, and so did a town constable who was nearby when the shooting occurred.

The constable spotted a man behind a dry goods sign across the street, and he ran in that direction while the head and shoulders of the man disappeared behind the sign. More constables headed toward the would-be assassin as they responded to the first officer's whistle.

Turning his head before the shooter ducked down, Brandon recognized him. It was Willard Lawson. Unhappy with the prospect of losing his family fortune to the woman whose cheek he had slashed, he apparently had decided to rid the world of the golden-tongued devil responsible for causing him to lose all his money and holdings.

Brandon stood and helped Elizabeth Rudd up, tipping his hat to her at the same time.

"Are you okay, miss?" he asked.

"Yes," she said, quite upset and traumatized, "I believe so. Thank you, sir. What happened?"

"I'm afraid, miss," he replied, "that a gentleman named Lawson was trying to shorten my life considerably, and unfortunately you and your companion were close to the line of fire."

"Why would he want to kill you?"

"I'm afraid I just cost him a great deal of money," Brandon said, "and he apparently has taken exception to it."

"How did you cost him so much?" she asked, "Are you a professional gambler or something like that?"

Brandon smiled warmly and replied, "Something like that, ma'am. Excuse me, my name is Brandon Rudd. Are you sure you're okay?"

"She's fine; my fiancée is fine, mister," Linford

Crowley snapped while walking up and holstering his pistol.

Brandon's face flushed when Crowley emphasized the word *fiancée*. He didn't like the shape of this man or his attitude. He smiled softly and said, "It's good you finally decided to check on her safety, since she is your intended, sir."

Linford's lips curled back in a snarl, and he subconsciously reached for his gun.

Virginia interrupted, "Linford, why are you carrying a weapon? I never knew you even owned a gun."

He was angry, and it was all he could do to maintain his phony demeanor in front of Elizabeth.

"Not now, Elizabeth. I'll explain later."

Brandon offered his hand to her. "Elizabeth is it? What a lovely name."

She blushed, and Linford flushed in anger again.

"Elizabeth Macon," she replied. "This is my fiancé, Linford Crowley, and I am sure he appreciates that you saved my life, Mr. Rudd. With this incident, I believe he has just forgotten his manners."

Linford was stuck now and could do nothing other than offer his hand. Brandon took it and the two shook with grips that were a bit too firm, and there was a deep smoldering fire as the two men stared into each other's eyes while politely smiling and nodding to each other.

Crowley had just started to speak when there was a commotion at the mouth of an alley almost directly across from the trio. Willard Lawson, breathing hard and bleeding from the nose and right ear, was led from the alleyway, in manacles, by three constables. He spotted Brandon Rudd and started screaming curses.

The constables led him across the street straight up to the trio.

The original law officer on the scene walked up to them to speak and gave a glance at the other constables. They clubbed the still-cursing Lawson across the back twice, and he decided that silence was a better choice.

The constable said, "Aye, and so his target was you, Mr. Rudd. 'Tis normally the young ladies yer attractin', good sir, but now 'tis bullets. Are the three of ya in good shape, with no holes in yer expensive clothing?"

Brandon laughed and shook hands with the constable, saying, "Yes, Constable Muldoon, we are all fine. Good work."

Lawson snapped, "And you and your client can both rot in hell, Brandon Rudd! You may have got her my family inheritance, but someday you'll feel the steel of my blade!"

"Client," Linford said. "What is he talking about?"

Muldoon said, "I would wager, sir, that this supposed assassin is yet another victim of the sharp wit and brilliant courtroom tactics of this fiery young attorney yer 'ere with on this dusty street."

"Attorney?" Crowley said.

"I believe very strongly in the law of the land," Brandon said.

He then wondered why he made such a statement. Was he trying to get under this man's skin? Why was he so irritated that this Crowley character was engaged to such a beautiful and classy young woman?

"Aye, Mr. Rudd, I'll be askin' ya and yer friends 'ere to come to the station and make a statement for me, if ya don't mind," Muldoon said.

The three escorted him to the police station, just

one block away. Crowley kept Elizabeth away from the tall arbitrator. He had noticed how his betrothed had stared at the attorney and Linford did not like it one bit. He wanted to keep her far away from the man and get her out of that station as soon as possible.

An hour later, as they were leaving the station, the two were halted by Brandon Rudd's voice. As he ran down the hall toward them, Elizabeth could not help but notice the athletic movement of his body, the width of his shoulders, and the broadness of his chest. Every time she looked at him, her breath was simply taken away, and she still felt extremely guilty for it.

Reaching them, Brandon stuck his hand out and shook again with Linford Crowley, then took Elizabeth's hand and kissed it while staring into her eyes. She tried to slow her quickening breath and felt sure that it was visible to all in the police station. Brandon handed each of them one of his business cards and couldn't miss the angry stare from Crowley after kissing Elizabeth's hand.

"I'm sorry that my troubles involved and inconvenienced both of you, but I hope this is over. May I take you both to dinner?"

"No," Crowley said, "I think we've had enough excitement for one—"

"Nonsense, Linford," Elizabeth interrupted. "After what happened, I think we should all share dinner and discuss what happened."

"Elizabeth," Crowley said angrily, "This day has produced too much excitement for you, I'm afraid, and I really should see you home."

Brandon said, "Miss Macon seems quite feminine but not too fragile, it looks to me, Mr. Crowley."

"Well, whatever she is, Rudd," Linford snapped, "it is none of your concern."

Elizabeth snapped now. "Linford!"

"No, Elizabeth," he said angrily, "I don't like it at all. Don't you see how he's trying to manipulate you?"

"Excuse me," said Brandon, "I'm sorry if my suggestion has angered you, but I do not believe I deserve to be insulted."

Really upset now, Crowley responded, "Nobody cares what you believe, Rudd. If Elizabeth wasn't here, I would snap you like a twig."

"Funny thing about teak wood," Brandon said calmly.

This made Linford cock his head to one side. Angrily, he said, "What does that have to do with anything?"

Staring Crowley hard in the eyes, Rudd said, "Heaviest wood in the world. Doesn't even float in water. Just to look at it, you would think you could break a stick of it in half, but the appearance many times is quite deceiving. You try to snap the stick and instead end up breaking your bones in the process."

Brandon tipped his hat to Elizabeth and said, "Miss Macon." He turned and started to leave but Crowley was beyond the flash point now. He took several steps forward and spun Brandon around by his arm. The cold stare he got sent a chill down to his black soul.

Brandon said softly, "Mr. Crowley, anger and words are one thing. Violence is another. I don't hold with it and will not put up with it, either."

Crowley gave a phony laugh and said, "What are you, Rudd, a damned coward?"

Brandon smiled softly again and said, "Why don't

you ask you fiancée? I was protecting her while you were busy looking for someone to fight with."

He again doffed his hat at Elizabeth, then turned and walking away. Linford Crowley didn't know what to say or how to respond, so he stood there doing a long slow burn. Elizabeth looked up at him and gave him an angry sigh, then turned on her heels and stormed away. He followed after her.

"Elizabeth!" he pleaded.

The next day Brandon received by courier an invitation to dinner with the couple. A Pinkerton detective, called the "eye," had already gotten back to Brandon with preliminary information about Linford Crowley when the lawyer had received the invitation. Brandon raised his eyebrow when he looked at the detective's report and saw that Crowley was indeed the unsavory character he suspected him to be. He was equally certain that the beautiful young lady had no idea how nasty Crowley really was.

He looked at the invitation and smiled, thinking how much Linford probably fought sending it. They were inviting him as their guests to dinner at a waterfront restaurant along the river called the Cajun House. It was quite popular with those in the know in St. Louis. Owned and operated by Creole French folks from New Orleans, it featured some wonderful Creole meals and had a fine imported wine list. Brandon had eaten there before and recalled how nice it was as long as one did not have his carriage break down on the way to or from; There were many seedy dives in the area, too. It was an exclusive restaurant, though, and even the chief of police dined there, so the lowlifes kept their distance.

Brandon decided this would be an opportune time to have the new suit made that he'd been considering. The tailor came by his office and fitted him; Brandon opting for a less conservative look, wanting deep down to impress Elizabeth. He chose a dark green double-breasted suit with an Edwardian collar.

Brandon couldn't wait for Saturday to arrive, and many of his waking thoughts were of Elizabeth Macon, who had obviously stolen his heart. He did not care that she was engaged to Linford Crowley. Brandon could tell that Elizabeth was intelligent; he figured that Linford would hang himself, given enough rope. The only thing he was really bothered about was the fact that the man would stop at nothing to gain what he wanted, including the hand of Elizabeth Macon.

On Saturday morning, Brandon Rudd went to the tonsorial parlor and got a hair trim, while the bootblack put a nice spit shine on his black high-top riding boots. When the time came to leave for dinner, the advocate stopped and placed the knife from the courtroom in his pocket, just for a little extra protection.

Brandon did everything he could to avoid carrying a gun. He did own an eighteen-shot Winchester .45 carbine for hunting, a standard Colt Peacemaker .45 for home defense, and a sawed-off American Arms twelve-gauge shotgun in his office. It had the stock sawed off, so there was just a pistol grip and the barrel was only about one foot long. That was hidden under his desk just in case there was trouble from sore losers like Willard Lawson who didn't play by the rules. As much as Brandon Rudd hated guns, he was not a fool and knew that some people knew nothing other than settling scores outside the law. He did, however, plan to go to the greatest lengths possible to avoid ever having to use a gun again against his fellow man.

Brandon Rudd didn't own a horse, although he

was an excellent horseman. He had no need for one, preferring to walk most anywhere or taking a carriage or buggy sometimes at night when going out for entertainment or with one of the many young ladies he was seen with around town. He took a carriage to the Cajun House.

The dinner was enjoyable; Brandon relished the blackened red fish, vegetables, and a salad. Elizabeth was radiant in a red velvet gown with white lace that squeezed at her tiny waistline and showed enough cleavage to make him wish he were not a gentleman and could stare all night long.

The one thing that really bothered Brandon, though, was how friendly Linford Crowley acted. The moment Brandon arrived, Linford stuck out his hand, big grin on his face, and had been extremely friendly ever since. Rudd knew that the man was not doing all this just to please Elizabeth. It was too much against his character.

Something was amiss, and it kept the attorney feeling unsettled all night. That was not all that upset Brandon. So did the looks of Elizabeth Macon. He could hardly keep his eyes off her. Her eyes held a sparkling zest for life that just glowed whenever she smiled. They could also penetrate deep into his soul, he thought, when he was saying something serious. Listening to Elizabeth speak, Brandon could also tell that she was very intelligent, and he loved that in a woman. Many men he knew wanted a woman who could cook, sew, and make babies, but didn't care about carrying on a decent conversation. That way, Brandon figured, they wouldn't have to worry about having their authority questioned in any way. It made them feel much more secure. But he wanted someone he could just sit and talk with for hours about a variety of subjects. He wanted a woman who had a brain and could make decisions to help make it successfully through life, which could become quite challenging at times.

Brandon just could not accept that Elizabeth would actually marry Linford Crowley. She seemed too smart to not see through the crooked millionaire, and Brandon was positive that somehow, some way, she eventually would. After an after-dinner drink and a cup of coffee, Brandon Rudd explained that he had to get up early the next morning for a promised fishing excursion with a local judge.

He rose to leave and shook hands with Crowley, who was still overly friendly and cordial. Brandon kissed the back of Elizabeth's hand and there was, he was sure, a hidden promise in her glance. If it wasn't there, he certainly wanted it to be there. Linford called for his carriage, as did Brandon and the two men waited with Elizabeth standing between them.

A man came out of the shadows and walked up to Brandon. The man was old and rough-looking, his face lined with too many years of staring at the sun. Half of his left ear was missing and another deep scar ran lengthwise down the side of his temple and cheek. He was dressed like a sailor and had the smell of the big river on him. A corncob pipe was firmly clenched in his teeth.

He spoke softly. "Aye, 'tis you, laddie, Brandon Rudd. Watch yerself this evenin,' me boy."

The man turned and started to walk away, but was stopped by Brandon's voice.

"Why are you warning me, and what are you talking about?"

" 'Member, laddie, a case you won fer an old widow woman named Alicia MacGregor?"

Brandon nodded.

The old man gave him a wink. He turned again to leave, but Brandon again stopped him.

"But what are you warning me about?"

The old man looked over at Linford Crowley, frowned, glanced at Brandon, smiled and winked, then turned once more and disappeared into the night.

Elizabeth said, "What a strange man. I wonder what he meant by all that?"

Linford smiled and said, "Crazy talk, my dear, That's all."

Brandon, not wanting to alarm Elizabeth, said, "He's right. It was just crazy talk."

The hoofbeats of two horses could be heard on the planks of the riverside street. Crowley's carriage pulled up, driven by a Negro driver with gray hair and a black suit. Rudd held the door open while Linford gave Elizabeth a lift into the carriage. They nodded and Crowley gave Brandon a last smile and wave that made the lawyer feel a chill run down his spine.

The young man who handled the buggies and carriages ran up to Brandon and said, "Mr. Rudd, sir, your buggy is gone. Two men took off with it from the stables out back where we hold them. I'm sorry, sir. I just gave chase, but they were ahead too far."

Brandon smiled at the upset lad and said, "Not to worry, son. I rented that rig earlier, and I'm sure that it will eventually end up back at the stable. Can you hail me a buggy ride?"

"Sir, it's late and they don't venture here much, I'm afraid."

"That's okay," Rudd said. "The moon is out and its a nice evening for walking."

He stuck a couple of coins in the young man's hand and walked off, whistling.

"Do be careful, sir. This is like the wilderness, Mr. Rudd—and thank you, sir!"

Still whistling, Brandon stuck up his right hand and waved without looking back. He couldn't really blame the boy for what had happened. He knew something was up and was now certain that the scoundrel Linford Crowley had probably arranged to sic some of his hounds on him. The question was simply when and how would he handle it.

Brandon could have stayed at the restaurant and waited for a more opportune time to leave or could have watched for a constable to walk by at some point and walk with him, but it just wasn't in him to handle things like that. As much as he abhorred violence and lawlessness, he hated cowardice even more.

All his senses were alert as he walked along the darkened riverfront. He heard the sounds of fights and songs and drunken cheering from many of the seedy joints along the way. In the distance, two dogs barked incessantly. Brandon watched darkened doorways and alleys, but when the attackers finally came, they seemed to appear from out of nowhere. Two shadowy figures appeared in the street in front of him and a rustle of clothing made him start to turn when something struck him hard on the back of the head.

He felt his knees buckle, and he heard men running up to him from the front and rear. His head was spinning and he shook it quickly to try to clear his vision. A boot kicked him in the ribs and he lost his wind, hearing a couple ribs crack with the vicious blow. Brandon fought back panicky feelings.

One of the men attacking him said, "Crowley said he should have money on him. He said take it and dump his body in the river with some chains wrapped around it."

Brandon thought to himself that they would not have such an easy time of it. Head clearing, he tried to stand, but a boot kicked his shin out sideways, the lawyer falling flat on his face. Another kick caught him on the hip and another on the left biceps. He felt his temper flaring and knew he had to move fast and hard or he was dead.

His hand went into his pocket and grabbed the knife handle. He rolled on his side, inviting a kick to the chest or stomach, and he saw a leg being cocked. His hand came out of the pocket, the blade flashing. He pointed it at the oncoming leg, and the man impaled his shin onto the blade of the deadly little weapon. He let out a scream of pain and grabbed his shin, falling to the ground.

In the meantime, Brandon rolled and jumped to his feet. Another man came at him and the lawyer sidestepped and slashed the man's right forearm with the knife. That man grabbed his arm and screamed in pain, running off into the night.

There were two left. Brandon replaced the knife in his pocket, making sure he could still get to it easily. He pulled out some bills.

He held them out to the closest attacker and said, "Here's my money. Take it but please don't hurt me anymore. My ribs are broken."

The man said, "Sure."

He reached for the money and his big hand closed on it while his other held a spring-loaded blackjack ready to club Brandon into death. As he tightened his fingers on the currency, Brandon's right foot came out and up and caught the man squarely in the middle of his groin. The man's air left him with a rush. He swung wildly and his fist caught Brandon on the left cheek, sending him reeling. The attorney recovered quickly and ran three steps and jumped up, both feet tucking up to his chest and kicking out, catching the big man on the chin and cheek. He flew backward and fell twenty feet into the big Mississippi River.

The other rushed Brandon and the lawyer rolled again and jumped to his feet, raising his hands in a boxer's stance.

"Boxer, are you?" the big man said.

In the darkness, the man was a giant shadow that looked like a mountain to Brandon.

The attorney replied, "Harvard boxing team."

The man chuckled and said, "Marquis of Queensberry won't help you here, Boy. On the river, we fight to win."

Brandon stopped and put up his hands, saying, "Well, we do have to have one rule."

The man stopped and said, "What's that?"

Brandon grabbed a plank lying across a barrel and said, "Well we set this plank down here."

He bent over and started to lay the plank on the street, but suddenly struck straight up with it under the man's jaw. The big man went up on his toes, his teeth clicking together loudly. Brandon then swung the plank like a club, the side of it catching the side of the moose's kneecap and sending his feet flying out sideways. He collapsed in a heap, yelling in pain.

Brandon said, "I always fight to win."

With that, he swung the plank again and hit the big man on the head, knocking him out cold.

He looked down at the moaning man with the stab wound in the shin and said, "I want you to give Linford Crowley a message for me."

The man angrily snapped back, "What?"

Brandon brought the board down over the man's head with a crash. He, too, fell unconscious. The attorney brushed his clothing and walked away, again whistling.

Brandon could hear the moans of the semiconscious men behind him, then the shuffling of footsteps. He wheeled and stared down the barrel of a Colt Russian .44. The man holding it had a cruel face and wore expensive clothing. He was average size and had brown hair and brown eyes, but the eyes were deep and simply looked evil.

The man spoke, "*Tres bien*, Monsieur Rudd. Your performance was most eempresseeve. You are quite a fighter, *n'est-ce pas?*"

"Who are you?"

"Oh, *pardon moi*," the man went on, "my name ees André Breton. I am een business weez Linford Crowley. We deal weez beautiful young ladies. Een fact, we take a load of zem in zee morning, and you shall escort us partway to Mexico."

André chuckled and said, "By zee way, Monsieur Rudd, how well do you sweem?"

He laughed even harder at his joke.

Pointing with his pistol, André said, "Okay, monsieur. Zere ees a buggy around zee corner. We must not have you walk een such a dangerous part of town, *n'est-ce pas?*"

When they reached the buggy, they were met by men dressed in black. Brandon turned his head to say something to André, and all he saw was the pistol right before it crashed down on his head.

Linford walked Elizabeth to her door, and she turned, a big smile on her face.

She said, "Oh, Linford, I'm so proud of you. I was so upset before at how jealous you acted toward Mr. Rudd, but tonight you were cordial and funny and interesting. I'm glad."

He smiled and gave her a kiss. She gave him a slight wave and turned, entering her doorway.

"Good night," she whispered.

He smiled broadly and said, "Good night, my dear."

Crowley wheeled and walked back to his buggy, whistling the song "Dixie" as he walked.

Brandon looked at the bear as it chased after him across the cornfield. He knew, from his pa's prior warnings, not to try to climb a thick tree, because bears could, too. He spotted a thirty-foot sapling with an eight-inch-thick trunk and jumped on it, pulling with his arms and pushing with his wrapped legs. He shinnied up the tree and let out a squeal as the angry sow swiped at his leg, her claws ripping through his trousers leg.

Her two little cubs watched with interest as the bear kept swiping at the boy's leg, just missing. Brandon's muscles wanted to give out and let him down the tree, but the boy was strong-minded. He held and held and started to cry.

"Pa!" he yelled. "Help me, Pa!"

Brandon kept yelling for his pa over and over while crying his eyes out. His arms and legs started to give, and he looked down at the big she-bear, frightened to death.

He opened his eyes and looked all around. Brandon felt the rocking of the boat and saw young women and girls, some asleep, laying all around him on big canvas bags of rice. They were in the hold of a ship. His head ached terribly, and he had no idea what was happening. Brandon kept looking around, a blank expression on his face, and he tried to figure out what was happening to him. He suddenly realized that someone was rubbing his forehead with a wet cloth and he looked up at the innocent faces of two teenage girls smiling down at him. One was holding his head in her lap and they both were wiping his forehead with wet rags.

He sat up suddenly and stared at them. One had bright red hair and the other was blond.

The redhead said, "Well, mister, you finally woke up. We wondered if you ever would. My name is Mary Nelle Meredith and this is Clara Lamborn."

"Where are we?" he asked, still confused.

Mary Nelle said, "We are in the hold of a ship in the Gulf of Mexico. All of us girls have been kidnapped and they are taking us to Mexico or Central America to sell us as . . . as slaves."

Tears welled up in her eyes and Brandon said softly, "Don't you worry. We'll get you out of this somehow. What happened to me?"

She said, "When you were brought in, you were knocked out with a nasty bump and cut on the back of your head. You came to twice and both times you tried to fight them and they knocked you out with clubs again. The last time I thought they had killed you. You have been knocked out for days. Clara and I have been taking care of you and giving you water and food every time you've started coming around."

"Thank you very much," Brandon said. "It is really hard for me to realize what happened because everything is very hazy and I cannot remember anything. I have a bad headache and I feel very frustrated."

Clara said, "The back of your head is healing, but you have a lump above your right ear and another right on top of your head from the other two times they hit you."

Brandon reached up and touched the spots, wincing while he did.

Mary Nelle went on, "They said that they want you awake when they kill you. I believe they intend to kill you before we get off the sea. André Breton and the others keep making cruel jokes about sharks and other things and what they will do to you."

Brandon said, "Is Linford Crowley aboard?"

"Linford Crowley!" Clara said, "Why, was he kidnapped, too?"

"Kidnapped!" Brandon said. "He is André Breton's partner!"

Mary Nelle exclaimed, "I knew it! I told my father not to have business dealings with him. I just didn't feel right about the man."

Clara said, "Well, I like him, but he had a business deal with my father, too."

Brandon said, "I just can't believe that St. Louis could have so many kidnappings of young girls that are apparently tied in with Linford Crowley and nobody has caught on."

"St. Louis!" Clara said. "What does St. Louis have to do with it?"

Rudd said, "You aren't from St. Louis?"

"No, I'm from Pittsburgh."

"What about you, Mary Nelle?"

Mary Nelle replied, "I'm from a little place in Kentucky, not far from Cincinnati."

With a sudden realization, Brandon said, "Along the Ohio River, which leads to the Mississippi, just like the three rivers in Pittsburgh lead to the Ohio River."

Brandon looked at the twelve other girls in the hold of the ship and said, "How many of you live near either the Mississippi River or a large tributary that pours into the Mississippi?"

Every one of the girls raised her hand, and they looked at each other in amazement.

Rudd then asked, "How many of you know if your family had any business dealings with a Linford Crowley shortly before your kidnapping?"

Five girls raised their hands. Brandon figured the

others simply didn't get involved in their fathers' business dealings.

Brandon said, "Amazing. He has traveled up and down the rivers making supposedly legitimate business deals and is actually looking all the time for young girls to kidnap. Well, our first challenge will be to get free. Then we'll deal with Mr. Crowley."

Mary Nelle asked, "But how are we going to get out?"

Brandon said, "I don't know yet. How big is this ship? How many crew members?"

Clara said, "Two large masts and some smaller ones. I don't know how many men, but they are all very scary. One tried to attack that girl over there and André Breton stabbed him in the stomach with a knife and killed him in front of us yesterday."

Mary Nelle said, "He yelled at the crew and said that nobody was going to spoil the merchandise. There must be ten or so men in the crew. They all carry knives and some have guns in their belts. One is dark-colored and has a short thick curved sword."

Brandon stood up and looked around the hold, listening to the creaking of the ship. It wasn't rocking too much, so he figured there must be calm seas outside. He looked around for something to use as a weapon, but there were only some crates and a couple of buckets to be used for the girls' body wastes. There was one bucket in the corner with water and a dipper for drinking.

Brandon heard a latch above starting to open, and he ran to the two girls and lay down, feigning unconsciousness. He squinted through his closed eyes and saw André and a large sailor coming down the ladder from above. They reached the bottom and walked toward him. He closed his eyes and breathed slowly.

He heard André's voice. "He still alive, leetle girl?"

"Yes, sir, I think so," Clara replied.

"Has he awakened yet?"

"No, sir," she said.

"Sacrebleu," André said.

He turned and walked away, followed up the ladder by the other man.

Brandon jumped up and went over to the wooden wall on one side of the hold to look through a crack where light was shining in. He saw nothing but blue water. Followed by Mary Nelle and Clara, he went to the other side of the ship and looked through another crack. There, about a mile off, he saw land. It might have even been less than a mile.

Brandon looked at the girls and said, "How many of you cannot swim?"

Five girls raised their hands, including Mary Nelle.

"How many can swim really well?"

Four others raised their hands.

Brandon said, "Somehow, I'm going to figure out a way to get us off this boat. It looks like an easy swim to shore, and when the time comes, I want each of you who can swim well to tie up with one who can't and help her. Mary Nelle, you go with me."

She nodded, and he went on, "When the time comes, everyone grab anything that floats, make toward shore, and don't panic."

"What are you going to do?" Clara asked.

Brandon said, "I'm going to have faith that we will make it."

He kept looking around the room desperately, searching for a solution. It did not matter that there were ten or more hardened men ready to kill him and the girls if they tried to escape. It did not matter that he was a man of letters, not guns and violence. Brandon Rudd did not give up when his mind was made up. He also would go to any moral lengths to win when he believed in what he was doing. That was just the way he was.

He knew that he was in the midst of more than a dozen kidnapped teenage girls, and he was probably the only man in miles who would even care that they needed to be rescued. He also knew that he would be killed, probably tortured first, as soon as André found out he was awake. He was also the only adult captive and felt totally responsible for saving these young ladies.

Brandon had an idea and rushed to the ladder. He summoned Mary Nelle and Clara and the three pulled on the edge of the fourth rung from the bottom. In two minutes, it started coming loose. They yanked harder and the board came free. They next pried loose the bottom board. Brandon set it aside, then asked Mary Nelle for several strands of her long red hair. She started pulling them out and he used them as little threads to tie the fourth-from-the-bottom board back into place.

Brandon knelt down behind a bag of rice near the bottom of the ladder and waited, the extra ladder rung in his hands. The two girls knelt near him and sensed that they shouldn't talk. They stayed there for a half an hour, only occasionally standing to stretch their legs and backs.

Finally Brandon heard the hatch being unlatched and his heart skipped a beat. It beat loudly in his temples and he could hear it like a giant bass drum. He started breathing hard and caught himself, concentrating on relaxing. He knew he had to keep a clear head or die.

Brandon watched and saw the legs of one sailor coming down the ladder first, then the legs of a larger crewman. The first sailor stepped on the rigged ladder rung and it gave way, sending him to the floor. Brandon concentrated on the other sailor, though, jumping up and grabbing the large man's ankle. The man came crashing down and hit the floor of the hold with a thud. Brandon swung the board hard and hit him in the temple, knocking him out cold. Something burned him across the back of his left shoulder and he swung around and hit the first man across the face with the board, the two nails sticking out ripping the sailor's cheek open. He swung it back the other way and hit the man solidly with the end of the board, rendering him unconscious.

Clara and Mary Nelle did not wait for instructions. They immediately searched the prone men for weapons. Clara tore off a strip from her petticoat and ran to Brandon.

"Hold still," she said, "you've been slashed by a knife."

Brandon looked back and saw a crimson streak across his shoulder blade. She wrapped the strip around his shoulder diagonally and tied it off. He thanked her and ran to the prostrate men.

Mary Nelle checked the neck of the larger one and said, "He's dead."

Brandon felt a chill run down his spine, then thought again that it had been either him or the man. This was survival.

They tied up the other man and gagged him. Brandon was handed the pair of knives taken from the culprits. One knife was a long sheath knife with brass knuckle handle. The other was a long throwing dagger, which he handed to Mary Nelle. Clara found a derringer, a Colt's first model .41 in the pocket of the other one. She proudly showed it to Brandon, then clutched it tightly in her hand. One of the other girls took the ladder-rung club that Brandon had used, while yet another grabbed the other rung.

They all sat around the bottom of the ladder and waited. They knew that another sailor or two would be sent if the first two didn't show up. It turned out even better than they had hoped. Two more came down the ladder and the first was André Breton. Brandon repeated his earlier actions, rendering the second man unconscious first, then turning on Breton.

Brandon gave the frightened Creole a sadistic sneer as he brandished the brass-knuckle knife. André started to reach back for his own and Brandon smiled broadly. He said, "Please do."

"Yes, please do, Mr. Breton," Clara said as she cocked her newfound derringer and stuck it against the kidnapper's temple.

He raised his hands slowly as another girl stripped him of weapons. Brandon stepped forward and held the point of his knife against André's throat. A drop of blood appeared on the end of the blade. Breton started sweating profusely.

"So, you have me, monsieur," André said nervously. "Keel me and have done weeth eet."

Brandon said. "Believe me, I want to, André, but I am saving you."

"Que est ce c'est?"

Brandon said, "You are going to testify in court against Linford Crowley."

"But why would I do that?" André asked.

Brandon smiled and said, "Breton, I have stood for the justice system my whole adult life, but when I think what you have had planned for these fine innocent young ladies . . . let me put it this way: If you go to prison, you could get out someday or maybe even escape. If you do not testify, though, I will turn you over to the fathers of some of these girls. I have the power to get the court to release you into my custody, and I will do it. Do you doubt me?"

Completely frightened now, André looked all about him and shook his head no.

From André and the other man, the girls and Brandon got two more knives and two more pistols. André was gagged and a stick was placed behind his back with his arms wrapped around it and tried securely.

Brandon checked the knots and smiled, saying, "Sure hope you can swim this way. If not, you won't have to testify."

Brandon led the way and pulled André behind him with a rope leash as the rest of the girls followed. He went up the ladder and out onto the deck of the ship, followed by André—who had to be helped up the ladder—and the girls.

At first they were not noticed, but one sailor turned and stared into the business end of a Smith & Wesson Frontier .44-.40, held in the right hand of Brandon Rudd. He raised his hands. Brandon silently signaled with his gun and the man descended into the hold.

The escapees stood on the deck and simply waited for men to appear like that, and two more were sent into the hold. The latch was set and Brandon led the girls to two lifeboats on the side of the ship. They were lowered into the water by the several remaining crewmen, who also lost their guns and knives and performed their good deed facing the barrel of Brandon's guns. Brandon waited until André Breton was loaded and held at gunpoint by Clara, and the rest of the girls were safely in the boats.

Brandon held two guns on the remaining men and escorted them to the hatch for the cargo hold. He told them to climb in and left the latch open. He then kicked the rungs off the top of the ladder and finally kicked the ladder support boards loose. Next he went over near the cabins and grabbed some lanterns and lit them. He walked back to the hatch and looked down into the hold.

He held the lanterns up to the men and said, "I'm leaving the hatch open. Hope you boys can figure a way out of there before the whole ship is one big ball of flame. Good day."

He heard a gruff voice from the hold yell, "You're a dead man, Rudd!"

Brandon looked down into the hold again, smiling sadistically. He had had it with these kidnappers of young girls.

"I shouldn't be hard to find. Just swim toward land. Of course, if you get there, you might learn that I can do better for myself on dry land. If you don't make it, I hope all of you think about the costs of the practice of kidnapping young girls and selling them as slaves."

With that, he tossed one lantern into the air toward one end of the ship and the other lantern toward the other end. Flames were soon shooting up into the air and fire started climbing a mast and large sail. Brandon went over the side and the girls started rowing toward shore. André Breton's gag was removed while all watched the ship slowly go up in flames. When they were about halfway to shore, they could make out the sight of sailors jumping overboard.

André Breton sneered at Brandon and said, "*Mais oui, mon ami*, you weel soon be dead now. My men weel rescue me and we weel roast you over zee fire, very slowly."

Brandon cocked his pistol and pointed it at the Creole, saying, "Maybe I'll just shoot you dead now, then."

The color drained out of André's face and his cheeks quivered. Mary Nelle laughed and Brandon uncocked the gun, sticking it in his belt.

They soon reached the breaker line near shore, and Rudd instructed the girls in both boats how to approach the line of waves pounding the beach, basing his words on common sense. The breakers were not too large and both boats made it to the shore without overturning. The girls got out and almost all of them dropped on the sand and started crying hysterically. Brandon was going to tell them that they had to keep going, as the sailors were still swimming toward them, but he decided they needed a few minutes.

Prodding André with the gun, he looked around while the girls cried, hugged, and comforted each other. Brandon took André over a large dune and could see arid mountains in the distance. He also saw some animals moving in and out of some small draws clogged with mesquite and sagebrush. Looking at the sun, he could tell that the shoreline was essentially running east and west and had been for some time. That made him feel that they must be standing on Texas soil instead of Mexican. He still had to figure out how to defend, feed, and care for these young girls and protect them from a very angry band of sailors headed their way.

Brandon prodded André back toward the beach and was surprised to see the entire group of girls standing there at the lip of the dune, waiting to follow him.

Mary Nelle said, "We better get going. His men are getting closer."

"Come on," Brandon said, "They'll rest a little when they hit the beach, but not too long."

He turned and headed toward the series of draws and brush that he had seen. The girls followed, as the young attorney tried to figure out exactly what he was going to do. He really had no idea. His first thought was to head toward the distant mountain range and climb them to perhaps locate a distant town or ranch. Then he remembered his uncle Anson Rudd telling his family how deceiving mountain ranges were out West. They would look like they were a short walk away and not that hard to climb and would turn out to be many days away. Unlike the mountains of Pennsylvania and New York he had seen back East on trips to New York City, Brandon heard from his uncle that these mountains were much larger up close than they seemed from far away. He decided to try to use the bushy draws for cover and to travel parallel to the coastline. Heading back easterly, he would at least be assured that he was not going to head into Mexico, and he figured they would eventually hit a coastal town.

The biggest challenge confronting Brandon was to somehow hide from the gang of vengeful hardened sailors following them. There was one more element of his plan that he would utilize when the time came. If the time came.

They headed toward the draws, and he kept a very rapid pace. André fell down twice on purpose and was slow to get up.

Finally Brandon said, "You are falling down on purpose, Breton."

André laughed and replied, "Ees too bad, *n'est-ce pas?*"

Brandon hit André in the rib cage with the pistol grip of the gun he was holding. André bent over in pain, the wind rushing out of him.

Brandon leaned forward and whispered in André's ear, "Hurts, doesn't it? I know, your friends broke my ribs and two of those sweet girls back there wrapped my rib cage very tightly. It hurts every time I breathe."

André's face was almost turning blue while he tried to get his breath back.

"Now," Brandon continued, "you have mistaken for weakness the fact that I hate violence. If your men catch up with us, they will rape and murder all those little girls, and I will not let that happen, and you will die before anyone. That is called justice. Every time you fall down or try to slow us down again, I will break another one of your ribs. *Comprendez-vous?* If so, shake your head."

André Breton nodded his head.

Brandon shoved him forward, and the Creole moved rapidly, almost outrunning the attorney in an effort to save his ribs from further injury.

Within a quarter of an hour the group was moving through the bushy draws. Brandon stopped the group.

"Clara," he called, "take these sticks and get one other girl to help you brush out our tracks behind us. Do not get too far behind the group."

Clara said, "Yes, sir. Then she added, "You know, after all we've been through, still none of us knows what your name is."

"Brandon. Brandon Rudd."

She smiled. "Okay, Mr. Rudd."

"Clara, we're friends. Please call me Brandon."

They rushed on for two more hours with still no sign of pursuit. There were so many draws, Brandon wound around and around through them with no concern about where they were heading. His first goal was to lost the sailors, who surely must be pursuing them. Brandon finally selected a place to stop for the night. It was a small draw completely choked with mesquite and other brush.

He had seen cattle in many of the draws that day and Brandon figured he would shoot and butcher one the next day if there was any evidence the escapees had lost the sailors.

He had the girls all lay together in a small tight group and assigned girls to take watches during the night. He took the last watch. The night passed without event and the next morning he got everyone ready to leave. They all were thirsty and hungry, and the next order of business was to locate water and get food.

Brandon assembled the girls to leave and, leaving André with Mary Nelle and Clara, he climbed up out of the draw they were in to a higher vantage point and see if there was any sign of the sailors. As soon as Brandon made the top, he almost fell back down, as he saw the sailors entering the draw where the escapees were camped. The dark-skinned sailor who had the curved blade apparently was a good tracker, and he was leading the group, his eyes scouring the ground for sign. Almost all the sailors were carrying rifles, apparently having gotten them from an armory before leaving the ship.

Brandon was almost in a panic. He half ran, half fell down the hill to the girls.

"Give me that gun," he hissed to Clara and Mary Nelle. "There's no time to talk. Take André and go. They're coming down the draw. Follow the draw until it plays out and keep going, no matter what. If they catch up to you, do not talk with them or give in. Keep fighting. Keep the ocean to your right and go until you find a town or can signal a ship. I have to go."

"What are you going to do?" Mary Nelle asked with tears in her eyes.

"I'll hold them as long as I can," he said. "Get going."

Clara ran to him as he started down the draw. She was crying hysterically, "Brandon, you can't leave. I love you!"

He smiled softly and held her by the upper arms, and at arm's length. "Clara, that makes me feel wonderful, but there is a huge difference in our ages and it would never work. Besides, I love another woman."

He kissed her lightly on the forehead and said, "Someday the right man will appear and you won't even remember my name."

She looked into his eyes and sniffled, saying, "I'll never forget your name. Good-bye."

She turned and ran after the others. Brandon headed down the gully to meet the sailors and pin them down as long as possible.

He shook his head and smiled, saying to himself, "Well, that makes it a lot easier to face death."

Brandon found a rock to hide behind and waited. He would pin down the approaching sailors and keep them down with sniper fire as long as possible. Fortunately, his father had taught him how to shoot well when he was a boy—not because he wanted young Brandon to become a shootist, but because ammunition was so darned expensive. If Brandon was sent out to shoot game for the family to eat, he was handed his dad's rifle and one bullet.

One time, the second time he hunted, Brandon got what had heard others call "buck fever." His first hunting trip had been after turkey; that was no problem. But on the second, he topped out on a rise overlooking their farm and saw a magnificent whitetail buck standing on his hind legs eating a crabapple. The deer dropped down on all fours and never knew Brandon was there, but the boy got so excited and nervous when he aimed that he jerked on the trigger and the bullet sailed passed the deer's head and knocked a limb off a sapling beyond. The deer took off at a dead run and the boy dropped on the ground and cried.

Brandon's pa hadn't ever said what would happen if Brandon didn't bring something home with one bullet, but the boy didn't want to find out. All he could do was picture his ma sitting there, a forlorn look on her face, eating pieces of bread at the table.

Brandon set his gun down after the buck was long gone and started making snares using his pocketknife. It took numerous tries, but he finally returned home well after dark with two rabbits he had snared. The father saw that there were no bullet holes in the carcasses and grinned at the young Rudd during the next several days, but nothing was ever said. Brandon never missed a shot after that. He went out behind the barn after his chores were done and practiced "dry firing" his pa's guns with no bullets, over and over again.

As a man, traveling to eastern cities or attending college, Brandon was always amused at dudes who spoke of western gunfighters shootings at rocks and cans and bottles and such for hours at a time, perfecting their quick draw. Nobody that Brandon knew could really afford to shoot up that much ammunition. It was too precious a commodity.

He didn't have to wait long for the sailors to come in sight. There were eight of them. Tears ran down both his cheeks as he aimed at the center of the lead sailor's chest. It was the dark-skinned one, apparently from the Far Eastern lands, he figured. The man seemed helpless, just staring at tracks in the ground, but Brandon realized what would happen if any of these men got their hands on those girls again. He would have to kill again, like he had as a boy. He wiped away the tears and set his mind to the task at hand. He squeezed the trigger and the gun boomed. The dark-skinned man flew backward, crimson splotch in the center of his chest. The other sailors just stared at his body convulsing in death; then suddenly they all dived for cover.

Brandon put one more shot in their midst just to make believers out of them, but he would not waste any more ammunition. He knew that they would eventually fan out, surround, and kill him, but for now he would buy as much time as he could for the girls to get away. Maybe, he thought, if he shot well enough, he could decimate their ranks enough that the girls could defend themselves against them.

He looked at the body of the dead man and felt sad. Then he got very angry at the man for making him have to kill him. He got angry at André Breton and Linford Crowley.

Brandon got the most angry at Crowley, because of Elizabeth, but also because Brandon saw how the man could be if he really wanted to. When they had gone out to dinner, Linford was pleasant and humorous and genuinely interesting. Brandon could never figure out why people had the tools for success but chose to take immoral shortcuts. Was it lack of morals, he wondered, character flaws, or maybe the excitement of doing something bad? It didn't matter. He could not change everyone in the world and wasn't about to try. He had enough trouble dealing with himself and trying to do what was right.

Brandon blinked his eyes as he strained for a

glimpse of one of the sailors. If he could spot a leg or arm, he would fire at it. Something moved and Brandon saw the lower leg of one of the kidnappers moving slightly as the man shifted his position. It was visible between two rocks the sailor was hiding behind. Brandon took careful aim and squeezed off his shot. The man screamed in pain and jumped up. Brandon fired twice and the man few backward, a bullet in his stomach. He writhed on the ground in pain and screamed at the top of his lungs for a full five minutes before he finally stopped and lay perfectly still. He was dead or close to it, but more importantly, Brandon figured the man's screams had to unnerve the others. It certainly must have given them food for thought anyway.

Brandon apparently was correct in his thinking, because the other sailors hugged the ground. He saw no movement and was excited, as he pictured the girls getting farther and farther away.

An hour passed. One large sailor who looked like he had been one of André's assistants suddenly sprang from behind a rock and dashed to a jumble of rocks that several sailors had taken refuge behind. Brandon got a quick snap shot at him and missed.

He waited, hearing the man yelling at the other men hidden down the gulch. Ten minutes later, a man peered over the rock the large man was behind and fired a rifle at Brandon, kicking up dirt five feet to his front. This was apparently a signal, as five more guns opened up on him with rapid fire.

As Brandon hugged the ground, he realized what was happening. Ignoring the withering gunfire, he stuck his head up and, sure enough, three men were rushing straight at his position, each firing at him with almost every step. Something slammed into his left shoulder and knocked him backward, but he jumped back up immediately, ignoring the pain. He fanned the revolver, wounding two of the three. One crawled for cover, while the other two lay on the ground holding wounds and moaning.

Brandon looked at his shoulder and realized there was a bullet in it. He quickly ripped the bottom of his shirttail off and bandaged the entry hole. The bleeding wasn't too bad, but the pain was incredible. He felt nauseated and dizzy, but he concentrated as hard as he could on staying alert.

The rapid gunfire started again, and he again looked. There was a flash and something struck his head. Everything went black and Brandon felt his heart start pounding with panic. He felt the back of his head and his back hit the ground.

The laughter seemed to be coming from behind a thick block wall. It kept getting clearer and clearer. Something was pinching both of Brandon's wrists and ankles, and he opened his eyes suddenly, shaking his head. He looked around him at the smiling, laughing faces of the kidnappers. They were making taunts and having a merry time at his expense. His wrists and ankles were stretched out and tied to two small saplings. He was spread-eagled. There was a large pile of dry brush and sticks piled around his legs and feet. Brandon realized he had been hit in the head by a bullet, apparently rendering him unconscious.

He was very frightened, but decided he would die bravely and not give these heathens the satisfaction of hearing him scream.

One of the sailors had made a torch out of a cedar stick wrapped with some cloth that apparently had been soaked in tree sap; the man lit it and a big flame leaped up. The man laughed and lit a cigar with the torch, and oddly enough, Brandon wondered how the man could have survived a shipwreck in the ocean and have a cigar to smoke. Then the man pulled a rolled up oilskin from under his shirt and passed out more cigars. Laughing and making jokes, the kidnappers passed the torch around, lighting their cigars. Each one pretended to light the pile of brush around Brandon's legs, but the brave young attorney feigned disinterest.

The leader finally came forward with the torch in his hand and held it toward the pile of dry tinder, saying, "Aye, yer slimy bloke. We'll now see how loud ye kin scream afore we send ye off to Hades to live with me ole father, Lucifer himself."

Brandon said, "Hate to disappoint you, sir, but you shall not hear a peep out of me. I'll die a man, as I have lived, and may you all rot in hell."

The sailor started to light the brush pile, but a loud gunshot from behind Brandon exploded and the torch flew backward from the man's hand. Several sailors raised their guns to fire and numerous shots rang out from behind Brandon. Within seconds, only four sailors remained standing, their hands raised high above their heads.

Three cowboys rode slowly forward, smoking guns in their hands. Each of them wore batwing chaps and were covered with trail dust. One was small, old, and leather-tough. Another was one of the largest and strongest-looking men Brandon had ever seen, and the third was very obviously the leader. He was over six feet tall, well-built, good-looking, and looked to be part black.

He gave Brandon a wink, then spoke to the new prisoners. "Now, sailor boys, I don't want to put any more holes in you gents. You might sink when you go back on the water, so why don't you lose all the iron real quicklike."

One of the kidnappers balked. He was a large man

and gave the black man a scowl that would scare a goblin and thought about lifting his rifle.

The black cowboy raised his Colt .45 Peacemaker and fired, the bullet catching the man full in the chest and driving him through the air and onto a companion. The other sailor pushed and shoved and struggled to get out from under the dying sailor. He jumped up and raised his hands skyward, eyes bulging in fear.

The cowboy leader said, "Mr. Rudd, the girls are okay. They're at my cow camp a few miles from here having beef and beans. Got some tough hands watching over them and nobody with trouble on their mind can get within five days' ride of them. They told me about you. You from St. Louis?"

Brandon nodded his head. Now that he could relax, he began feeling very weak. Everything he looked at seemed to start spinning and then got darker and darker. He passed out cold.

Brandon was lying in bed and it was cold October morning. His ma had heated a couple of stones in the fireplace, wrapped them in a blanket, and placed them in the bottom of his bed to keep his feet warm. She always did that on cold mornings, and it really made Brandon feel comfortable and cared for. He wanted to stay in bed and sleep, but she kept shaking his shoulders. He had to awaken and go to school, but he just wanted to stay under the blankets and keep warm.

She kept shaking him, so he finally opened his eyes, blinking them against the morning light streaking through the window. It was not his mother. He sat up and looked around. The woman shaking him was a nurse and the room was an ugly shade of green. It smelled of alcohol. He looked down and saw a fresh scar where he had been shot in the shoulder. He reached up and felt where his hair had been cut very short, and he could feel another fresh scar on his forehead and the top of his head.

"Welcome back, Mr. Rudd," the nurse said, "I'll be right back; I have to tell the doctor you're finally awake and send someone for Miss Macon."

"Miss Macon!"

"Why, heaven's yes," the nurse went on. "She has hardly left your bedside all this time. She was the one who argued with anyone who said you'd never come around. She'd give them the what-for and let them know you'd be just fine."

"How long have I been, asleep?" Brandon asked. "Where are we?"

"Well, we're in St. Louis, of course. You had been unconscious two weeks when they brought you in here, and another three weeks since you've been here.

"Five weeks!" he said, totally shocked.

"Mr. Rudd, "you had one nasty bump on your head and you lost a lot of blood from your other wounds."

"Wounds?" he said, even more shocked. "I thought I only had a shoulder wound."

She laughed and said, "You had a bullet through your thigh and another through the lower right part of your abdomen. Look at your scars."

Eyes open wide, he pulled the sheets back and looked down. Sure enough, there was a bullet-hole scar on his lower right side. He twisted and saw the exit scar on his back. He had another pink scar on his right leg.

"The girls?" he said suddenly.

She smiled and said, "The ones from St. Louis ask about you all the time. Each one of them, I think, fell madly in love with you, and you'll always be their hero. Everyone is safe and sound."

"Linford Crowley?"

She said, "André Breton testified against him before they hanged him. Several of the others identified him, too, before they were hanged, but unfortunately, he fled before they could arrest him. He swore vengeance against you, but I wouldn't pay attention to it."

"They've already hanged Breton and his crew?"

The nurse said, "I believe the folks in south Texas don't cotton to men who kidnap young girls. Mr. Colt and his men turned them over to the nearest sheriff and his good citizens relieved the sheriff of the responsibility of having to feed and care for the prisoners. I don't think he argued too much."

"Who is Mr. Colt?" Brandon asked. "Was he the Negro gentleman who saved me?"

"Joshua Colt of the Coyote Run Ranch in Colorado," she replied.

"Why, the Coyote Run is owned by Chris Colt, the famous scout and gunfighter." Brandon said.

"Well, Joshua Colt is Chris Colt's half brother and part owner of the ranch. He is half white."

Brandon was excited. The Coyote Run was only a day's hard ride from Canon City, and Chris Colt was very famous.

He said, "Did Mr. Colt leave? I have to thank him and his friends."

"I do not know, sir, but I believe Miss Macon knows. She should be here shortly."

Brandon's heart leaped in his chest. The nurse smiled and left the room. Brandon pictured the beauteous Elizabeth Macon, and he smiled to himself. He suddenly felt very tired and closed his eyes for a second.

"Mr. Rudd, are you awake?"

The voice came out of the blackness and made Brandon want to swim to the surface. His mind came up through the veil of blackness, and he opened his eyes, focusing them in the bright afternoon sunlight streaking through the windows.

He looked at the figure in the bedside chair and gulped. It was Elizabeth Macon.

She wore her hair piled atop her head and had on a white ruffled blouse with a high neck, over which she wore an ivory cameo necklace. She also wore a brightly colored gingham skirt. To Brandon, she was the most beautiful woman he had ever seen.

Elizabeth looked at the handsome young attorney looking so helpless in bed, his wounds not totally healed. What a hero he was. She wondered how one man could possess so much courage. The sheet was halfway down his chest, and she glanced at the large rounded muscles of his shoulders, the strong muscles in his upper chest. She realized he was now seeing the direction of her glance, and her face flushed. Well, he was a new friend, she decided, and there was certainly nothing wrong with admiring a friend.

"Miss Macon," Brandon said. "What a pleasant surprise."

Brandon got so angry with himself. He was supposed to be a man with the ability to effectively communicate. He had been, it was said, born with a golden tongue. Here he was fumbling over his words and saying "What a pleasant surprise." Why, he wondered, couldn't he think of something more intelligent to start the conversation with? He decided he was really being foolish. He had seen plenty of pretty ladies in his day. Brandon wondered why he was acting this way and why he should worry so much about his selection of words.

"I heard you've visited a lot, Miss Macon," he went on. "I sincerely appreciate it."

"Well, Mr. Rudd, I consider you a friend," she replied. "and I wouldn't think of not looking in on you."

"Again, thank you very much. I'm sorry to hear about the disappointment you must have endured. I am speaking, of course, of your fiancé and his shortcomings—and please, call me Brandon."

"Well," she replied, "I am so grateful that I discovered he was a scoundrel and a cur before we married. If I had gone ahead with our betrothal and then found him out, well, I just shudder to think about it. I thank you so much for exposing him."

"I didn't do anything."

"Mr. Rudd," she said with a laugh," you are too modest."

"Brandon . . . please," he said.

"Brandon."

"Now, what about Joshua Colt?"

"Oh, I will be spending a good deal of time with Mr. Colt very soon," she said.

"Oh?"

"Yes," she went on. "He came to Texas on a cattle drive to ship cattle from the coast. That's when he found you and the girls. He was going to proceed to Independence and purchase some bulls. He brought you here and decided to stay a few days to see how you were doing, and he met a rancher here who had fallen on hard times and wanted to sell a very large herd for very little money, so Mr. Colt bought the whole herd. He is driving them back to Colorado and is quite a businessman. He made a deal to escort a large wagon train to Colorado and supply them with beef along the way. He will stop in Independence and buy his bulls, incorporate them into the herd, and they will start seeding the herd of new cattle along the way."

"How does this mean you will be spending a lot of time with him?" Brandon asked.

"Oh," she said genuinely embarrassed, "I am moving. I am going with the wagon train."

"You are!" he said, surprised and upset. "Oh, have you decided to put this place behind you and erase the memories?"

"Sort of," she said, "but my aunt has always been trying to get me to move to Colorado. She was one of the first settlers of the small town I am going to. I figured that this would be a good time to go."

Brandon's heart was now beating with excitement. His uncle had been making him eager to see this magical country for years now. Uncle Anson, too, had been one of the pioneers of his small town, Canon City, and Brandon now had an excuse to go there. Elizabeth Macon would be living in the same state.

Brandon said, "That is certainly a coincidence, Miss Macon. I am moving to Colorado, too."

Elizabeth corrected him, "Elizabeth, please," but it was now her turn for her heart to leap in her own chest. She didn't know why, but she was quite excited that her new friend was headed for the same state, and she wondered if he would live near her.

"Why, we will be neighbors, I suspect," she said.

"I suppose we will," he replied. "My uncle also was an early settler of his town and is a community leader. He has told me so many stories about the area that I have been in love with it for years. The stories are so rich and the people sound so strong and colorful. His son was the very first child ever born there, and I have wanted to help spread the Rudd name there myself."

Her face flushed.

Brandon continued, "When the first big wagon train traveled there, one woman's baby was kidnapped by Cheyenne Indians. Do you know what that woman did?"

Elizabeth was shocked as a big smile spread on her face.

"I certainly do," she said, and Brandon stared in shocked disbelief. "She and her husband, John, and several men trailed the Indians to their encampment. Then she and her husband rode into the encampment and found the baby. A Cheyenne woman held the baby tightly in her arms and the Indian who appointed himself as interpreter said she claimed that she loved the baby very much. Mary Virginia Macon—my aunt, sir—walked forward and snatched my cousin out of the woman's arms and stated that she loved her, too, but it was her baby. My Uncle John and Aunt Virginia—we don't call her Mary—mounted up with the child and rode out of that village without so much as a look behind them."

"Oh, my goodness," Brandon said. "You mean to tell me that of the entire American frontier, of the millions of square miles of the Wild West, we both have been planning to join our respective relatives in Canon City, Colorado?"

"Apparently so, Brandon. A coincidence indeed. Are you sorry?"

"Absolutely not!" he responded too emphatically, and embarrassed himself again. "I mean . . . you and I are fast friends now, Elizabeth, and I am delighted that we shall live in the same community. Just delighted."

Delighted? Brandon Rudd could hardly catch his

breath he was so overwhelmed with joy, but he could not understand so much happiness over a friend he hardly knew.

Brandon struggled to sit up in the bed, his eyes sparkling with enthusiasm. "Then your aunt is the lady who put the cat in the piano?"

Elizabeth started laughing and said, "That's Aunt Virginia."

They were referring to an incident which actually occurred several years earlier in the early 1870s. Mary Virginia and her husband John had built a fine house in Canon City and, along with Anson Rudd, John's brother Augustus, and a few others, actually donated much of the land and organized the building of the city, which had just about been deserted during the Civil War years and had to start over. Anson Rudd had actually greeted their wagon train and helped every one of the forty-some families get situated in town.

One of the items carried the many miles from Missouri to Canon City by Mary Virginia was her beautiful hand-carved mahogany upright piano, which she delighted people with by playing for them from time to time in her parlor. Anson Rudd and some other leaders in the area had befriended the great Ute chief Ouray, whose tribe always wintered at Canon City, as it was their winter hunting grounds. Ouray had, in actuality, prevented a great Indian war and all the settlers went out of their way to be friendly with the Utes. Friendships developed, and in the case of Mary Virginia Macon, a large group of Utes started showing up daily at her house, asking her to play tunes for them on her piano.

She did not want to offend the tribes' members, but several hours of each day were being spent entertaining the same Utes with the same tunes. Mary

Virginia racked her brain to figure a way out of her predicament without hurting the feelings of her Indian audience.

She finally struck upon a solution. The big grandfather clock in her foyer was about to strike noon, and just as reliably, she saw the large group of Utes coming down the road toward her beautiful home. She ran to the kitchen pantry and opened the door, where she had placed one of her cats, a large, black, very good mouser named Midnight.

She ran back to the parlor, placed the cat inside the piano, and walked quickly to the front door just in time to greet the large group of Utes in front of the house.

They started to enter, led by an old sourpuss warrior, who said, "Play music."

Mary Virginia tried her best theatrical performance with a very concerned look on her face.

"Wait," she said, before the group entered the house.

Having remembered that the spiritual world was a very important part of American Indian life, she put the next part of her plan into effect by saying, "I am afraid I can no longer play for you."

Another English speaker in the crowd said, "Why, no play music?"

Mary Virginia let a phony chill run up her spine and hunched her shoulders as if suddenly engulfed in an icy draft.

She said, "Bad spirits have gotten inside my piano. I cannot play it. The bad spirit wants to."

Her words were translated and a great murmur went up among the crowd, which by now was quite curious about the possessed musical instrument, and they started streaming into the house toward the parlor. The noises frightened the already traumatized feline even more than the weird vibrations the strings were causing under his feet. He ran back and forth across the piano strings in a panic, causing the piano to emit noises that one might imagine while on a lonely visit to an ancient graveyard on a moon-filled night. The exit the Utes made was immediate and quite hasty, and they never returned to hear any more of Mary Virginia Macon's melodic piano recitals.

Elizabeth and Brandon had stopped speaking but were staring into each other's eyes without realizing their conversation had stopped. They both jumped when the door suddenly opened and in walked Joshua Colt, an imposing figure to say the least.

"Miss Macon," he said, removing his dusty black Stetson.

His smile was infectious and his bright white teeth contrasting against his dark-colored skin made it even more so. Elizabeth stood and offered a handshake to the mulatto rancher. He politely kissed the back of her hand, and she giggled in embarrassment. She smiled broadly and seemed quite pleased to see him.

"Well, well, Mr. Rudd," Joshua said, extending his hand, "glad to see you're back with the living. I'm Joshua Colt. Last time I saw you awake, you were in a pretty good fix."

Brandon said seriously, "And were it not for you, sir, I would be quite dead right now. I owe you my life, and I will be eternally grateful. You ever need an attorney, just call."

"And if it weren't for your courage and quick thinking, a whole lot of pretty young girls would not be alive right now. Shame you live here in Missouri. My brother and I are looking for a good attorney right now."

"Oddly enough, I am preparing to move to Canon City," Brandon said.

"Why, that's wonderful, sir," Joshua said.

Brandon felt quite good, as he could tell that unlike many Negroes he had seen in Missouri, this man only said "sir" to people he chose to address in that way. Having dealt with many victims and criminals alike in his law practice, Brandon had become a pretty good judge of character, and he definitely knew that Joshua Colt was a real man. Brandon knew that this black man must have really been through hard times to be a successful rancher in a society with so much racial prejudice. Many white men, Brandon knew, would have pulled out a six-gun just for Joshua kissing the back of Elizabeth's hand. Brandon grinned as he thought to himself about how few men would probably be able to pull the trigger if they did draw a six-gun on Joshua Colt.

"When are you moving?" Joshua said.

Brandon hadn't even thought of it.

He suddenly blurted out, "Now is as good a time as any, I suppose. I've put it off long enough. Do you suppose the captain of the wagon train you're taking would allow me to come along?"

Elizabeth said, "Oh, I'm sure he would, Brandon," and she blushed, as both men gave her an amused look.

"I'm having breakfast with him in the morning," Joshua said. "Name's Carter Reasoner. I'd be happy to bring him by the hospital and you two can parley about it."

"Thanks. Thanks very much, Mr. Colt."

"Joshua," Colt replied.

"Joshua," Brandon went on, "you mentioned needing an advocate. For normal ranch paperwork or a special case?"

Joshua grinned broadly, even chuckled, and replied, "It seems that, if your last name is Colt, there's always some coyotes nipping at your behind. Pardon the expression, ma'am."

Chapter 2

>>>>>>>>>>>>>>>>>>>>>

Wamble Uncha

The horse the man rode was magnificent. He was one of those horses men dreamed about owning if they could be somebody important. A black and white Ovaro pinto, he had many big swirly patches of white and black over his muscular body. The mane and tail were long and flowing and were both pure white. Around each upper foreleg were three red coup stripes and there were red handprints on each hip. Additionally, there were three eagle feathers braided into the mane of the sixteen-hands-tall stallion and two more braided into the tail. This was the way the horse was decorated when he was received as a gift from the Oglala war hero Crazy Horse, and this was the way War Bonnet would always be decorated.

The mountain was so steep that the rider's right foot could almost touch the ground as the big paint made his way along the rocky mountainside. The deer trail he was on was only about six inches wide and the big horse instinctively put one hoof in front of the other, without stepping on any loose round rocks or loose sand that might give way and send him and his master tumbling down the mountainside. The horse even knew not to step on dry branches or anything that could crack and make a lot of noise, because he had been raised and trained to walk in secrecy. It could mean the difference of life or death for the big man on his back.

The man, a white man, would have to look slightly down when speaking with a six-footer, and his shoulders and chest showed years of hard work and self-discipline. They were the kind of shoulders and chest that would make women stare as he passed by and men feel uncomfortable.

His saddle was a U.S. cavalry-issue McClellan rig, but behind it was a bedroll with an unstrung Cheyenne bow and quiver of arrows rolled up within. Beneath this was a pair of tanned elkskin saddlebags with fancy beadwork and porcupine quillwork decorating them, just like the man's fringed buckskin Lakota (Sioux) war shirt. The large bone-handled bowie knife on his right hip was also in a fancy decorated beaded sheath.

His hat was the floppy leather kind that scouts traditionally wore with a beaded band and one single plumed eagle father adorning it.

Like his saddle, his trousers were military issue. A gold stripe running up the outside seam, they were royal blue in color and were tucked into a pair of high-topped rough leather cowboy boots. On these were a pair of fancy large-roweled Mexican spurs that had little tiny brass bells hanging on the outside of the rowels which added extra tingling noises when the man walked in them. For clandestine movement, he had a pair of soft-soled Lakota moccasins with red and green porcupine quillwork all over them.

The weapons the man carried were most impressive. The gun belt that held his beaded knife sheath was a double-rig quick draw set up in natural leather and had been carefully oiled and cared for. The holsters had been worn from much use. Within each holster there was housed a very clean and oiled Colt

.45 Peacemaker with an engraved mother-of-pearl handle. The engraving, a special edition from Colt firearms, featured a design from the Mexican flag. It was a bald eagle proudly perched atop a curving serpent which was clutched tightly in its talons and its beak. Additionally, the barrels were hand-engraved in scrollwork.

In the saddlebags were a pair of spare guns, Colt short barrel .45 Peacemakers with four-and-three-quarter-inch barrels. On the right side of his saddle there was a scabbard containing a Winchester .44-caliber eighteen-shot carbine, and it was decorated Indian style with a pattern of brass upholstery tacks driven into the stock. There was one single eagle wing feather adorning it.

The scabbard on the left side of his saddle held a similarly adorned Colt twelve-gauge revolving shotgun.

In his right boot, there was a small leather holster holding a Colt Third Model .41 derringer.

Down his back, between his shoulder blades, was a second bowie knife in a plain leather sheath.

Ironically, the man was a man of peace, but his work and reputation sometimes called for violence. When it did, he was ready.

He looked up and saw the edges of a billowing storm cloud trying to force a storm over the bare windswept peaks above him. He was very close to timberline and could make out little yellow alpine flowers and hear the whistles of the many marmots feeding on the sparse summer alpine grasses. The trees above him were large and covered with dark green needles, and it seemed that next to each one was another one, dead, which had been pushed over by an avalanche years before. Patches of snow, some twenty feet deep, wedged themselves between house-shaped rocks on the peaks above, and the warmth of the summer sun sent tons of crystal-clear water splashing and gurgling down the mountainside in roaring little creeks in almost every place there was a depression.

The man looked at the big horse's ears as they quickly pointed off to the side, and he reined up. He dismounted on the uphill side of the mountain, then walked out in front of War Bonnet and watched down below. The wind shifted, and he heard the faint sound again. The horse did, too, and his nostrils were flaring as if a certain smell was exciting him, as well.

The man strained his ears as his eyes passed from left to right in arches down below him, each glance a little bit farther down the mountainside. Just like a deer or an elk, his eyes were looking for something moving, causing shine, or seeming out of place with the environment.

Leading the stud by his reins, he went straight down the hill, watching out of the corner of his eye for rolling boulders from the horse's sliding hooves. Tail dragging, War Bonnet's rump almost scraped the ground, the mountainside was so steep as they went down the side.

Three hundred feet down, he stopped and the horse did, too, after struggling for several seconds trying to get a foothold and gain balance. They listened and now the noise could be heard more clearly. It was the definite meowing of an injured cat, a baby.

The man went down the cliffside faster and emerged on a rocky outcropping, where he could now clearly hear the cries. He dropped the reins and left the horse, moving forward. Down below, he saw a mother lion and a spotted kitten standing on the edge of a cliff looking below. He moved forward, and the big cat turned toward him, her ears laying back flat against her head. She hissed and spit, her fangs bared in warning, then gave her kitten a smack, sending it scurrying away.

The lioness faced him for a while, but finally backed away as he kept moving closer to her. She kept looking back at him as she cautiously melted into the shadows.

Many people talked about attacks by mountain lions but it very seldom happened, except with children, or if a lion was starved. They were extremely shy animals and kept very far away from humans. One thing that cougars did that might have added to their reputation for being dangerous was to stalk or trail men in the wilds. Colt understood that this was simply done out of a cat's normal instinctive curiosity, just like a housecat might do with smaller prey.

The cougar took a place under some cedars and kept watch on the big man. The kitten was now out of sight. Hearing cries from down below, the man crept forward and looked over the cliffside. On a two-foot-wide rocky ledge, twenty-five feet below, another kitten stood crying, his sad mournful eyes staring up at the man. His tawny fur had little spots, and his meows were desperate-sounding.

The ruggedly handsome man turned, whistling, and War Bonnet came trotting down to him, stopping right at the cliff's edge. The man quickly took his braided Mexican riata off the right front part to the saddle and slipped the loop over the saddle horn, tightening it.

He removed his buckskin war shirt, and what was revealed underneath told a story. This white man had two large scars above his nipples. The scars had been created from wounds resulting from eagle talons, in the hands of a shaman, being pushed through his flesh, and wooden pegs were placed through the

holes. The wooden pegs had been attached by
leather thongs that ran over a pole in a lodge and
down to some heavy buffalo skulls. He had been
fasting and steam-bathing before this ceremony and
was already weak from that. He then did a dance
pulling back on the pegs while staring up at the sun
through a hole in the ceiling. This, the sun dance
ceremony, went on until the man was ready to drop
unconscious and have a vision. He was eventually
lifted up in the air by the thongs, the skin of his
chest stretching out to grotesque proportions. Although he was white, this man bore the scars of the
sacred sun dance ceremony of the Sioux and Cheyenne.

There was a bullet-hole scar that entered below
his left shoulder with the scar of a large exit wound
on the back of the same shoulder. There was a
knife-slash scar across his washboard stomach, a
small pucker scar on his cheek near his left eye
which only appeared when he smiled a certain way,
and four large claw marks running down his massive right biceps, the marks of a fight with either a
bear or a mountain lion. There were other less sig-
nificant scars, but these certainly told a story of adventure.

The other thing that was quite noticeable was the
massive bulk and clear definition of his muscles.
This man had lived a rough and tough life, and he
obviously was no stranger to hard work, grueling
hard work. The sinew and musculature clearly
showed that. Any woman looking at this man's bare
torso would certainly breathe a little bit heavier, and
any man would toe the scratch line against him to
avoid a no-holds-barred fight.

He now held the buckskin shirt in his teeth,
quickly and easily climbing down the rope hand
over hand to the ledge where the frightened kitten

was. The tiny cat hunched his back and hissed, swiping at the man with its left paw. The man held the rope with his right hand, and with his left he tossed his buckskin shirt over the kitten, trapping its legs and covering its head, with its sharp little teeth and fangs.

He snatched it up under his arm and yelled to the horse above, "War Bonnet, back!"

The big pinto started backing up, his nostrils flaring in and out as he smelled the strong danger odor from the big cat. There was no smell from the kittens, as mountain lion kittens were born with no scent, part of nature's protective system to increase their chances for survival.

Soon the man pulled himself and his little bundle over the edge of the precipice. He immediately released the little cat, and the mother ran forward from the trees, urging her offspring to safety. The kitten ran to its mother, and the big cat sniffed it all over. The man worried that she might reject the kitten because of the man-smell on it, but with a smack of her paw on its little rump, the two disappeared without a backward glance. The man didn't expect them to do anything but flee. Anything else would not have been their way. Thank-yous were not needed in nature. The sight of the cats rejoined was enough for the man.

After patting War Bonnet on the neck, he coiled his rope and tied it below the horn, then swinging up into the saddle. The big horse proudly went on along the mountain game trail.

Some of the man's cattle had been rustled, and the rustlers thought they would get away cleanly by pushing the cattle along the front of the big mountain range.

The man's eyes scoured the ground in front of him, sweeping back and forth from left to right,

right to left, his gaze moving out another ten feet with each sweep. He didn't watch them but was also constantly aware of the ears of War Bonnet, which would hone in on any noises that were too slight for the man's ears or smells that were too sensitive for his nose.

Cattle, especially high-altitude cattle, have a tendency, like man, to follow specific game trails when walking along the faces of mountains. It was easy for the rustlers to push the small herd ahead of them and even easier for the big man to follow them. Their tracks had been lazily following the bovines along the wooded Sangre de Cristos, but now the man discovered they had turned off suddenly and ridden a little higher than the trail.

This was the clue the scout had been looking for. An expert tracker has to read an entire story into a set of tracks and figure out what his quarry was trying to accomplish. These men were not very good at rustling, nor were they very good at hiding their intentions. They would look for a good ambush site overlooking the trail and try to bushwhack him. He needed only watch for a good ambush site as well.

It took only fifteen minutes before he spotted a clear slide area above the trail. Above that was a jumble of boulders and trees, offering good cover and clear fields of fire to the trail. Winchester carried carefully across the swells of his saddle, he was ready for action. Before coming to the clear area in the trail where he would be a sitting duck, he spotted a large boulder that would make good cover.

It took one minute to reach it and two seconds to dive behind it before pouring searching fire at the trees and boulders above. He only needed to see the sudden twisting of War bonnet's ears in that direction to know that the ambushers were indeed there.

The big horse knew what to do while his master dealt with the dry-gulchers. The man smiled to himself as he stopped firing and lit a small cigar while reloading. The gunfire from the rustlers began in heavy volume, then tapered off to short bursts.

Christopher Columbus Colt knelt down behind the black and gray boulder as two more shots rang out from the trees above. He spotted and memorized the looks of each man. The five men were all white, all bearded, all very large.

They had started riding south along the eastern face of the Sangre de Cristo range, which towered over his ranch some ten miles to the north and northeast. By the time they got to Horn Peak, the rustlers had decided that they had had enough of being chased and set up an ambush to dry-gulch Chris Colt.

Famed chief of cavalry scouts, Chris Colt worked as an independent contractor for the U.S. government. He had recently returned from New Mexico and Texas, where he was the chief of scouts for the famed black Ninth and Tenth Cavalry "buffalo soldiers." They had hunted down the notorious Mimbres Apache chief Victorio and fought numerous battles with him before he was finally killed in Mexico.

Colt had arrived home at his ranch to meet his new son, Joseph, named after Colt's friend the famous Nez Percé chief. He spent time with his beautiful auburn-haired wife, Shirley, and he helped his half-brother Joshua. Joshua really was the expert with cattle and horse husbandry, so Chris had given him part of the ranch and put him in charge of the operation so it could be run as a profitable business. Chris, in the meantime, would sometimes scout for the U.S. cavalry and try to prevent other Wounded

Knees and Sand Creek Massacres from happening to the American Indians he revered and respected so much. His first wife and daughter, in fact, were Minniconjou Lakota, but had been killed by Crow warriors.

The Colts also had a young Nez Percé who lived with them and had become like Chris's younger brother. Named Man Killer, he was a fine young man who was fast learning how to master both the white man's world and the red man's. Man Killer, who had been in Joseph's band, was a teenager and was madly in love with a girl down the valley named Jennifer Banta. She lived with her father just southwest of Westcliffe.

Chris, nephew of the famous Colonel Samuel Colt, the man whose invention made "all men equal," had studied guns at the side of numerous gunsmiths while growing up. He could have become a famous gunfighter, he was so good with firearms, but he chose to be a chief of scouts. His name was as legendary as Bill Hickok, the Earps, John Wesley Hardin, Doc Holliday, and others. He was also famous among the tribes as either Colt or by his Lakota name Wamble Uncha, meaning "One Eagle."

Chris could not understand why these fools who now had him pinned down had picked his cattle to rustle. He was modest, but he was not stupid. He saw how women and men looked at him. He heard the whispers as he walked by. He saw the way white children and Indian children ran up to him in a crowd whenever he rode into a population center. Colt had a reputation as being a fair man, but one that nobody should ever want to cross.

It was almost as if that reputation acted like one of those magnet gadgets he had seen, he thought. He figured that, if he were a different person, he would never try to stir up trouble with someone like himself or his brother. It would be like trying to pet a rattlesnake. It made no sense. For some strange reason, however, it sometimes seemed that some people would occasionally try to prod the Colts. He had no respect for the intelligence or sense of these people, but he would have to make believers out of them.

Colt knew that the men had stopped and were above him because of some fresh elk tracks he had seen down the face of Horn Peak. Elk wouldn't be coming down to water out of the high dark timber until near evening, and this was midmorning, so they had been spooked. Normally in the Sangre de Cristos when elk were spooked they ran uphill and crossed over to the steep San Luis Valley side of the majestic range, the western slope, but these had not, so the men who had spooked them had to be above Colt and a little to his front.

Earlier he may have chased the men many miles and harassed them to teach them a lesson and then let them go, but now they had tried to kill him. In cases like that, Colt believed you should never play the tune if you aren't willing to dance the dance. They would learn what many others had learned. It took an awful lot of killing to get rid of a Colt.

He met one of the Sacketts in New Mexico and their family had the same reputation. So did the Earps, and a few others. These families were the backbone of the West. The rest of the families were the flesh and blood, but these particular families were the backbone that held everyone else rigid and upright.

Colt whistled for War Bonnet, and he heard the big paint coming from down below. War Bonnet was a warhorse, and he had a few scars just like his master. He was totally loyal and devoted to Chris, but he knew when Colt bailed out he should get out of the way of the loud things that could hurt him. It was instinctive.

Colt stripped off his fringed buckskin and quill-decorated war shirt. He quickly made a frame with green sticks which he tied with little pieces of leather thongs from his saddlebags. He pulled the shirt over the frame and placed his floppy leather scout's hat over the fake head he had created.

Chris then tied the frame in the saddle, anchoring it to the saddlebags and the saddle horn. He pulled his Cheyenne war bow and quiver of arrows from his bedroll and strung the bow. Colt then pointed the big horse down the deer trail running along the face of the mountain and slapped his rump. War Bonnet knew what to do and took off at a canter to the south, bullets flying all around him from above.

Colt, in the meantime, scampered on his elbows and knees along a depression heading north and went headlong into a crystal-clear ice-cold glacial runoff stream cascading down from above timberline, not far above. He held his breath, stuck his head under the cold water, and started climbing upward rapidly. The icy water chilled Colt all the way to his soul, but a rush of adrenaline kept him climbing. Every minute, he would carefully stick his face barely out of the water, check the dry-gulchers' position with a sidelong glance, then duck back under the rushing water and keep climbing.

Colt finally left the stream when he knew he was about a hundred feet higher than the ambushers. He found a spot where some bushes grew thick along the crest of the ridge, and he used that for cover. He had removed his boots earlier and now wore soft-soled Sioux moccasins, which he carried in his saddlebags. He only wore his blue-and-gold-striped cavalry trousers and his arsenal of weapons. This included his pair of matched ivory-handled Colt Peacemaker .45s.

Colt had the bow and arrows slung over his back as he crept down and sideways toward the unsuspecting ambushers. He could see the five fools now as they strained and pushed their necks out trying to spot him down below.

The frame with shirt and hat had been knocked off by a branch, and two of the men got a glimpse of the riderless horse galloping away and figured they had shot Colt.

With the soft-soled moccasins, Colt could keep his eye on the men and not have to look down at his path; he could feel sticks and stones through the soft soles. He didn't stare directly at the men, either, but a little off to the side. This was a hunting and war trick he had learned from the Indians. They knew that prey, human or animal, could sometimes sense someone staring directly at them.

Colt slowly made his way down the steep timbered slope, pulling out the bow and nocking an arrow on the string. The man highest up the hill was half turned toward Colt, and Chris felt he was the biggest risk. Colt stopped, raised the bow, and drew the arrow back. He had to lower the odds. There were five of them with rifles. He released the arrow, and it sliced through the left center of the man's back and side. The arrow came out the other side and actually pinned the man against the tree he had been hiding behind. As the lifeblood quickly drained out of him, the man slowly slid off the arrow and dropped backward like a rag doll.

The other four didn't notice, still preoccupied with trying to spot the dead or wounded man downhill. Colt moved closer and finally felt he was close enough to try another shot. All four of them were on about the same level. He would shoot one more arrow, drop the bow, and draw his guns.

Colt looked at the holsters of the four men and selected the one which was worn from more use and was placed properly on the man's side, not too low or too high. That one would be the most dangerous with a gun and would be the next to take an arrow.

He raised the bow and drew back the arrow. The nock of the shaft was held gently between Colt's index and middle fingers and the end of his ring finger also wrapped around the string. He held the crook of his thumb against the lowest point of the right side of his jaw and took a breath, exhaled partway, and slowly let the string roll off his fingers. The arrow swished through the air and penetrated the outlaw's skull with a soft thud. It killed him instantly and the other three, turned, bringing their rifles to bear.

One turned his head to stare at his dead partners, totally shocked. Colt ignored him and felt his two Colts buck in his palms. The man on his right was slightly faster than the other and Colt's bullet smashed the man's rifle as he raised it, then the bullet glanced off, and tore a slice open in the man's cheek and ripped the tip of his right ear off.

The man on the left dropped his rifle and tried to draw his pistol. Incredibly, the bullet from Colt's left-hand gun struck the pistol of the man on the left and sent it flying backward just as he cleared leather. Unfortunately for the man, his thumb also flew backward with the smashed firearm.

Chris Colt was an outstanding shot with a pistol, but what had just happened was an incredible coincidence. When Colt fired at a man in a gunfight, he employed the principle used by the military: Fire at center mass. Whatever object he was shooting at, he tried to hit in the center of its thickest, widest part. In the case of a man, he would fire at the torso.

When he shot the man's gun out of his hand and holster, it was actually a miss. Hitting the other's rifle stock and knocking it from the man's hand was also an accident. However, the bullet would have caught the man in the belly if the rifle would not have been in the way.

Nevertheless, Chris Colt would never tell a soul that he was not aiming for those guns. The fact that he had shot the guns out of the two men's hands would get around the country and add even more to his legendary status. Colt knew that each time the story was retold, the number of his adversaries would increase, but he also knew that such stories might ward off at least some fights from young ruffians.

The man who had hesitated while he looked at his dead compadres had shucked his rifle as soon as Colt's guns came out. His hands were raised and his face was the color of the big cloud billowing around the peak above them. The other two fell on the ground and held their hands, one yelling in pain and the other staring daggers at Colt. Colt motioned for them to stand.

They both stood and Chris said, "Left hand. All three of you unfasten your gun belts and let 'em drop."

They complied, but the one who stared daggers hesitated at first. He looked into Colt's eyes and saw that he meant business.

Finally the hard case said, "You backshot our pardners."

"What the hell were you dry-gulchers trying to do to me?" Colt said.

"Makes no matter," the hard case said, "I git half a chance, I'm a gonna kill ya, Colt."

Colt chuckled and said, "Mister, if I were in your boots, I'd look down at my bloody hand and stare down the muzzles of these Peacemakers, then figure that I'm not very darned good at this killing business. Now, you know who I am. Why would you pick my cattle to try to rustle?"

The hard case looked at the frightened one and gave him a threatening glare. That look told Colt volumes.

He addressed the frightened one and said, "Who hired you to rustle Coyote Run cattle?"

The man glanced at the hard case, then back at Colt.

Finally the hard case blurted out, "Keep yer mouth shut, Slim. He can't do nuthin' but take us to the law. Just keep shut."

Colt smiled warmly, turned his right-hand gun, and shot the hard case in the right thigh. The man went down like a sack of feed and clutched at his wounded leg, cursing and screaming.

Colt looked at Slim and said, "I can do anything I want. I'm holding the guns. Now take a look at your amigo, Slim. I can put more holes in him or you if I want. We can make this long and painful or settle it right now. Your choice."

"His name is Millard, Preston Millard," the man said nervously.

"Fool," the hard case said, "you've done it now. We're all goners."

Colt said, "Mister, I have plenty of bullets left."

The man shut up and began trying to bandage his leg and hand.

Colt said to Slim, "Of the Millard Mining Corporation?"

The third man said, "Thet's the same durned

one, Mr. Colt, and he has more money than the good Lord. We are all dead now fer spillin' the beans."

The hard case said, "We didn't. Slim did."

The third one said, "Makes no never mind. He's our ridin' partner. Ya shoot at him, yer shootin' at me."

Colt said, "Friend, I don't go around looking for trouble. In fact, I do everything I can to avoid it, but it seems to me you must enjoy getting into trouble. Now we are going to take a ride down to Westcliffe and pay a visit to the Custer County sheriff. If you want to save yourself the ride, I can hand you back your guns and we'll have at it right here and now. It's your choice."

The hard case spoke up immediately. "Boys, let's see if'n he's man enough to take us up on that. I don't want to die of hemp fever nohow."

Colt felt the gauntlet was going to be taken up, and his mind immediately bent upon ways to even the odds a little bit. He would have to if they wanted to fight it out. The other two, however, showed no interest and the hard case lost his right away.

It was shortly after sunset when Chris Colt rode into the town of Westcliffe with his prisoners in tow. Each had his hands tied behind his back, his ankles tied under his horse, and was facing toward the rear of the mount. The sheriff walked out the door, followed by a tall, good-looking lawman with a badge on a black leather vest.

The sheriff said, "Well, lookkee here. Mr. Colt's been out huntin' varmints. Ya gonna skin 'em and sell the hides?"

"Naw, Sheriff," Chris said, "thought I'd turn 'em over to you and see if you can stretch their necks out, maybe get a longer hide."

The good-looking lawman had a friendly smile

and twinkle in his eyes. He said, "I'll just bet you that you want to stretch their necks because you do not admire their artwork."

Colt liked the man immediately and replied, "You got that right, partner. They didn't like the shape of my brand on my cattle and were just gathering up a bunch of those cows so they could rework the art with those running irons they got carrying on their saddles—or were those just extra cinch rings you carry, boys?"

The hard case turned and glared at Colt, and Chris said, "Guess they aren't in the mood to talk. You know how those artsy folks can be."

The stranger-lawman and sheriff chuckled, and the stranger stepped forward, offering his hand to Colt as the scout dismounted. They shook, while the sheriff summoned a deputy to assist him with the rustlers.

Chris said, "Howdy, Marshal, name's Chris Colt. Got a ranch north of here."

The man smiled broadly. "Whooey, I've sure heard of you, Colt. Just passing through. Delivered an escaped prisoner down at Canon City and thought I'd visit this old geezer here. Name's Destry."

"Destry," Colt said. "Heard of you, too. Nothing but good things. Welcome to southern Colorado."

"Sure is beautiful country," Destry said. "Ran into one of the Sacketts on the way here, and he said he met you down in New Mexico. Told me to tell you hallo if I met you."

Colt said, "Sackett was being modest. He saved my bacon down in New Mexico, or my scalp might have been hanging on old Victorio's belt. Those Sacketts are some good men."

"I'll say they are. Well, I got to get an early start. Nice meeting you, Colt. Real pleasure."

They shook again.

Colt said, "You, too, Marshal Destry. Safe trip."

With that, Chris walked into the sheriff's office to swear out a complaint. Destry disappeared into the darkness, heading toward his hotel room and a soft goose-down mattress.

Colt spent the night in town and headed toward his ranch at daybreak, knowing that Shirley wouldn't worry. Man Killer, his young Nez Percé sidekick, was at the ranch and would watch over her almost as well as Chris could. The lad was in his late teens and seemed much older than his years. He had been following a stolen horse herd and was taken in by Colt in his early teens. He wanted to learn how to live in the white man's world and was constantly learning from one of the best teachers possible. He knew what the future held, but he also had great pride in being Nez Percé, especially being from the band of Hin-Ma-Too-Yah-Lat-Kekht, "Thunder-Traveling-to-Loftier-Heights," but better known to all white men as Chief Joseph. Man Killer was in love with a gorgeous blonde down the valley named Jennifer Banta, and she with he. He was also becoming legendary for his own feats of bravery, but Chris Colt was his hero and his mentor.

In the morning, Colt rode up to the ranch house by a circuitous route which took him along the banks of Texas Creek. He would glance down at the rocky bottom and see shiny little streaks of brook trout, passing from rock cover to rock cover eating bugs. Colt seldom took the same route to any familiar locations. He had too many enemies about. He put War Bonnet up in the barn and gave him a bait of grain and fresh hay, after a good rub-down.

Chris walked toward the ranch house and heard sobbing from inside. Too much bad had happened to his wife previously, so he crept forward, .45 gripped tightly in his right hand, expecting the worst. He crouched down and dashed to the window below the kitchen pump. He peered in the window and saw his beautiful auburn-haired wife, Shirley, staring out at the nearby "big range," tears streaking down her high cheekbones.

Colt holstered his gun and ran back to the cover of the trees. He knew what he was looking for. He ran until he was out of breath, but he came to a small meadow not far from his home which was covered with numerous types and colors of wild-flowers. He quickly picked a large bouquet and headed back toward his house.

Colt went in the door with a big smile on his face and Shirley quickly tried to wipe away and hide her tears. He handed her the flowers, lifted her into his arms, and kissed her long and hard and full on the lips. She just squeezed his neck then, and buried her head in his neck and sobbed. He carried her into their bedroom and laid her down gently. Colt sat on the bed, pillow in his lap, and stroked his wife's hair while she cried. He never asked for an explanation. He just stroked her hair and waited.

When Shirley's sobs subsided, Chris got up and walked out of the little room. He returned with a cup of steaming coffee, handing it to her. She sat up, smiling, and accepted it, carefully sipping.

Colt finally spoke. "You know, Shirl, you are such an incredibly strong person. Many times you hold up your troubles the way a big dam holds back tons of water. Sometimes a lot of the water behind the dam has to be released or the whole thing could just break."

Shirley smiled and said, "Chris, sometimes when you are away overnight or longer, I don't worry about you, I just get scared. I remember the past."

She started to sob again but caught herself.

He smiled softly. "Honey, you cry if you need to. I'll hold you till spring if you want. I caught the rustlers. Turned what was left of them over to the law."

She said, "Figured that. You know, I was looking up at the snow on Spread Eagle Peak blowing around today, and I thought about my winter that I was a hostage of the Cheyenne. That one brave was going to offer three ponies and buy me, and here comes Chris Colt with a whole herd of horses and traded them for me. My hero."

She smiled and Chris blushed.

She got serious again and said, "It struck me strange. The white men call Indians savages, yet they never touched me. That . . . that Will Sawyer. He was the savage. Even if he would have . . . would have forced me only one time, it might be easier to cope with. He didn't, though, Chris. He raped me repeatedly. It was daily and in front of those other men, while they cheered."

Shirley burst into tears again and threw herself against his big chest, sobbing heavily. He held her tight and rocked her from side to side.

Chris looked out the window and spoke softly. "They're all dead now, except in your memory, and they won't die there, but they will fade away some with time."

She had stopped crying again and Colt held her at arm's length and looked deep into her eyes.

"What's important for you to know is that I love you, Shirley Colt, with all my heart, and always will. You also need to know that you didn't do anything wrong to deserve what happened, except to be in love with me. But that bully got his comeuppance, like bullies always do. You didn't do anything wrong, but you did a whole lot right. You survived, didn't you?"

"Chris Colt, you are such a wonderful man," she said. "I love you so much, my darling."

She melted into Colt's arms and they kissed again. He lay down and held her tight until she fell asleep in his arms.

Shirley Colt awakened and sat bolt upright in bed. She looked around from left to right and noticed that it was dark outside. Everything was at first a fog, but she quickly realized she had fallen asleep while speaking with Chris. She wondered where he was and what time of night it was.

She got out of bed and heard giggling. She walked to the doorway and saw Chris Colt seated in front of the fire, cigar in his mouth, giving their little toddler boy, Joseph, a "horse ride" on his foot. Colt was beaming with pride and his little son was giggling with enthusiasm. A tear forming in her eye, she watched her two men and smiled. She enjoyed watching, but as usual, Chris always knew what was going on around him.

He never looked or glanced. He just said, "Hi, Sleeping Princess. You hungry?"

"Starved. Why?"

He got up and handed Joseph to his mother, walking over to her Dutch oven. He grabbed her leather pot holders and opened the door, pulling a crock out of the oven. Steam poured off a casserole dish while Chris took it to the table and set it down. That was when she noticed the candles and vase of flowers, along with dishes and silverware. Colt gave a whistle that sound like that of a marmot, and seconds later, Man Killer appeared in the doorway. He came in the house and took Joseph from Shirley's arms.

He said, "Nice nap, Shirl?"

She gave Chris a quizzical look and smiled at the

Nez Percé saying, "Yeah, thanks. What are you doing, Man Killer?"

He held Joseph in his left arm and picked up a parfleche of Chris's in his other. Shirley saw the edge of some diaper cloths sticking out of it.

He said, "Joseph needs to learn some of the games of the Nez Percé. We will have fun in the bunkhouse tonight."

He walked out the door tickling the little boy, while Shirley gave Chris another amazed look.

Colt said, "Thought you were starved, Shirl."

He held the chair for her while she sat at the table. The giant oak table had been handcarved by a local German furniture maker, but her pride and joy were the chairs at the table. Chris had made them all by carefully matching and intertwining the shed antlers of mule deer bucks around a frame made from shed elk antlers. The antlers were all fashioned into high-backed chairs and were then tightly bound in several places by rawhide thongs. She had made cushions for the seat of each one, and everyone who visited talked about them.

Colt served her an antelope stew he had learned from the Comanches to make when he scouted against them. There had been a love-hate relationship between Colt and the Comanches, and some had befriended him, as he was highly respected. The stew had carrots and potatoes cooked in the juice along with some sage, wild onion, pepper, salt, and other local spices. He also served her coffee, bread, and fresh tomatoes from their garden. The meal was delicious.

Eyes again glistening, she said, "You know, Christopher Columbus Colt, you are a legend as a chief of scouts and gunfighter. You are famous all over the country, but nobody knows that you are probably the most wonderful husband in the world."

Colt thought back into his own past to his former Minniconjou Lakota wife, Chantapeta, and daughter Winona. They were long since dead. He also remembered a special woman, Sarah Guthrie, a widow he had shared his loneliness and sorrow with intimately. Like him, her family had been snatched away by a Crow war party.

Colt knew that he could never ever take this woman he loved for granted. He knew she could be taken away too easily.

The beautiful Sangre de Cristo mountains held many secrets, and one of those secrets was that their beauty was offset by their harshness. It was a savage and tough land and the hardy people who lived on it could be taken away in the flash of an eye by a lightning bolt, bullet, arrow, avalanche, blizzard, grizzly, or many other dangers. Like so many things in nature, the pristine countryside around them was a contradiction. It could provide so much sensory fulfillment, or it could kill you, just like that.

When they finished dinner and a slice of the apple pie she had made the day before, they sat across from each other, smiling. Again she got a tear in her eye.

Colt said, "Must be that time of month?"

"No," she said, chuckling, "that came and went while you were on that short scout for that renegade out of Old Bent's Fort last week."

"Oh," Chris said, and bowed his head in mock embarrassment.

She said, "I just realized again how very special you are, Colt."

Like others, she loved to call him by his last

name. Sometimes he jokingly called her "Colt," too.

"I'm not, so much. You make me anything good I might be."

She stared at him and shook her head in wonder.

Colt stood and walked around the table, extending his hand. She took it, and he helped her up.

"Care to dance, Mrs. Colt?" he asked.

She said, "But there's no music."

"Wanna bet?" he replied, and led her outside on their new plank porch. "Listen."

The wind blew down off the mountains and across the meadows, making a soft whistling sound. Not far from the house, Texas Creek gurgled along its grassy banks, and off in the trees were the sounds of thousands of crickets rubbing their hind legs together. On top of that, a far-off bird made a constant whistling sound.

Colt said, "Prettiest music in the world."

He swept his pretty wife into his arms, and they started dancing.

Colt didn't tell Shirley about the mining company. She didn't need to worry about that as far as he was concerned. Colt and Man Killer would deal with that the next day.

The road that ran west of Canon City was called the "river road," as it went up across Eight Mile Hill, by-passing the Grand Canyon of the Arkansas, which became known as the Royal Gorge. It kept on west and down a steep hill to the western apex of the gorge canyon, where the angry churning Arkansas River carved its way through the thousand-foot sheer walls. There at Parkdale was the crossing, and the river road continued on next to the whitewater river toward Salida.

Preston Millard's Millard Mining Corporation was

headquartered on the river road toward Eight Mile
Hill, but actually carried on mining operations in
that area and all the way up Copper Gulch Stage
Road and up into the Sangre de Cristos.

Colt and Man Killer arrived in the rocky foothills
overlooking the Grand Canyon of the Arkansas late
in the afternoon, pushing their horses hard. They
rode down Copper Gulch, cut over through Pine
Gulch, and down to Grape Creek, which they followed all the way to its mouth at the east end of the
gorge. They forded the Arkansas right there and
traveled back west, climbing slowly up a thousand
feet in the process. They stayed close to the rim of
the gorge canyon and held to the piñons and stunted
cedars that grew all over the Eight Mile Hill area.
Several times they wound out of the trees and rode
along the canyon rim, looking straight down from
the cliffs over a thousand feet and saw the churning
river below. From that height, though, the Arkansas
looked like a small blue ribbon that wound between the giant rock walls. In fact the rapids in the
Royal Gorge were the toughest of any stretch of
the Arkansas, having claimed several lives each
year.

The two men made camp in the trees in a little
hollow not far from the canyon rim. They made a
small smokeless fire and fixed lunch, not having
stopped for any earlier in the day. Man Killer had
selected their camping site, because there was a
small glade nearby where the water gathered after
storms and the sparse gramma grasses grew a little
thicker. The two horses had worked hard, alternating
between a ground-eating canter and a fast trot to get
the men down to the Royal Gorge that day. Colt
packed some sweet feed for them with some barley,
corn, and molasses mixed together, and the two big

steeds ate heartily. They would not leave the glade area and could be summoned with a whistle.

Colt wasn't worried about camping where they did, because they were in close proximity to Canon City and could easily explain to anyone why they were in the area. He would just say they were spending the night on their way from or to Canon City. But in fact, before daybreak and during the next day, the two experts would scout the Millard Mining Corporation and see what they could detect.

When he was in Westcliffe, Colt had hired a couple of out-of-work ranch hands to drive the small herd of cattle back to the Coyote Run and to gather the rest of his cows that they could find. He wanted them better protected while he was gone. His brother Joshua, who actually ran the ranch operation, was gone to Texas and Missouri to drive cows back. With him were the Coyote Run's two top hands, old Tex Westchester and the giant Muley Hawkins. That had left Chris and Man Killer to mind the ranch, which they enjoyed doing anyway. It was hard, rewarding work and a great diversion from their scouting duties.

Chris Colt used his razor-sharp bowie knife to shave off slices of bacon into the small cast iron frying pan. Man Killer, in the meantime, mixed biscuit dough in his metal coffee cup. He stirred it with a green cedar stick, then twisted the wet stick around, wrapping the dough around it into a biscuit shape. Each little roll was saved to be fried in the grease when Colt finished the bacon. Chris also had a pot of coffee boiling on the fire. He shaved pieces of potato into the pan with the bacon strips, along with small slices of carrot.

After dinner, the two men smoked rolled cigarettes and Colt looked up at the stars, formulating plans for the next day. Man Killer sat by the campfire and read "The Pit and the Pendulum" by Edgar Allan Poe. Ever since meeting Jennifer Banta, the handsome Nez Percé had become a voracious reader. Man Killer was acutely aware of his ancestry and the racism in white American society, but he was determined to become successful in both the white man's world and his own. All the while, he would do so as a Nez Percé warrior. That was his legacy.

They ate again after dark and went to sleep early, awakening several hours before daybreak. It was still dark when Colt and Man Killer arrived at the Millard Mining Corporation headquarters off the river road. The place was quiet and nobody was working the several open prospect holes on the grounds. There were several armed guards and Colt wondered what that meant. Why would a mining company without even a shaft of a gold mine on its property have a number of heavily armed guards? he wondered. The sentries each wore double six-shooters, carried Winchester repeaters, and had crossed bandoliers of ammunition for the rifles.

There were four buildings: the wood frame headquarters building, an outhouse, the tool shed, and an explosives shed. Leaving their horses back among the rocks, the two went forward on foot. Man Killer remained behind on a small red hilltop and kept watch on the sentries, while Colt sneaked forward to the headquarters building. He had to time his approach to avoid the sentries. He imagined they were being well paid. Their clothing and guns were in good shape, and they were alert, which was unusual for any kind of sentries. Even on Indian campaigns in dangerous territory, Colt often found guards napping on duty.

Moving carefully and quietly, wearing his soft-soled moccasins, Colt made his way to the head-quarters building. He hid underneath the plank porch and waited for the two nearest sentries to walk away from the building. He used his knife to pry open the door and closed it quietly behind him, making sure the lock was still set.

Colt immediately went to the large hand-carved desk in the corner. He pulled the desk drawers out and started leafing through piles and papers, crouching under the desk and striking matches one at a time for light. He found nothing. There were several pieces of paper atop the desk with the bottom half of the top paper torn off. At the top of the page were the words "*Coyote Run.*" Colt found nothing else, but he did look in the wastebasket for the bottom half. It wasn't there.

Colt looked on top of the desk, near the window, thankful for the full moon's light. He found paper ashes and a burned match in an ashtray on the big desk. Colt knew that it must be the ashes from the bottom half of the paper from the other desk. Millard was certainly being careful, he thought. Colt knew that he would find nothing in the office if the man was that careful. He did have an idea, though. He grabbed the blank sheet of paper laying on the desk under the torn sheet. He carefully rolled it and tucked it inside his buckskin shirt. With that, he checked to make sure he had not dropped any of his burned matchsticks and crawled toward the door.

Chris rejoined Man Killer with no incident and the two men retreated to their horses, leaving the mining area just before daybreak. They rode back to the cliffs overlooking the Royal Gorge and found a steep cut going down. They followed it and found shelter under the cliff overhang in a small area where the horses could carefully graze, though one misstep could mean a fall of over a thousand feet.

Colt and Man Killer were too smart to return to their previous campsite, unless it was an exceptional and well-hidden one.

They started to set up camp, but Colt said, "Wait, we'll go to Canon City, get a hotel room, and snoop around for a day."

They were checking into the McClure House Hotel within the hour. On the way, they flagged down the colorful Colorado Stage and Express Company six-horse Concord stage. It departed each morning for Silver Cliff and Rosita at seven-thirty, arriving there at three in the afternoon.

The driver was a tobacco chewer and spitter named Ruby Granby.

When Colt heard the man's name he immediately asked the story behind it.

The gruff man laughed and said, "Mr. Colt, I was sech an ornery creature even at birth and before thet. My sainted ole ma jest had a horrible time with me, and my pa would fuss and holler. No matter what, though, ma always said I was her little gem. Mebbe she was expectin' a girl. So's anyhow, oncet I was born, my ole pa and his rotten sense humor ups and names me Ruby on account ma kept sayin' I was her li'l gem."

A monarch butterfly fluttered by the stage and the old man took careful aim and spit, narrowly missing it.

Colt handed him a note for Shirley and asked him to give it to the sheriff, with directions to have it dropped off to her by anyone heading toward Texas Creek or Cotopaxi.

Chris just wanted to let her know where he and

Man Killer were and the fact that they were staying in Canon City.

"Pleasure meeting you, Ruby," Colt said. "I know you're on a tight schedule. Sorry to hold you up."

Ruby spit a giant brown stream at a hummingbird on a roadside bush and said, "Hell, Colt. You neen't never apologize noways. My home is up in Silver Cliff and ever since you bought yer ranch hereabouts, stage holdups and sech mischief has really gone down. Whene'er ya want sumthin', jest name it."

After checking in, the two men went to the Canon City Hot Springs. Single baths were advertised for $1 and tickets could be bought for $4.50 per dozen.

Man Killer had been here once before with Chris, but this time was interested in the writing on the hotel's advertising. It read:

Among the diseases in which the most marked benefit has been noticed by use of the bath, may be mentioned rheumatism, cutaneous diseases, catarrh, torpidity of the liver, diseases of the kidneys, and all scrofulous affections.

The Springs have one of the finest sanitary locations in Colorado. The altitude being about five thousand feet (nearly two thousand feet less than any other hot springs in the State), they offer to the new comer an especial advantage, as it is not safe or desirable for invalids to go immediately into a high altitude.

There was also a sign on the wall which read:

"Of all the mineral waters of the West which I have analyzed, I find those of Canon City the best."
                    Professor Lowe, the Wheeler Expedition

A chart on the wall showed the percentage of grains of various minerals per gallon of water. Still another stated that the constant temperature of the water was 104 degrees.

Man Killer, as usual, received many stares as he entered the hot springs bathhouse, with his braided hair and carrying his book of Edgar Allen Poe. Nobody dared say anything, though, since he was in the company of the famous shootist and ruffian Chris Colt.

Reading all the material in the place, Man Killer finally said, "Tell me, great scout, what does all of this mean?"

Colt smiled and said, "It means the water's hot, so it feels good for sore muscles and sinew."

Man Killer smiled and slid into the comfortable steaming water, opening his book to the marked page.

That night, over steak dinners, Colt and Man Killer met three men, two of whom were obviously distinguished-looking easterners. The third was obviously a man of importance, but he was a man of the West. Chris learned he was H. Hufhus, the superintendent of the Astor Mine and Milling Company at Galena, near the Custer County border. The other two were William Shepherd, the company president, and its secretary, G. O. Pearce, both of these men being from New York City. They were out to visit and inspect the mining operation, just one of their many holdings.

Colt bought these men drinks and tried to find out what he could about Millard Mining, but only Hufhus had heard anything, and that was that Millard was a simply a local mining operation, was very popular, and there were some rumors about claim jumping in the Sangre de Cristos, but sometimes that just went with any successful mining operation. They hadn't hit any large strikes; he did know that. The men had a branch office at the Astor Hotel in New York and told Colt that they would be happy to check for him when they returned, and would let him in on anything they discovered.

That night, in the hotel room, Colt pulled out the rolled-up blank sheet of paper. Man Killer watched with interest. Next, Colt went downstairs where the big stone fireplace stood in the lobby. He returned to the room shortly with a charred piece of wood from the fire.

Finally the brave could no longer contain himself and said, "What are you doing, Colt?"

Chris winked and said, "Tracking."

Colt smoothed out the paper sheet on his dresser top while the Nez Percé looked on. Next, Colt held the flat edge of the charcoal lightly against the paper and rubbed it up and down the page, carefully, gingerly.

He explained to Man Killer that this was the paper directly under one on which Millard had written something pertaining to Coyote Run. Colt hoped that the man had pressed hard with his pen and left an indentation on the next paper. He had.

Below *"Coyote Run,"* which Colt had already seen in the office, it read: *"Chris Colt—Lost Brother."*

Colt felt a rush of adrenaline course through his body, and he looked at Man Killer, saying, "Joshua's in trouble. I have to go after him. You have to get back to Coyote Run and watch over Shirl, Joseph, and the ranch."

Man Killer headed toward the door, grabbing his war bag on the way, saying, "I will go now."

"No," Colt said. "We'll sleep and both leave in the morning refreshed. I'll draw some money from the bank and ship War Bonnet and myself on a train part of the way."

Chapter 3

»»»»»»»»»»»»»

Man Killer

The next day, Man Killer left before daybreak.
Colt had to draw some money from Fremont
County Bank and laughed when he heard a tale going around that apparently was totally true. The
bank's only competitor was directly across the street
from Fremont Bank and the president was considered a harsh and judgmental old windbag. A week
earlier, he had refused a loan for a prominent and respected rancher and his wife, who were some of the
earlier settlers in the valley. The rancher was a typ-
ical western cattleman. He could give his handshake
and word on something and to him that was a legally
binding contract.

The rancher's wife apparently took exception to
the loan refusal by the banker despite her husband
giving his word that the money would have been
paid back. She decided to give the would-be money
lender a piece of her mind, so she set off for down-
town Canon City one morning and waited outside
the bank. She held something in her hand, but nobody saw it. At midmorning, the bank president left
for his usual two-hour lunch. When he walked out
onto the street, the tough frontier woman raised her
hand and blew an entire handful of red pepper into
the banker's eyes. While he screamed in agony,
she gave him a piece of her mind, then stormed
off.

Colt bought passage at Beaver for he and War Bonnet to ride in a boxcar on the Denver & Rio Grande Railroad.

Man Killer was almost halfway up Copper Gulch road when he spotted some cattle tracks going up Sunset Gulch. There were plenty of cattle and cattle ranches around, but one thing stood out. Any other tracker, with the exception of Colt, would have missed it, but Man Killer saw one track out of the tracks of fifty cow-calf pairs that caught his attention. It toed out at an odd angle, and he could tell the cow's size and weight by the depth of the track and size. It was about a seven-hundred-pounder.

Men like Chris Colt and Man Killer, like smart bank tellers learning to recognize a person's signature at a glance, could look at a cow, man, or horse track a few times and commit it to memory. Each one had something a little different. This particular cow had gotten her leg caught and broken way up north on Cottonwood Creek and the leg healed at an odd angle.

The warrior pulled his Winchester out and walked slowly into Sunset Gulch, knowing that a bullet with his name on it could come from any direction without notice. His eyes scanned the tracks of the cows, trying to see where the herd had been pushed. Man Killer rode slowly up the gulch for a half an hour until he finally came to what he had expected, an expedient log corral fashioned by poles placed across the mouth of a steep gulch.

He rode up the side of the gulch and around the fence across its mouth. Moving slowly through the trees, he looked for signs of man, but saw nobody. There was a small spring in the end of the gulch and a cistern had been dug out and shored up with rocks. Several cows stood around the water tank, and a small group of calves played around the spring.

Each cow and calf had been freshly marked with a brand in the shape of a tomahawk. Conveniently, its design would fit right over the top of Coyote Run's brand, which was simply the rough outline of a Colt revolver. Man Killer spotted the ashes of the large branding fire. He rode to the mouth of the corral and waited atop a nearby ridge, finding a good hiding spot among the trees.

Within an hour, two cowpunchers rode up to the gate.

They dismounted at the sound of the Winchester being cocked and Man Killer's voice from the side saying, "Lose the hardware, boys. I'm in the mood for taking scalps."

They dropped their guns on the ground and raised their hands. When they saw Man Killer riding down the hill toward them, however, they wanted to grab for the discarded firearms.

He taunted, "Go ahead. Dive for them. Maybe you'll make it before I plug you."

One of them said, "Are you a real Injun? I never heard no redskin talk like that."

"No," Man Killer said sarcastically, "I'm no Indian. I'm Italian."

"What do you want with us, Redskin?" the other rustler said.

"I want to see you hanged for rustling, Whiteskin."

The first said, "Rustling, ha! How do you think you're going to prove rustling? These are our boss's cattle. All legally branded."

"And you boss, I suppose, is Preston Millard."

Did Man Killer detect a startled look on one of the men? A raised eyebrow on the other?

The first said, "Don't matter. These are his legal cattle, and you can't prove no different."

Man Killer spotted the lame cow and drew his belly gun, a walnut-handled Colt .45 Peacemaker, and fired. The bullet took the animal through the head just below the ear, and it dropped like a sack of flour. The Nez Percé spun the gun twice and replaced it in his waistband.

Man Killer rode up to the rustlers and dismounted, grabbing his leather braided riata in his other hand. He replaced his rifle with his right-hand .45 and slipped the lasso over the first man, tying him to a corral post. He then tied the second man to the next post and then put his gun away, pulling out his razor-sharp bowie.

Man Killer walked over to the dead cow, bent over, and cut the hide in a big square around the brand. He turned the piece of hide over and showed the two rustlers the other side. On the inside of the hide, the colt brand scar was clearly visible, with the new tomahawk brand atop it.

Without saying a word, Man Killer loosened the bonds on the now quite nervous outlaws.

"Now what?" the first rustler asked, obviously frightened.

Man Killer smiled and said, "With the Nez Percé, I had a favorite saying."

"What's that?" asked the second rustler.

Man Killer said, "Kill white men."

He laughed at his own joke and signaled for the two to mount up. He started to mount up as well, but a rifle shot made his horse jump sideways and Man Killer did a somersault, after yanking his carbine from the rifle scabbard. He came up running and firing at the third rustler, who had dismounted and was firing from a kneeling position at the bend of the gulch.

The man flew backward with a large patch of crimson on his chest. Man Killer started receiving fire from the other two, though, who had retrieved their weapons. He dropped his rifle and stood, drawing both short guns. Firing from the hip, the angry warrior walked forward, shooting with both guns and ignoring the fire from his enemies. When both his guns were empty, he actually stopped and realized what had happened. Both rustlers lay on the ground, riddled with bullets and quite dead.

Man Killer released the cattle and started pushing them further up the gulch. He figured he could find a place where he could turn them to the right and head the cattle over to Copper Gulch. From there, he would head them by Deer Mountain, down into Turkey Gulch, cross over a low saddle into Heck Gulch, and bring them out along Texas Creek, just a few miles from the ranch. After getting the cattle to Coyote Run, he would head to Westcliffe and notify the sheriff about the shootout.

It was well after dark when he arrived, but Man Killer managed to get the herd to the ranch. He rode to the house exhausted, after stopping at the bunkhouse and giving directions to the new ranch hands there.

Man Killer knocked on the door and Shirley opened it with a smile. She told him to sit down right away, and she handed him a steaming cup of coffee. Going to the oven and grabbing her pot holders, she pulled out a steaming bowl of beef stew and placed it on the table for him.

Over dinner, he explained everything that had happened.

Shirley thought for a minute and said, "Well, Man Killer, it looks like someone's coming after us. I don't know why, but we will defeat them. It's happened before and it will happen again. I accepted that when I decided to marry a man such as Chris Colt."

"Regret it?" he asked.

"Not a second of it. If I were killed today, I wouldn't have a regret. Marrying Chris was like being granted a special privilege from God."

Man Killer reached into the humidor and pulled out one of Colt's cigars, lighting it. He smiled softly and stared at the flames in the fire.

Shirley walked over to the coffeepot and brought it back to the table, a knowing grin on her face. "By the way, how is Jennifer Banta doing?"

"Oh, fine I guess," Man Killer said.

"Why don't you invite her over for supper on Sunday?"

Man Killer blushed. "Oh, with the trouble that's beginning, Shirl, I don't know if—"

"Nonsense. We are not going to stop living just because some weasel wants to invade our henhouse."

Man Killer smiled. "Okay. What time?"

"Five o'clock."

He blew a long stream of blue smoke at the ceiling and smiled. Then he stood. "Thanks, Shirl. I'm going to turn in."

"Turn in?" she said. "Aren't you starting to sound like a cowpuncher with braids?"

He laughed and walked out the door with a wave.

The U.S. cavalry set fire to the numerous lodges in the Nez Percé village.

Looking Glass ran out of one and Chief Joseph yelled, "No!"

It was too late: the rifle bullet took the old chief between his eyes. Suddenly he became Man Killer's dead brother. The smoke from the lodges swirled toward Man Killer and he could smell it, as the flames crackled.

Smoke! Man Killer's mind screamed, and he flew out of bed in the bunkhouse. His guns were in his hands before his clothes and he looked out the windows of the small building and spotted flames crackling up from the new barn Muley Hawkins had been building. The big giant Muley was with Joshua on the cattle drive but hated to leave the barn project he had started. It was his idea to replace the old barn, and the new one was Muley's pride and joy.

Man Killer yelled at the other hands, "Fire! Get up! Grab buckets make a line to the trough!"

He sprinted out the door and ran toward the big house, his guns drawn. Reaching it, he circled, looking inside. He saw nothing.

He ran to the back door and burst through. "Shirley! Shirley! Are you okay?"

Joseph started crying and Shirley came out of her room, nightgown and robe on.

She gave him a queer look and Man Killer said, "The barn's on fire. See if Joseph's all right."

She ran to the little boy's trundle bed and picked him up, stroking his hair.

"He's okay," she said.

"Lock the door," Man Killer commanded, and ran out to fight the fire.

It was a lost cause, however, because the building was sending angry flames licking up at the night sky, orange tongues of fire shooting fifty feet into the air. Man Killer pulled the men back, and they watched helplessly. He used the big light from the fire to carefully search for tracks and saw that three men on horseback had gone toward the big range. They were smart, he thought; it would be too hard to follow them in the dark forests of the big range at night, and they could turn toward either West-cliffe, Cotopaxi, or farther west, perhaps to Salida.

With nothing left to do that night, Man Killer told everyone to go to bed, assigning the men to take turns keeping watch on the fire so a hot ember wouldn't blow into the trees or another building and start a new fire.

The next morning, he ate breakfast with Shirley and Joseph, assigned chores to the men, and pre-pared to leave for Westcliffe. Shirley came out of the old barn, dressed for riding.

She said, "Is my horse saddled?"

Man Killer gave her a quizzical look.

She said, "You are riding into a white man's town to report a shootout you had with three men, in which you killed them. Think about it."

"The sheriff for Custer County trusts me."

Shirley countered, "What if he's out ill or chasing a bad man? What if a deputy is in charge, and he doesn't care for Indians? You know there's many like that about?"

Man Killer said, "I'll get your horse."

Seconds later, he led a beautiful Palomino geld-ing from a stall and started saddling it. Shirley walked over and handed it a cube of sugar from her pocket, while Man Killer gave her a disapproving look.

She said, "Buttercup, you want to go into town, boy? Here's some sugar."

"That's not a good idea."

"Why?"

"First, Indians never had bad teeth until the white man came. The sugar does it, but the bad thing is that a horse who gets treats all the time that come from your pocket will bite your pockets when you are not looking. Many times your skin is close to your pockets, so it gets bitten, too."

"Okay, I'll remember that," she said. "What about carrots, if I carry them from the garden or house?"

Man Killer smiled, saying, "Maybe Buttercup will eat too many and become a rabbit."

Shirley laughed and placed the bridle over her horse's head. Man Killer tightened the cinch and removed her canteen from the saddle, carrying it and his own to the gravity-run water pipe. The water came through a pipe from a spring behind and slightly uphill from the ranch.

Shirley gave Buttercup a pat and turned toward the door, saying, "I'll be back. I have to get Joseph ready."

When Man Killer had both horses saddled, he mounted up and led Man Killer out into the ranch yard. Shirley walked out the door carrying Joseph and a canvas feed bag. Man Killer chuckled as she hung the feed bag over the saddle horn and placed Joseph inside. His little legs stuck out holes she had cut into the corners of the bag, then reinforced with stitching. The little boy looked up at Man Killer and giggled, mumbling something unintelligible. Shirley handed the reins to the Nez Percé and ran back into the house, reappearing with a Winchester eighteen-shot lever-action .45-caliber carbine. She also carried a saddle scabbard which she strapped to her saddle under the right stirrup fender, shoved the gun inside, and mounted up. The two rode down to the road and turned right toward Westcliffe.

After he heard Man Killer's story, the sheriff got some deputies together and led them off toward Copper Gulch, then headed northeast towards Canon City. He would bring the bodies back and investigate the scene of the shooting, but he believed everything Man Killer told him. The next day, he would come out to the ranch to investigate the arson, but Man Killer told him the trail would be too cold and difficult to follow. The sheriff also promised he would try to dig up the dirt on Preston Millard, but he was sure the man probably had covered his tracks well. As for the tomahawk brand, he said would have known if a new brand would have been registered in the area. He promised to wire the state brand board to double-check.

In Kansas, War Bonnet cantered over some small rolling hills. It had been totally flat for miles, but once Colt got more into the eastern half of the state, he found depressions in the landscape, which gave way to the rolling hills. He was well east of Fort Leavenworth when he reined up on top of a large grass knoll with a sweeping view of the Santa Fe Trail. At a distance, Colt saw a very long column of Conestoga wagons headed west, followed by a very large herd of cattle comprised of Hereford, black bollies, black-white faces, and a few longhorns. This was probably the operation his brother Joshua was working in. Everything looked normal at that great distance, but Colt had been around too much to trust that. Joshua was in danger and Colt had to be there to help him when the danger, whatever it was, threatened to strike. He would circle the giant train and herd before approaching it, looking for any signs of trouble.

It was hours later, and Colt had made a giant circle around the portable town when he did find a sign of potential trouble. There were the tracks of twenty men watching the massive column. They had been watching from a knoll overlooking the Santa Fe Trail from the east while Colt had originally watched from the west.

Colt found several spots where the watchers had

been smoking rolled-up cigarettes. One man had smoked a pipe, and Colt found his dumped-out ashes. He also found an impression in the dirt where the main group had squatted and watched. Someone had used binoculars and laid them down on their side. The main thing the tracks told him was that the group of men watching had not wanted to be seen. They stayed inside the trees. Their horses, watched over by three of the men, had been kept on the other side of the hill out of sight of the train.

The group had gone from the area after the wagon train passed, but not before it had passed from sight. Colt could tell by the age of the tracks and freshness of the horses' droppings. The gang went on toward the west but veering south somewhat. Chris figured that they would pick up the wagon train again farther along. Maybe they would go to a town for supplies, but he did feel that they would strike sometime before the train and drive got to the really flat western part of Kansas. He was sure that a group that size had to be after the herd of cattle, and there were a lot more hiding areas in this half of the state.

Colt finished his circle and found no more sign, then galloped ahead to catch up with the cattle herd and remuda. Colt spotted Joshua, who happened to be riding drag, and Chris grinned to himself knowing his brother was doing this to set an example for his cowpunchers. Joshua was part owner and ramrod of a major ranch operation. He didn't have to choke on trail dust and follow a large herd.

Colt was going to ride down and join his brother, but then he noticed a single rider holding a good ways back behind the big herd. Colt decided to watch the man for a while to make sure. He had to protect his older brother, and staying out of sight seemed the best way to do it right then.

Whoever was planning on killing Joshua, Colt decided, was going to have to learn an expensive lesson. You go after one Colt, you might as well be going after the others, because you're going to have to deal with them. The lesson would be so expensive because the price would be paid in blood. Colt decided to follow along the ridges as much as possible. The man following the herd was really bothering him now, because the lone rider was pacing the herd and not trying to overtake it.

As Man Killer and Shirley left the sheriff's office, the young Nez Percé said, "Can I buy you lunch today, Shirl?"

"Okay, I'd love it. Thank you," she replied.

Man Killer beamed.

He said, "Why don't we ride down the road to Silver Cliff? I know a good place."

The road east out of Westcliffe ran almost straight into Silver Cliff, as the city limits of the two towns almost met each other. Shirley noticed a six-story red brick hotel with a nice yard. Located at the corner of Dewalt and Main streets, it looked very clean, and for some reason she felt that was where Man Killer was taking her. Indeed it was, and Man Killer led her up to the front of the building and they tied their horses at a hitching rail under some planted trees in front of the concrete fence.

The sign in the front read:

POWELL HOUSE
THE FINEST HOTEL IN THE CITY
ABELL & BRACKEN, PROPRS.

When they walked through the front door, into the fancy foyer another sign read:

This house has been newly furnished from cellar to garret, and has all the conveniences of FIRST CLASS HOTEL. The tables are suppled with the best the market affords, with polite and attentive waiters. CHARGES REASONABLE—SPECIAL RATES TO FAMILIES.

They were seated, although Man Killer received a number of stares, and the entire dining room got very quiet.

Man Killer said aloud, "I guess, Shirley, these people have never seen a woman with auburn hair."

Shirley chuckled out loud. A few throats were cleared and people resumed their conversations and culinary activities.

The two nodded as glasses of water were poured and menus handed to them; and a few minutes later, Man Killer just beamed as a gorgeous young blond woman about sixteen or eighteen approached their table. She had hair that fell to below her buttocks and looked as if it had just been dipped into a bucket of honey and it was running off the ends. Her eyes were very light, bright blue. Shirley glanced at her and smiled, then looked over at Man Killer with a "that-explains-it" look.

Shirley said, "Jennifer Banta, how in the world are you?"

"Just fine, Shirley. It's good to see you," Jennifer replied. "Hello, Man Killer."

"Hello, Jennifer. "How are you?"

Shirley grinned to herself and concentrated on her menu as she watched the new lovers almost fall all over each. She excused herself and took Joseph from the room to change his diapers.

When Shirley returned, Jennifer was in the kitchen and Man Killer told her that he had ordered for her.

"When did Jennifer start working here?"

"Last week."

"Oh," Shirley said, "but you were simply hungry today and invited me to eat with you?"

Like a chameleon, changing into his poetic Nez Percé conversational pattern, he said, "Good friend, sister ... you do need put food into your stomach when it growls like a cornered badger."

Shirley smiled and said, "Great brave, if I were cornered by an angry badger, I would stab him with a pitchfork."

Laughing, Man Killer held his fork out and brought it in for his stomach, pretending to stab himself. He feigned dying and both laughed while Jennifer walked up with their food.

The two talked during the meal and laughed at Joseph, who kept falling asleep sitting in Shirley's lap, his head bobbing up and down.

When they had eaten, after a short conversation with Jennifer they walked outside to the horses. Man Killer spotted a problem immediately. There was a group of four hard cases near the two horses. One was leaning against a tree and another against the hitching rack. A third whittled on a piece of wood, and the fourth was checking the loads in a pair of much-used Russian .44s. Man Killer sensed trouble by the sidelong glances they gave each other and the muttering under their breaths as he approached.

He grabbed Shirley by the forearm and turned her around, handing her her son, whom he had been carrying.

"What is it?" she asked, alarmed.

"Those men. Trouble."

Shirley Colt knew enough of her husband and Man Killer not to ask how they knew if either sensed trouble. They were experts at recognizing it.

Man Killer steered them quickly back toward the restaurant.

In front of it, Man Killer gave out the loud whistle of a marmot, twice. Hawk, his sixteen-hands-tall black Appaloosa, threw his head up and pulled back from the hitching rail, his reins unwrapping. He ran forward and vaulted over the concrete fence and was soon followed by Buttercup, the Palomino not wanting to be left behind.

The men came forward, but Man Killer helped Shirley mount up and followed suit, riding off in the direction of Westcliffe. Man Killer looked back to the group of men and grinned. One of them kicked the dirt hard with his toe.

It was past nightfall when they arrived back at the ranch.

The stars were plentiful over the clear Kansas sky and Brandon escorted Elizabeth outside the circle of wagons. They had made their circle, as usual, near water and the cottonwoods cast long shadows. The mile-wide Santa Fe Trail was clearly visible as it headed toward the west. Stopping by an old fallen tree, Brandon helped Elizabeth to sit on it. They looked out at the prairie, up at the moon and the Milky Way, then into each other's eyes.

Elizabeth said, "This is so far from civilization, so far from where you can practice law successfully. I understand the West is full of the lawless: heathens, and bullies, and ruffians. You must be leaving so much potential to accumulate wealth in St. Louis."

Brandon looked out at the sweeping panorama in front of them and said, "For so long now, Elizabeth, I have felt alone. I believe in the law, but I have not felt like what I am doing is important. Thomas Paine said, 'Man must go back to nature for information.'

That's what I must do, Elizabeth. I believe that people like me are needed in the new frontier."

"But Brandon." she said. "you are a successful advocate. You could have surely taken a train and shipped all of your belongings, as well."

"I did not want to."

"But why?" she asked, genuinely curious.

Brandon blushed and cleared his throat. He looked out at the prairie again and said, "You were not on the train."

Elizabeth blushed now.

He turned his gaze back at her eyes and was totally entranced. Suddenly Brandon swept her up into his arms and held her close. Their noses were now inches apart. She smiled slightly, and their lips came together slowly. They kissed, softly at first, then let their lips melt into each other's. They pulled apart and he smiled down at her, then kissed her eyelids slowly. They hugged.

"Wal, wal, wal, ain't this jest purty, now," a voice came unexpectedly.

Brandon and Elizabeth, startled, turned their heads and stared into the business end of a Spencer rifle. It was being held by Willard Lawson, the man who had taken a shot at Brandon earlier after losing the lawsuit to Brandon's client. The man's clothes were filthy, his beard unkempt, and his eyes had a crazed look. Previously he had been impeccably dressed always, and a tonsorial example of excellence, with neatly trimmed beard and hair.

Brandon shoved Elizabeth behind him and held her there with one arm. He could feel her body quivering.

Brandon said, "Lawson! You were imprisoned."

"Wasn't I, though, you bastard, and your black heart!" Lawson raved. "But, Rudd, you should see the pretty work a red brick does on the head of a jailer. Ha, ha. Split it like a melon, and I have chased you down for miles and days, Brandon Rudd. And now I'm a gonna send ya ta hell with a lead express ticket."

Brandon said, "Fine, but let's let the lady leave first. You have always been quite the gentleman, Willard, and I know you don't want her to witness this."

"On the contrary, you son of a mongrel bitch," Lawson said, "I saw the look in your eyes. I think I'll gut-shoot her first, then come back in a day or two, after you've had a chance ta watch her suffer good."

Brandon said, "Now, Willard, as I said, I know you're a true gentleman and a real man, but your jest may frighten this young lady. We should let her return to the wagon circle. Then you can have done with me."

"Naw, Rudd. Good try, but she's the one ya love, so ah'ma gonna plug 'er oncet or twicet."

"The one I love," Brandon said. "Ha—she's just a harmless Jezebel I met on the wagon train, and I paid her handsomely for an hour of her time in the moonlight. You saw the way she kissed me."

"Reckon yer right there, but no matter. She seen me, an I ain't leavin' her fer no witnessin' agin me." He raised the rifle and cocked it.

Brandon got a very serious look on his face. "All right, Lawson. You are going to shoot me, but before I die, I'm going to get my hands around that skinny neck of yours and you will not shoot her. Elizabeth, when I rush at him, or if he shoots me, you run and don't look back."

Elizabeth was so scared she couldn't even speak.

Lawson aimed his gun and grinned evilly.

"Mister, I don't think that would be a very good idea," a voice said from the darkness.

All three looked to the side and saw a smiling Chris Colt leveling his twin-eagle-gripped Peacemakers at Willard Lawson.

Lawson stared at the big man. "Who are you, mister?"

Chris motioned for the man to drop his gun. "Name's Colt."

"That's Chris Colt," Brandon exclaimed. "I've heard so much about him, I know that's who he must be."

"So yer Colt, huh?" Lawson said. "I figgered you'd be ten feet tall, all the tales I heerd of ya, but you don't look so much ta me. I ain't throwin' no gun down. Now, I'm aimin' at this purty little gal here, so's how about you droppin' yer hoglegs?"

Colt dropped his Peacemakers and Brandon's heart sunk. Lawson chuckled and started to swing the rifle toward Chris, but the scout dived forward, reaching down the back of his shirt. He did a somersault as the rifle boomed and the bullet cracked by his left ear. His hand flipped forward and a large bowie knife came out of the back of his buckskin shirt and spun through the air. It buried itself between the collarbone and shoulder blade of Lawson, and the man let out a howl. Colt dived back for his guns, hit the ground, and rolled while the rifle boomed again and the bullet kicked dirt into his right eye. Chris grabbed the right-hand gun and fired it at the man, his eye closed with dirt in it. Without both eyes functioning correctly, Chris fanned the gun and put five more shots into the man's chest. Willard was dead by the second bullet. His back hit the ground with a loud thud and Colt dug at the dirt in his eye.

Elizabeth ran over and gently grabbed his eyelid and pulled it down. "Oh, Mr. Colt, are you all right?"

"Fine, ma'am, just fine," Chris said. "Thank you."

Brandon felt a twinge of jealousy as he saw Elizabeth attend to the famous scout/gunfighter. Then he realized he was being silly, and he walked up to Colt and offered his hand.

"The name is Brandon Rudd, Mr. Colt, and this is Miss Elizabeth Macon," the attorney said. "It is indeed a pleasure to meet you, sir. I have heard so much about you. You saved our lives, sir, and I don't know how I can ever thank you."

Colt doffed his hat to Elizabeth, saying, "My pleasure. I have heard good about both of you."

They gave each other questioning looks and Colt explained, "My brother wired me about you. Mr. Rudd, I may have helped save your life, but it seemed to me that you saved Miss Macon's. I don't believe that man could have gotten a bullet near her with you standing there."

Elizabeth took Brandon's arm and gave it a squeeze. She was amazed at how hard and large the muscles were for an attorney.

Brandon went on, "That man, Willard Lawson, was insane. He had a grudge against me because of a previous disagreement."

Elizabeth laughed. "Disagreement! Brandon's being modest, Mr. Colt. He is an attorney-at-law and won a huge case against that man. Brandon's client, a poor scarred woman, got an enormous settlement which ruined the man. He went over the edge and blamed Brandon instead of himself."

Colt laughed and said, "That's the way it always is, Miss Macon. It's a lot easier to blame someone other than ourselves for our problems."

By this time, there were numerous people from the wagon train gathering around, all men, guns in hand. The captain of the train, a husky man in his fifties, rode up on a tall red thoroughbred with four white stockings.

With a thick Nordic accent, he said, "Everybody back! Now, you sur, yust tell me what ees happening?"

Chris doffed his hat and Brandon stepped forward. "Captain Swenson, this is Joshua Colt's famous brother Chris Colt. He just saved our lives. That dead man there was named Willard Lawson and has followed us from Missouri where he apparently escaped prison. He intended to kill me and grabbed Miss Macon as a hostage when Mr. Colt intervened. Mr. Colt proved that the stories about his proficiency as a shootist were certainly not exaggerations."

The captain dismounted and walked forward, hand outstretched, saying, "Mr. Colt, it is sure a fine pleasure to meet you, sir."

They shook hands and Chris said, "Well Captain, pleased to meet you, but I'm afraid that this dead man was not your only problem. A large group of riders has been keeping watch on the train and the herd. I assume the herd is what they're after. They have probably been looking for a place to strike and run off the cattle. I would assume it will be soon, before we get to really flat terrain."

"Yah," the captain said, "I am sure dat the riders you saw vere interested in de wagon train, but mebbe yust curiosity, I tink."

"No," Chris said, "not curiosity. The people watching were up to no good."

"Just how do you know, Mr. Colt?"

"It's my job to know."

"If my brother tells you something pertaining to danger," Joshua Colt said, riding up, "you have two simple choices: Heed his advice or die."

The tall mulatto cowboy dismounted, a big smile on his face, and swung down off his gelding, his big batwing chaps slapping against the front of his calf. The rowels on his big Mexican spurs jingled as he walked forward to his half brother. The two clasped hands in a firm handshake, their left hands grabbing each other's upper arm, reaffirming their affection for each other. They looked almost like twins, although Joshua had wavy black hair and dark skin.

"Why are you here, Chris?" Joshua asked.

Colt said, "Time for that later, Josh, over black coffee."

That sentence told Joshua volumes, and he knew that Colt had bad news which wasn't for anybody else's ears.

Joshua responded, "Well, we got plenty of that, brother. What happened here?"

Chris grinned and said, "Oh, I tried to warn that man about reading the tracks of some bad hombres, and he didn't believe me, so I shot him."

Brandon Rudd chuckled aloud as captain Swenson's face turned beet red and he cleared his throat in embarrassment.

Brandon asked Colt if he could join him, as Chris accompanied his brother back to the cattle drive chuck wagon and fire. On the way, they stopped at the last wagon in the train and Josh showed Colt the large hand-carved rocking chair he had purchased in St. Louis as a gift for Shirley. Chris admired the piece and thanked Joshua for the thoughtfulness.

On the way to the chuck wagon, Chris explained what had been happening back in Colorado, and Joshua told Chris all about the events that had occurred with Brandon and Elizabeth.

Colt enjoyed the hot black coffee as the three men sat down at the campfire and talked.

He said, "Well, Mr. Rudd, we do not have an attorney for the ranch. What do you think, Josh? Shouldn't we start him out, as his first clients?"

"Absolutely," Joshua replied. "I have a feeling we are going to need a good attorney before this is all over. First, Chris, we need to discuss these men who were watching the train."

Colt said, "They weren't watching the train. They're after the herd."

Unlike Captain Swenson, Joshua knew and respected his brother's tracking skills and knowledge. Whatever Chris read in the tracks told him that the group was after the herd, and that made it gospel in Joshua Colt's mind.

"They must have awfully powerful medicine to think they can take us on, Chris," Joshua said. "It really bothers me."

Colt said, "Me, too. It seems like there must be something more to it, but I cannot figure it out. I am positive they will strike shortly, because we will be reaching the flat treeless prairie soon, and a herd that size would be a lot harder to find and round up quickly there."

"Not only that," Joshua said. "they'll probably try to take the herd straight to Dodge City, Wichita, or one of the close cattle markets and get rid of the cattle as quickly as they can."

"Who would try to steal our cows?" Chris said. "Do you suppose this could be tied to Preston Millard?"

"I don't think so," Brandon chimed in, "if you don't mind me rendering an opinion."

"No," Chris said, "we appreciate it. Why don't you feel he would?"

"He's essentially a prospector, with a lot of equipment and other men doing the digging for him. He wouldn't have an interest in cattle. That's not his bailiwick."

Joshua looked over at Chris and raised his eyebrows. "Makes good sense."

"Sure does," Chris replied, smiling at Brandon. "I suppose reading a man's sign is an important part of being an attorney."

"Probably *the* most important part," Brandon replied. "You look at a track and can tell all kinds of things about the person or thing that made it, but to most people it is just a mark or two in the dirt. To you, it's like the pages in a book. To be a good advocate, you must be able to read men the way you yourself read a track, Mr. Colt."

Chris corrected him, "Chris or Colt, but not 'mister', please. Pa was Mr. Colt."

"Very well," Brandon replied. "From what you have told me so far, I believe that this Preston Millard is not against you, necessarily. As I say, his passion is gold. He probably wants your land for some reason. Do you have any precious minerals on your land?"

Colt smiled. "Only my wife, Shirley. She's a diamond."

Brandon smiled.

Chris went on, "No, no mines or anything like that. Our land runs up to the base of the Sangre de Cristo range and most of it is open green pastureland. There's a few little creeks running through it, including Texas Creek, which is a little bigger than the others. I know people have found sign in Texas Creek, but would he want our land for that reason?"

Brandon said, "No. I have been doing some

studying about mining, ranching, and ranch and mining law ever since deciding a couple of years ago to move to Canon City. Panning for gold can give you some nuggets or dust, but it usually is mostly an indicator of where to go to dig in the ground for the main source of the gold. For example, if you pan for gold and you get a few nuggets in your pan and they are rounded, that means they have flowed downstream quite a ways from the main source of the gold. If the nuggets have sharp edges, the current hasn't had time to wear down and round the edges, and it indicates that you are close to the source of the gold. That is when men usually start digging. Are there any old mines on your property?"

"No, not at all. Like I said, it's mainly pastureland with a few thickets of trees or scrub oaks here and there. It raises uphill toward the big range, but it is not hilly and doesn't have any mountains or ridges on it."

Brandon said, "Well, my guess is that he is after your land for some reason, but we can take some measures to stop him when we arrive in Colorado. As far as the people who are after your cattle, with the reputation that you enjoy, Chris, I cannot imagine anybody being stupid enough to attempt larceny against your property. But after several years of having dealings with larcenous scoundrels, I do not have much respect for the intelligence of criminals. After all, if they were smart, they probably wouldn't break the law, would they?"

Joshua bit off a piece of jerky and chewed on it, while swallowing the hot coffee.

Brandon watched him with interest and Joshua explained, "Just realized I've been too busy working the herd today. Haven't eaten since breakfast."

"Wal, Hell, why ain't ye eatin' sumthin' substantial, boss?" were the words of old wrinkled Tex Westchester as he walked over to Joshua carrying a large slice of apple pie from the chuck wagon.

Brandon admired the wrinkled old cowhand with the twinkle in his eye. He looked like he was ageless and had probably spent his entire life in the saddle. He nodded at Chris as he winked and poured a cup of coffee.

"Howdy, Colt," Tex said, testing the hot liquid with his upper lip. "Who's the dude?"

"Tex Westchester," Joshua said, "Meet Brandon Rudd, our attorney."

Brandon grinned and stepped forward, his hand outstretched. Tex grabbed the handle of his old .44 Russian and started pulling it out of his holster.

"Did you say he was a lawyer?" he asked.

Everyone laughed and Tex shook hands with the advocate.

Joshua said, "They're both funning, Chris. Brandon met Tex before the drive even started. He saw Tex back in Texas, but I doubt if he remembers much about that, he was so full of bullet holes."

"I certainly don't remember that. It was a bad time," Brandon said.

The grizzled old ranch hand started rolling a cigarette, saying, "Yep, last lawyer I seen had been bit by three different buzztails."

Brandon said, "What's a buzztail?"

Joshua replied, "Rattlesnake."

Tex lit his cigarette. "Man. it was sumthin' turrible. Plumb turrible. All thet durned writhin' and moanin' and foamin' at the mouth. Then before the ole grim reaper showed up, a whole bunch of shakin' and twitchin'. I mean to tell ya' all, it was one of the worstest things I ever witnessed. Fact, we had one ole boy thet rode fer our brand, and he shore as heck held a considerable affection fer them bottles a amber liquid thet sets fire ta yer throat. Well, he had been makin' love to one a them bottles all day, but when he seen the aftermath a them three rattlers bitin' thet lawyer man, he got sober right then and swore off the stuff."

Brandon said, "Oh, my goodness. That poor attorney. What a horrible way for him to die."

Tex puffed on his cigarette and said, "The hell you say. What ya talking about? The lawyer man was fine. I was talkin' about the snakes dyin'. It was plumb turrible."

Everyone laughed heartily and Brandon's face turned beet red, but he did laugh at himself, earning the respect of the other three men.

"Where's Muley?" Chris asked Tex, inquiring about the other top hand from Coyote Run.

"Aw, he's out singin' to the cows. Don't know why old Muley does thet, though. If'n they wanna act uppity, he's so big all he needs ta do is smack oncet upside the head, and thet'll straighten 'em out or scramble their durned brains."

"Got a couple nice bulls, Chris," Joshua said. "Think they'll be a good addition to our herd."

"The ones you told me about before you left?"

"Yep, good breedin' stock."

Tex took a sip of coffee and started rolling another smoke, saying, "Yep, when I was out there ridin' nighthawk, I kept seein' sumthin' in the dark, and it bothered the hell outta me. Well, I was a hankerin' ta git away from Muley's guldurn singin' anyhow, so's I sauntered out into the big herd kinda slow-like. I seen a couple big shadows movin' around in the herd, an' I figgered we had trouble brewin' with a couple a silvertips."

"Silvertips?" Brandon asked.

Colt said, "Grizzly bears. Tips of their hair around the shoulders and chest area are colored silver. Go on, Tex."

All eyes were on the ancient cowhand while he reached out and grabbed the steaming coffeepot off the fire. He poured a cup and took a small sip, grimacing.

"Dammit ta hell and beyond! Burnt my durned lip again."

Joshua said, "Tex!"

"Okay, so anyhow, I seen these two big shapes in the herd, and I shucks my Winchester outta my scabbard and jacks a round in the chamber. The cattle wasn't actin' skitterish, though, so I dint worry too much. Of a sudden, the clouds move away from coverin' the moon, and I can see better. Wal, there they was. Them two new bulls. Now, they was out there waltzin' from cow to cow handin' big bouquets of flowers to the old gals. I swear them boys is gonna spoil our heifers."

The gunshots came from the east and the rumble started immediately.

Joshua jumped up and hollered, "Stampede! Rustlers!"

Numerous cowhands, previously asleep in bedrolls and unnoticed by Brandon Rudd, jumped up all around the outer reaches of the fire's illumination. Within seconds, all were in the saddle, carbines and rifles in hand. Not to be left behind, Brandon, albeit unschooled in handling stampedes or rustlers, vaulted into the saddle himself and followed Chris and Joshua Colt. He felt a little ashamed when, two minutes later, the old silver-haired Tex Westchester blew by him on a little sorrel mustang gelding that made Brandon look like a loaded freight wagon being passed by a team of runaway thoroughbreds pulling a doctor's buggy.

Tex hollered back, "Foller me, sonny! I'll watch out fer ya!"

Chris and Joshua were already out of sight in the darkness and everything was total confusion. Brandon could not figure out how anyone could sort out who were rustlers and who were ranch hands. Tex led him toward the loudest part of the thundering sounds. Brandon pushed his horse and came up alongside the cowboy.

"Ya got ya a hogleg?" Tex hollered.

Brandon said, "A pistol?"

Tex winked.

"No!"

Tex hollered, "Foller me! We gotta git to the head of the stampede and turn the herd back in a circle!"

Brandon followed the oldster as they sped through the tall prairie grass, soon pulling up alongside the thundering herd. There were numerous gunshots off to Brandon's right, and they produced little stabs of flame, which at that distance across the sea of cattle looked like so many fireflies. They raced beside the panicked bovines and Brandon made out the forms of each one as he slowly overtook them individually. Before long, he found himself right behind Tex and whooped and hollered at the herd, like the old man, as they slowly made the lead cattle turn to their right, back toward the shooting, which now was becoming more sporadic and fading away.

They kept pushing the frightened bovines for another fifteen minutes when it seemed the herd finally started slowing down. Brandon's horse was laboring when he topped a small rise with the herd alongside his right stirrup, and he reined up sharply, face-to-face with two guns, both being held by men with red bandannas over their mouths and noses. Tex had swung to the left seconds earlier, after a small group of cattle that followed a little dip in that direction. Brandon was now faced with two rustlers pointing rifles at his midsection.

Suddenly the two flew forward off their horses and under the hooves of the thundering herd. Brandon looked beyond their horses and saw Chris Colt, smoking six-gun in each hand, looking just like one of the legendary heroes written about in the dime novels back East. His reins were between his white teeth. He quickly replaced his guns into his holsters, smiled at Brandon and doffed his leather scout's hat, then rode off toward the shooting.

Brandon saw another faction of the herd split off to the left and noticed that more cowpunchers were joining in turning the lead element. They literally were turning the front of the herd back into the main body. Brandon took off at a gallop after the small element and topped out on a small hillock overlooking two grassy arroyos. The small split was racing down the second arroyo, which joined with the one running on his left. With horror, he saw Tex in the bottom of the junction of both draws and his horse was rearing, while he was surrounded by the first split element of cattle, and the second bearing down on him.

Brandon didn't even take time to think. He slapped the reins to his big lineback dun and kicked his spurs into the horse's ribs. The quarterhorse saw the danger and was already excited by chasing cows, an instinctive job with him. He raced down the gentle ridge toward the old man, now lying flat on his back in the midst of wild-eyed cows. Brandon saw one cow step on the cowboy's left leg and another kicked his head, running by.

He slid the horse to a stop and piled off, almost falling on the unconscious puncher himself. The panic-stricken small herd headed right at the pair and Brandon's horse pulled away and dashed off in abject fear. Again there was no time to think, just react. Brandon grabbed Tex's carbine off the ground and aimed between the eyes of the lead steer. The animal fell to the ground and slid for several feet, another steer and a heifer behind him broke their legs over his prostrate body. Brandon fired into their heads as well. He dragged Tex with one hand as he shot from the hip with the carbine at the rest of the oncoming cattle. Running out of ammunition, he dropped the gun and grabbed Tex by both lapels, pulling him forward as fast as he could move. He pulled Tex right up next to the small pile of dead cattle and lay down, covering the man with his own body.

The herd poured past, but the small pile of dead cattle prevented them from trampling the two men. The herd went on by and Brandon stared after them, his heart pounding and his breath coming out in gasps. Tex's voice made him jump.

"Jest 'cause I shook hands with ya, youngster, dint mean we was gettin' hitched."

Brandon sat up quickly and started laughing at the man's sense of humor at the height of adversity.

Tex sat up, shaking his head and looking all around. He shook his head again, apparently trying to clear out the cobwebs.

He finally spoke again. "Looks like ya used yer head. Never seen the like, a lawyer what can think. Thank ya, boy. Ya saved my life, 'cept now

I spose I'm gonna have to listen to more a Muley's singin'. Wal, I guess I could shoot 'im if it gits too bad."

Brandon said, "Well, I suppose the first order of business is to get a splint on your leg. Then—"

"The hell it is, mister," Tex interrupted. "You catch thet nag of yourn and help git the herd settled. Then ya can git help for me."

Brandon started to argue, but Tex held up his hand, saying, "Look. I don't go in no courtroom tellin' you how to attorney. I'm a cattleman, and I ride fer the brand. Now, my boss's herd is scattered from hell to Californy and part a my job it ta see thet they git back where they belong. Now git."

"I'll be back with help," Brandon said.

"Aw, hell, young un, I know thet. Now git!"

Brandon was able to grab Tex's horse almost immediately, yanked the slicker off the back of the cantle and covered the cowboy, then mounted up.

"What the hell ya gonna do, read me a bedtime story and lullaby me ta sleep? Git!"

Brandon waved and took off on the little red horse. Within minutes he was with the main herd, and the cattle were now milling around. He rode straight to Joshua and explained what happened, leaving out his own heroics.

Thirty minutes more time found Tex on his own horse, his leg in a splint expediently constructed by Chris Colt. Brandon had his horse back. Muley hovered over Tex like a mother hen, and most of the cattle were with the main herd. Chris Colt and two of the cowboys held guns on three captured outlaws. They were tied backward in their saddles, their hands behind their backs.

A number of rustlers lay dead on the prairie and

one Coyote Run ranch hand was killed as well. The Colt brothers, along with Brandon and two other punchers, escorted the prisoners to a grove of trees. The punchers immediately threw ropes over a stout cottonwood limb.

Brandon said, "You can't do this, Joshua, Chris!"

Joshua said, "Have to, Brandon. There's no law out here and these men are rustlers and responsible for the death of one of our hands. Justice for rustlers has to be quick and harsh or every cattle drive will be plagued by herd cutters."

Brandon said, "I understand. It's just hard for me."

"Want to ride on to the train?"

"No," Brandon replied. "If it must be done, it must be done. I'll stay."

The nooses were placed over the men's necks and one of the Coyote Run punchers told them they could pray if they liked. All three laughed.

Joshua said, "Who you men riding for?"

One of the three rough-looking hombres responded, "Big crazy feller named Lin Crawford. Hey, you Chris Colt?"

Chris nodded.

The man laughed and said, "See ya in hell, Colt."

He kicked the sides of his own horse, and it bolted, dropping him off the back, his neck breaking with a loud crack. This unnerved one of the other rustlers, who wet himself and started screaming. The third was expressionless, looking straight ahead.

The puncher slapped the two remaining horses on the rump, and they bolted. The job was finished.

Colt turned his head to see Brandon urging his horse in a mad dash toward the wagon train.

Colt said, "Guess it did bother him."

Joshua said, "No, I was watching. The name. That's it. Linford Crowley was the man who was Elizabeth Macon's fiancé. That man said his boss was Lin Crawford."

Chapter 4

>>>>>>>>>>>>>>>>>>>>>

More Trouble

The two Colts raced after Brandon.

Brandon's heart was ready to explode when he arrived at the assembled crowd at the train. Captain Swenson came forward. The Colts were riding up in the near distance.

Brandon said, "Elizabeth Macon—where is she?"

Captain Swenson said, "I'm shoore sorry, Brandon. When you were all shooting back there, we got raided and aboot ten men, dey rode in here and kidnapped her right out of her wagon. They rode off over that ridge while we were all pinned down."

Brandon slapped spurs to his horse and let out a spine-chilling primal scream. "No!"

The attorney sped his horse off in the direction the kidnappers had fled. Chris and Joshua slid their horses to a stop and dismounted.

Colt said, "What happened, Captain? Where'd Brandon head to?"

The captain explained quickly what had happened.

Joshua looked at Chris and said, "How do you want to handle this?"

Chris said, "Get some sleep and let these worn out horses rest. We'll take off after her at first light when I can read sign."

"What about Brandon Rudd?"

Chris smiled. "Must love her an awful lot. He didn't even take a gun with him. I'll take an extra horse. He'll probably kill the one he's on. All our horses are exhausted, Josh, and you can miss some important signs at night. We can do Miss Macon a lot more good by waiting until morning. I'll go. You'll need to stay with the herd and take care of it and your men."

"Chris, you can't go alone!"

Colt gave his older brother a raised-eyebrow grin and Joshua said, "Okay, so you can go by yourself. Why don't you take some men with you?"

Chris said, "No, you need every man you can spare. You know that. Besides, I came here to protect you in case there is a death threat on you. I'd rather you have plenty of loyal men around you."

Joshua gave Chris a raised-eyebrow grin and Colt laughed. "Okay, so you can take care of yourself, too. I'm going to put up War Bonnet and give him a rubdown. You got any corn or grain?"

Joshua replied, "Yeah, check with Cookie at the chuck wagon. He's got some nose bags, too, you can put on to feed him if you want. Tell him to have you some traveling grub and full canteens in the morning."

"Yes, Mother," Colt said sarcastically.

Joshua slapped his younger brother on the shoulder and Chris vaulted into the saddle. He gave a wink and rode back toward the herd.

Captain Swenson said, "Well, I yust cannot wait until morning, Mr. Colt. I am going to organize some men and go after Miss Macon immediately."

Joshua snapped his glare toward the captain and saw the Swede's Adam's apple bob up and down.

Very softly and quietly, Joshua said, "No, you're not. My brother will handle it."

He mounted his horse and rode off. Nothing else needed to be said. The elder Colt's look, soft words, and demeanor said it all. The wagon train leader decided it was better to leave the tracking to the expert tracker. Besides, he had a lot of other people he was responsible for.

Chris Colt lay rolled up in his blanket, writing a note for Joshua by the firelight. He wanted his brother to wire Shirley from Wichita and check on how things were at the ranch. Chris had left a small amount of money in Silver Cliff at one of the mercantiles. Whenever wires were sent for his ranch, the telegrapher would deliver the wire to the shopkeeper, who would hire one of the town hangers-around to ride out to Coyote Run and deliver the message.

Colt finished the note for Joshua and closed his eyes. He mentally decided to awaken about a half hour before dawn and fell asleep almost immediately. But soon a presence made his eyes open slightly to see who approached. It was Tex Westchester, struggling horribly on man-made crutches and obviously dizzy from his bandaged head wound.

Colt opened his eyes and didn't speak as Tex dropped his well-worn holster, gun belt, and Colt .44 Russian next to the scout. He also dropped a leather pouch full of extra .44s.

"Reckon that young lawyer fella'll need a good weapon an' some powder an' lead," Tex said. "Ya know his mount's probably dead or stove up?"

Chris nodded affirmatively.

Tex went on, "Take 'im my sorrel mustang, too. He'll do for 'im. I'll ride from the remuda till ya'll get back. Guess thet's 'bout it. Staked the horse out near yer big paint, saddle's nearby. You'll find it—yer Chris Colt, ain't ya? Luck."

Tex turned and hobbled away.

"Tex," Chris said, "Don't worry. I'll keep him alive."

Tex stopped and faced Chris. "Hell, Colt, I know thet. I work fer you and yer durned brother. I don't work fer no pantywaist wished-I-wases. I only work fer men. G'night."

He turned and hobbled away and Colt called, "Thanks, Tex."

The cowboy waved without looking back.

Chris lay back and covered up with the blanket, wondering how his wife was. Was she safe?

The moonlight seemed to bounce off of the crusted snowpack on the big peaks of the Sangre de Cristo Mountains and brighten up the Colorado night sky. Down below Spread Eagle Peak and the forested ridges running off of it lay the pastures of the Coyote Run. The house and outbuildings were all dark but clearly visible in the moonlight. So were the three masked desperadoes carefully prying open the front window of the Colt household.

They finally worked the window open and carefully climbed inside. Once inside, they tiptoed carefully around the big room, trying to see by the red light of the hot embers in the big stone fireplace.

The lead man was a hawk-faced gunslick named Jasper McCall. He was followed, as usual, by a big lummox named Bull Smith, and the last man was an out-of-work ne'er-do-well called Max Barnes. They had been hired by Preston Millard to terrorize the wife of Chris Colt, with constant and emphatic assurances that the chief of scouts was thousands of miles away on a scouting mission for the U.S. cavalry. They had heard about Man Killer, but in their minds he was just another "red nigger" to be moved out of the way.

In his right hand, Jasper held his well-used Smith & Wesson single-action Schofield .45, a gun he favored because it had been a favorite of Jesse James. The other two followed closely behind him as he inched around the room.

He looked in the small room near the fireplace and saw the sleeping figure of little Joseph Colt in his trundle bed.

He saw one more door against that wall and knew it had to be the bedroom of Mrs. Colt. Jasper turned his head and grinned at the other two. He was actually excited about frightening a woman and making her scream. It had been that way ever since he was young. Nobody knew about the four occasions when he had actually taken women by force and beaten on them at the same time. He loved to see the terror in their eyes and the degradation when he stole their private secrets and injured them.

As bad as most of his friends were, he dared not ever tell him of his sexual assaults because of the Code of the West. Women were a very rare commodity out West, so even outlaws had lynched other outlaws for assaulting women.

Jasper's two cohorts were as bad as they come, just about, but he didn't want to push his luck and tell all his secrets. Still he did start wondering what this Shirley Colt looked like. He had heard in town that she was a handsome woman—a real looker, in fact. Maybe he could get the two to stand watch outside the bedroom while he entertained himself a bit.

He signaled for Bull to grab the oil lamp off the table and bring it to him. His plan was to go in the door quietly, lamp in one hand, gun in the other.

The woman would be scared to death as women always were, but he would have to immediately indicate the gun and tell her not to scream or make any noise. He didn't want to alert the bunkhouse or have any crying brats around. Millard just wanted the three to sneak into her house and confront her, maybe suggest moving off the ranch, then leave. The closer Jasper got to the bedroom door, however, the more his heart pounded with the memories of previous women he had violated.

He lit the oil lamp and held it in his left hand, motioning for Bull to open the handle for him. He walked into the room and saw the sleeping beauty named Shirley Colt, long naturally curly auburn hair flowing all over her pillow. Jasper was excited. He moved in closer and was followed into the room by Bull and Max.

Shirley opened her eyes and smiled softly at the men. This shocked them all.

She said sweetly, "Hi, boys, want to dance? Let me start the music."

With that, the blanket covering Shirley exploded, as well as the oil lamp. Jasper, almost ripped in half, flew backward into Bull and Max, each of whom had been hit with several twelve-gauge double-ought buckshot pellets. Both men screamed, covered with Jasper's blood and parts of his body. Shirley threw the covers back and cocked the other hammer of the double-barreled sawed-off scattergun. The two climbed all over each other scrambling out the door and vanished into the darkness as Shirley's second shot smashed into the side of the doorjamb and part of her wall.

Joseph was screaming and Man Killer, clad only in a breechcloth, fired two quick snap shots at the two men fleeing into the darkness. He ran straight to the main house.

"Shirley!" he yelled smartly before charging through the door and then dived headfirst into the room, a pistol in each hand.

He hit the floor in a shoulder roll and came up looking all around.

Shirley yelled, "They're gone!'"

He quickly looked at Joseph, saw he was unharmed, and lifted him up, carrying him into Shirley's room, still clutching a gun in each hand.

Shirley took the crying boy away and patted his back, while she sniffled and sobbed. Man Killer placed his left arm around her and Joseph, and she cried on his chest.

She regained her composure after a minute or so, as several of the temporary hands finally poured in from the bunkhouse, guns in hand.

One of them said, "Mrs. Colt, are you okay, ma'am?"

"Yes, thank you!"

He went on, "What do you want us ta do, Man Killer? How many were there? Should we look for sign?"

"No," Man Killer said, "just organize the boys into guards for the main house. I'll check for tracks, but I think they're gone for the night. I need a volunteer to get the sheriff. Mrs. Colt sent one of these boys home."

"I'll go to town," the hand said.

"Good," Man Killer replied. "Tell him there were two more. Mrs. Colt saw them."

He glanced at her for her confirmation, and she nodded. The man ran outside and Man Killer walked over to the stove, lit several lamps, and put some wood inside. He placed the coffeepot on top, then added wood in the big stone fireplace.

Shirley, in the meantime, changed Joseph's diaper and got him back to sleep and put on some clothes.

She joined Man Killer near the fire and accepted a cup of coffee. Man Killer lit one of Chris's cigars from the big leather humidor.

While they waited for the law to arrive, Man Killer went outside with a lantern and checked for sign. He found the tracks of the three men's horses. Bull's horse had a corrective shoe with an unmistakable bar across from one shank to the other.

Man Killer returned to the house and joined Shirley over coffee at the table.

"If you want to get some sleep, I'll be right here," he said.

"No," she replied, "I imagine the sheriff will be wanting breakfast when he arrives. Think he'll be here by daybreak?"

"No, it will take a few hours more, I think."

A lone deputy rode up to the ranch house two hours after daybreak, escorted by the ranch hand. The lawman was young, tall, and slender. His guns, a pair of standard Peacemakers, were worn low and the holsters were well worn from thousands of practice draws. He looked more like a professional gunfighter than a peacemaker, but he did wear a badge.

Deputy Wolf Keeler was good-looking but had a checkered past. He had lived in other states and territories under different names with different occupations, but he knew how to talk the talk, so he was hired as a Custer County deputy. In 1868, both of his parents were killed by a Comanche raid on his west Texas homestead. His mother had been assaulted and had her head bashed in, and his father had gone down with twelve arrows in his hide. Wolf didn't care so much about him, as he felt the old man had a black heart, but his ma had kept him from getting his hide skinned off by his father many a time.

He had to raised himself and a younger sister from then on, and he put his nose to the grindstone, not even allowing himself the opportunity to think about revenge. When his sister was fifteen, however, she ran off with a half-breed Kiowa/Mexican man who treated her like a queen. Wolf hunted them down, shooting and killing the man from ambush a week after their wedding, riding off to Montana afterward hoping the guilt feelings would go away. They never did.

Instead of blaming himself, Wolf blamed Indians and Mexicans.

Now he dismounted and nodded at Shirley Colt as he wrapped his reins around the hitching rack in front of the porch. He tipped his hat to her and walked forward.

Man Killer said, "Where's the sheriff, Deputy?"

Wolf stared daggers at Man Killer as if the young man had just insulted his ancestry.

He said, "I don't talk to no red niggers, boy. I'm here to talk to Mrs. Colt. Now butt out and run along."

Man Killer didn't like being spoken to in that manner, and it clearly showed on his face. Wolf Keeler's hands hovered over his guns and Man Killer did the same.

Shirley said, "Deputy, what's your name?"

"Wolf Keeler, ma'am"

She went on, "Well, Deputy Keeler, Man Killer is not only a close friend, he is like a member of our family, and you will not come on my property and speak to him or anyone in that manner."

Keeler started to speak, but she cut him off. "My husband, brother-in-law, Man Killer—who has a large herd of Appaloosa horses here—and I pay a lot of money in taxes, which pays your salary. Now, as usual, I guess we'll just have to handle our own problems or wait until the sheriff returns, wherever he is."

"He's chasing some escaped convicts from down to Canon City, ma'am—" Keeler said meekly, but she cut him off again.

"Fine, we'll talk to the sheriff when he returns. In the meantime, you get off my land."

He got angry at this and said, "Now, listen, I'm the law—"

"You might wear a badge, but you're no more the law than the three men who broke into my house tonight. One of them's dead, and I'll send the body in today on a buckboard. Now get off my land."

"Ma'am, I don't care what you say. If you have had a shootin' here, I have to check it out. That is the law."

Shirley relented. "You are right about that, so you investigate, but understand this: If you speak that way to Man Killer again, I'll slap your face so hard your ancestors will feel it."

Man Killer grinned as he turned away, and so did the three Coyote Run hands standing nearby. Shirley took the deputy into the house and showed him the dead man, while explaining about the break-in. The sheriff's deputy returned to town an hour later, towing the dead man's body tied over his saddle, after Shirley had Man Killer locate and track down the horse. Man Killer also found the tracks heading north on the main road to Westcliffe and Silver Cliff.

The young Nez Percé did manage to tell the young deputy about the bar across Bull's left rear shoe. It was hard for him to speak to the supposed lawman, but he did want to try to learn how to handle things properly in the white man's world, and especially so in this case for Shirley and Chris's sake. Wolf minded his manners, though, and took the information without emotion. Apparently Shirley Colt's warning did not fall on deaf ears.

At noon, Man Killer appeared at the house and spoke to Shirley. Hawk was loaded up with full saddlebags and two canteens.

"Shirl, I have to go after those men. The trail will be easy to pick up. I have the men watching the house in shifts. You will be okay."

Shirley smiled and handed him a burlap bag.

"What is this?"

"A bagful of grub," she replied, "I knew you'd be going. I also put some of Chris's cigars in there for you to enjoy."

Man Killer smiled, gave Shirley a kiss on the cheek, and went out the door. Holding the bag in one hand, he easily vaulted into the saddle and kicked his moccasined foot to the horse's rib cage.

Hawk's mile-eating fast trot got his master into town while it was still early afternoon. He went straight to the Powell House in nearby Silver Cliff. Jennifer was working but got relieved by the manager's wife, who adored her but did not know why the beauty was so taken with an Indian. On the other hand, the woman did have secret, very private thoughts about some of the Indian warriors she had seen, although she never would have believed that other white women shared those same thoughts. It was something she would think about briefly and then shoo it out of her mind and never breathe a word about it.

Jennifer and Man Killer stood outside the tall brick building and talked under a tree. He told her what had happened at the ranch and about Wolf Keeler. Three man rode up while they talked and Man Killer was certain that one was Preston Millard. The other two were Bull Smith and Max Barnes. Max was a left-handed gunfighter and Man

Killer had already determined that the smaller intruder at the ranch had been left-handed. He could tell this by the way he angled his feet when mounting, dismounting, and crawling in the kitchen window. The other man, the big one, certainly fit the size of the man he had tracked and was described by Shirley. Additionally, Bull Smith had on boots with riding heels and Max wore old hob-nailed teamster's boots.

The clincher would be the bar across the hoof of Bull's horse.

Man Killer said softly, "Go inside."

Jennifer had learned enough about the young man to know not to argue. She smiled and walked inside. The three men headed toward the restaurant, whispering something to each other as they approached.

Preston Millard had cruel, very light blue eyes. He also walked with a slight limp. He stood about Chris Colt's height and weighted well over two hundred pounds. He looked soft, but Man Killer knew better. Like Colt, he was a very good judge of men. He had to be.

When they were just a few feet away, the scout was ready to say something, but Preston beat him to it. "Say, aren't you the young redskin that's the protégé of Chris Colt?"

Man Killer said, "You know I am, Millard."

The familiarity and the fact that Man Killer knew his name upset the miner. Nobody else could have detected this, but Man Killer read it faintly on his face.

Millard said, "I understand you two have been making a lot of inquiries about me and some wild speculation, too?"

Man Killer said, "Me Injun. No speak good. No savvy."

Preston Millard was now visibly upset and responded, "You persnippity young pup, I'll—"

"You'll what?"

Max chimed in, "Maybe lift some scalps, kid."

Man Killer laughed and decided to take his shot in the dark, saying "How could you two do that? You couldn't even handle a lone woman, with a partner helping you."

Well, there it was. He had thrown down the gauntlet and both men immediately knew that he would have to be eliminated before he had a chance to tell his accusations to the law. They were scared. Both had heard about him, but still he was a kid to them and was not Colt himself. Preston Millard was simply thinking, plotting, scheming. How would he handle this situation and come out on top?

Man Killer instantly decided that the smaller one would be faster and would take his first bullets. He didn't worry about Millard. The man put his hands on his hips, pulling the sides of his jacket back. The Nez Percé knew the man was doing that on purpose to let him know he was not carrying a sidearm.

Man Killer would try to wound both men, so they could be arrested and tried for the break-in, and so they could testify against Preston Millard. He would attempt a shoulder or upper chest shot on them and figured that he could accomplish it quite easily if he simply remembered what he had been taught.

Max went for his gun and Bull followed suit, although not anywhere near as fast. Man Killer's right hand swept down and up, and he felt the familiar recoil of the .45 as a stab of flame shot out and Max Barnes spun half around, his gun flying and left arm going out limp in an odd angle, his shoulder bone shattered. Man Killer fanned the gun, as he turned it on Bull, and two rounds went into the man, one hitting him in the collarbone and the other tearing through his bicep and upper arm.

Suddenly something slammed into Man Killer's head from the side. There was blackness.

The voices seemed to be miles away, but one of them clearly was the deputy, Wolf Keeler.

"Man Killer. Man Killer, you moved. I know you can hear me." This voice was unmistakably Shirley Colt's, but the scout wanted to sleep.

He was so tired.

Another voice! Jennifer Banta said, "Look Shirley, his eyes are flickering. Man Killer! Wake up!"

He had to awaken and see Jennifer again. Man Killer opened his eyes and saw numerous lights flashing off and on. He finally saw everything come into focus and saw Shirley and Jennifer standing on the other side of bars. Bars! He was shocked and confused. The scout jumped off the cot and got very light-headed. He grabbed the bars and held on while a wave of nausea passed. Finally his head cleared and pounded like a drum, but he could handle the pain. Man Killer was still confused.

He said, "What happened?"

Shirley said, "You were shot in the side of the head, but the bullet grazed you."

"Why am I in jail?"

Jennifer said, "You were arrested for murder. Oh, Man Killer, it's horrible."

She started crying, and he stuck his fingers through the cell bars. In the background, Wolf Keeler sat at his desk and gave him an evil grin.

"Murder?" he said, shocked. "Who do they say I murdered?"

"Those two men with Preston Millard," Jennifer said.

"I did not kill them!" he insisted. "I shot both men in the shoulder."

Shirley said, "But Preston Millard had no gun and the big one had no gun, either. Both men were shot in the shoulders, but both also had a bullet hole between their eyes."

The young Nez Percé shook his head.

Jennifer went on, "It's terrible. Many people have been talking about lynching you. You must escape and run far away."

"No!" he said flatly and angrily.

Jennifer started crying again.

Shirley said, "He won't leave, but Man Killer, you will have to escape somehow and hide out until I can get Chris back here."

Man Killer said, "But I am trying to learn how to live in the white man's world. I must respect the law, and it will protect me."

"This country is not that way yet," Shirley went on. "Sometimes we have to watch out for ourselves because the law doesn't."

Man Killer wistfully looked out the window at the mountains.

He turned to the women and said, "I am trying hard to learn to live in your world because the white man's way will become the way of this country, but many times it is hard for me to try to live by your rules. In my tribe, I would tell elders that I did not kill the men I am accused of killing, and it would be over. I think I should stay here and try harder."

Jennifer choked back tears, saying, "Man Killer, they will hang you."

"There are many things worse than dying," he said.

"But you mustn't die!" Jennifer cried out, and started sobbing again.

Shirley put a comforting arm around her as Wolf Keeler walked up from the desk. His face was beet red.

"Awright, visiting time's up," he said.

"Just one minute more, please?" Jennifer pleaded.

He took her by the upper arm and started pulling her from the bars, saying, "No, you should be ashamed of yourself anyhow. A white woman like you carrying on over a worthless red nigger."

Jennifer started to swing her hand at his face, but Man Killer's words stopped everyone. "Keeler!"

The deputy tilted his head up and Man Killer said, "Take your hand off her, or I'll kill you."

The words sent a chill down the deputy's spine, but he laughed it off and said, "You ain't gonna do nothing but stretch a rope."

His hand did release Jennifer's arm, however.

She blew Man Killer a kiss while she and Shirley left the jail. Outside an ugly crowd had gathered.

Wolf walked up to the bars and gave Man Killer an evil grin. The two stared at each other for several minutes and Wolf made a sound and walked back to the desk. Man Killer lay down and went right to sleep. He let his subconscious mind work on an escape plan.

When Man Killer awakened, it was dark and there were the sounds of a drunken mob outside, screaming about lynching him. Several times men came in the jail and spoke to the deputy. Man Killer could tell by his laughter and whispers that the racist was planning on turning him over to them. He would probably wait until the solid citizens of the town went to sleep.

That would be good, Man Killer thought, because the jail cell bars were steel, and the floor and wall were concrete. The ceiling was concrete with steel bars in it. He could not escape from within the cell, so he would have to be taken out by the lynch mob and take his chances with them, or somehow trick Wolf Keeler into moving him out of the cell.

Man Killer looked at every nook and cranny inside and outside of his cell for an idea or for something he could use to help him. All he could find was an old dirty sock left under the bunk by a previous prisoner. The floor was covered with tiny pebbles and sand from deteriorating concrete. Man Killer thought, *What can I do? Throw sand at him?*

Suddenly a thought struck the young scout, and he grinned broadly. He grabbed the sock and dropped to his hands and knees, scraping the sand and tiny pebbles into it. He saw movement out of the corner of his eye and quickly sat back on the cot, holding his stomach. Wolf Keeler walked over to the cell carrying an Overland shotgun, a twelve-gauge double-barrel greener sawed-off to a total length of about eighteen inches.

"What the hell you doin', red nigger?" the deputy asked.

Man Killer moaned and pointed at his stomach.

Wolf chuckled and said, "Aw, does yer little tummy hurt cause yer so scared? Wait a bit more, boy, 'cause they're damned shore comin' to stretch yer sorry red neck tonight. Ya ready ta bring up yer supper? Go 'head. I'll make ya lick it up off the floor. Ya know, sometimes when a man hangs, his eyeballs pop clean outta his head and he goes in his drawers. Bet it all happens ta you, nigger boy."

Man Killer just moaned and dropped to the floor. Wolf laughed and walked back to the office, sitting down behind his desk and looking through a stack of wanted posters. Man Killer curled up on the floor and started scraping more sand and gravel into the sock. He kept this up for fifteen more minutes until the sock was filled up and packed solid.

Next, Man Killer clutched the sock firmly in his right hand and held it between his legs. He started writhing on the floor and pretended to vomit. He made horrible retching sounds, and finally the sadistic lawman walked back over to the cell, again wearing his evil grin.

"I warned ya, boy. Good 'n' sick now, huh? This is awright. It's plumb awright," he said. "Now, what I want ya to do, nigger, is ta—"

Boom! Man Killer straightened up like a snake striking, that sock came from between his legs, and his right arm shot out, straight at the lawman's face. The heavy expedient blackjack hit Wolf Keeler right between the eyes with a loud thud. The man's nose was smashed flat and blood spurted in every direction as his eyes rolled back in his head and his legs folded underneath him. He caught the deputy by the lapels with his left arm and pulled him against the bars as he slumped forward.

Dropping the sock, Man Killer caught the shotgun with his right hand and pulled it between the bars. He quickly stripped off the man's belt and holster and pulled it into the cell with him in case anyone barged in the door. He searched the man's pockets but couldn't find the keys, then saw something almost sticking out of the right boot. It was a boot knife in a sheath, and inside the sheath was a large key. He pulled it out and tried it in the steel door. The key turned and the tumbler clicked. The mighty steel cage door released and Man Killer felt his heart skip a beat. He smiled, then went back to his task at hand. He dragged the injured deputy into the cell, bound his hands behind his back, and gagged him as well.

* * *

Brodie Pace had worked for Preston Millard for ten years and helped his boss do some mighty ruthless deeds to achieve some selfish end. Millard just liked to conquer and Brodie simply liked to get into scraps and come out on top. He was always looking for ways to make his life exciting, and when he accomplished one, it would only be a matter of days before he was ready for more action.

His job this night was simple: He was given a wad of bills by Millard and told to buy drinks for men all night and whip them into a frenzied lynch mob. Brodie had been succeeding. He now had two dozen angry drunken men assembled in front of the jail, carrying torches and lanterns. He held a stout hemp rope, which someone had tied into a hangman's noose. Arrangements had already been made with Wolf Keeler to drag the young Indian out with no protest from the lawman. They would simply string him up from the nearest tree, and Millard would be one step closer to taking over the Coyote Run Ranch.

The appointed hour had come and Brodie waved with his arm, yelling, "Come on, boys, let's string up that redskin murderer!"

With shouts of agreement, he led the way into the jail and was surprised to see the deputy's chair empty.

He yelled, "Wolf!"

To that shout, he was greeted with a muffled sound from the cell area. He led the crowd inside and found Wolf Keeler, with broken nose and face covered in blood, gagged and his arms up over his head, wrists tied to the bars of the small cell window. His ankles were tied with the bed sheet to the frame of the cot, and he seemed to be in great pain.

Brodie couldn't figure out what had happened to

the Indian, as the outside had been watched all night for any possibility of escape. The men looked all around the jail, but there was no sign of Man Killer. Finally one of the men hollered for Brodie and Wolf, who was now free. They ran into the office and the man slid the large desk to the side and showed them where three of the floorboards in the office had been pried loose, but they had been out of anyone's sight, blocked from view by the massive desk.

"Son of a ..." Brodie exclaimed. "Quick— outside! He couldn't have gotten very far."

Outside, a single buckboard with two drunken men driving it back to their ranch was all that moved.

Brodie hollered at the men, "Here, you two, hold up there!"

The men reined the wagon and the crowd rushed up to it, leaving the drunks quite bewildered. Wolf Keeler, pinching his nostrils, looked over the side rails, and one man jumped up into the back of the wagon, looking under a trap and even under the buckboard seat to be sure Man Killer was not there.

One of the drunks giggled at his friend and said to Brodie, "I kin see you boys admire this wagon a lot, but it ain't fer sale."

Brodie said quietly, "Go on. You can go."

The second drunk found his friend's joke quite amusing and his raucous laughter echoed off the buildings in the deserted street as the two rode away. Wolf and Brodie were beside themselves with anger.

Minutes later, the wagon turned the corner and passed by the livery stable. From beneath the slow-moving vehicle a shadow dropped to the ground, a knife in each hand. Man Killer lay in the middle of the road and put his two knives back in their sheaths. His arms and legs ached and shook from the exertion of hanging underneath the wagon, knives stuck into the wood and toes gripping the edges of the bottom of the floorboards. He found Hawk right away and saddled him up, sticking his rifle in the scabbard and quickly checking the loads in the guns he had retrieved from the sheriff's gun rack.

Man Killer heard the voices of the crowd in the distance. They were getting closer. He looked out both doors of the livery stable and saw men coming in both directions. Figuring he would go for his horse, they had split up into two groups. If he made a sprint out either door, he would be shot to ribbons.

Minutes later, Wolf leading one group and Brodie leading the other, the lynch mob entered the doors of the livery stable, guns drawn. They went straight to Hawk's stall and found the horse, saddle, and tack were gone.

"Damn the luck!" Wolf exclaimed with a very nasal voice.

Brodie chimed in, "The red scoundrel made his escape right from under our noses. He's a slippery one. Well, boys, Millard Mining Corporation takes care of its employees, and I am authorized to offer a reward of a least five thousand dollars for the body of Man Killer. Mr. Millard may even increase the reward when I speak with him in the morn."

The crowd scattered, many deciding to try to follow the Nez Percé this night and get a jump on the rest. Most would try to ride to the Coyote Run and catch him, and a few even reasoned he would head for the Banta ranch. Within seconds, their sounds died out and something stirred in the big bedding straw pile.

Man Killer climbed out of the barrel of feed he

had been hiding in and ran to the straw pile, pulling away the golden weeds. He grabbed the edge of an Indian blanket and jerked it out of the straw and Hawk stood up, shaking bits of straw off his body and saddle. Man Killer smiled, patted him, and led him quietly out into the night.

He walked the horse between buildings and down alleys, avoiding all eyes, then rode toward the high lonesome. If these men were going to find him, they would ride through grizzlies, storms, rocks, trees, and misery to get to him. He would be up high in the Sangre de Cristo Range, where most men feared to tread. First he would climb straight up Horn Peak. Then, riding above timberline, he would make his way south along the range to Spread Eagle Peak, where he would be able to still maintain a vigil over Shirley and Joseph and the Coyote Run until Chris and Joshua returned.

Chris Colt surveyed the tracks before him and saw a line running from each front hoofprint from Brandon Rudd's horse.

"Oh-oh, War Bonnet, Brandon's horse didn't even make it as far as I thought he would. He's almost dead."

Colt rode on and found the horse lying dead, fifteen minutes up the trail. The saddle was still on him, with only the canteen missing as far as Chris could tell. Colt saw the tracks of the man go on after the more obvious tracks of the kidnappers. He took off after Brandon at a mile-eating trot.

Seeing the dead horse brought back horrible memories for Chris Colt. He thought back to his teen years and a very difficult lesson he had learned. When his father's estranged brother, Samuel Colt, died in 1863, Chris felt really sad, so he entered the Ohio National Guard on a whim and went off to fight with Company G of the 171st Regiment in the Civil War. Although only fourteen years old at the time, he was able to pass easily.

When the war was over, Chris felt decades older and was so anxious to get back to northeastern Ohio, he killed his horse by riding it so hard. It was just like Brandon had done except Chris had to watch his horse drown. Trying to swim the exhausted mare across the Tuscarawas River in southern Ohio, the young Chris Colt watched the animal drown, because its intestines knotted up while it tried to swim. He swam to the bank and lay there crying for an hour, he felt so bad. The young veteran vowed that he would never mistreat an animal again. His horse would get fed and watered before he would, and would be treated like a friend instead of a tool.

Brandon saw Elizabeth a mile off atop a high mountain. She was tied to a large pole and there was a brush fire built around her legs. Even at that distance, Brandon could hear the brush crackling as it burned. With Linford Crowley giving the commands, ten men were in line in front of her in a firing squad formation. They were going to shoot her while she burned.

She spotted Brandon and screamed, "Shoot me! Quick, shoot me!"

Brandon cried, "I can't! I have no gun! I don't believe in them!"

The flames leaped higher around her and she screamed at him, "What? You fool! Kill me, please, someone kill me!"

Brandon saw the men in the firing squad grin and pull the triggers. He jumped up and looked into the smiling face of Chris Colt. A small fire crackled in front of the scout and steam came out of the spout of a blackened coffeepot. Colt had unloaded one of his pistols and was cleaning it, cocking and dry-firing it every once in a while.

"Nightmare?" Colt asked.

Brandon said, "Mr. Colt."

Chris said, "Colt, or Chris, please?"

"Colt," Brandon said, "I must have passed out on the trail. Do you have a spare firearm, sir?"

Colt grinned and tossed him the weaponry, saying, "Tex said to lend you this, but you don't have to return the bullets. He also sent his horse along for you. It's mustang and meaner than Lucifer. He'll do for you on the trail."

Brandon smiled, strapping on the gun. "Thank you. You're not going to try to talk me out of it?"

"Think you could talk me out of it if it was the woman I loved?"

Brandon grinned.

Colt poured them both coffee.

Chris offered Brandon a cigar, which was refused. He tossed him a strip of venison jerky and some hardtack. The lawyer ate ravenously.

Colt said, "You walked on another ten miles past where your horse gave up the ghost. Know how to shoot that pistol?"

Brandon nodded.

Colt went on, "I know you want to save her, and you can, but you have to let me be in charge. This is my courtroom."

Brandon replied, "I know. I will do whatever you ask of me."

Colt said, "Good. Finish your coffee and mount up. We have some tracking to do."

The kidnappers had made good time and a wide swing back toward the east, heading north initially. By midday, Colt found their night location. They had camped out in a grove of cottonwoods, leaving at daybreak. Colt was relieved to find sign that Elizabeth apparently had simply been tied to a tree and slept there. She was also loosened and allowed to go into some bushes to relieve herself. That was a relief as well, as a similar instance might be an opportune time for him and Brandon to grab her and escape.

On the other hand, Colt kind of wanted to tangle with these hombres. They had stolen and terrorized a woman. He didn't cotton to bullies at all.

As often happened when he was dealing with those who would intimidate, Chris grinned as he remembered a conversation with one of the gunsmiths in his uncle's firearms factory. The man had become one of the very first gunfighters ever, winning many battles, until a rifle-toting lawman missed his chest and put a bullet through the back of the man's right hand. His youth and his wild gunfighting days were over, so he decided to settle down and learn a trade. He became a master gunsmith.

The man and young Chris Colt were having a conversation about courage one day when the gunsmith said, "Young'un, the difference betwixt a coward and a hero is about one minute in time."

Chris was perplexed by that statement, and it bothered him for a long time afterward, but he finally got a handle on it. He got into a fight with two brothers whose family owned a farm just outside Cuyahoga Falls. Their family and his had attended the same church, but the two brothers were about the furthest thing you could get from walking the Christian walk of life. They were troublemakers from the get-go. The two bullies simply beat up everybody, and finally Chris's turn came. Anyone they confronted simply backed down from the bullies because they were so tough and brutal, so they would chase the person down and still beat him senseless.

When one of them started picking on Chris, he tried everything he could to avoid getting into a fight. When one of the two, however, made some disparaging remarks about a girl in Chris's church whose father had been arrested for public drunkenness, Chris had finally had it. He was very scared. Their brutality had become legendary locally, but Chris was beyond caring at that point.

He was so ferocious in his demeanor alone that the two even started to look a little unsettled. Colt had heard somewhere that a man using his head has a much better chance in a fight than one who just uses his muscle, so he tried to think his way out of trouble. When the first punch was thrown, it landed square on Chris's temple and sent him reeling to the ground. His right hand closed around a smooth egg-shaped rock lying on the ground, and he grabbed it surreptitiously.

The two brothers ran up and both kicked him in the rib cage, knocking the wind out of him and severely bruising his ribs. Most boys would have folded over and cried, but this simply made Chris furious. He came off the ground with a fury and tore into both brothers. His fists were swinging so wildly and quickly, nobody noticed the rock sticking out of the ends of his right fist. The faces of the bullies, however, showed that they had made contact with the rock. Within a minute, both brothers were lying on the ground unconscious sporting two black eyes and a broken nose each. Chris dropped the rock behind his back and nobody saw it.

He became the hero of the young girl he had defended, and of the community. His reputation grew and the story of the fight became more elaborate with each telling. In actuality, part of the reason he went off to fight in the Civil War was that he was worried about the two bullies trying to get retribution. It bothered him that he left like that, but as he grew and gained confidence, he realized how smart he had really been.

One thing he never forgot was the butterflies he felt in his stomach when he had to face the two bullies, and the great fear that clutched at him. It would have been so easy to start his life out as a coward back then; instead Chris Colt chose to act like a man. That decision made him a hero. It was one in which he had about a minute to think and react, and the opposite decision would have made Chris Colt a different man.

Colt said, "Brandon, can you keep on? We are going to push these horses far tonight and make up for a lot of time while the kidnappers sleep tonight. We can travel in the dark now because I know where they are headed."

"You do?"

"They're headed back east and they can only cross the big river in a few spots. It's pretty easy to figure out where they will cross. We'll slow down when we see likely ambush spots or places where they might be camped. They've pushed it hard, but their horses have slowed a lot now and the men will figure that there's no pursuit now. They probably spotted you on their tail from a distance and maybe figured you were the lead man in a column. They probably figure now there's no one, because they have held men back all along the way as rear guard, but their sign shows they dropped off watching the back trail. Now we can put spurs to our mounts and make up lost ground. War Bonnet can handle it and so can that wiry mustang of Tex's, but can you?"

Brandon gave Colt a queer look and said, "You have to even ask?"

Colt grinned and pushed War Bonnet into a fast

trot. He lifted his canteen to his lips and took a sip while the big paint cantered across the prairie.

After a three-hour rest for the horses and nap for the two men, they got back in the saddle shortly after midnight. While the kidnappers slept, the rescuers would travel.

It was shortly after daybreak when Colt discovered the new campsite in a grove of cottonwoods. Replacing his spurs with his Lakota moccasins, he bade Brandon stay with the horses and handed the attorney his Colt revolving shotgun.

"You cannot take on all these men alone," Brandon whispered.

'I know. I'll ask for your help, but I don't want you to come until I'm ready or in trouble."

The chief of scouts walked to his saddlebags and dug around, pulling out some small braided rawhide strings. He disappeared into the darkness heading toward the campfire. Two men sat at the fire, one smoking and rambling on about how the country was going to hell, and the other drinking coffee and staring at the flames. Brandon checked the shirt Colt had placed over the nose of the sorrel to keep him from whinnying to the other horses; it was in place. War Bonnet was indeed a warhorse and, although a herd animal, knew not to whinny when they were in a strange location. It had brought him bullets before when he was owned by the mighty Oglala Lakota war hero Crazy Horse. He had learned.

Brandon leaned against a tree and watched the campfire and the shadows around the cottonwoods. He couldn't see a thing of Chris Colt, just the two sentries and sleeping forms around the fire. It was almost daybreak when Brandon finally heard a noise and Chris Colt suddenly appeared, leading someone through the shadows. It was Elizabeth.

She ran into Brandon's arms and started crying. He looked at Colt with amazement. This famous frontiersman was indeed everything the legend had described for him. He had marched into a camp of armed men and stole her out from under their very noses.

Colt whispered, "I'm going to sneak back in and get her a good horse and scatter theirs, then you can take her out of here while I settle accounts with them."

Elizabeth said flatly and firmly, "No, you will not."

Both men looked at her, shocked. Her jaw was set, though, and it was obvious that arguments would prove futile.

Colt said, "What do you mean, Miss Macon?"

"First, if you stay behind to fight these hooligans, you'll get killed. There are eleven of them. Second, Brandon won't let you go alone, so he'll want to go down there and shoot it up with them. Third, if we leave and try to escape, they will try to overtake us and we'll be on the defensive. On top of that, some of them might escape justice and that cannot happen."

Colt grinned and whispered, "Well, ma'am, you sure figured all that out in a hurry. What do you propose?"

"Give me a gun and the three of us will shoot it out with them," she said matter-of-factly. "That will help the odds considerably."

Brandon said firmly, "No, absolutely not."

"But Brandon," Elizabeth said, "I can shoot a gun and—"

Colt interrupted her with a very quiet but conversation-ending no.

She knew that further discussion would be a waste of time.

Colt said, "You stay with the horses, and we'll go down. If we are killed, you mount up on War Bonnet and tell him to take you home. He'll lead you to Joshua. First scatter their horses. It will be worth the danger and give you a good head start. Let him have his head and travel at his own speed. The mustang will follow him."

Colt dug a Navy .36 out of his saddlebags and handed it to her. He grabbed his carbine and jacked a round in the chamber.

"Come on, Brandon," he said, moving toward the fire in the near darkness.

They went forward and Colt signaled for Brandon to drop down and crawl. The attorney felt his heart in his throat as they crawled closer to the camp. Before he knew it, they were near the first sleeping snoring bodies. Chris crawled up to the first man and slowly, carefully wrapped one of the rawhide thongs around the man's wrist and tied a knot, which wasn't tight enough to awaken the sleeping scoundrel but apparently good enough to bind him. Colt repeated this with the other wrist. He then crawled up behind the two men at the fire and stood up right behind one, a gun in each hand. Brandon, at Colt's gesture stayed where he was, between two sleeping men. He had never been so scared. What amazed him was that neither man moved or acknowledged the scout's presence. Brandon suddenly realized that both had fallen asleep sitting up. Colt's right hand went up and the butt of his gun smashed into the temple of one, and he caught the man before he fell and laid him gently by the fire.

Chris walked over to the second and smashed him in the head as well. That man dropped, too, but his arm flopped into the fire and he came to quickly with a yell. Colt held his guns, one Peacemaker and his carbine, out in both directions and faced the sleepy men, now jumping up, going for their guns.

Brandon jumped up and smashed the barrel of the shotgun into the face of one, then butt-stroked the other in the solar plexus, finishing him off with an uppercut butt-stroke that stood the man up on his tiptoes, and he dropped on his back like a sack of potatoes.

Seeing this, Elizabeth held her breath. Chris Colt was a gun man and great fighter of some note, but Brandon Rudd was an attorney, and he was . . . what was he? she wondered. He was the man she loved. Yes, that was it. She loved him through and through, and she knew that she did. The beautiful young woman wanted to leap up and down, but on the other hand, she was worried sick for him.

Brandon unloaded the shotgun into the body of one gunfighter who was drawing and had a chance at Colt's back. Flames stabbed out of Colt's rifle and the handgun barked angrily six times in a row. Colt recocked the Winchester with one hand between shots. The lawyer noticed the one man Colt had tied and two others he apparently had tied while freeing Elizabeth.

Brandon saw a streak of blood appear across Colt's left calf muscle and the man never flinched. He just shot and shot and kept reshooting. Three men stood among the moaning mass, their hands raised. Four more lay wounded and complaining on the ground, and four more lay dead. The center man among the three was Linford Crowley and Brandon walked forward to face him.

Colt said, "Hold up, Brandon. All of you that are down, toss your guns toward the fire with one hand when I point at you."

The first complied, but the second one stared daggers at Colt. Chris raised the rifle, pointed it straight

at the man's face, and pulled the trigger. The bullet
went between his eyes and took the back of the kidnapper's head off. The rest tossed their guns as
quickly as he pointed at them.

When Brandon reached Colt, the scout whispered,
"When you are vastly outnumbered, you have to be
very bold, decisive, cold, and gruesome. This will
turn the tide in your favor most times."

Brandon said, "I'm learning, Colt."

Colt said to the three standing men, "Now, you
three, left hands only, toss the guns toward the
fire."

They complied, but Linford smiled broadly at
Brandon and said, "If it was just you and me, laddie
boy, and we had no weapons, I'd tear you limb from
limb."

Brandon handed the shotgun to Chris, who set
down the carbine. He unbuckled his gun belt, ready
to take on the kidnapper in a fistfight, when he heard
Elizabeth screaming, running toward them.

She yelled, "Brandon, no!"

Brandon smiled at her, and she ran up to him,
grabbing his arms.

"Brandon," she said, "please don't. It came out at
the trial: He won all his money originally in brawls
on barges on the river."

Brandon didn't speak. He grabbed her gently by
the arms, kissed her on the forehead, and placed her
by Colt. He walked forward to meet the giant
fighter.

Colt whispered to Elizabeth, "Something he's got
do."

She bit her lip.

Laughing loudly, Linford said, "I'm gonna rip
your arms off and feed them to you."

Colt said, "Brandon, wait. Come here a minute."

The lawyer told Linford, "I'll be right back. Don't worry."

Brandon came to the chief of scouts' side.

Colt whispered, "You know how to fight?"

Brandon whispered, "Boxing and wrestling at Harvard Law."

Chris said, "Good, but fight dirty, too."

Brandon said, "Like I told you, I'm learning."

Brandon walked back to Linford and the big man started to say something, but the lawyer kicked him viciously in the groin and punched the big man square in the face. Linford shook his head and started laughing again.

He came forward trying to sweep up the smaller man in a mighty bear hug, but Brandon dropped to the ground, hooked a leg in front of the giant, and kicked the back of Crowley's knee with his other foot. Linford flew forward face first into the campfire then came off the ground with a roar. He dived into the attorney, head-butting Brandon in the face. Brandon felt his knees buckle and tasted blood as it ran down his throat from his split lips and loose teeth.

Brandon jumped aside as Crowley rushed again, and the lawyer kicked the big man in the left knee-cap. Linford turned sharply and swung a left that missed, a right that hit Brandon in the shoulder and paralyzed it temporarily, and a left that sent the lawyer flying backward to the ground. Brandon shook his head, which was spinning like mad. It started to clear, and he saw the big man ready to drop on him from above. Brandon stuck his foot up quickly, and it caught Linford in the ribs, spinning him off to the right. Brandon rolled away and jumped up, shaking his head again.

Linford jumped to his feet and charged headfirst, screaming like a mad bull. Brandon sidestepped and hit him hard in the temple with an overhand right as the big man charged by. As soon as Crowley turned, Brandon hit him with a left jab into the nose, another, and still another. Each one snapped the man's head back and sent blood streaming everywhere. Brandon followed this with a right cross, left uppercut into the solar plexus, and another right cross. The second one spun Crowley half around. He turned and grabbed Brandon in a mighty bear hug, but the attorney head-butted him full in the face, knocking out several of the man's teeth. Crowley's face was puffing and changing colors in numerous places now, and Brandon didn't look much better.

Crowley stood there weaving, his big sides heaving in and out. Brandon loaded up and hit him so hard with a right cross that Brandon felt it jar his entire arm and part of his back. Crowley's eyes crossed and closed, and he fell forward.

The handsome attorney walked toward Elizabeth, and she ran forward, wrapping her arms around him. He winked at Colt and fainted.

When Brandon came to, he was lying on the ground in Elizabeth's arms. She smiled down at him, tears dropping off her cheeks. Colt was tying up captives.

She whispered, "Thank you so much for coming after me and saving me."

"Wild horses could not drag me away," he said. "I love you."

Her breath caught and she said, "I love you, too."

She bent forward and kissed him and Brandon winced in pain.

Elizabeth giggled, saying, "I'm sorry."

He said, "I need to rest my eyes a minute."

With that, Brandon fell asleep, and Elizabeth helped Chris Colt.

Brandon awakened suddenly, opening his eyes to the sharp light of the midmorning sun, and sat up, wincing with pain emanating from several places in his body. He looked all around and blinked his eyes. There were five dead men stacked side by side not far away. Back in the trees, Brandon saw some more people. He made it to his feet and swayed slightly, caught himself, and went forward. He found his gun belt sitting by the fire, which was still going with Colt's coffeepot on it. He replaced the gun and walked to Chris and Elizabeth under the trees.

Linford Crowley had his neck in a noose and sat bareback on a large horse, hands tied behind his back. His face was grotesque, one eye swollen shut and the other almost closed. His nose was broken and both lips were split and very puffed up. There was also a large bruise and swelling on one cheekbone, and it was partially split open.

He laughed again through obviously sore lips and said, "Well, lawyer, you're supposed to stand for law and order. Are you going to let him lynch me?"

Brandon walked forward to Linford's horse and said, "You kidnapped little girls and sold them into slavery. You kidnapped the woman I love, and you ask me that. No, I won't let him lynch you. This is justice and I will be responsible for it as an officer of the court. May your black soul rot in hell."

Brandon took off his hat and slapped the horse on the rump. It took off with a lunge and Linford's neck snapped like a dry branch.

Elizabeth turned her head, a tear running down

her cheek. Brandon walked over to comfort her, but she turned back, setting her jaw.

"See here," she said, "this is a messy business, but it must be done. We have miles to go, no towns around, no lawmen within miles. We cannot take these men at gunpoint all those miles and our survival is of primary importance. They kidnapped me and were part of a plot to rustle cattle, both of which are hanging offenses. I saw them all, Brandon, there is no doubt about their guilt or innocence, so they must be either let go or hung. Let's finish."

Brandon said, "No, Colt and I will finish. You might want to make some food for us. Do you not have some food in your saddlebags, Chris?"

Colt nodded and Elizabeth, obviously shaken, walked to the horses.

Brandon said, "I hate this, but let's get it done."

Colt said, "I'd rather fight a grizzly with a toothache."

They hanged the rest of the crooks and returned to the fire. Brandon simply accepted what had to be done, because what Elizabeth said made perfect sense. The three then sat around picking at their food.

Colt finally set down his plate and said, "Nobody with any sense can stomach killing anybody for any reason. The faces will fade away with time. Men cannot live without laws or law enforcers. If either of those are not around, it becomes the survival of the fittest. What we did had to be done, or we would have had to let them go and someone else would have been kidnapped or murdered."

Brandon said, "Colt, I believe we both understand and agree with you totally, but that doesn't make taking the life of another any easier."

"I know," Colt replied, "I've been through it too many times myself. It just helps to know that what you did was all that you could do. There was no choice in the matter."

Elizabeth finally spoke. "Mr. Colt, I would wager a shiny copper or two that you do not even understand why you are such a legend. You don't, do you?"

Colt blushed and didn't know how to respond. He stood and walked to his saddlebags.

He explained, "I'm ready for a cigar. Want one, Brandon?"

"One of life's great pleasures."

Colt took longer than usual to find the cigars. He thought to himself, *Legend. Why do people say that? I only do what I have learned to do, try to be honest, try to do what's right. Why do people call me a legend like that?*

Very uncomfortable, he lit Brandon's cigar and his own and thought of things to say to change the conversation.

Blowing a blue trail of smoke skyward, he said, "There are very few things in life like a good cigar, especially after a meal."

Brandon puffed his and added, "One of the few bastions of male expression left in our great country, sir."

In mock anger, Elizabeth said, "Just what do you mean by that, Mr. Rudd?"

"Exactly what I said, Miss Macon," he replied. "This is one of few pleasures which men can share without worrying about suffragettes and the like. You know, today's modern women, like Lemonade Lucy?"

"Nonsense," she replied.

Brandon said, "You know Lemonade Lucy Hayes, the First Lady, the wife of our illustrious president who will not allow any alcoholic beverages to be served in the White House . . . and I'm speaking of the suffragettes. You know who they are?"

Colt said, "Women who want all women to have the vote?"

"Exactly," Brandon said. "One of them is even going to run for President under the Equal Rights Party banner."

Chris Colt laughed and said, "So what?"

A little perturbed, Elizabeth said, "Yes, so what about it?"

Brandon laughed. "There's nothing about it. I'm just having a little fun with you."

Elizabeth turned and started to huff away, saying, "Well, I'm not laughing."

Colt and Brandon took long drags on their cigars and blew the smoke skyward. Elizabeth disappeared into the trees, apparently to take care of personal needs.

Chris looked at the long plume of smoke. "Well, Mr. Legal Man, you sure figured out a good way to get her mind off the hangings and get angry at something else, didn't you?"

Brandon said, "I think it was bothering her more than she was showing."

"I think you're right. Tough woman. She's got bottom to her. You're plumb crazy if you let her get away."

"You think she'd even consider marrying me?"

Colt chuckled.

"What's so funny?"

Colt replied, "You ought to see the way she watched you, partner. She'd marry you in a minute and stand by you through every broken bone, heartache, and sandstorm."

"Are you positive?" Brandon asked, very excited.

Colt said, "It's my job to read sign. It's not always tracks on the ground, you know."

Brandon took another deep puff and blew a smoke ring, then grinned proudly.

Colt stood and said, "We need to get away from here. That will do you both more good than anything."

"What about burying the dead men?"

"When you were resting up from the fight, I let several of the wounded men go. They seemed to have learned their lesson and aren't going to be in much shape to harm anyone else again. They can bury them."

"But Colt, they won't come back. I know it doesn't matter to dead men, but it seems uncivilized to just leave their bodies out."

Colt said, "This is a hard country. That's the responsibility of their friends. Our responsibility is to live and survive and make it back to the wagon train."

The two men struck camp, saddled the horses, and confiscated the rest of the remuda to take back to the wagon train. They took saddles and tack with them. Elizabeth came out of the trees and Colt could tell she had been crying. He pointed it out to Brandon and the attorney went to her with the horse he had saddled for her.

"Elizabeth, I'm sorry if I offended," Brandon said. "I was only teasing."

She smiled. "I know, Brandon," she said softly. "It was seeing those men die, even though I prayed for that very thing just hours before."

The three mounted up and started to leave. The other horses were saddled and would follow the three.

Elizabeth asked, "What about burying the dead men?"

Colt said, "Buzzards have to eat, too."

He touched his calves to War Bonnet's flanks and took off at a trot, eyes on the western horizon. The other two followed.

That night, they made camp in another cottonwood grove and sat around the fire talking long into the night. Colt said they should take it easy on the horses, especially his and Tex's. He also wanted the horses fairly fresh in case of any other emergencies.

Brandon and Elizabeth seemed to have an unlimited number of questions about Canon City, the Arkansas Valley, the terrain, climate, wildlife, and frontier life.

Colt enjoyed telling them about the mountains, especially the majestic Sangre de Cristos. He described the view in the Wet Mountain Valley southwest of Canon City, where his ranch was located. The mountains swept up from the valley floor and many went up to over fourteen thousand feet, stretching side by side, north and south all the way down in New Mexico and turning west up past Salida, connecting to the Collegiate Range. The two listened intently as Colt described the green lush pastures of the Wet Mountain Valley giving way to thickets of scrub oaks, which in turn led to the evergreen forests that swept up the many gentle ridges. There were numerous glacier-fed streams running off the big range and lots of lakes, many landlocked above timberline. Colt described the rough rocky peaks above timberline and the alpine-covered bare tops with many marmots grazing on the sparse grasses, their warning whistles signaling the others to scurry to their holes.

He spoke about the groves of quaking aspen trees and the brilliant gold patches along the sides of the mountains in the autumn, and the ferocious winter

storm winds that could almost blow a man off his
horse near the peaks in the wintertime. He talked
about giant avalanches tumbling down the moun-
tainsides in great chutes, beavers making dams
across the fast-flowing streams and creating trout-
filled ponds up in the tall timber, and he talked about
the large herds of mule deer, bighorn sheep, harems
of elk, pure white mountain goats, cinnamon-colored
bears and mighty silvertip grizzlies, numerous
mountain lions, and giant herds of pronghorn antelope running freely up and down the floor of the big
valley.

Colt told them about the extremely mild winters
around Canon City, and they were amazed to learn
that many times there were blizzards in places like
Denver and Colorado Springs, while Canon City
and Pueblo would have sunshine. They were
shocked to learn that the Canon City area would
usually get a few inches of snowfall at a time that
would usually melt away within twenty-four hours.
They were further stunned to learn from Colt that
there were very few snowfalls in Canon City in the
winter, and there were many days of sunshine when
a coat wasn't even necessary. Like most people, the
two easterners simply pictured the entire state of
Colorado as being covered with a giant blanket of
snow half the year.

The two were even more excited about moving
there than before. Telling it, however, made Colt
very anxious to get home to his wife and son.

The horses seemed to recover well, for the party's
travel was unhurried now. A wagon train often never
made more than just a few miles in one day's travel,
so three people riding three saddle mounts could
easily overtake a wagon train without their mounts
getting winded.

* * *

What Colt did not want was to come face-to-face with a Pawnee war party. Unfortunately, there was one scouting the train, hoping to cut some stray steers or possibly run off with the remuda. Finally giving up, the thirty-two warriors decided to cut back east and see if there were any easier pickings, because Joshua Colt had provided such good security for the herd and the train was too large.

That was when they spotted the trio of riders coming toward them from the distance. Thirty-two Pawnee warriors against three white men—after observing from a hillock, they saw that one was a woman. Those were odds that Laughing Hawk, their leader, liked. He had a very prominent nose, bulging muscles, and many coups and scalps collected over his thirty years. The strip of hair that ran the length of his otherwise shaved head held one eagle feather tilted off to the right. He carried a round-headed war club and bone-handled knife, but his pride and joy was the Smith & Wesson .44 pistol and conch-covered holster and gun belt that he took off a hapless gunfighter who wanted to parley over a deer the white man had just killed. Laughing Hawk fancied the man's horse, gun, saddle, and deer, so he simply killed him, scalped him, and took everything.

The Pawnee chieftain suggested that the war party ride ahead of the white eyes and keep a vigil. They would camp nearby at night and send sentries to keep a vigil on the three and take them at first light. They would count coups on the men, kill them, have their way with the woman, kill her, then take their horses and possessions. Half the Pawnee warriors had guns.

That night, camped in yet another grove of cottonwoods on a small stream, Colt spoke again of Canon

City and its surrounding beauty. In the middle of the conversation, though, he grabbed his stomach and bent over painfully.

"Colt, what's wrong?" Brandon said.

Colt said, "Bad vittles. I'll be back."

He went off into the trees. The three sentries watching him each laughed, although they were at different locations around the camp. Long Otter had been assigned ahead of time to follow any of the white eyes who left the fire, so reluctantly he moved into the trees where Colt went. He did not really want to observe a white man, or anyone, with diarrhea, but he had to.

He moved in close and found the man squatted down and unmoving. He watched and blinked his eyes against the darkness and the shadows. Suddenly a gun cocked and he felt the cold steel of the barrel stick into his left ear.

He slowly turned his head to look at the smiling face of Chris Colt, standing next to him in the darkness, totally naked except for a gun belt and twin holsters. Colt winked, then quickly raised his right-hand gun and brought it down on the forehead of Long Otter, who watched it, eyes crossed, descend toward his head.

Colt tied the Indian, then took his buckskins and hat off the sticks and bushes he had fashioned into a dummy.

Dead Skunks laughed to himself as he watched the man and the woman by the fire bring their lips together, and he wondered if he would watch them plant seeds by the fire. Although it was impolite to pay attention to a man and woman breeding, these were enemies, so he reasoned it would acceptable.

He heard a noise behind him and smelled tobacco. His hand went down to his knife and clutched it. He spun around and was greeted by a work-hardened fist. Everything spun in circles, then went black.

Many knives knew that Dead Skunks and Long Otter were good warriors and would maintain a careful watch, so he decided he could nap. But something awakened him and he jumped up to his feet and grabbed for his war club. But it was gone, and so were his knife and Spencer rifle. He looked into the gun barrel of a tall white man clad in quilled buckskins of Lakota origin, with a Nez Percé choker necklace around his neck. The man also wore soft-soled, quilled Cheyenne moccasins. Many Knives knew he was in trouble. His gun was clutched in the left hand of the white man and his knife and war club were tucked in the man's gun belt. The smiling white eyes gestured with his gun and Many Knives walked into the trees.

Brandon was just getting ready to propose, or at least winning the fight with himself about it, when there was a noise and the two lovers stared, mouths open, as Chris Colt walked back from the depth of the trees with three Indians, hands tied behind their backs. One had a pair of swollen lips. Another had a large blue lump on his forehead above and between the eyes. The third looked okay but quite upset.

Cold had them all sit cross-legged by the fire and this just about unnerved Elizabeth. All three wore war paint and had shaved heads except for a strip of hair running down the middle. Two wore a feather from their scalp locks. All three wore only breechcloths and moccasins, although the eldest wore a breastplate.

Colt sat down and ate dinner, which Elizabeth had prepared. It was sumptuous. He untied the hands of the three braves and handed each one a biscuit and an antelope steak. They at first resisted, then devoured the meal. Colt then made them lay down and tied their hands and ankles behind their backs. He kept them near the fire.

While all this was going on, he explained to Brandon and Elizabeth that they had been watched by a war party of Pawnee all day.

Brandon said, "Why didn't you tell us?"

Colt chuckled and said, "What would you have done, file an injunction against them?"

Elizabeth chuckled this time.

Colt explained, "No sense three people worrying about something they have no control over instead of one."

Brandon said, "But what if they would have attacked?"

Colt responded, "They didn't."

"That's true. What about these three?"

"You keep an eye on them while I'm gone. I'm going to parley with their riding partners."

Elizabeth said, "Oh, my goodness, Chris. Isn't that dangerous?"

Colt smiled broadly and said, "Of course."

He walked over to War Bonnet and saddled him, then rode off into the night. One of the mares, in estrus, fussed a lot, wanting to follow the stallion, but the horses were all in a large brush and rope corral made of lassos and windfall logs. The big paint stud had been off feeding by himself.

Colt rode in the direction he figured the Pawnees would bivouac for the night and didn't even look for the tracks of his three captives. They would not have come directly from their own campsite and would have made a different route into his camp.

Colt found the Pawnees in a smaller grove of cottonwoods less than three miles from his own spot. He carefully left War Bonnet outside the little bowl where the grove of trees lay. Chris went forward down the grass-covered hillside on his hands and knees. He slithered into the trees and spent an hour reconnoitering the Pawnee location. One young warrior guarded the horse herd and another watched over the campsite.

Colt went to the horse herd first. He crept up close to the sentry's position. The guard heard a noise in the trees behind him and walked forward cautiously, an arrow cocked on his bowstring. He looked all around but found nothing. The man turned and started back to his position, walking under a tree with large branches jutting out. Chris Colt swung down, hanging by the back of his knees, and smashed the sentry on the point of his chin with the butt of his rifle. The young man dropped like a hailstone.

Colt wrapped up in the man's blanket and walked toward the campfire, carrying his bow and arrows. The other sentry was putting some sticks atop the fire and nodded at Colt without paying much attention. When the scout got right up to the fire, he walked up quickly to the guard, who finally realized he was an imposter. Too late. Colt flipped the blanket over the man's head and struck him with the barrel of the carbine. He caught the falling man and lay him by the fire.

Colt pulled a cigar out and lit it with a burning brand. He then got the entire pile of firewood and placed it all atop the flaming embers. Soon the fire was licking golden tongues up at the Kansas night sky. Firelight danced on the leaves and branches of the surrounding trees.

Colt sat on a log and smoked his cigar while he

waited for the remaining Indians to awaken one by one. He had only to wait until the flames reached their highest peak. Bewildered Pawnees rose and stared at him. Several grabbed for weapons when they saw him, but Colt's accurate shooting with the carbine sent weapons flying into splinters. Finally he spun a man around with a bullet through the shoulder. At the same time, another reached for his Henry, and Colt's quick draw with his left hand while holding the carbine in his right made believers of them all.

He stood by the fire and used his weapons to discourage any more from reaching for their own. He grinned at the Pawnees and clamped down on the cigar with his white teeth.

Colt said, "Who is the leader among you, Pawnee brothers?"

Laughing Hawk, wearing his pistol, stepped forward. "I am Laughing Hawk, and you call us brothers yet wear the clothing of our enemies, the Lakota and Cheyenne."

"I am called Wamble Uncha, One Eagle, by my brothers, your enemies, but I am not enemy to the Pawnee. I am brother to all those of the red skin. I pass through here to join my black brother who takes many cows to the land of the Ute, where I live."

The Pawnee said, "You speak and act boldly, but why do you think you can come in here and not be struck down like a lame deer?"

Colt stared at Laughing Hawk. He smiled, puffed on his cigar, and dropped the carbine across the log, spinning his left-hand Peacemaker backward into the holster.

He said, "I see you are wearing a gun. Why don't you strike me down like a lame deer?"

Laughing Hawk was no coward. Die or not, he would try, and try he did.

His hand went down to his .44, but as his hand touched the handle of the pistol, flames shot out from both of Chris Colt's guns, already in his hands. Dirt kicked up next to Laughing Hawk's feet. He let go of the handle of his pistol like it was a hot coal.

Another brave reached for his bow and arrows and Chris turned both guns and fired from the hip. The bow shattered in pieces as a bullet from the left-hand gun struck it. Because he had fired both pistols at the same time, the Pawnees were unaware that he had missed with the other gun.

He deftly spun both guns forward, caught them on the second fingers, and sent them spinning backward and holstered them in the midst of the rapid back-spin. The Pawnees were overawed by this show of expertise and daring. They could not believe that this man, who apparently took out their sentries and came into their midst, would now even holster his guns. He was counting coups and had very strong medicine.

Colt said, "Hear me, my brothers. I have killed none of you, but I could have. Back at my fire, your three scouts sleep by the flames and are warm. When I go back, their bonds will be cut and they can come here to you. My hands have been touched by the lightning in the sky, and my guns are like the thunder. I have come here because my brother and sister at my fire are much better fighters than me, and they want me to learn."

Laughing Hawk's Adam's apple bobbed and he said, "The two at your fire can fight better than you."

Colt said, "Yes, they are just teaching me to fight. I am like the young child in their presence."

Laughing Hawk thought a second and said, "Do you have more of that tobacco you smoke?"

Colt said, "For my friends and to make many gifts to the Great Mystery. He smiles on me and makes my medicine very strong."

Colt whistled like a red-tailed hawk and War Bonnet came galloping up over the hill and down into the trees. He ran right up to the fire. All the warriors admired the big paint.

Laughing Hawk said, "You are the one who was blood brother to our great enemy Crazy Horse, who now walks the spirit trail. I thought so, but now I see. This was the horse he gifted to you."

Colt said, "My great brother has now gone beyond."

Laughing Hawk said, "They sing about you in the lodges of our enemies, One Eagle. You are also called Colt?"

Chris said, "I am Colt, so is my brother who looks like me but wears dark skin. The one whose cows you could not steal."

That was a guess on Chris's part, but he could tell by the embarrassed smile on the chief that he had hit the mark.

Colt grinned and Laughing Hawk grinned back, saying, "He guards his beef well. He truly is the brother of the mighty Colt."

Chris tossed a cigar to the Pawnee, and the man walked forward, lighting it with a flaming brand.

Colt mounted his horse and said, "I go in peace."

The chieftain raised his hand and said, "Go in peace, Colt."

At Colt's fire, he amazed the three captives, and his two companions, by handing the Indians the leads to their war bridles and their weapons.

He spoke to them in sign language by pointing at the ponies and placing his index finger and middle finger on either side of his fingers with his other hand turned sideways. He then bounced the hand along, indicating riding the pony. He pointed in the direction of their camp and then stuck his fingers of his left hand upward and spread apart, indicating people, and he drew his right index finger backward over the fingers in an arc, indicating chief over the people. They understood and rode off without looking back.

Brandon and Elizabeth sat at the fire looking at Colt with the kind of stares children would give to their father, waiting to see if he has cut them a Christmas tree. Elizabeth handed the scout a cup of coffee when he sat down. He thanked her and sipped the hot brew.

"Well?" Brandon asked.

"Well . . ." Colt replied. "Oh, the Pawnees you mean? They want us to come over tomorrow at four for tea and crumpets."

The couple laughed, while Chris rolled a cigarette and lit it.

He said, "I spoke with them, and we came to kind of a peace treaty. We can turn in safely tonight and leave in the morning, I think. I'll keep War Bonnet here to warn us."

"Warn us?" Elizabeth said.

"A good horse is better than a watchdog," Colt said. "His ears are bigger. Nose is bigger. Eyes are bigger, too. If someone tries to sneak up in the night, War Bonnet will whinny and snort, and you only have to look at where he's staring and where his ears are aimed to pinpoint the intruder."

"Amazing," Elizabeth said.

They caught up with the train late the next day

and Joshua told Colt about the telegraph he had received from Shirley. Man Killer was arrested, obviously framed for murder, and was now hiding, probably in the Sangre de Cristo Mountains.

Chapter 5

>»»»»»»»»»»»»»»

Quick Action

Chris told Joshua he would have to leave immediately for Coyote Run. Colt worried about Joshua's health, but also felt that his brother was well protected and aware of possible danger. The chief of scouts would travel south to the nearest railroad and take trains all the way to Canon City.

Brandon Rudd said, "I'm going with you."

"The hell you say," Colt said.

Brandon explained, "If this young protégé of yours has been framed for murder and is a fugitive, he obviously needs an attorney very badly, does he not?"

Chris said, "That's okay. I'll take care of him."

"Oh, what if he's been recaptured by the time you get there? What will you do, break him out and become a fugitive yourself?"

Colt was a little frustrated, as he was used to handling things, being in control.

"If I have to," he responded.

Brandon said sarcastically, "Oh, I'll bet that Mrs. Colt would certainly appreciate that."

Joshua stood by and grinned, even chuckling lightly.

Colt said, "You don't have a horse."

"Fine," Brandon said, "let's go purchase one from Captain Swenson. You help me pick it out."

Colt finally laughed at himself and clapped

Brandon on the shoulder, saying, "Brandon, anytime I have to go to court, I don't want anybody but you representing me."

"If you mean that, Colt, let's understand something right now," Brandon replied. "If we are surrounded by Indians or outlaws, or lost in a blizzard, or anything like that, you are totally in charge. If it comes to legal matters, however, you do exactly what I say without arguing. Agreed?"

"Fair enough," Chris said, and stuck out his hand.

Elizabeth Macon just looked at Brandon Rudd, her heart all aflutter. He was so professional and manly in her eyes. She was a little sick to her stomach thinking of him leaving the wagon train, but she was very proud of him nevertheless. After they had gotten back to the wagon train earlier, Colt had told her privately how Brandon took off after her immediately, ran his horse to death, and continued on foot until he fainted. This was the man she wanted to spend the rest of her life with, definitely.

Colt took Brandon to the remuda and found a solid, tall roan gelding. He had a nice saddle already that he picked out from the kidnapper's booty. They saddled the horse and rode it to Captain Swenson, who negotiated halfheartedly and finally gave in for a good price.

Chris and Brandon returned to the attorney's shared wagon and got supplies for the trip, along with some good grub from the chuck wagon. Colt was ready to leave, but Brandon wanted to make one stop. He rode to Elizabeth Macon's wagon, and signaled for her to stop. She reined up her team and he rode up to the wagon seat, reached out his hand, which she took, and he whisked her off the wagon and into his arms. Elizabeth was overwhelmed and her heart pounded mightily.

While many of the other married women on the train watched and got moist eyes, Brandon said softly, "Leaving you here without me is the hardest thing I've ever had to do, but I must help Chris. Besides that, we will have our lifetimes to spend together."

"We will, will we?" she said.

Brandon said, "Count on it."

He swept her up in a big hug and pressed his lips against hers for several minutes. Then Brandon said, "I love you Elizabeth Macon, and if you don't marry me, I'll never marry another, for I could love no woman the way I love you."

Tear spilled down her smiling cheeks and she said, "And I could not bear thinking of spending my life without you, Brandon Rudd. I love you, too, with all my heart."

They kissed again, and he placed her back on the wagon seat, spun the roan around, and spurred it away. Colt was already walking War Bonnet south toward the nearest rail line. Brandon caught up with him a mile out from the train.

As they rode along, Colt said, "I'm going to be traveling fast."

Brandon said, "What is this, Colt? Are you going to keep putting me on trial because I'm a dude? Go fast. I wouldn't expect you to go slow if your friend is in trouble."

Chris halted his horse with a sliding stop and Brandon did, too. Colt noticed that the attorney could handle a horse. He didn't know that Brandon's father couldn't afford saddles when Rudd was a boy. Those were luxuries, so Brandon, by the time he was twelve, was helping his pa break horses without the benefit of a saddle. The Missouri farmer supplemented his income by breaking and training horses for city folks from St. Louis and a neighbor who bred and sold Morgans.

Chris stuck out his hand and shook with Brandon. "Look, I am sorry if I have made it sound like I'm looking down my nose at you or feel you are a dude. Believe me, you may not be a westerner yet, but you are definitely not a dude. I have a lot of respect for you, Brandon, and I like you, as well. So does my brother."

They both noticed a rider cantering toward them from the far-off train.

Colt went on, "When I made the remark about going fast, I suppose it is because I am used to working alone. I apologize."

"Thank you, Chris," Brandon said, "Having a man like you say you respect me means more to me than just about anything anyone can say. Who do you suppose the rider is?"

"Tex Westchester. That's his little sorrel and nobody sits a saddle like him in a lope."

Tex slid the horse to a stop, and it was obvious he was still in pain from his wounds. His broken leg was splinted and hanging straight down past the stirrup on one side of the horse.

"Wal, wal, whatcha know 'bout thet," he said. "This ole lawyer boy is so anxious to git to Canon City thet he leaves that purty little thing back there alone with me. He'll be sorry, Colt, when the wagon train arrives and he learns I up and married her."

Brandon laughed and said, "If she had that kind of taste, I wouldn't want her anyway."

The oldster said, "Wal, I am so busted up, I ain't got no use fer my short gun till I git to Canon City. I'll be ridin' in a durned wagon like a little kid, so why don't you hold my gun fer me again till I git there?"

Tex reached in his saddlebags and started to hand the attorney the old used gun and holster, but Brandon pulled back the left side of his coat. In a shoulder holster was a Colt Sheriff's model Peacemaker .45, a shorter version of Colt's guns and not quite as fancy.

"Thanks," Brandon said, "but after what happened with Elizabeth, I decided that this country is still too wild not to wear a sidearm."

"Where'n hell d'ja git that?" Tex asked.

"Out of my trunk. I just hate guns and was hoping I would never have to use it, but if I do, it will be handy."

"Well, I'll be durned. A man owns a hogleg an' keeps it in a trunk. Why, thet's like ownin' a horse and keepin' the saddle in the barn an' ridin' bareback all day. Boy, I swear, the kids these days."

He waved at the two and turned his horse, walking it back toward the wagon train, mumbling to himself, "What's this country comin' to? No respect fer ole folks no more. Forward men. Wild women. Young'uns thet keeps their shootin' iron in a trunk, then when they wear it they stick it up unner their dad-blasted arm where they cain't draw it fast enough, cain't swing a rope over their head, and then they hide it unner their durn jacket so no man cain't see thet they got a weapon and shouldn't be messed with none."

Brandon and Colt just watched the old man, laughing at his rantings.

They turned and headed toward the railroad line running to the west and home for Chris Colt. It was also a new home for Brandon Rudd, a home which was now offering to him one of his greatest challenges ever. Colt wondered how Man Killer was handling the challenge he was facing.

* * *

Man Killer was on a long ridgeline running the length of Marble Mountain. When he saw the posse sweeping down the valley and up toward his perch on Spread Eagle Peak, he took off carefully along the faces of the southern-adjoining mountains, not wanting to leave any sign that he was on or near Spread Eagle. The farther he could keep people away from Shirley and the Coyote Run, the better. Reaching Marble Mountain, far to the south, he built an obvious, and too large, cooking fire and placed a few green sticks on it to make it smoke better.

That was all that was needed and the large posse was now coming for him. Not only that, Man Killer spotted two other posses coming across the valley floor. Apparently there had been a prearranged plan to somehow signal each other or get messages to each group if one group found his sign. An hour later, he spotted the Spread Eagle segment signaling with a mirror to one of the other groups. Man Killer estimated that, with all three groups, there must have been over a hundred men coming after him.

He wished Chris Colt were here with him, but Man Killer knew that he would somehow figure out a way to evade all these men. Chris Colt and Chief Joseph had both taught him how, and that was to develop an attitude that you cannot be defeated.

Chris Colt told him, a couple years earlier, "It's not really so important what happens to a man. It's how the man handles the problem in his mind that's really important."

The scout walked to his mount Hawk and swung up into the saddle. He walked him down the mountain directly toward the posse coming at a fast trot out of the town of Westcliffe. Nobody could see him because he was well up in trees and still a good distance from them.

One branch of the angry men was coming straight at him, another group was miles to his south, and the third miles to his north. He figured that they would try a giant pincer movement, but he had plans that would not work well with theirs, he hoped.

Man Killer kept watching the approaching riders as he rode straight down the mountainside. Up above timberline on Marble Mountain, almost directly above him, was the top entrance to the Caverna del Oro, the Cavern of Gold. At the entrance was the breastplate of a Spanish conquistador with an arrow sticking in it right over the heart. Man Killer and Chris Colt had journeyed there and entered, but the entrance was snowed in ten, sometimes eleven months out of the year. There was a vertical drop of hundreds of feet and there was a Maltese Cross on a rock marking the entrance. The two gave up on the difficult top entrance and went down the mountain hundreds of feet to the bottom entrance. Chris warned Man Killer that this entrance would not long be available to enter because a large avalanche chute clung above it and was filled with giant boulders.

When Colt pointed them out, he told the young scout, "Someday, all that will be down there covering the cavern entrance."

Everyone knew about the big cavern, and legend had it that the Spanish explorers holed up there while attacked by Indians, and hid thousands of tons of gold treasure inside the bowels of Marble Mountain. Some hardy souls explored the mountain and a few found the entrances, especially the top one, but the terrain was too rugged and the mountain too unforgiving to accommodate most want-to-be gold discoverers. Man Killer knew how to get to both entrances and figured on using them as a temporary hideout, but for this night, he had other plans.

The scout rode downhill until he was close to the bottom of the wooded mountain. The riders were still approaching at a fast trot, and he hoped they would soon slow to a walk. No sooner had Man Killer thought this than he saw the group slow their horses to save them for the climb up into the big mountains. They would soon be entering the trees, and he was not far from the edge. Man Killer directed his Appaloosa down to a grove of scrub oaks running down a slight ridge and into a gully.

Hopping off his horse near a big growth of vines and brush, he pulled out his bone-handled bowie knife and made preparations.

Wolf Keeler himself was the leader of one group of the posse, and he thought back to his first experience chasing after a man like this. Wolf, as a young boy, liked a girl named Sally Belle King who went to his school. She had bright red hair, that flamed like a bonfire, and bright blue eyes.

Wolf was the oldest boy in the school and the largest, so he had become a bully, always picking on the other children. One of the boys who stood up to him, though, was a good-looking boy named Tom McGregor who was several inches shorter than Wolf.

One day during lunch, Wolf asked Sally Belle to go skinny-dipping with him after school at a secluded swimming hole. This suggestion unnerved her so much, she started crying. Tom McGregor asked her what was wrong and tried to comfort the girl, and the sight of this completely upset the young bully.

Wolf tore across the schoolyard and lit into the smaller boy, who put up a game fight but finally went down. Wolf picked up a clay brick on the ground and started hitting the smaller boy in the face and ribs, breaking several bones and causing numerous bleeding wounds. On top of that, he broke away from the schoolmarm twice and kicked the unconscious boy viciously. Young McGregor almost died but finally survived until his eighteenth summer, when he was shot from ambush by a cowardly sniper. The dry-gulcher was never caught, but many in the community felt that Wolf Keeler was the only boy who would have anything against the hardworking, good-looking young man. Wolf was also the only man in the county that some thought would be mean enough to do such a thing.

Although Wolf was expelled permanently from school as a young boy, he genuinely loved to bully people, and it had become a habit that followed him into his adult life.

Man Killer continued his preparations and saw the second part of the posse riding west two miles north of the town headed toward the big range. In the meantime, the first part of the posse was now less than a mile away. Man Killer finished his preparations and rode slowly forward through the trees. The posse spread apart and entered the forest at thirty-pace intervals.

Man Killer stopped the big horse and placed a rag over his nostrils to help keep him from whinnying when he smelled or heard the posse's horses.

The men came through the trees, one man twenty-five paces to Man Killer's left and Wolf Keeler himself thirty paces to his right. He scratched his horse's neck with his fingers, but aside from that, he and Hawk were motionless. The men were watching all about but saw nothing. Man Killer did not move un-

til he could no longer hear them high above and behind him in the hardwood forest.

Finally he chanced looking around and uphill and
breathed a sigh of relief. They were out of sight
and earshot. He lifted the giant veil of twisted vines
and branches off Hawk's back and head, and the big
black and white horse shook all over. Man Killer admired his handiwork. He had used one long thin
branch as a spine and had woven other branches together as two large screens of twisted vines and
leafy branches for the sides. He waited five more
minutes, then headed south one hundred yards and
rode down into the shallow scrub oak–filled draw.
He found a spot where the trees and brush were the
thickest and waited.

It was an hour after sunset before the Nez Percé
scout felt it was safe to move. First he poured out
his canteen in a small hole he dug in the thicket and
mixed the water and dirt together. He grabbed large
handfuls of mud and rubbed it into the white rump
of Hawk. There was a sliver of moon, and he didn't
want the horse to be spotted easily. The white spotted rump could be like a signpost if the moonlight
struck it just right. From above, where the men were
carefully searching for him, not only could the entire
Wet Mountain Valley be seen, but the western slope
of Pikes Peak, as well. That was over fifty miles
away as the crow flies. If Man Killer was spotted by
the men up on the mountain, he figured they would
just assume he was an elk, deer, or possibly a cow
roaming the valley, because from up above and in
the dark, he would just be a dark blob.

The young man walked his horse slowly toward
the northeast. He headed the big mount across the
pastures with one single purpose in mind. His eyes
checked all about him, but he focused on a large
ranch house and outbuildings.

* * *

Up above, Wolf Keeler walked away from the campfire of the center posse. He carried a telescope with him and looked all over the valley.

Man Killer was very educated in the ways of the white man for an American Indian in the early 1880s, but there were some disadvantages to not having grown up white. Man Killer had used a spyglass and binoculars several times but usually relied more on his extremely keen eyesight. One thing he was not aware of, however, were the light-gathering properties of a telescope or binoculars. Such optical devices had an inherent ability to gather the available light from moonshine and stars at night and focus it into one small field of vision. Because of that, a person looking through such a device at night could see things not only more close up, but much more brightly than the naked eye could make them out.

One object that kept getting Wolf Keeler's attention was a large bull elk walking slowly across the pastures. Another man walked up behind him while he glassed the bull.

Pointing, Wolf said, "Toby, ya ever see elk walking across those pastures down there?"

Toby said, "Shore, Wolf, every night I seen 'em."

Wolf replied, "Ever see one walk all the way across those nice fields without stopping to graze along the way?"

"Why, hell no," Toby responded. "Elks is a grazin' animal. They cain't no more walk crost a pasture without grazin' than I could walk past a saloon without at least havin' a beer or two."

"What I figured," Keeler said.

Man Killer was just outside the ranch yard, arriving there in a little over a half an hour's time. He reached up and cut the two large branches off the sides of Hawk's bridle. He had stuck them up in the air to look like antlers in the darkness while he walked the horse.

Wolf took the glass from his eye and grinned in the darkness, saying, "Tell the boys to saddle up, quick."

Man Killer left Hawk ground-reined behind the barn and scouted around the grounds. He spotted two men camped out at the end of the long drive-way to the ranch. He made his way through the shadows to a spot below Jennifer Banta's window. He tossed a little pebble at the window and waited. A second stone brought the beautiful young woman to it. She looked down at Man Killer and beamed. Jennifer pointed toward the road and Man Killer nodded his head, letting her know he had seen the lookouts.

The scout jumped up to an overhead branch of a cherry tree next to her house. He swung up and hooked a leg over the branch, pulling himself up. He climbed up through the branches. While Jennifer watched eyes and mouth open wide, he balanced himself, walked out on a branch and dived to her window, grabbing the sill with both hands and hang-ing on for dear life. By this time, Jennifer had opened the window. He pulled himself up and inside the bedroom.

He grabbed her by the shoulders and moved her to the side where she couldn't be seen from the out-side. Man Killer swept Jennifer into his embrace and kissed her. She felt faint almost.

When they finished and stepped back, she said, "Man Killer, what are you doing here? They'll shoot you dead. They've been out looking everywhere for you and Millard Mines put a ten-thousand-dollar bounty on you."

He grinned, saying, "I had to see you and tell you how much I love you."

Tears formed in her eyes and she said, "You didn't have to risk your life to do that!"

"Yes, I did. You are very much worth it, Jennifer."

"Oh, I love you so."

She melted into his arms, and they kissed again, parted, and stared deep into each other's eyes.

Then he stepped back. "I must go."

Jennifer headed toward her door, saying, "Wait. I'll get you some food."

She opened her bedroom door and gave out a little yelp. Her father stood in the hallway holding a burlap bag of food in his hand. Man Killer grinned as the skinny white-haired cowboy stepped into the room. He pulled out his making and started rolling a cigarette, handing the fixings to Man Killer.

Old Man Banta said, "Wal, young'un, I reckon I would unner normal circumstances bring in a greener to give the what-fer to any suitor I'd catch in mah li'l gal's bedroom, but since these is special circumstances, I s'pose I kin unnerstand ya' sneakin' in here ta see Jennifer. S'pose it's purty hard to come in the front door when half the county's out to stretch yer neck. Besides, if'n I was to plug ya with a greener, I reckon Miss Purty here would let me have it with a Gatlin' gun."

Jennifer chuckled and blushed.

Chancy Banta went on, "Now, lookee here, young'un. You come back here if'n ya run inta trouble, need food, or jest git ya another hankerin' ta talk with Jennifer, but ya keep yer nose inta the wind an' ride with yer rifle cocked and crost yer saddle. They're after ya and want ya bad."

Man Killer nodded and grinned. He was amazed at the kindness and understanding this old rancher had shown him ever since they had first met. Up until then, many of the white men he had dealt with, aside from Chris Colt and some of the missionaries when he was growing up, had treated him as either a second-class citizen or with out-and-out racial hatred.

Man Killer had been recuperating from wounds he had received fighting some Utes that were after Jennifer. He had been willing to sacrifice his life to save Jennifer and sustained numerous wounds fighting off the Utes. He had been unconscious for some time. When he opened his eyes, he almost jumped with a start, but a pain in his side and leg kept him from rising. He was in a bed in a frame house. That much he could tell. He looked out the window and saw the nearby Sangre de Cristo Mountains, snowy caps glistening in the moonlight. From this window he was looking almost directly across at Hermit Peak and Horn Peak, so he must be in the large ranch house which he had earlier decided was Jennifer Banta's

A man walked into the room, smiled at Man Killer, and turned his head, hollering, "Wal, Jenny, reckon ya' oughta git up here! Yer young hair-liftin' hero's up 'n' about!"

The way the man said it, and the smile in his eyes, made Man Killer like him immediately. There was no judgment on his face about the young man's skin color. He could sense respect from the leathery old cowboy.

Slight in frame with graying hair and a handlebar mustache, he was whipcord tough-appearing and had the look of a man who knew cattle well, and one you would want on your side in a range war. He was bowlegged from way too many hours in a saddle, and a rolled-up cigarette dangled from his thin lips.

" 'Fore she gits here, youngster," the man said,

"want to thank ye. Jennifer's the most important thing in my sorry ole life."

Chancy Banta turned away and Man Killer saw a tear rolling down his wrinkled brown cheek. Jennifer walked in the room, while her father bent over, pretending to straighten a water pitcher on the floor. She wore a white cotton dress and a happy face.

"How are you feeling?" she asked.

Man Killer smiled and said, "Thank you for taking care of my wounds. Do I still have bullets in me?"

She said, "No, the doctor removed them. You'll be okay, but it will take a long time to heal."

He sat up suddenly and felt very light-headed, but he refused to lay back down. She tried to gently push him, but she felt she may just as well have been trying to push Marble Mountain. She also felt bad because he seemed friendly but a little more distant than before. He grabbed the headboard and hoisted himself to his feet.

Jennifer said, "Man Killer, you can't."

"I must. How long have I been asleep?"

"We arrived here almost a week ago," she said.

"I have a job to do and Chris Colt waits for me in New Mexico. Thank you very much for saving me and for the care your family has given, but I must go right away. I must get dressed."

Chris Colt had been hired as chief of scouts for the Ninth Cavalry, the black buffalo soldiers, in their pursuit of the renegade Mimbres Apache Victorio.

Jennifer quickly slipped out of the room and Man Killer stood up and started dressing. It was difficult because he had no strength, but he knew that would return.

He was impressed. She was smart enough to have

placed his weapons within easy reach and someone
had carefully cleaned and reloaded them, even hon-
ing a new edge on his knife. He grabbed his war bag
and slowly made his way downstairs. Jennifer and
her father sat at a hand-carved table, and Man Killer
noticed, out of the corner of his eye, her father
gently grabbing her arm as she tried to rise to help
the Nez Percé down the stairway. He stumbled once,
but made it to the table and sat down.

Man Killer held his back straight, although he saw
many little light-colored bugs flying around in his
eyes.

He stuck out his hand to the father and said, "My
name is Man Killer, sir, and I want to thank you for
your help."

The man shook with him and said, "Name's
Chancy Banta. Jennifer put ya up a bit of grub ta
carry with ya, an' I can give ya a horse ta pack supplies on, if'n ya want. Girl shore learnt how ta cook
after her ma went under, nigh on seven year ago
now. Yer horse's in the barn. Far as thankin' me, I
cain't never thank ye enough, son. Long as I got me
a roof, yer welcome to sleep unner it. Ye saved my
little girl."

Man Killer said, "You are not bothered that I am
red?"

Banta didn't answer, but instead took out the fixings and offered them to Man Killer. They both
rolled cigarettes and lit them. Jennifer smiled and
left the room.

Finally Chancy took a long slow drag and
breathed the blue smoke toward the ceiling and said,
"One time this dude come out here from back East.
He was a Banta, too, cousin or sumthin'. He asked
me ef'n I could help him buy hisself a horse, so's I
took him to the livery down to Bent's Fort, on account a they kept a good supply, bein' on the Santa

Fe Trail and all. Wal, I reckon I picked him out the best old bay gelding ya ever did see. Straight cannons, straight back, good head, big bunchy muscles. I worked him on a couple calves and the durn thing could stop on the head of a pin, do a roll-back, cut left and right without fallin off'n the pin."

Man Killer grinned.

The man continued, "I tell him to lemme do the talkin' but he had to git hisself that hoss on account a he would have to search far and wide ta find a better one. Wal, that ole son of a buck tells me he's been lookin' at this ole white mare thet seems real flashy, and his heart's set on it. I tole him ya never buy a horse fer color, ya always buy 'em fer confirmation, stoutness, and sech. Wal, we argued, but his heart was set on thet white mare 'cause she looked so purty."

Banta took several puffs and Man Killer waited patiently, knowing this man enjoyed telling stories. It reminded him of Ollikut, the giant brother of Chief Joseph, who also joked and told many stories.

Chancy went on, "Wal, my ole cousin bought the durned horse an less'n two weeks later, the blasted nag bucked on a mountain trail and started pitchin' a fit and sent him over her head flat on his back. Only problem was jest beyond thet mare's head was a two-thousand-foot cliff. Yep, my cousin shore hit thet ground hard."

Jennifer walked in the room carrying two plates full of meat and potatoes, along with sliced tomatoes. She set them down in front of Man Killer—who nodded his thanks—and her father. Chancy took a big bite of steak and smiled while he chewed on it.

He swallowed and said, "Yes, sir, sonny, don't

never buy a horse fer color. Thet ain't what makes 'em a good or bad critter."

After four helpings of food, Man Killer felt a little better and made his way to his horse. He found out that Jennifer's horse had died from exhaustion, and her dad was going to take her to buy a new one.

Man Killer sat his saddle proudly and looked down at the beautiful girl and her father.

He said, "Don't forget, don't look at the horse's color when you pick one out."

Chancy grinned, as did Man Killer, but then the warrior added, "Unless it's an Appaloosa."

Chancy tipped his hat and walked off to the house. Jennifer remained and appeared irritated.

The young scout said, "You are angry?"

She shuffled her feet. "You have been so . . . so distant. I thought you were concerned about me before."

Her face reddened, and she was just as angry at herself for making such a stupid statement.

Man Killer had smiled. Then "I simply must go. I have a job to do and must do it. Concerned? Someday I will marry you, Jennifer Banta, but for now I must go do my work."

She had watched him openmouthed while he wheeled his big horse and rode off toward the south. Jennifer was breathless and speechless, she was so shocked, but her heart skipped several beats, and she wanted to leap for joy.

Then she had wheeled, saying aloud to herself, "What conceit!"

She thought back to that same incident now herself and grinned.

Man Killer's voice brought her out of her daydream. "You are smiling. Why?"

She said, "Oh, I'm just happy."

Chancy backed out of the door and closed it quietly behind him, after giving Man Killer a wink.

Jennifer threw her arms around him and they kissed again.

She stepped back and said, "I am so worried about you, but I believe in you, darling."

He heard a noise outside that Jennifer couldn't hear.

Man Killer said quickly, "I must go. Tell Shirley to give messages for me to you. You leave them behind your barn under the chopping block. I will leave messages there for you, too, sometimes, but do not check during the daytime."

She started to speak, but he interrupted, "I must go. I love you, Jennifer."

She tried to kiss him, but he dashed for the window. As he reached it, the front door of the house opened and he heard men run in and Chancy cursing. Man Killer looked across at the branch he would jump to and several guns cocked below him.

A voice said, "Go ahead, red nigger, I love snap-shootin' crows. Try to fly, and I'll sent ya ta redskin hell."

Man Killer backed away from the window, grabbed Jennifer by the upper arms, and flung her across her bed. He drew his Peacemaker and the belly gun he carried in his waistband.

The door flew open and a posse member came through with Chancy Banta in front of him, the barrel of the man's .44 to his temple.

Chancy growled, "Shoot the son of a—"

Boom!

Nobody expected the shot, but the man holding Chancy flew backward, a large hole between his eyes and the back of his head splattered across the hallway wall. He crashed into Wolf Keeler and another man behind him and all three fell down the stairs together, the dead man's limbs mixing in the live ones. Man Killer looked at Jennifer, and she waved.

"Go quickly," she urged. "We will be fine."

Man Killer looked at Chancy and the old man said, "Hey, nice shootin' boy. Now git the hell outta here."

Man Killer walked near the window, tried to disguise his voice, and hollered, "Hurry, boys, the nigger's goin' out the front door!"

Jennifer and Chancy laughed as they heard people outside scurrying around to the front. In the meantime, Man Killer backed up several steps, as Wolf and the others ran back up the stairs.

The scout winked and smiled at father and daughter, then ran toward the open window and dived out headfirst as Jennifer screamed. In midair he heard the door open and gunshots followed him outside, cracking by his ears. His hands were stretched out and hit a branch, grabbing hold, and his momentum swung his legs down hard until his lower abdomen struck another branch. HIs wind left him in a rush, but he let go of the other branch and grabbed this one, letting himself drop quickly. He looked down and saw the ground not too far below.

He heard a man upstairs say, "Let go of me, you wench!"

Man Killer heard a slap, and he dashed around the corner of the house, reloading his pistol. The men who had been at the tree now came dashing back around the house and Man Killer dropped to the ground and rolled right up against the side of the building, letting them run by. He jumped up and ran silently to the front porch, swung up and vaulted over the railing, and walked in the front door, gun in each had. He went up the stairs noiselessly two steps at a time and kicked open the door to Jennifer's bedroom.

Wolf and another man just stared at him in awe. Jennifer held a red cheek and her father was getting off the floor with a swelling cheekbone and eye.

Man Killer gestured and the two white men dropped their guns. He tucked away his belly gun.

Looking at the men, Man Killer asked Jennifer, "Which one hit you?"

Chancy said, "Thet ugly one with the red hair."

Man Killer looked at the man next to Wolf and said, "Wrong thing to do."

He punched the man flush on the tip of the jaw. Still holding his gun on Wolf, he quickly hit the man in the ribs, then punched him square in the nose, sending him backward into the wall. The man crashed into the wall and slid to the floor unconscious.

Man Killer asked Jennifer and Chancy, "Are you hurt bad?"

"Naw, son, we're okay," Chancy replied. "I'll take care of her. Ya git outta here."

Wolf Keeler laughed and said, "He ain't goin' nowhere. I'm callin' my men in here and we're puttin' him under arrest."

Man Killer smiled at Chancy. The old man chuckled and Jennifer put her hand over her mouth. Man Killer turned to Wolf and grinned. His pistol came up and smacked the deputy across the nose and his eyes rolled back in his head, his legs buckled, and he dropped to the floor. Man Killer ran to Jennifer, gave her a quick kiss, and, holstering his pistol, walked out the door.

Jennifer fell into her father's arms, and he stroked her golden hair, saying, "Sweetie, I don't care what

color his skin is. Thet boy ya got there ain't no boy.
Ya got yerself a real man, and girl, yer plumb crazy
if'n ya ever let thet one git away. I want his blood
runnin' through my grandchilluns' veins along with
ours."

Jennifer said, "Me, too, Daddy. Me, too."

Man Killer was angry. The woman he loved had
been slapped and a man he loved had been punched.
Their home had been violated, and he was tired of
being chased. At least for this night he was sick and
tired of it. He walked down the stairs, out the door,
and into the night.

Walking around the corner of the house, he
headed for the barn, not caring if anybody spotted
him or not. Man Killer was maybe inheriting this
trait from his mentor Chris Colt, because Colt had
gotten this way sometimes. The young scout actually
kind of hoped someone would try to stop him. His
blood was boiling.

He got his wish. Two other posse members ran
around the barn right before he entered. He didn't
even give them time to react. Man Killer drew his
pistol and his belly gun, firing several times into
both men very rapidly. They both flew back, dead or
gravely wounded, without getting off a shot. Without thinking, as taught to him by Colt, he ejected his
spent shells immediately and reloaded. Over his
campfire that night, he would tear the guns down
and thoroughly clean and reload them, if he survived
that long.

Man Killer vaulted onto Hawk's back, where the
horse had been eating hay, and rode out the back of
the barn, jumped the little irrigation ditch, and
headed back toward the mountains. He saw torches
from another part of the posse coming down off Hermit Peak, so Man Killer wheeled his horse around

and headed right back at the house, where he heard shouting and horses starting to leave. The posse from the house was coming after him, so he simply rode back into the back door of the barn, while they thundered past the big barn, on both sides. When they were out of hearing, he walked his horse out the front door of the barn and rode right next to the house.

As he went by the front porch, Chancy Banta's voice brought a grin to his face. "Yes, sir, sonny, you'll do ta ride the river with. Mind yerself at the end of the drive. Them two sentries is still there. I got yer back covered from here."

Man Killer turned his head and looked at the grinning old wrinkled face, saying, "Mr. Banta, there's no one who I would rather have covering my back than you. Take good care of her."

"Always have, son."

Man Killer rode very slowly down the driveway and the sentries didn't even pay attention to him until he was upon them. As he approached in the darkness, the two turned, thinking it was just a posse member heading home. They stared into the business ends of two walnut-handled standard Peacemakers. Man Killer held the reins in his teeth and used leg and voice to control his horse.

Quietly he said, "Drop your guns and belts."

They complied and he said, "Kick them over here."

They both looked very nervous as they again complied.

He went on, "Take off your boots and socks."

Both men wondered if this savage red killer they had heard so much about was going to hang them above a fire and roast their feet. They removed their footwear.

Man Killer said, "Toss them over here beyond your guns."

They did so.

"Now turn and walk back to town."

They were both shocked he spoke English like a white man.

One said, "It's several miles back to town. What about our horses?"

Man Killer rode several feet to their two mounts, untied them, and shooed them away while the questioner moaned.

The scout said, "They will find their way home."

"Our feet will be raw by the time we get there," the second man said.

Man Killer said, "You should not ride after an innocent man."

The first man wanted to say something, but decided it would be smarter to keep quiet. With Man Killer slowly following them on his horse, they started walking back to Westcliffe. He kept after them until they had gone far enough that he could let them return for their guns and boots. He rode on at a canter without looking back.

Man Killer rode right into Westcliffe, went through the town and straight on into Silver Cliff. Here he was finally spotted by two cowpunchers. Both had been drinking and playing billiards, and when they spotted the fugitive, the younger cowboy thought he might give it a try and win the bounty on Man Killer.

The scout had an evil grin on his face, as he was fighting mad. His hand hovered over his pistol, and he stared at the two punchers.

Finally Man Killer said, "It's a lot of money. Why don't you try it? Go ahead—please."

The puncher moved his hand slowly away from his gun and his partner pulled him in the opposite direction at a fast walk. Man Killer rode on through Silver Cliff and past the little mining town of Rosita. If anyone wanted to shoot it out with him right now, they could. He was ready for it, but there were no further incidents.

An hour later, all three posses had converged on the town and numerous people had come out, many in bedclothes, to tell about the "killer Indian" riding his big Appaloosa horse right through the middle of town, just like he owned it. They went on to Silver Cliff, where they ran into the two punchers, who related their story, except their version had Man Killer backing down and cowering out of town. This brought chuckles and derisive comments from the giant posse, especially those members who had already had run-ins with the scout.

The posse rode off to the east into the Wet Mountains, which some people called the Greenhorns, after the Ute chief Greenhorn and the peak which bore his name. Wolf Keeler wondered what Man Killer was up to. Why, he wanted to know, did the Indian leave the relative safety of the giant mountain range and cross the valley floor to the smaller range of mountains with smaller and more scarce trees and cover? Many others in the posse had the same thoughts.

What they did not realize was that Man Killer wanted to be on this side of the valley so he could move around more easily. On the big range, he could move laterally north and south, but crossing over the mountains, moving east and west was quite difficult and impossible on many of the ranges that were sheer granite peaks. On the eastern side of the valley, however, if pursued, he could move in all directions, easily crossing over smaller mountains if he wanted, or easily traveling around them. There were also plenty of gulches and canyons he could use as escape routes and he could travel greater distances, but on the big range, he could travel only basically north or south and the posse members knew it. This side of the valley also provided cover in many places right up to the main roads running out of Westcliffe, Silver Cliff, and Rosita. He knew they would now watch Jennifer Banta's ranch much more closely, and they would have very close surveillance on Coyote Run.

The big posses now numbering over one hundred men, each carrying a bedroll, saddlebags, and grub, headed into the Greenhorns after one man. Hundred-to-one odds against someone who was still a teenager, but Man Killer was definitely not a boy. He did not receive the name Man Killer for no reason.

Shirley Colt looked out the window of her warm house up at the big mountain range. She wondered where Man Killer was and if he was up in the cold, snowy, rocky hell above timberline. Was he snuggled up in a warm cave with a fire going? Was he shivering and hiding in some trees, not wanting to build a fire for fear of being discovered? She wished Chris were back. She would ask him to go out right then and find Man Killer. He was such a fine young man. He had become a member of her family, and she and Colt loved him as such.

Man Killer walked his horse in past the miners. They stayed in a ramshackle cabin just around the bend from their big mine. They had found some considerable color one year earlier and were digging their way through the mountain on the side of an unnamed gulch which ran east off of Spike Buck

Gulch. Many mines Man Killer had seen were basically glory holes in the ground and some were little crawlways where the hapless miner ended up with arthritis from stooping over and digging all day. This mine, however, was large enough to house Man Killer and Hawk for the evening and keep them quite comfortable. He just went back deep in the mine and built a fire. There was an air vent which had been dug straight up out the top of the mine and it served as a natural chimney for the smoke.

Man Killer would sleep peacefully during the night, then extinguish the fire and leave at daybreak before the miners came to work. A piñon and sand-covered ridge of maybe one hundred feet in height acted as a giant wall which kept him totally out of the sight of the miners' cabin. Nor could they smell his smoke from the fire, as it was filtered out among the trees.

Man Killer fried bacon, biscuits, and apple slices, of which he ate ample portions along with two full pots of hot black coffee. He rolled himself a cigarette and smoked that before turning in.

At one point he awakened and thought about Jennifer. Water was dripping down the chimney hole, so he rolled another cigarette and walked to the mine entrance. Rain poured down from the dark Colorado skies. A half dozen miles away, the sentries of the one-hundred-man posse kept trying to keep the campfires going while the men huddled and shivered in half sleep under their slickers and blankets, water running down their faces from the leather saddle pillows they used.

It was just shy of daybreak when Man Killer rode out of the mine and headed down into Spike Buck Gulch. Spike Buck ran off Lookout Mountain, continuing downhill a couple thousand feet to the wild, angry, churning Arkansas River. The gulch was steep and rocky, with a spring-fed intermittent stream running down its middle, occasionally running underground. It was rocky, wild, and remote and a favorite crossing and bedding area for mountain lions and bears both. Rocky Mountain bighorn sheep inhabited its rocky piñon- and cedar-covered ridges, as well as some elk and lots of mule deer.

Lookout Mountain had a well-deserved name, as it was a lone rocky sentinel on one side of the valley which had served as a lookout point for outlaws as well as Indians. Rogers, Likely, Spike Buck, and Five Points gulches all ran off of it in different directions between its long rocky fingers, along with a number of smaller gulches. Directly or indirectly the water flow off each in a storm would end up draining into the mighty Arkansas. Man Killer, for now, would ride down the gulch he was in to the Arkansas, ford the river west of Spike Buck, and travel west to Long Gulch, if Hawk could handle the whitewater current. The scout would hide out in the even more rugged country on the other side of the river. They were having a lot of grizzly bear trouble north of the river and he figured people would be less likely to hunt for him there, or at least not as many people would be anxious to venture there. He would go through the Big Hole and Little Hole country heading northwest and hole up on either Loco or Waugh Mountain, where there was plenty of game and water. In fact, Waugh Mountain, covered with aspens on the top, was loaded with elk and deer, so he would probably go there.

Billy One-Eye was a Comanche tracker and scout and enjoyed a reputation for being one of the best.

Charlie Wolf Killer was a Ute with a similar reputation, and these two headed up the party of scouts hired by Preston Millard to track for the hundred-man posse. Man Killer hadn't been too careful yet, because he was not aware of the scouts or the lengths that Millard was willing to go in order to hunt him down, but he had a premonition, and being a man of nature, he had learned to pay attention to such feelings.

Billy One-Eye looked at the jumble of tracks around the miners' cabins and outbuildings. He dismounted and led his horse while staring at the ground. The men in the posse saw the tracks, too, and wondered how he could possibly make sense out of so many, but for Billy it was no problem. Hawk was a large Appaloosa, with very large hooves. He also had a longer stride than the average horse, so Billy walked around the perimeter of the cabin and outbuilding area, where there was less horse activity. He looked at the tracks coming and going until he spotted the large-hoofed, deeper-imprinted tracks of Hawk heading downhill toward Spike Buck Gulch. Charlie rode next to him and the two compared notes.

Both men looked at a likely place to camp, as the tracks had been made before the previous night's storm. They both spotted the large mine entrance on the side of the rocky ridge and gave each other knowing looks. There was some activity around the mine, but the miners all stopped when they saw the giant group of armed riders. They all walked forward, some stopping to get water from a bucket and dipper.

Wolf Keeler said, "See anybody?"

And the front man shook his head no.

Charlie Wolf Killer surprised the deputy, though,

when he asked, "Last night. Someone make fire. Your cave? Huh?"

"Aye, laddie," the front man said, "they damned sure did, but we never seen them, just the ashes."

Charlie and Billy rode on down the gulch and picked up Hawk's tracks again, with Wolf and the posse following shortly after. They turned north into Spike Buck Gulch and started following it downhill.

Spike Buck was an interesting gulch, in that it started out as a sloping valley one-quarter to a half mile wide, but a couple of miles downhill from Lookout Mountain it narrowed to a spot called the Narrows by the locals. The stream ran underground there and the rock walls rising straight up on each side could crush a man's feet, if he got them caught between a fat horse and the walls. This hourglass apex would slow the posse considerably.

They entered the Narrows traveling through one at a time. Charlie Wolf Killer was the first man through with another scout, with Billy One-Eye following.

As taught to him by Chris Colt, Man Killer decided to check his back trail before entering the Narrows. He couldn't go through with Hawk and then backtrack, so the Nez Percé sent the Appaloosa through by himself while he scaled the western ridge and looked back up toward Lookout Mountain. He saw the giant posse come out of the side draw and turn into Spike Buck. The familiar scout clothing of both men in the lead told him that he was not being tracked by tinhorns. He would run along the side of the ridgeline, then go back down into the gulch and summon Hawk with the whistle of the red-tailed hawk, the summoning call that both he and Chris used for their horses.

Charlie squeezed through the Narrows, pulling his feet out of the stirrups and letting them be pulled back when they hit rock. He was followed by another Ute scout.

Charlie Wolf Killer saw it too late. It was a braided leather riata crossing the trail and it ran up a narrow but long crack in the rock wall. Up above he saw a configuration of three large notched sticks that formed the figure of the number 4. The main stick was the trunk of a pinion sapling growing between two rocks. The one lashed to it, pointing down at an angle, had a notch at the bottom, and the bottom stick, the trigger, had a pointed end stuck into the notch, and it was lashed to the main stick. It was also tied off to the rawhide rope, which Charlie's horse had just struck with his front leg. The trigger stick came out of the 4 and the log being held by the upper arm of the figure came loose—and so did the pile of boulders behind it. Charlie put the spurs to his horse, but it was too late.

Billy One-Eye was the third man, and he looked up and yelled, "Look out!"

Several good-sized boulders raining down upon them. Charlie and the other man, as well as their horses, were struck and instantly killed by falling rocks. On top of that, the rock slide that came down blocked off the Narrows, and the rest of the posse would have to ride or probably lead their horses up the steep rocky ridgeline on either side, bypass the Narrows, and go back down the slopes into the gulch.

While the two men died under the crushing rocks, Man Killer attempted crossing the angry, swollen river. This particular summer was hot and the winter snows up in the Sangre de Cristos and the Collegiate Range were very deep. The snowmelt was still affecting the churning water, which dropped over one mile in elevation in its course from Leadville down to Canon City. Knowing he was being followed by a gigantic group of men, Man Killer had no choice. He would have to brave the high river.

The big Appaloosa snorted and reared slightly as Man Killer tired to urge him into the water. Across the river, there was a break in the tall rocky cliffs and there was a smooth sloping ridge, covered with grasses and stunted piñons and cedars, along with a herd of bighorn sheep enjoying the afternoon sunshine. There were whitewater rapids upstream just above Man Killer and directly below him. One slip and he and the horse could be easily killed.

They eased into the water and started slowly across, Hawk stepping gingerly in the ice-cold water, feeling his way along the rocky bottom. The water, rushing at hundreds of cubic feet per second, pulled at the big horse's legs, but Hawk was too surefooted to panic like most horses would. Man Killer was genuinely frightened, but he went on. If he could make it across, the posse would be hours behind him, because they would surely have to go several miles upstream to cross on the bridge at Texas Creek or several miles downstream to cross the bridge at Parkdale.

They had made it three-quarters of the way across the river when Hawk tripped on a rock that rolled sideways. The water was already halfway up his rib cage, and he had almost been swept away several times already. Man Killer stayed in the saddle and talked quietly to the horse while the river swept them toward the nearby rapids. The big mount kept kicking with all four feet and suddenly his front feet struck rock, then his hind feet. He lunged forward, fighting panic, and scrambled the rest of the way across the river and up the far bank. Man Killer dismounted, lay on his stomach, and carefully replaced all turf, rocks, and grass from where the horse had scrambled out of the river and up the bank. Then he swung up into the saddle.

On the far side, Man Killer immediately rode Hawk up into the trees and went down the back of the gentle hill, finding a gulch running north up between big ridges. He rode back about a quarter of a mile and stopped, unsaddled, and let his horse roll. Hawk was still breathing heavy from adrenaline and exertion. The Nez Percé warrior made a smokeless fire, knowing it was shielded from across the river, and stripped down to a breechcloth. He made a drying rack and hung his saddle blanket and bedroll on it, along with his buckskin leggings and homespun red shirt.

The big horse stayed nearby, enjoying the sun and occasionally grazing on the sparse mountain gramma grasses, while Man Killer got his cooking utensils out and prepared a meal. While the venison and potatoes cooked, he cleaned and oiled all his weapons. The scout ate his meal, replaced his clothing, and rolled a cigarette. After smoking that, he took his Winchester, and letting his exhausted horse nap and gaze, he worked his way back to the small wooded hilltop and watched for the posse.

A half hour later, they appeared and Billy One-Eye found his tracks crossing the river road and the spot where his horse entered the river. There was some discussion, with Wolf Keeler and the posse eventually heading east toward Parkdale, the opposite direction than Man Killer had planned on going.

He finally figured that the scout had reasoned that Man Killer's horse could not have possibly made it across the roaring river and was swept downstream. That was, in fact, exactly what had happened.

Man Killer, well hidden in the trees, lay motionless for the next forty minutes and watched until the last man disappeared out of sight around the bend downriver. Many people traveled the river road, plus there were now trains running on tracks on his side of the watercourse, so the scout would travel crosscountry to Waugh Mountain.

It was his second full day on Waugh Mountain when Man Killer was discovered. A miner from Nesterville went up on the mountain to harvest an elk for his family and happened to come upon the scout's lean-to while Man Killer was fetching water. The man rode back down to Nesterville without being discovered, gave the alarm, and two riders hightailed it down the mountain to Cotopaxi on the Arkansas. They telegraphed Westcliffe, and Wolf Keeler and his posse were soon on their way toward Waugh Mountain.

"You certainly present a good argument, young man," the Colorado governor said.

"Well, sir," Brandon Rudd said, "I haven't time to utilize formal channels, and I certainly appreciate you offering me time out of your very busy schedule. An innocent man's life may depend on my ability and legal right to practice law in the state of Colorado."

The governor said, "Well, Mr. Rudd, your reputation precedes you and it is impressive, to say the least. It also does not hurt you in the least that your uncle, Anson Rudd, was the very first lieutenant governor of this great state and also served as sheriff of Fremont County. You, sir, take this letter with you, from me, and you do your level best to represent this young Indian we spoke about. As of right now, you have the right to practice law in this state. I'll personally see to the paperwork. If there is anything else I can do for you, just wire me. Now, get to Canon City and welcome to Colorado. You are a welcome addition to our legal machinery."

"Thank you so much, Governor," Brandon said.

He left immediately.

Chris Colt found Hawk's days-old tracks where he and his master crossed the river road and entered the water. When Colt and Man Killer first came to the ranch, they would sometimes take one- or two-day excursions to become familiar with the general area within a couple days' ride of the ranch.

Colt had said, "If you don't know your own backyard better than your enemies, you're in trouble."

He looked across the river and imagined where Man Killer would have gone after crossing the river. Colt saw the small tree-covered hill that stood sentinel over the entrance to a steep gulch. Colt knew Hawk could get Man Killer out of there over the rocks when other horses couldn't, and figured Man Killer would have hidden behind the hill and watched his pursuers from the trees. Seeing them go east, he would have headed west.

Colt and Man Killer had discussed good places to hole up where there was water, game, cover, and plenty of graze for horses. Waugh Mountain, Loco Mountain, Black Mountain, the plateau above the Big Hole? It would be Waugh Mountain. Man Killer had remarked on the cover and the elk and mule deer sign in the area.

The posse looked like a giant swarm of ants as Man Killer looked down at them from the aspens atop Waugh Mountain. The distance was still so great, he could not hear them or their horses, but he could see the men, spread apart, coming across the high mountain meadows down below. They had already climbed steadily several thousand feet higher than Cotopaxi.

He tried to formulate a plan for escape, but one thing he did not want to do was to just bolt and run without a reason. The posse stopped and Man Killer made a circle with his palm and looked through it, like a telescope. Colt had taught him to do that with his hand, and it helped concentrate his eyesight on one particular spot. He spotted Wolf Keeler looking toward him with a telescope.

Oh, was Man Killer angry at himself. A white man's invention that he was totally familiar with, and he had not thought about it. That was how they had spotted him going to Jennifer Banta's! He remembered one of the lieutenants in the Tenth Cavalry, during the Victorio War in Texas, teaching him to look through binoculars at night for better vision. He also knew that he and his big horse had been spotted now. He would never forget this lesson, he knew as he watched the posse cantering up the gentle meadowed side of the mountain toward him.

Man Killer wheeled his horse around and kicked him toward the scrub oak thicket fifty yards above him. Beneath the quaking aspens, he rode into the thicket and Hawk's ears turned to the left and his nostrils flared as he snorted. Too late! Something from the depths of hell roared, slamming into the Appaloosa's side with the force of a cyclone, just as the panicked horse slid to a stop and started to rear. Man Killer flew sideways with a terrible force, and the eight-foot-tall grizzly was on him in a second.

Man Killer had learned from Colt and his tribal leaders to not panic in an emergency. In a millisecond he quickly analyzed the situation.

The posse was heading toward him, and to fire a shot would mean instant discovery and inevitable death, because he knew they would not take him back alive. To not shoot would mean death also, because the grizzly would surely kill him. He respected the grizzly more than he did humans. Man Killer reached for his .45, but it was gone, having flown out of the holster while he fell. His belly gun was tucked away in his saddlebags. He felt panic and caught himself, steeling his nerves.

The young scout yanked out his big-bladed bowie and yelled, "Go, Hawk! Go home! Go home, Hawk!"

He knew he was in trouble and his only hope now was that his big horse's presence alone might alert someone. Hawk took off at a gallop.

The bear was furious. He was a twelve-hundred pound mass of anger, teeth, claws, and sinew. Charging forward a few feet, it swatted Man Killer as if he were a rag doll, and the scout flew into a scrub oak, two of his ribs broken. He felt a stabbing pain in his side and struggled to breath. He tilted his body to the side, favoring his rib cage. There was no way he could stab this beast. The big bear knocked him down again with a mighty paw, its long claws raking Man Killer's chest. It bit into his leg and shook him like a bone. Man Killer wanted to cry out in pain as the bruin's fangs penetrated his shinbone and calf muscle, but that was not the Nez Percé way.

Man Killer struggled to remember something Colt had taught him. Chris had said, if fighting and running didn't work with a bear, play dead, because then the bear would have no challenge and would leave him alone; bears didn't like the taste of humans anyway. Man Killer rolled over on his stomach, wrapped his arms over the back of his neck to protect his spinal column, and went limp. He gritted his teeth against the pain he knew would come. The bear's breath smelled like rotten carrion, and the smell made the Indian gag, but he didn't move. The bear sniffed him, then bit his right buttocks, sending excruciating pain through his entire body. The animal stepped on Man Killer's other leg, walked up to his shoulders, and clamped down on Man Killer's skull. The pressure made the scout feel his head would pop like a watermelon. Man Killer felt faint, but he fought to stay conscious. He wanted to scream, and the grating sound of the bear's teeth on his own skull was horrifying. The pain and pressure were unbearable. Fortunately, the teeth scraped along the skull on both sides, only tearing away hair and skin. Man Killer felt blood running all over his face, and it actually blinded him, it was so excessive. He forced himself to not move or panic.

The bear sniffed him some more, then stopped, stood on its hind legs, and the scout could hear it sniffing. Man Killer heard the far-off sounds of horses galloping toward him. They got closer and the bear dropped back down, sniffed him, then gave him a swat. He rolled under some more scrub oak, but didn't move. The bear ran out of the thicket as suddenly as it had appeared.

Man Killer heard the giant posse and heard a voice yell, "Look out boys, a griz!"

Another voice yelled, "Look at the size of that son of a buck!"

Still another yelled, "Look how fast he can run!"

Man Killer then heard the hated and familiar

voice of Wolf Keeler yelling, "Forget that! Look at the dust cloud. He just ran over that ridgeline. Come on, boys, hells-a-poppin'! Five thousand greenbacks for the one that puts 'im under!"

Man Killer rolled over on his back, tears running down his cheeks mixing with the blood. Many white men thought that Indian warriors never cried, but it was just that they never cried in front of anyone. Racking sobs came out of his mouth for several minutes, then subsided. He wanted to sleep, and he pictured Jennifer Banta floating above him in the clouds. Her golden hair was made out of the rays of sunlight. He smiled and then started laughing and decided to float up to be with her.

Suddenly his thoughts about his love were interrupted. He saw Chief Joseph's face in the clouds above him now, and there was a stern look on the man's face.

Joseph said, "Any warrior can walk the spirit trail when he has been wounded, but a true warrior never gives up the fight. Sometimes it takes more of a man to live than to die."

Man Killer suddenly understood those words, and he shook his head, blood splattering all over the leaves around him. He tried to stand but couldn't. He knew he must bind his wounds to stop the bleeding before he fainted, or he would die. Man Killer decided that would not happen without a fight. That was all he knew. He was a warrior.

It was an hour later, and the posse was galloping through the sandy-bottomed Maverick Gulch. They rounded a bend, and the leaders pulled up short, facing the twin .45 Peacemakers of Chris Colt, leading Hawk by the reins back up the gulch.

All the posse members drew their guns and Wolf

Keeler said, "You shore as hell ain't gonna kill us all, Colt."

Colt quickly assessed the situation and knew that he had been had. He thought about opening up with both guns, then hightailing it back down the gulch, but he spotted several Sharp's and a Spencer with a scope. He thought better of it. Besides, this posse was after Man Killer, not him, so he holstered his guns and raised his hands.

Wolf Keeler said, "Whitey, collect his weapons."

A light-blond-haired puncher rode forward and seized Colt's weapons. Wolf Keeler gave a hand signal and several men rode up and yanked Colt off his horse.

Colt said, "What are you doing, you fools?"

Wolf said, "The mighty Colt, huh? You don't look so legendary to me. You are hiding a fugitive, so we're gonna stretch yer neck. Right, boys?"

The men yelled in agreement except for two who rode up to Keeler. Both men looked like tough cowpunchers but had honest looks in their eyes.

The leader of the two said, "Look, we came out here with a posse to arrest a killer. Chris Colt's a hero, not a killer. We'll have no truck with hanging an innocent man."

"To hell with you two, then. Git!" Wolf snarled, his hand hovering over his .44. "He's the boss of that cold-blooded murdering redskin and he brought him to this valley. Now he's hiding him from us. Look, boys, he's got the red nigger's horse."

Wolf went on, "Don't worry, Colt. We won't lynch ya. We'll give ya an even chance."

What he did took less than five minutes.

The deputy then said, "Last chance, Colt. Where did ya hide that red nigger killer?"

Chris sneered, "Go to hell."

Wolf Keeler said, "See ya around, Colt. Hope that horse a yours has plenty of stay in him. C'mon, boys, let's find the red nigger."

Colt simply said, "Mister, you just made a big mistake."

Wolf Keeler laughed aloud and slapped his horse with the reins. The posse followed Keeler back up the gulch and left Chris Colt standing there on the back of War Bonnet, both hands tied behind his back, noose around his neck, tied to a low-hanging cottonwood branch.

Chris spoke softly, "Steady, boy. Stand, War Bonnet."

His mind worked quickly, calmly, and methodically. Chris Colt had gotten himself out of near-death situations before by thinking his way through it, but this seemed awfully scary.

He kept speaking softly to the now-nervous paint horse. Colt wished now he would have gone home first to see his wife and son. At least he would have seen them before he died. On the other hand, in emergencies like this, there was no quit to Chris Colt.

Man Killer was completely naked, except for his bandages: His pants legs cut off and wrapped tightly around his rib cage, his bloody shirt was wrapped around his head, and his shirtsleeves were tied tightly around his calf.

The scout was weak, but he would not give up. He reached out, stabbed his bowie knife into the ground, and dragged himself another two feet farther down the mountain. It had been hard, but he had made it a hundred yards so far. The grizzly had not returned, and he was thankful for that. Man Killer kept crawling, passing out three different

times. Fortunately, he was crawling downhill, and
his head was lower than his feet, so he would regain
consciousness fairly quickly. His heart pounded
with the least bit of exertion, he had lost so much
blood.

The posse rode toward Big Hole, because Chris
Colt had wisely confused and hidden his trail before,
and after, finding Hawk.

"Easy, boy, easy," Colt said.

He could tell that the scent of a mountain lion or
bear was in the wind, by the nervous way War Bonnet was now prancing and tossing his head around.
His nostrils flared in and out, and he whinnied nervously.

"Stand, War Bonnet. Easy, boy."

Colt had an idea. He kept talking softly to his
horse and walked back onto the horse's rump. This
really made War Bonnet nervous. Chris remembered
a trick he had been teaching the horse, and he
prayed now that the horse would remember the trick
as well.

Colt, still on war Bonnet's rump, bent his knees
and said, "War Bonnet, kick!"

The horse's hindquarters went high in the air as
he kicked with both hooves. At the same time,
Chris Colt jumped and bent his body forward, landing stomach first on top of the branch. Colt lay
there on the branch, tears in his eyes, and he
breathed a heavy sigh of relief. He mentally said a
prayer of gratitude and lay there catching his
breath. War Bonnet pulled at some mountain
grasses down below.

Chris Colt had a large antler-handled bowie in a
sheath between his shoulder blades, but he had to
figure out how to get it into his hands now. At least

he had gotten on the branch, so he didn't have to worry about his neck becoming two feet longer, but how would he get his hands free? Colt slowly worked his way up to a sitting position where the tree limb forked, and he worked his hands back and forth until his raw wrists started to bleed, but the bonds were too tight.

Finally Colt stood up gingerly on the forks of the limb. There was a small branch above him that forked slightly. Colt started chewing on the skinny branches and in a few minutes chewed through two of them, creating a stick with a fork at the end. He positioned himself so it went down the back of his shirt and kept working it until he finally, carefully, extracted the knife from the back of his buckskin shirt. The fork of the stick held the handle of the knife and it hung point down above Chris. Now he carefully turned around and held his bound hands back behind him. He flipped his head back and tapped the knife loose, and it fell into his grasp. It only took a minute of sawing with the scalpel-sharp blade and he was free. Colt slipped the noose off his neck and called War Bonnet over. He dropped onto the big horse's back. Chris then called for Hawk, and he wandered over. He reached into his saddlebags and pulled out an extra gun, slipping it into his right-hand holster.

Chris Colt was angry. He had a score to settle with Wolf Keeler and his posse. It didn't matter to him right then that the odds were over one hundred to one. If it was unfair, they could go get some reinforcements. First, however, he would have to find Man Killer. Chris was pleased that they didn't know where the scout was. There was a good chance that he was still alive, but Colt was very much bothered that Hawk was off by himself.

He knew one thing: He had apparently guessed

right about Man Killer going to Waugh Mountain. It
was nearby, and Colt headed there at a gallop. He
didn't lead Hawk. The mount would follow War
Bonnet.

Colt cantered and fast-trotted his horse for a little
over a half an hour and arrived at the base of Waugh
Mountain. Man Killer was at the last of his strength,
but he spotted his mentor far down below. He had
emerged from the aspens and had crawled over a
quarter of a mile. Seeing Chris, he stopped and
started gathering together dry sticks that he could
reach. Man Killer pulled out a matchstick from the
bandage he had made out of his pants. He lit the tinder and fanned the flames with one hand. The fire
started burning, and he grabbed several handfuls of
green grass and set them on top of the fire. Smoke
started pouring out of the fire, and the young man
grinned, then fainted.

Upon finding him, Chris literally carried the
young Nez Percé back to the aspens and found a
good spot to build a fire. He put water on to boil
and replaced Man Killer's expedient bandages
while covering the wounds with a poultice. Man
Killer remained unconscious, except for coming to
one time to briefly smile at Chris, who just winked
at him.

Colt prepared some mountain lion steaks, wild
onions, potatoes, and biscuits. Mountain lion and
antelope were the two favorite meats of mountain
men, trappers, and scout—especially mountain lion.
They considered it the best tasting of all wild game
meats.

Man Killer did not have a fever, although Colt
was expecting it to happen. Colt awakened the
young man and helped feed him. The meat and vegetables seemed to perk him up, as well as a hot cup

of coffee. While Man Killer drifted off again, Colt cut some saplings and lashed them across the front of Man Killer's McClellan saddle. He then lashed Man Killer's blanket behind the horse and formed a travois. Chris carried the young scout and placed him on the travois, then covered him with a blanket. Next he rolled and lit a cigarette for him. Colt mounted up and led Hawk, with the travois behind him, down the mountainside, and they continued downhill for Cotopaxi.

At the bottom of Waugh Mountain, Colt now turned left instead of right and rode into the small berg of Nesterville. He enlisted the aid of a local miner and they placed a mattress in the man's buckboard and lay Man Killer on it. The Nez Percé was unconscious, had a fever, and was stirring a good bit in his sleep. Colt checked on the time of the next eastbound train going into Canon City. If he could move fast, he could flag it down. Colt removed the saddles and bridles from War Bonnet and Hawk and paid the man for the use of his rig, with a promise to leave it down at Cotopaxi.

Chris put the reins to the team of horses and headed down the wagon road toward Red Hill and down to the Arkansas River. The pair of horses were well lathered when he arrived, and he hired a man at the general store near the bridge to take care of the team. Colt heard the train whistle in the distance and learned it was not supposed to stop this day. He saddled War Bonnet and rode out onto the tracks and started flagging the train down as soon as he saw the engine riding along the rock canyon walls on the north side of the river.

The train came to a complete stop directly across from the general store at Cotopaxi. Colt climbed aboard and quickly explained to the engineer what had happened. They soon had Man Killer and the two horses loaded on the train in an empty boxcar.

Chapter 6

>>>>>>>>>>>>>>>>>

Canon City

Two hours later, Man Killer was in a clean bed in Canon City, being tended to by an older doctor with a friendly face and cheerful disposition. The physician, Dr. J. Reid, had started the first pharmacy in the town in the early 1860s, and he was loved and respected by one and all. He now lived in Black Hawk and frequently returned to Canon City to see patients. Not able to find a horse to use, he had once walked fifty miles to Greenhorn, fifty miles away, to treat an old man who couldn't make it to a doctor.

Dr. Reid told Colt to go about his business and not worry about his young friend. The doctor would soon have him on the mend.

Colt went straight to the telegrapher's to get word to Shirley about his whereabouts. From there he went to the sheriff's office and met with the current Fremont County sheriff, Benjamin J. Shaffer, whom Colt had met before and liked. Chris explained the situation with Man Killer as he knew it, and the sheriff told him about the rumors that had been going around about his young Nez Percé friend and the vast reward put up by Millard Mining Corporation.

Shaffer said, "Mistah Colt, ya know ahm gonna have to place him under arrest?"

Colt said, "Yes, I do, Sheriff Shaffer. That's what I'm counting on. You'll protect him here."

"The hell you say," Shaffer said. "I should say so. Ain't nobody gonna take a prisoner outta the Fremont County Jail on my watch without a judge's order."

"Good," Chris said. "My attorney, Brandon Rudd, will be here anytime, and he'll see to Man Killer, but I want him safe while I do some snooping around myself."

Shaffer said, "More power to ya, son. Anything ah kin do ta help, ya jest give a hollah. Thet boy's under mah protection now, so you don't have to worry none 'bout 'im. By the way, Sheriff Schoolfield's back in Custer Country, an I hear he farred thet Wolf Keeler deputy thet has been causin' ya'll so much trouble. Thet's what the driver jest tole me comin' down from Rosita. You have a powerful reputation, specially 'round these parts, but the evidence against this Man Killer is awful badlookin' fer him. Still and all, I know yer a damned good judge a character, but I gotta do what I gotta do."

"I respect that, Sheriff," Colt said, "just so long as you watch over Man Killer."

"No problem. Ya take care, son. Luck to ya."

Colt left, stopped by the doctor's to explain to Man Killer that he would be arrested but would be in good hands, then he headed west to see his wife and son.

It was well after dark when Chris Colt walked in the door of the Coyote Run ranch house. Shirley had a giant cast-iron pot of stew cooking on the swing-out iron hook in the giant stone fireplace. Coffee was boiling on the stove and two apple pies were cooling in the window over the sink. Joseph was asleep in his trundle bed, and Shirley sat in the giant rocker stitching one of Colt's buckskin shirts.

She jumped up as he came in, tears streaming down her cheeks, and threw herself into his arms. He picked her up without saying a word and carried her into the bedroom. Chris Colt missed his supper that night.

Brandon Rudd immediately got himself a room at the McClure House, then checked around town for office space and a law library to use, at least until his books and supplies arrived with the wagon train. His uncle, Anson Rudd, had insisted that Brandon stay at his fine home, but the young attorney wanted to take care of himself without family help. Having the name Rudd had helped him enough in southern Colorado, but he wanted to make his own mark.

After meeting several attorneys, he made arrangements to temporarily rent space and the law library at Macon and Cox. They were only too happy to accommodate him, as they had heard so many good things about him in letters from Elizabeth. Thomas Macon, the senior partner and one of the most prominent citizens of Fremont County, spent as much time as Brandon wanted to spend to offer advice and tell Brandon who he could count on for help in Fremont and Custer counties. Macon's firm also specialized in mining laws, and their library was very adequate in that regard.

Rudd visited Man Killer, who was now in a cell in the Fremont County Jail; the conscientious Sheriff Ben Shaffer had had a hospital bed brought in and the cell scrubbed down totally. Dr. Reid had already been there twice that morning to look in on Man Killer, who was covered with bandages and had his leg in a cast. Brandon wanted the man to be released on his own recognizance, but the county judge, Robert A. Bain, explained that Custer County had jurisdiction over Man Killer and Fremont County was only holding him for them because of the gravity of his wounds and the danger involved in attempting to move him. He let Brandon know that he would have to take it up with Judge W. A. Offenbacher, the Custer County court judge. Because of the evidence stacked against Man Killer, that conversation would not be his top priority.

The courtroom in Custer County would become Brandon's battlefield, and he would have to learn as much as he could about the principles and the terrain of that battleground. He also had an awful lot of research to do and would need help with that.

That night, he had dinner with his uncle and aunt and met his cousin Anson Rudd, Jr., who was the first president of the Band of Hope, Youth's Temperance Society, and spoke quite enthusiastically about it and the evils of drinking.

After dinner, Brandon accepted a fine cigar from his highly respected uncle and listened with fascination as the white-bearded man recited a poem he had written, one of his favorite pastimes:

Our Wives and Children
Our wives and children, precious terms that move
And thrill our being with a sacred love.
Divine afflatus! from our inmost souls
It wells and bubbles, every sense controls;
Exalts and purifies, refines, restrains:
It soothes our sorrows, modifies our pains;
Subdues our passions, lifts our souls above
Earth's sordid pleasures to elysian love.
In fact earth's joys would fade and round us gloom
As deep and dark as in the silent tomb
Would gather, till life's brightest beams would seem
The horrid phantom of some troubled dream.

If 'twere not for these precious gems to light
And cheer our pathway thro' this earthly night.
God bless our wives, first, last, best gift to man,
The crowning beauty in creation's plan;
Our guiding star that points to heav'n above,
Where all is joy and harmony and love.
Our children, also, sparks that scintillate
From love's bright realm where forms ecstatic mate.
May they be spared to cheer our varied lives
As we go journeying heavenward with our wives.

After the recitation, Brandon heartily applauded, along with Anson, Jr., and Mrs. Harriett Rudd. Their only daughter had died as a youth, and Anson, Jr., was now around twenty years old. The three men all shared cigars and cups of coffee on the porch.

Brandon glanced at his younger cousin and thought about how proud he seemed to be to be included with the after-dinner cigars and males-only conversation. Rudd thought about some of the little things that made a young man feel like he had finally become a real man. It was mainly little things, not major events.

Brandon still remembered when he was a teenager and had gone to the local mercantile to purchase some flour, baking powder, roofing tacks, and a bolt of blue cotton material for his mother. The memory was so clear he still remembered the list of items to be purchased.

The mercantile was normally operated by a big Frenchman named Francois Marchand, and he was very jolly and amiable. His wife, however, was curt and tactless, driving many customers away from his business. Born in Erie, Pennsylvania, she was not French but came from a Scotch/Irish and Pennsylvania Dutch background which was actually German in derivation.

When the young Brandon walked in the door, she kept staring at him in a peculiar way, and it made the young man very uncomfortable. He started fidgeting but finally walked up to the counter and told her the list of goods he wanted. She brought the flour, set it down very hard on the hand-carved countertop, and gave him an exasperated look, hands on her hips.

She said, "Young man, when was the last time you shaved yourself?"

Brandon said, "Several days ago, ma'am."

She replied, "Well, the next time you shave, I would suggest that you stand much closer to the razor."

She turned to get the rest of his items and muttered, "A boy that age growing a beard. I just do not know what is happening with the youth these days. We are all headed for judgment and the wrath of the good Lord. Young people have no respect anymore. They are so vile and vulgar and rebellious."

She worked herself up so much, she spun around, pointing a finger at Brandon, saying, "You young people are going to be the ruination of this country. Mark my words. We shall not even make it into the twentieth century. The Lord shall destroy the world by fire first. You just remember that."

Brandon said, "But ma'am, I really don't—"

"Just yesterday, another young pup was in here and do you know what he said? It was the McAllister lad. Do you know him?"

"No, ma'am."

"Well," she went on, "he tried to convince me that someday there will be over one million people living in New York City. Can you imagine that? He expects me to believe him when he said there would be over one million people living in New York City.

How ridiculous. Now, can you answer me a question?"

Brandon said meekly, "What's that, ma'am?"

"If there were one million people living in New York City, where would they find the room to stable all their horses?"

She had stared at him with a victorious look on her face, knowing she had stumped Brandon with such a well-thought-out question.

He had said, "I don't know Mrs. Marchand."

"Good cigar, Brandon, isn't it?" Anson Rudd, Jr.'s voice snapped the attorney out of his daydream.

Brandon took a long puff and blew a long slow stream of blue smoke at the engraved copper ceiling.

He smiled and said, "That it is, cousin. That it is."

After the cigars, Anson, Jr., excused himself, and Mrs. Rudd brought the two small snifters of brandy.

Anson Rudd handed one to Brandon and kept the other himself, clipping and offering Brandon another cigar, lighting one for himself.

Dipping the unlit end of his cigar into the brandy, then puffing, he said, "I prefer not to imbibe in front of Junior. He has such strong reservation against the partaking of alcoholic beverage, but I feel a small snifter helps take the chill from the night air. Don't you agree, nephew?"

Brandon said, "Yes, sir, I do, and it's a fine liqueur, I might add."

"Ah, yes," Anson replied. "Imported, and a good year."

Anson went on, "James Clelland is a Scotsman by heritage, emigrating from Glasgow some years back. After a number of successful business ventures elsewhere, he settled in Canon City in 1871. He is a man of great import and keen insight in matters of business and shrewd investing. He is far superior to others in executive ability and is noted for such.

"Mr. Jonathan A. Draper is another, dear nephew. One of our earliest and finest citizens and a man of superior business acumen, he stands as one among the foremost in matters of public enterprise. His foresight and keen investing has enabled Mr. Draper to be one of the holders of some of Canon City's finest architectural masterpieces, including his own home."

Brandon said, "Should I meet these men, sir?"

Anson replied, "Indubitably. If Preston Millard has the devil in hiding in his closet, and his objective is the attainment of some shrewd and improper business deal, maybe Messrs. Draper and Clelland can help you sniff it out. If there are riches to be had around here, those two men can locate them, generally. Except they can attain those riches by legitimate means."

Brandon met with both men the following day, and they each had interesting theories about what Millard's motivation might be. However, neither one struck a chord with the young attorney.

Brandon spent the next two weeks preparing for the murder trial of Man Killer. Chris Colt worked on the ranch until Joshua's arrival, by train, with the herd. Because he wanted to get back as quickly as possible to resume his duties on the ranch, and because the herd he pushed was primarily breeding stock they would keep, Joshua decided to load the cattle onto boxcars in Kansas. He also loaded Brandon's wagon contents into wooden shipping boxes and brought them on the train, as well.

As an added surprise, Elizabeth Macon also loaded her goods on the train and escorted the herd and Coyote Run hands to Canon City. She had purchased a Conestoga wagon for the trip, but Captain Swenson was happy to purchase it from her. Her idea was to assist Brandon with his case preparation.

The day she arrived, she went straight to the home of her uncle and aunt, apologized to her very understanding aunt for having to be so busy right away, and went to her uncle's office. She first visited with him, but her real goal was to see Brandon again. Much to her relief, he swept her into his arms and gave her a wonderful kiss.

"I missed you," he said.

"I missed you, too," she replied.

Elizabeth blurted, "Do you have a secretary?"

"No, things are too uncertain," Brandon replied. "I have a tidy savings and some investments, but until I establish myself in Colorado and have a thriving practice, I want to take some things slowly. I have to build a clientele base and illustrate my capabilities in a courtroom out here before I can even think of hiring a secretary or establishing my own office."

"Well," Elizabeth said, "I would assume that you'll need a secretary or assistant of some sort to help with your case preparation. Now you have one."

Brandon said, "Elizabeth, I appreciate your thoughtfulness very much, and an assistant would be most helpful now. However, I am ill prepared to make provisions for such a person at this time."

"Pshaw," she replied. "Uncle Thomas will provide me with whatever materials I need, and you needn't compensate me in any manner. I shall work for you for free."

"But why?" he asked.

Elizabeth smiled coyly and said, "Let's just say that I am making my own investment in my own future."

She embarrassed herself with that remark and Brandon felt his entire face flush as well. Brandon hugged her.

She stepped back and said, "If you allow me to help you, I will be treated as an employee and will conduct myself in that manner, too. It could prove to be too uncomfortable for you, mayhaps, if I did not do so."

"Oh, Elizabeth, working with you truly would be heaven," he finally relented. "Do you mean what you say?"

She said, "Yes, I most certainly do. Will there be much preparation?"

"For this murder trial? Come with me," Brandon said.

He took her outside and walked her down Main Street a short distance to a small eatery where they walked inside. There were several small tables and Brandon seated Elizabeth at one. He walked over to the counter, which held freshly made baked goods in its glass-covered innards.

Elizabeth looked at the gold-leaf lettering on the window and translated it, after reading it backward. It read: A. WALTERS, BAKERY AND CONFECTIONERY, then in small letters it read: ICE CREAM AND SODA WATER. In even smaller letters, it read: FRESH OYSTERS IN THE WINTER, SERVED ANY STYLE.

Brandon sat down, placing an ice-cream sundae in front of her and himself. The thick-stemmed glasses had been frosted in ice, and this really seemed like something most welcome on a hot day like this.

"Thank you, Brandon," she said, genuinely enthusiastic, "this looks like the perfect thing to have right now, although I am afraid it will make me look like an elephant."

Brandon quickly interjected, "Oh, no, not you. You could never look anything but beautiful."

He again flushed with embarrassment, but Elizabeth smiled demurely and felt her heart start pounding harder, like it so often did when Brandon was near her.

He said, "You asked if we would have much work in the case preparation. You have seen Chris Colt handle firearms and have heard numerous stories of his acumen, correct?"

"Yes."

"Well, how do you suppose he got so proficient with weaponry?"

Elizabeth said, "I imagine Mr. Colt has probably spent hour upon hour practicing drawing his pistols, then putting them back in the holsters, then drawing them again. He probably has spent at least an equal number of hours practicing firing at targets so he can hit them after he draws his guns. On top of that, I would assume he practices many more hours shooting bows and arrows, throwing knives, and the like."

"Precisely," he said. "Now, when Chris Colt has been in a gunfight with another shootist, let's say, the entire episode may last five minutes, ten minutes, even less. Look, however, at the countless hours and hours and days of preparation prior to that five or ten minutes.

"Now, I have been told that the frontier courtrooms are far less organized and properly procedural than the ones I have been used to. However, I still will not spend much time in the courtroom practicing law compared with the countless hours I must spend preparing for that short appearance."

Elizabeth said, "Where do we get started?"

"I want you to find out as much as you can about Preston Millard and Millard Mining Corporation, to begin with. I am going to try to piece together a puzzle."

Elizabeth said, "What's that?"

"Colt obtained a paper that Millard had in his office and it read, *Coyote Run—Lost Brother.* I am going to try to figure out what that signifies."

"When we return, why don't you visit with my uncle? Maybe he will have an idea about it."

"Good idea."

Elizabeth asked, "Is that all there is for us to do?"

"I should say not," Brandon replied. "We are just getting started, dear girl. You do not know what you have let yourself in for with your spirit of volunteerism."

When the two returned to the office, Brandon excused himself and went to meet with Thomas Macon. Another man with long mutton-chop sideburns sat in the office drinking tea. Thomas Macon, a distinguished-looking gray-haired gentleman, offered Brandon a seat on his leather-covered oak couch.

Brandon first shook hands with the mutton-chopped man, while Thomas said, "Mr. Rudd, I wish to present Mr. Carl Wulstein, late of Rosita, where he is in great demand as a civil and mining engineer. He not only examines mining properties, but he also plats and reports them from underground, as well, utilizing the latest in engineering instruments. You may speak freely in front of Mr. Wulstein."

Brandon nodded and smiled as Thomas said, "Mr. Wulstein, this is Mr. Brandon Rudd, nephew of the man himself, and he has just traveled here from St. Louis, Missouri—and, I suspect, from what I keep hearing from the womenfolk, will be joining my family in the not-too-distant future."

Wulstein looked at Brandon appraisingly.

"By way of my lovely niece Elizabeth Macon," Macon explained, "who also just journeyed here from St. Louis."

A secretary walked in the door carrying a clean china cup for Brandon. She also had a tray with a fresh pot of tea, fresh cream, and sugar, from which she freshened the cups of the other two.

After she left the room, Thomas Macon said to Brandon, "What can I help you with, sir?"

"Well, Mr. Macon, I was just wondering if you could possibly help me solve a puzzle. My client's employer and mentor—you know who I mean—discovered a paper with the name of his ranch written on it."

Thomas interrupted to explain to Carl, "Brandon just arrived and he already has a major murder defense case he is working on."

Looking then at Brandon, he said, "As I mentioned, Carl can be trusted with confidentiality on any matter."

Carl said, "Oh, you must be the new one defending the young Indian charge of Chris Colt. Just going by rumors, you have a very tough case to handle, Mr. Rudd. You've heard the expression 'baptism by fire.' Well, you certainly will have it with this case, as far as practicing in Colorado goes."

Brandon said, "Well, I believe you are quite right, sir, but battles are never won by commanders who sit in their fort headquarters cowering and whimpering about how they cannot succeed in their military campaign."

Carl smiled at Thomas. "Thomas, are you certain that this young man is related to Anson and not your wife? He's full of the fire, is he not?"

Thomas teased, "He will be a welcome addition to my extended family."

Brandon said, "All right, Mr. Macon, you made your point."

Carl Wulstein laughed some more. "You know, Mr. Rudd, we could use some fighters in my family. I have a couple of very ugly cousins, but they have some land that goes with them."

All three men laughed.

Brandon said, "On a more serious note, this piece of paper named Mr. Colt's ranch. Then there was a hyphen and the words: *Lost Brother,* with both of the words capitalized. I haven't a clue what that might mean."

Carl Wulstein said, "Well, I certainly do, Mr. Rudd."

"Brandon, please."

"Very well, Brandon," Carl went on. "I am positive that I have the answer to your puzzle. One day in 1868 a stranger knocked on the door of a ranch house in the Wet Mountain Valley. That is where my home is located along with Westcliffe and Silver Cliff and your client's beauteous ranch. The man's name was Bill Skinner and stated that he was seeking his long-lost brother George, who had come to the Wet Mountains in 1860 from Illinois, and nary a word from him had been heard by the family since that time.

"Bill Skinner explained that he had traced his brother first to Denver, where he met a man who owned a grocery store and knew his brother. George had come there to buy provisions and left a considerable sum of money with the merchant to be held until his return in the spring. Apparently George had no use for banks whatsoever.

"From conversation, the grocer had deduced that George Skinner had been in the Wet Mountain Valley, and more specifically the Big Range, and was returning there with his provisions. The main thing was that several years had elapsed and George had never returned for his money.

"When Bill Skinner explained all of this to the rancher here, he was invited to spend the night, although the rancher had never heard of his brother. But the rancher did feel consumed by the young Skinner's story, so he told Bill that the next day the two of them would begin asking questions of Wet Mountain valley residents and see if they could develop a lead on George Skinner."

Brandon leaned forward, getting interested in the story.

Carl went on, "The next day, true to his word, the rancher took Bill around the valley, but not a soul had heard of or had seen George Skinner. This seemed to satisfy the rancher, but Bill Skinner's curiosity was piqued, so he asked around for several more days, then finally hired a local guide, familiar with the area mines, to take him up in the Sangre de Cristos to search for his long-lost brother.

"The two hiked up into the mountains, where they searched for the entire summer. Near fall, they decided to give up and started back toward Westcliffe, and many believe they stayed on Horn's Peak one night.

"In any event, they awakened in the morning to a great chill and several inches of new snow. They were fortunate, however, in that they had camped near timberline and spent the night in an old miner's cabin they had discovered. Bill Skinner found some old utensils and a dirty old black wallet wrapped up with baling wire. He tossed it into his knapsack. They quickly returned to Silver Cliff, where Bill Skinner got himself a room above Ed

Austin's Horn Silver Billiard Saloon, across from the post office."

Mrs. Canterbury, the secretary came in and freshened everyone's coffee. Carl stirred in a little sugar and cream, while Brandon attempted to wait patiently for the engineer to finish the story.

Carl Wulstein continued, "Skinner was exhausted from the long trek and slept almost a full twenty-four hours. The next day, after he awakened and finished a big breakfast, he decided to go through his pack and inventory what he had remaining after the difficult summer. He came across the old wallet that he had found and forgotten, and unwrapped the wire and opened it.

"Well, don't you know it. The wallet had belonged to none other than George Skinner himself. In it, Bill discovered a handwritten letter from his brother to his family in Illinois and the letter had been dated back in 1860, one-half year after his brother had left home. It told the family about discovering a very rich mine in the Sangre de Cristos, and it further explained that George was heading for the "settlements" to winter there and prepare himself for a great mining venture in the spring. He would stock a great deal of supplies for his venture.

"Bill Skinner worked at odd jobs all winter and stayed in Silver Cliff, then hired the same guide in the spring to go back up in the mountains to find his brother and his mine. However, he kept to himself what he had read in the diary. He just told the guide that he wanted to return to the cabin and continue looking for his brother. The guide, however, saw him reading the letter at night on several occasions when Bill thought the guide was fast asleep. Bill Skinner also confided in several people, over liquor, in the Horn Silver Billiard Saloon, on several other occasions during the lonely winter months."

Brandon was totally engrossed in the story now, and Carl continued. "When he and the guide got to the cabin site on Horn Park, they found that, as usual, everything had changed in those mountains in the winter. Avalanches, rock slides, and high winds are always attacking those mountains like a mad sculptor, carving them out in many new and sometimes wonderful ways. The cabin was gone completely, so Bill Skinner and the guide remained in the mountains once more until fall, searching to no avail.

"This time, however, they took a totally different trail back home than the ones they had previously used. That trail ran along a sheer cliff face on the side of a deep canyon. The route was certainly a murderous one, with signs of numerous rock slides and avalanches all along the way.

"At one point, the path gave way and one of their pack mules fell down the steep cliff to its death. Well, Bill Skinner and the guide had to have the supplies that were lost, so they rigged some ropes and pulleys to descend and retrieve their supplies. When they completed their descent, there lay the skeleton of another pack mule, and alongside it a man. It was the remains of George Skinner, rest his poor soul."

Brandon poured more tea for himself without even looking down.

Carl continued, "Along with the weathered skeletons were numerous large gold nuggets and a black, weatherbeaten, but still legible booklet, which turned out to be George Skinner's diary. He explained that he had written the location of the mine in another letter kept in his cabin in the mountains. The other letter had also instructed the finder to mail the contents of the letter Bill had found to his family in Illinois, but unfortunately the letter with the mine's location had not been discovered. At least by Bill, it hadn't.

"Bill Skinner buried his brother George there on Horn Peak and returned to Illinois to inform his family.

"He came back the next spring, however, to give it one more try to locate the mine. Mother Nature had further changed the complexion of the mountain, and he finally gave up, returning to Illinois to his family. That was about a dozen years ago."

Brandon asked, "So George Skinner's mine is referred to as the Lost Brother Mine, correct?"

"Certainly," Thomas said. "I've heard of the Lost Brother Mine. Many speak of it, but most feel it is a simple legend with no bottom to it."

Carl Wulstein said, "No, it's real enough, all right, but many searched all over Horn Peak for the mine and never found a clue. I have it on very good authority that the mine was located on Spread Eagle Peak, the upper reaches of Chris Colt's ranch."

"That's it, then," Brandon said smiling at Thomas Macon.

Then, looked at Carl, he said, "On good authority, huh? How so, sir?"

"Bill Skinner's guide," Carl said, "was my best friend."

Brandon and Thomas both stared at Carl in awe and wonder. Thomas smiled and saluted Carl with his teacup. Brandon grinned and followed suit.

Brandon said, "Millard must have found some clue or heard from someone that the mine was on Spread Eagle and wants the Coyote Run to be his."

At the end of the work day, Brandon said to Elizabeth, "May I walk you home?"

"Certainly," she replied. "I would enjoy that very much. I am staying with my aunt and uncle for the time being."

They walked west on Main Street, turning north on Fourth to head the few blocks to her aunt and uncle's street, but instead they ran directly into a gang of toughs. Brandon took Elizabeth by the arm and tried to pass around the group without making eye contact, but several of the men blocked their path. Without saying a word, Brandon spun Elizabeth to the rear and tried to head back to the office, but their retreat was blocked as well.

Brandon said, "See here, if you have foul play planned, we shall address that momentarily, but first you will let this lady pass freely and out of harm's way."

The leader, who looked like he had lost a fight with a bulldog as a young child, said, "Why, of course, Mr. Rudd, we would never do harm to a lady. Ma'am."

He doffed his hat and the men parted to let her pass, but she crossed her arms and said, "I am not moving and you shall not harm a hair on his head. He is an officer of the court and you all shall swing from the gallows, gentlemen, if you so much as cast him a sidelong glance."

"Wal, now, ain't thet sweet, Butch," one man said. "The lawyer man here has hisself a lady what kin do all his fightin' fer him."

"No, actually, I've seen him fight, and he needs help from no man or woman," Chris Colt said as he rode around the corner on his impressive pinto stallion.

"Who the hell are you sticking your nose in our business, mister?" Butch said.

"Chris Colt," came the reply, and all the men gave each other nervous looks.

Chris said, "This young lady and this young gentleman are very good friends of mine, so anybody that has trouble with them also has trouble with me. Now, gents, do any of you have trouble with either of them?"

He stared at each man in the gang, and they each cowered at his gaze—with the exception of Butch, who apparently fancied himself as quite tough. Chris knew anyway that this man was very much the leader of the gang, so taking him down in front of them should totally diffuse the trouble.

Colt smiled and said, "Brandon, it looks like this ugly hombre here has a problem with you. You're an attorney. If you stretched him out it would be self-defense, after the things he said, wouldn't it?"

Brandon immediately picked up on Colt's goal and concurred. He simply said, "Yes," and his right fist arched up from his side, catching Butch flush on the point of his jaw.

The impact of the punch was so hard, it jarred Brandon's arm all the way to the shoulder, but he stepped in before Butch could react and swung again, with a left to the bully's midsection. Then he followed that with another right to the temple, and Butch fell into and on top of two of his followers. They stood and let their unconscious leader drop on the board sidewalk.

Colt rolled a cigarette, hooked his leg over the saddlehorn, and said, "Yeah, I remember when I was down in St. Louis and was out drinking with the old attorney here. We left one of those old waterfront dives along the Mississipp when this old gang of cutthroats tried to jump us, just like you boys. 'Course, there's ten of you, and there was only seven of them. Well, actually there's only nine of you now, since the ugly one there is napping on the sidewalk."

Colt pulled out his right Peacemaker in a blur of speed, making the gang members all jump, then spun it backward into his holster.

He said, "I was just going to shoot them all dead in cold blood, which I'm known to do with gangs of bullies who team up against less than their number. You know, I just get in this fighting rage and can't control myself. It's kind of like both of my guns come out and start going off real fast. Anyway, Brandon here said, 'Relax Chris. I need a workout,' and he waded into that crowd and came out of it with just a black eye and them all laying on the ground bleeding and such. He gouged the eyes out of two of them. Then, after all that, him being an attorney, he prosecuted them all for assault, and they all went to jail, to a man."

One of the men, quite frightened, said, "Mr. Rudd, Mr. Colt, we've heard enough. We have no truck with you. Butch there was hired by Preston Millard to run you out of town. He was s'pose to hire a bunch to help him. That's us, but not no more. See you around. Sorry, ma'am."

With that, the gang disappeared around the corner as quickly as their legs could move. Brandon, Elizabeth, and Colt all laughed heartily.

Brandon said, "Chris, you should have become an attorney yourself. Hey, I want you to meet my new secretary, Miss Macon."

Colt doffed his hat, saying, "Elizabeth, nice to see you again. May I buy you folks dinner? I'd like to discuss the case with you."

Brandon said, "As soon as I get someone to haul this trash off the street and off to jail. I will need this man as a witness against Preston Millard."

Colt took a lasso off his saddle and expertly roped

Butch, who was still lying unconscious on the walk. He rode up and poured his canteen on the man's face until he came to and sat up, looking all about him as one in a stupor.

Colt drew his gun and said, "Stand up, Butch."

Butch stood, weaving slightly, and shook his head several times. He tried to rub his jaw but saw his hands were pinned to his sides.

Colt said, "March yourself to the sheriff's office."

Still wearing a dreamy look on his ugly visage, Butch started toward the jail.

They started down the street and Colt said over his shoulder, "Want to eat over there at Boyd's House?"

It was a fine and well-known local hotel and restaurant.

No sooner had he asked the couple walking behind him than a shot rang out from up above and to the front. Colt spun in the saddle and fired his left-hand gun six times, by fanning it, through a second-story window where gunsmoke still swirled out in the early evening hours. Chris's six shots were fired so quickly, the last of them were still echoing before Butch's dead body hit the ground, the sniper's bullet lodged in his brain.

Colt dropped the rope and drew his right-hand gun, starting to lunge War Bonnet toward the building when he heard a sawed-off double barrel being cocked.

The deputy sheriff holding it brooked no funny business when he said, "Hold up there, and hands up!"

Chris stopped and raised his hands skyward.

He pleaded, "Deputy, there's a dry-gulcher getting away. He shot from that building with a rifle."

The deputy thought for a second, then all four of them heard hoofbeats while someone sped away from behind the building.

Colt dropped his hands and said, "Damn!"

Then he quickly turned and doffed his hat to Elizabeth, saying, "Sorry, Elizabeth."

She replied, "Your language is not a problem with me, Chris. I agree with you."

Brandon chuckled despite the situation. The deputy still looked perplexed.

Brandon stepped forward and said, "Deputy, you saw that Mr. Colt was making this man walk to his front, rope tied around his arms. If he or Miss Macon or myself had shot the man, the hole would be in the back of his head, wouldn't it? As you can plainly see, he was shot from the right front at a high angle, which would indicate the same window Chris Colt just mentioned."

The deputy took off at a gallop as fast as he could spur his mouse-colored roan. He hollered, "Sorry. Tell the sheriff—and tell him I'm after the shooter."

It was at the end of the meal, over wine and cigars, when the sheriff came in to the Boyd's House to inform Chris and Brandon that the deputy couldn't overtake or track the killer.

Colt said, "Where does Preston Millard live?"

Sheriff Shaffer said, "Big spread along the river road."

Colt said, "That's where he would have found the man hiding. Too late now."

Sheriff Shaffer said, "This ain't a-gonna help your case very much, is it, Mr. Rudd?"

Brandon said, "What do you mean, Sheriff?"

Shaffer replied, "You know that other lawyer's gonna claim thet you all was takin' in thet good-fer-nuthin' thet got kilt, an he'll try ta twist it so's it looked like Colt here backshot him."

Brandon smiled and said, "The other attorney will try, but he won't succeed."

Edward Ellsworth Carrington III, Esquire, turned toward the jury and vehemently said, "And that's when the accused murdering redskin's boss, Chris Colt, pulled out his six-gun and blew a hole in the head of poor Phineas Filbert."

"I object strenuously, Your Honor," Brandon yelled, jumped up, "He characterized the accused as a murdering redskin and tried to implicate one of the leading citizens of this entire country as a murderer when it has been very clearly proven that Mr. Filbert, who was known by one and all as Butch the Butcher, not Phineas, was shot from ambush by a cowardly sniper."

"Objection sustained," the Honorable W. A. Offenbacher said. "The jury will disregard the remarks of Mr. Carrington in his feeble attempt to slander the accused as well as Mr. Colt, to whom this entire country owes a great debt."

Carrington sat down and took a swallow of water, trying to hide his anger and slow his racing heartbeat. "No further questions, Your Honor," he said.

"Cross-examination," the judge said.

Brandon stood and walked slowly, deliberately to the jury box, staring and smiling at each juror individually. He faced the witness.

"Deputy," Brandon said, "we have already established that Mr. Filbert was shot in the head by a Henry .44-caliber rifle being fired from a second-story window at 624 Main Street. Why do you suppose he was shot?"

Carrington rose triumphantly. "Objection, Your

Honor. Mr. Rudd is calling on supposition from the witness. We want to hear hard facts."

Brandon said, "Your Honor, I am asking for the deputy's professional opinion, as it is already in the court record that he has served this county faithfully as a deputy for over fifteen years. I believe that would certainly qualify him as an expert, Your Honor. Therefore, his opinion would be admissible in a court of law as an expert witness."

Carrington jumped up, saying, "An expert of what?"

Brandon thought quickly, faced the jury, and quietly said, "Shootings."

"What was that?" Judge Offenbacher said, not sure he had heard correctly.

Brandon turned, smiling, and said, "Shootings, Your Honor. Deputy, how many shootings have you investigated or been involved in over the years?"

The judge ordered, "Do not answer that. We still have an objection before the court which needs to be ruled on."

Brandon stared at the judge, a polite smile on his handsome face.

Judge Offenbacher thought for a second, then said to the witness, "How many shootings have you been involved with, Jesse?"

"Plenty, Judge. Hell of a lot more than thet there lawyer dude," the deputy replied, indicating Carrington.

The judge grinned to himself as he rapped the gavel to quiet the chuckles in the courtroom.

Judge Offenbacher said, "He is qualified as an expert witness. Objection overruled."

Carrington made a face and sighed while Brandon faced the jury with a broad toothy grin.

He went on, "Deputy, I was asking why you thought Mr. Filbert was murdered."

The deputy said, "Wal, hell, thet's easy, Mr. Rudd. To shet him up. Everyone hereabouts knows thet."

"And who do you suppose would want to shut him up?" Brandon asked.

Carrington again jumped up and yelled, "Objection! That calls for speculation on why he was shot, not how. That has absolutely nothing to do with being an expert witness."

Brandon quickly interjected, "If it please the court, Your Honor, it most certainly does. The deputy has investigated numerous shootings over the years and would qualify as an expert investigator as well as expert on shooting. His opinion would carry much weight as evidentiary opinion."

"Nice argument, Mr. Rudd," the judge said, smiling, "But it doesn't hold water, sir. Objection sustained."

Carrington clasped his hands together under the table and smiled slightly.

Brandon went right on, "Deputy, do you know factually and for certain why Mr. Filbert was murdered?"

"Yup," the deputy said, "I shore do."

Carrington was shocked. How could this man know?

The deputy continued, "He was shots so's thet he couldn't tell no one thet he was hired by Preston Millard to git hisself a gang and run you outta town, Mr. Rudd."

"Objection, Your Honor," Carrington snorted, rising again. "How does he know this factually?"

The judge said, "Good question. How do you know for certain, Jesse?"

The deputy turned to the judge and said, "Common sense. Heerd it around, and it makes perfect sense, Judge."

Carrington slammed his pen down on his table and stood, hands on his hips.

The judge said, "Objection sustained. The jury is instructed to disregard Jesse's last remarks regarding his suspicions and conjecture about Preston Millard. Do you all understand that?"

The jurors all nodded their heads.

Brandon smiled and said, "No more questions, Your Honor."

He returned to his table and grinned at a very angry Carrington all the way.

The judge said, "You can step down, Jesse. Thanks."

"Shore, Judge, anytime."

Judge Offenbacher said, "The court will stand in recess for lunch. Be back here in your seats at one P.M. precisely."

He rapped his gavel on the block and everyone rose, until he walked from the court room. Brandon walked out the door, Elizabeth on his arm. Chris and Shirley Colt met them at the back of the courtroom. Joseph was at home with the nanny Chris had hired to help Shirley out.

Colt said, "Buy you two lunch. You are doing just great, Brandon. I'm impressed."

"Thanks, Chris," Brandon said, "but what is important to me is for Man Killer not only to be freed, but his name totally cleared and Preston Millard implicated."

Shirley said, "That is of the utmost importance to us, too, Brandon. We do not want anyone in this county to have any doubts whatsoever about Man Killer's innocence."

Chris said, "And you will figure out a way to make that happen, Brandon."

The four rode a surrey, borrowed from Thomas Macon, to the Powell House in Silver Cliff for lunch. Once there and inside, they were immediately seated. Brandon was fast becoming famous in the two counties because of this murder trial, and Chris Colt was famous everywhere.

Over fried chicken, assorted vegetables, and homemade bread, the four discussed the case, but all during the meal Brandon seemed distant, and indeed he was. There were a few things he was missing.

Suddenly he got enthusiastic. Brandon had carried his briefcase from the courthouse and now pulled some of his printed letterhead stationery out. He quickly wrote a letter and handed it to Chris.

"Colt," he exclaimed, "can you take the rails, your horse on the freight cars, the Pony Express, or whatever, and fly your way to Fort Robinson, Nebraska, and back as fast as the wind?"

Colt read the letter of introduction and grinned, saying, "I'm halfway there and back already, Brandon. You'll see to my lovely wife's comforts, sir?"

Brandon said, "Guard her with my life."

"Chris, you're leaving now?" Shirley said.

"This minute, darling. Watch how fast I get back here."

Shirley said, "What are you two cooking up?"

"He'll explain. Ladies. I'll take care of the check on the way out, and the tip."

He gave Shirley a kiss and departed quickly.

Brandon said, "Shirley, I did not want to tell Chris until he's back from Nebraska, but on top of everything else, Millard Mining Corporation's lawyers filed an injunction this morning against the Coyote Run Ranch to prevent you from doing any type of mining operations on the ranch or ceasing any such operations."

Mrs. Colt said, "I'm not certain I understand the meaning of filing an injunction."

Brandon said, "Well, technically, when you legally enjoin someone or file an injunction, in legal language, it is defined as a writ granted by a court of equity whereby one is required to do or refrain from doing a specified act."

Shirley smiled, took a sip of tea, and said, "Fine. Now, how would a normal human being say that?"

Brandon grinned. "It means Millard Mining claims that there are some legal grounds or reason for the court to order you to stop, or simply not start, any mining operations on your property."

"How can they do that?" Shirley asked.

Brandon said, "They can't do that without committing some sort of foul play somewhere. I only received a note about this from a friend right before we left the courthouse, so I do no know on what grounds they claim to attempt their obvious desire to take over your property."

Shirley said, "When can you find out?"

Brandon said, "When we go back to the courthouse, but I have some ideas what they might have up their sleeves. With that in mind, Shirley, we will prepare for it ahead of time."

He pulled out another piece of paper and began writing.

Elizabeth gave Shirley a smile and a look of obvious pride in her professional and efficient beau. Shirley smiled, but was also secretly smiling to herself, impressed and touched by the obvious love that Elizabeth felt for Brandon. There were many character traits and mannerisms that the slightly younger woman had that reminded Shirley of herself. She liked both her and Brandon Rudd and felt that they made a handsome couple who definitely should be together.

Brandon finished writing and handed the paper to Elizabeth. He said, "I put money on deposit at the telegrapher's at Western Union before the trial started. Elizabeth, will you please wire this message to the head law enforcement officer of every city and town that you know of in Colorado, Utah, New Mexico, Wyoming, and Kansas?"

"Of course, Brandon," she replied.

Brandon went on, "Then you'll want to check for replies for the next several days, starting this afternoon."

Elizabeth said, "Would it be wise to first send this message to all towns which have a major prison nearby?"

Brandon said, "Excellent idea. Yes, absolutely."

The three left the restaurant, with Shirley being escorted to the courthouse by Brandon, while Elizabeth rode with F. A. Raynolds, the president of Custer County Bank and Fremont County Bank. At Shirley Colt's request, he was glad to give Elizabeth a ride to the Western Union office in his little buggy. In fact, Mr. Raynolds was happy to do anything that the Colts requested, as they had their money deposited in Fremont County Bank in Canon City, and he knew the exact amount they had deposited, and it was considerable.

In court, a cowboy was called by the prosecution, who claimed to be a patron of the restaurant at the time of the shooting involving Man Killer. He identified himself as Reb Holder and an employee of a local ranch in South Park.

Carrington asked the expected questions of Reb Holder, and the man told about watching the gunfight from the window of the restaurant, and he gave what sounded to Brandon like a rehearsed rendition of what he had seen. His testimony implicated Man Killer as a murderer who wounded his intended victims, then walked over and blew a hole between the eyes of each one in cold blood.

Finally the judge asked, "Mr. Rudd, would you like to cross-examine the witness?"

"Indeed I would, Your Honor," he replied.

"Mr. Holder," Brandon said, smiling at the man, "how did you get the name Reb? Are you from the South?"

Reb smiled and drawled, "Yas, suh, ah'm from the Sandhills Region a North Carolina. Not too far from the Atlantic Coast in the southeastern part of the state."

Brandon said, "Been out West long?"

Reb smiled. "Yas, suh, all mah adult life."

Brandon said, "I'll bet you were eating at the Powell House that day for the same reason I do. I bet living close to the ocean growing up, you acquired a taste for fresh lobster tail."

Reb smiled more broadly. "Yas, suh, I jest love lobster tail. It's my favorite food."

Brandon said, "So that's why you, a ranch hand, came all the way to Silver Cliff from South Park? To eat lobster tail?"

Reb stumbled a little. "No, suh, uh, ah din't work in South Park at that time."

Brandon smiled more warmly and said, "Tell me, who do you punch cows for in South Park?"

Reb seemed to relax a little, replying, "Ira and Joshua Mulock, suh."

Brandon walked over to him and leaned forward, his hands on the walnut wood separating him and the witness.

Looking into Reb's eyes, Brandon said, "Just how long have you worked for the Mulock brothers?"

The cowboy looked down, shuffled his feet, and replied, " 'Bout a week an' a half."

Brandon walked away from the witness stand and stood by the jury box, saying, "I'm sorry. That was kind of hard to hear. Would you repeat how long you've worked for the Mulock cattle operation?"

Loudly now, Reb said, " 'Bout a week or so."

Brandon said, "Oh, well, where did you work before that?"

Reb said, "An outfit in Canon City."

Brandon said, "What's the name of that outfit?"

Carrington arose saying, "Objection, Your Honor. This is totally irrelevant and has nothing to do with witnessing a murder."

Brandon said, "Your Honor, if you will grant me a little leeway, I'll show relevance shortly and illustrate how this leads to a credibility issue."

"Very well, Mr. Rudd," the judge said, "I'll work with you a little here. Objection overruled. Mr. Holder, answer the question."

Disgusted, Carrington sat down.

"What question, Jedge?" Reb asked.

Brandon said, "What outfit did you work for in Canon City?"

Reb said, "Millard Mining Corporation."

Rudd said, "Oh, you mean the outfit owned by the only other witness to the shooting, Preston Millard, the man seated right over there."

Reb said, "I s'pose so, but that ain't got nuthin' ta do with it, mistah."

Brandon said, "I believe it has plenty to do with it. Tell me, Mr. Holder, were you working for Mr. Millard at the time that the shooting occurred?"

"Yas, suh, so what?" Beads of perspiration now appeared on Reb's brow.

He wiped his forehead and Brandon made it a point to say, "Hot, isn't it?"

Reb seemed relieved with the easy irrelevant question, saying, "Yas, suh."

Brandon said, "That's funny. I feel quite comfortable."

Reb started squirming and kept looking over at Preston Millard.

Brandon said, "Were you paid to testify here today?"

Reb cleared his throat and said, "No, suh. Hell, no."

Brandon went on, "Why did you leave the employ of Preston Millard?"

Reb said, "Wal, uh, Ah don't right know. He din't need me no more."

"Except to testify?" Brandon said.

"Objection!" Carrington yelled, jumping up.

The judge said, "Sustained. Watch your step, Mr. Rudd."

Brandon said, "Yes, Your Honor."

Brandon said, "Now, let me make sure I have it clear here. You were eating lobster tail at the restaurant and saw the accused shoot Max Barnes and Bull Smith between the eyes after wounding them in the shoulders?"

Reb said, "Yas, suh."

Brandon said, "Did you work as a miner?"

"Naw," the man said, "a security guard."

Brandon went on, "But while your boss was outside the restaurant having his life threatened in a gun fight, you watch from a window inside the restaurant, still enjoying a relaxing meal?"

"I strongly object, Your Honor," Carrington raged, on his feet once again. "My able opponent is leading the witness."

Brandon smiled and said, "Mr. Carrington, if you

feel I am an able opponent, why do you keep inter-
rupting me with these stupid objections?"

Everyone in the courtroom chuckled and even
Judge Offenbacher had a smile on his face.

He rapped his gavel, saying halfheartedly, "Order."

Brandon said, "Your Honor, I am not leading the
witness. I am just clarifying his answers thus far."

"Objection overruled," the judge said. "I've got
my eye on you, Mr. Rudd. One false move . . ."

Brandon said, "Mr. Holder, if you were a security
man for Mr. Millard, why in the world would you sit
in a restaurant watching him being assaulted and
possibly gunned down in a gunfight. Are you coward?"

Holder jumped up, reaching for a gun on his hip
that wasn't there. His face was beet red and he
stared daggers at the handsome, smiling attorney.
Between curled lips, he hissed, "Nobody calls me a
coward, ya gussied-up purty-boy sumbitch."

The gavel was banged down hard by Judge Offenbacher, who said, "Order! Order in the court!"

Pointing the gavel at Holder, he said, "You, sir, sit
down. I'll have you jailed if I see one more outburst
such as that. Do I make myself perfectly clear?"

"Yeah, Jedge," Reb said, sitting down.

Brandon walked up to Reb Holder and leaned
across the front of the witness stand, his face inches
from the irate cowboy.

The lawyer said, "Mr. Holder, I eat all the time
at the Powell House, a very find restaurant and
hotel. And they do not serve lobster tail. Why
don't you tell the court who paid you to lie here today?"

Holder jumped up and raged, "The hell with you
. . . with ya'll. I'm leavin'. I don't need this!"

There was a loud cocking sound as Reb jumped

out of the witness box and started for the door. The right half of Judge Offenbacher's black robe was tossed aside, and he held a wood-handled Starr double-action Army .44 revolver in his right hand. It was pointed at Holder's body.

The judge said, "I warned you. Deputy, escort this man to the rooming accommodations that Custer County just decided to provide him with. We will talk later, sir, about your contempt of court and maybe some charges of perjury. By the way, you are discharged, Mr. Holder."

The trial continued for several more days with several more prosecution witnesses, including Preston Millard, who was unflappable when it came to cross-examination. That was until Brandon Rudd brought something out in court.

Brandon walked over and picked up several pieces of paper, showed them to Carrington, then the judge.

He said, "Your Honor, I would like to enter these as pieces of evidence for the defense."

The judge nodded and Brandon showed them to Preston Millard.

The attorney said, "Mr. Millard, do you know what these pieces of paper are?"

Preston said, "Yes, one is an injunction signed by the good judge here filed by my corporation against the Coyote Run Ranch. The other is a deed my corporation owns to all the mineral and water rights on the same ranch."

Brandon said, "Who owns the ranch?"

Millard replied, "Mr. and Mrs. Chris Colt."

Brandon said, "Who are the other owners?"

Preston Millard said, "I don't know what you mean."

Brandon said, "I mean who are the other owners of the Coyote Run Ranch?"

Millard said, "Just Colt."

Brandon held up another piece of paper, which he showed to Carrington, then the judge, and finally to Millard, explaining it was another piece of evidence for the defense.

Brandon said, "Can you tell the court what this piece of paper is?"

Millard said, "It looks like a deed to the Coyote Run Ranch."

Brandon said, "And does it not have a date of the year before last, almost two years ago today?"

Millard said, "Yes, I suppose so."

Brandon said, "Would you, sir, kindly read to the court the names of the owners exactly as it appears on the deed?"

Millard looked it over and sighed, then said, "It states that sixty percent of the ranch is owned by Christopher Columbus Colt and Shirley Ann (née Ebert) Colt, thirty percent is owned by Joshua Colt, no middle name given, and ten percent is owned by Man Killer, a Nez Percé Indian of the band of Chief Joseph of the Wallowa Valley, Oregon."

Brandon said, "Well, isn't that the defendant you are testifying against?"

Millard said, "I suppose it is."

Brandon said, "You suppose it is. Wouldn't it be most convenient for you, sir, if one of the owners, at least, was out of the way by maybe dying of hemp fever? Namely Man Killer?"

Again, Carrington jumped to his feet. "Objection, Your Honor! He is questioning the motives of morality of my witness. This may indeed be grounds for slander."

Brandon said, "Or a long jail term or rope, maybe, for your witness, when I prove my case."

The judge rapped his gavel on his desk and said,

"Order in the courtroom. Mr. Rudd, watch those snide remarks, sir. Objection sustained."

"No more questions right now, Your Honor," Brandon said, "but I will probably want to recall this witness at a later time."

"Mr. Millard," the judge said, "you may step down, but avail yourself to this court, as you will soon be called back upon the stand."

Preston Millard said, "Of course, Your Honor, I'm at your beck and call."

For the next two days, as Brandon presented his case, he paraded numerous character witnesses testifying on behalf of Man Killer, including the sheriffs of both Custer and Fremont counties, several county commissioners, lawyers, businessmen, ministers, Joshua Colt, Shirley Colt, and two retired cavalry generals. Everyone spoke about Man Killer in glowing terms.

When he put Man Killer on the stand, the young Indian spoke honestly and in a straightforward manner. Carrington, in cross-examination, tried everything he could to rattle the scout, but Man Killer was cool, calm, and collected. Seated with Shirley Colt, Jennifer Banta stared at Man Killer on the witness stand and love oozed from her gaze. Shirley glanced at her with an amused look and saw the way she viewed the young Nez Percé. Shirley was reminded of the way Elizabeth and Brandon looked at each other, and the way she and Colt did. She also noticed that every time Man Killer looked her way, which was quite often, a smile appeared on his face. Brandon redirected with Man Killer after Carrington's cross-examination. This was only done to stall for time and control the situation because of the telegram Colt had sent him.

Mrs. Canterbury suddenly came into the courtroom, and the gray-haired lady rushed forward, handing a note to Elizabeth. Elizabeth read it, a big smile appearing on her face, and signaled for Brandon to come to the defense table.

Brandon turned saying, "Thank you, Man Killer. No further questions, Your Honor."

The judge said, "Mr. Man Killer, you may step down."

Man Killer, in shackles and cuffs, was held by one deputy and led to his seat at Brandon's table.

Brandon said, "Your Honor, I have a surprise witness who has just arrived from Fort Robinson, Nebraska, to testify."

Carrington jumped up, yelling, "Objection, Your Honor, I object."

Judge Offenbacher, mildly amused, said, "On what grounds, sir?"

Carrington was frustrated and said, "I wasn't told anything about this."

With dry humor, the judge said, "That, sir, is why we have the term 'surprise witness.' Who is your witness, Mr. Rudd?"

Brandon looked at the back of the courtroom and the doors opened with a crash as Chris Colt, with trail dust and a week's growth of beard and dirt on his face, walked in, followed by a contingent of war-bonneted Indians and several cavalry soldiers.

Brandon said, "Your Honor, I call as my next witness the honorable Chief Joseph of the Nez Percé nation, currently held in Fort Robinson, Nebraska, but formerly of the Wallowa Valley in Oregon."

As the calm-faced chief walked forward, he looked deep into Brandon's eyes and his eyes seemed to light up. He was resplendent in his eagle feather double-trailer war bonnet and other colorful accoutrements.

The judge leaned forward and said, "Are you, sir,

the same Chief Joseph who led the U.S. cavalry across seventeen hundred miles a couple years ago, outfoxing them at every turn, while they tried to kill your women and children?"

Joseph said, "I tried to help my people get to Sitting Bull of the Lakota. We were stopped by General Bear Coat [Miles]."

Joseph was sworn in and sat in the witness stand. Chris sat in next to his wife, and they held hands.

Brandon said, "Sir, will you please tell the court your full name?"

Joseph said, "My name cannot be pronounced well by your people. It is Hin-Ma-Too-Yah-Lat-Kekht. It means Thunder-Traveling-to-Loftier-Mountain-Heights. My Christian name is Joseph. Some of your people call me Young Joseph, because my father was also named Joseph by your missionaries. I grew up in the land of my father and his father before him in the Wallowa Valley. My land was stolen by the grandfather in Washington."

Brandon pointed at Man Killer and said, "Do you know the defendant?"

Joseph said, "Yes, a fine warrior. He is like a son to me. His name is Man Killer. Why is he tied in iron ropes? Is he not being a good Indian for your people? Does he not do good tricks like a proper dog?"

Colt grinned broadly.

Brandon said, "Probably not, Chief Joseph. How did Man Killer get his name?"

Joseph said, "He was a young boy named Ezekiel. He and his brother were guarding a horse herd which was stolen by some bad white men. Ezekiel and his brother tracked them many days' ride from our village to steal back the horses. Ezekiel's brother was murdered by the white men and Ezekiel was stabbed and tortured, but he fought and never gave up. He became friends with the great warrior Wamble Uncha, who you call Chris Colt. He sits there."

Chris blushed and Shirley squeezed his hand.

Joseph continued, "The sight from the mighty Colt's eyes were taken by a great bear, but Ezekiel became Colt's eyes. They fought the bad white men and many more who came to kill Colt. They won and rode many days to return to us our horses. I changed Ezekiel's name to Man Killer, a proud and noble name for a warrior such as him."

Man Killer felt a strange lump in his throat and sat up very straight.

Brandon looked at the judge and said, "Your Honor, I not only want Chief Joseph here as a character witness for Man Killer, but as an expert witness on the tribal traditions, laws, and mores of the Nez Percé nation."

Judge Offenbacher said, "Well, Mr. Rudd, if Chief Joseph here could not be considered an expert witness about the societal lifestyle of the Nez Percé Indians, I suppose no man could."

Brandon said, "What happens to a brave in your tribe who tells lies?"

Joseph said, "Men of the Nez Percé do not tell lies. If a man did such a thing, he could no longer be a Nez Percé."

"Why?" Brandon asked.

Joseph said, "There is no honor in it."

"Is it that important to you?" Brandon asked.

Joseph looked at the jury and said, "If things such as honor were not important to a man, then nothing else would have importance."

Brandon, knowing that the chief's eloquence would impress judge and jury alike, asked him to expound.

Joseph said, "There are many good things that men can share with each other: a battle victory, a good hunt, a meal, looking at a beautiful woman or the setting sun, a dance, a shared story, or a quiet smoke. But without honor none of these things can be shared, because a man with no honor is not a man. He would no longer be a Nez Percé but a man with no people."

Brandon said, "If Man Killer, the defendant over there, is found guilty of two counts of cold-blooded murder, he can be hanged by a rope being put around his neck and he would be dropped from a high place so the rope would break his neck. Knowing this, Man Killer said he was innocent. Would he do so because he was afraid of hanging?"

Joseph said, "The only fear Man Killer has is to not walk the spirit trail when he dies. If he had no honor, he would not walk the spirit trail. If he is asked and says he is innocent if he truly is a murderer, then he is hanged anyway: He would not walk the spirit trail. His spirit would wander forever, lost and alone."

Brandon said, "So you're saying he would not lie, even if he wanted to, for fear of being damned."

"Objection, Your Honor," Carrington fumed, jumping to his feet once more. "Chief Joseph is already internationally renowned as one of the world's greatest orators. Mr. Rudd does not have to act as a translator and twist it so the jury hears what he wants."

Joseph turned to the judge and said, "Who is this man? He speaks like a fool."

Red-faced, Carrington sat down.

Offenbacher grinned and said, "Objection overruled."

Joseph, clearly perturbed, looked at Carrington

and said, "This man who is talking to me is a friend of my friends Colt and Man Killer. When we first looked at each other this day, his eyes looked into mine and mine into his, and I saw a man of honor and truth. Yet you call him a liar. If I were him, I would remove your tongue from your mouth with my knife."

Carrington got very red-faced and he took a long swallow of water, while trying to think of what to say.

Brandon broke the ice and got chuckles from all by saying, "Thank you, Chief Joseph. Maybe that's not a bad idea if the prosecution gets too carried away. I'll remember that tactic. Thank you, sir, and thank you for your comments. No further questions."

Judge Offenbacher said, "Mr. Carrington, cross-examination?"

Carrington got up and tried to confidently stride over to the jury and then directly to Chief Joseph.

Joseph looked at the jury and said, "He tries to walk straight and tall to hide his fear."

The courtroom broke up with uproarious laughter until Judge Offenbacher finally rapped his gavel and called for order.

Joseph looked at the judge and said, "That wooden war club might be a good thing for a chief. You make all here get quiet. I should have one to hit on the heads of my people sometimes, so they will listen. Maybe someone should hit the grandfather in Washington on the head so he will listen to my people."

There were more chuckles and murmurs. Judge Offenbacher pulled out his pistol again and laid it down where the gavel lay.

Smiling, he handed the gavel to Joseph, saying, "I

would be honored if you would take this wooden war club from me as a gift."

Joseph took it and gazed at it proudly saying, "This is a good thing."

Tucking the gavel in his belt, he removed a conch shell and bone-hair pipe choker necklace from his neck and handed it to the judge.

Before the judge could protest taking a gift from a witness, Joseph said, "When chiefs from different tribes can give each other gifts instead of bullets, that has honor, too."

Carrington said, "Chief Joseph, we kind of got off on the wrong foot. You are very famous and celebrated, sir, and I do not want you to think I do not respect you."

Joseph said, "I know about your court. You cross-examine. You will ask me questions and speak to make me look bad in the eyes of those people. The grandfather in Washington took away my weapons, but Colt there is a great warrior and my friend and brother. If you call me a liar, he will cut your tongue from your mouth."

Colt nodded affirmatively. Judge Offenbacher and others smiled.

Carrington cleared his throat, saying "Ah, no questions, Your Honor. Thank you, Chief."

Judge Offenbacher said, "Chief Joseph, sir, you may return home to Fort Robinson. I am deeply honored to meet you and be in your presence. I read about you and your people every day during your long trek and, like many others, hoped you would make it to Canada or get yours lands back. Thank you for coming here to testify, and have a safe journey back to Nebraska."

"I came because Colt asked me. That is what friends do. That is called honor," Joseph said, then added simply, "Fort Robinson is not my home. It is my prison, given to me by the grandfather in Washington. It is the gift the white man gives you if you try to lead your people and honor your ancestors."

With that, he turned and walked from the courtroom without looking left or right, except to smile at Colt and Shirley, who joined him at his side. Even the soldiers guarding him treated him with great respect, even awe. Man Killer carefully looked around and brushed a tear from his eye.

Brandon stood and said, "Your honor, I have another witness I would like to recall. Dr. Edmund J. Stanlick, the Fremont County coroner, who also serves Custer County, since you have no coroner."

The judge said, "Is he here?"

Brandon said, "Yes, he is, Your Honor."

Dr. Stanlick came forward carrying a piece of paper.

The judge said, "Doctor, I remind you that you are still under oath."

The doctor said, "Yes sir," and sat down.

Brandon said, "Your Honor, as you know, yesterday I asked you to sign an order to have Dr. Stanlick exhume the bodies of Max Barnes and Bull Smith."

The judge nodded and Carrington jumped up, saying, "I object. What does that mean?"

The judge said, "It means that the good doctor here dug up the remains of the two decedents, Mr. Barnes and Mr. Smith."

Carrington made a face, saying, "I never heard of that, Judge. Can that be done?"

Judge Offenbacher said, "I believe it already has, Mr. Carrington."

Colt and Shirley walked back into the courtroom, along with Joshua Colt and quietly sat down.

Brandon went on, "Dr. Stanlick, did you exhume the bodies of Max Barnes and Bull Smith?"

The coroner said, "Yes, I did."

Brandon said, "And did you cut them open and dig out the bullets?"

The doctor said, "Yes, I did."

Carrington jumped to his feet. "This is blasphemous! Cutting open dead bodies! I object strenuously, very strenuously, Your Honor!"

"Careful, Mr. Carrington," the judge said, "Mr. Rudd may want to take Chief Joseph's advice. Objection overruled."

There were numerous low chuckles throughout the room.

Brandon continued, "And what did you learn, Dr. Stanlick?"

The coroner said, "The bullets I took out of the shoulders of both men were big and looked like they came from a .44 or .45, but the bullets I took out of their skulls—"

There were murmurs. The judge rapped his gun butt.

The doctor resumed. "Those bullets were much smaller and so were the bullet holes between their eyes."

"Could those bullets possibly have been .44s or .45s or maybe pieces of them?" Brandon asked.

The coroner said, "Absolutely not. The holes and the bullets looked to be probably .32-caliber."

Brandon went on, "When you conducted your inquest, sir, you read the report by the arresting officers about what weapons were taken from the accused?"

The doctor said, "Yes, indeed I did."

Brandon said, "And was a .32-caliber weapon found on the accused or in his possession?"

The coroner responded, "No, sir, nor was one found anywhere near the scene."

Brandon said, "Only Colt .45 Peacemakers, correct?"

The coroner said, "That's right."

"No further questions," Brandon said, sitting down beside Man Killer and giving him a reassuring pat on the arm.

"Cross-examination?" the judge queried of Carrington.

The prosecution stayed seated and said, "Are you absolutely positive of this evidence, Doctor? Couldn't you be mistaken?"

"Absolutely not," the coroner replied.

"Then," Carrington added, "where is the murder weapon? Couldn't Man Killer have thrown it away?"

"No," the coroner came back, "the area was thoroughly combed for more weapons. It couldn't have happened."

Carrington said, "Couldn't?"

"Well," Dr. Stanlick came back, "I suppose if there was some small hiding place that nobody thought of . . . but that is extremely unlikely."

Carrington smiled, saying, "No further questions."

The judge said, "You may step down. This court is recessed until eight o'clock tomorrow morning."

He rapped his gun butt on the desk and everyone stood up. He holstered the gun and walked from the courtroom. Man Killer was led away and Brandon and Elizabeth joined the Colts and Jennifer. Brandon was pleased to see his old friend Tex Westchester seated in the back of the courtroom, and he waved him over.

Tex walked up to the group, a noticeable limp bothering him. He said, "I'll tell ya what, lawyer boy. I been a watchin' ya, and I gotta say, you kin shore fork this kinda bronc and ride it. I didn't know half them fancy words ya used, but I could tell ya was shore beatin up on thet old Carrington dude."

Brandon said, "Tex, from you, that means an awful lot to me. Come on, everyone. Dinner is on me."

Elizabeth said, "Where do you want to eat?"

"Let's eat at the Powell House," Brandon said. "I would like to find out if they serve lobster tail. I've never had it."

Shirley Colt said, "But you said in court—"

"He was under oath. Not me."

Brandon discussed strategy for the next day for some time with the group and then bid them adieu. Chris rented a room at the Powell House, and he and Shirley spent the night, after he got a full shave and a hot bath. She washed out his buckskins, trousers, socks, and scarf, hanging them on the windowsill of their room on the fourth floor of the plush hotel.

Like many previous nights working on the case, Brandon, too, spent the night at the Powell House, and Elizabeth did as well. Brandon was careful to rent her a room on a totally different floor at the opposite end of the hotel from him. But before he fell asleep each night, his mind pictured numerous scenes of her sharing his room with him.

Elizabeth loved Brandon before, but by now, she was in total awe of him. If this man did not marry her, she thought she would absolutely explode like a cannon shot. Each day, the courtroom was loading up with more watchers and even Thomas Macon and Anson Rudd came up from Canon City to watch the young man's performance, even though Thomas Macon was also establishing a practice in Denver 120 miles away, which was now consuming a lot of his time.

"Your Honor," Brandon said, "I have a surprise witness."

"Jumping Jehosaphat!" Carrington blurted.

Judge Offenbacher said, "I suppose it will be actress Lillie Langtry, maybe, or perhaps the President."

Brandon smiled. "No, Your Honor. Defense calls Lucky Charlie Silverman to the stand."

Sheriff Schoolfield came in from the hallway, escorting a cuffed and shackled prisoner, who was dressed like a dirty unkempt riverboat gambler. He walked him to the witness stand, where he was uncuffed and sworn in.

He identified himself as Luciano Charles Silverman but had gone by the nickname of Lucky all his life, and even explained that his mother was Italian and gave him his first name, which he never used "on account of" he couldn't hardly pronounce it correctly himself.

Brandon said, "Mr. Silverman, you do not look so lucky to me right now. Can you tell me why you are here in shackles and cuffs, a prisoner of our illustrious sheriff?"

"Yep," Lucky said, "I got caught again over in Durango forging some bank notes, and they're gonna send me back to prison."

"Back to prison?" Brandon said.

"Yep," he went on, "been in Yuma twicet. Don't reckon I'd enjoy the trip again. Maybe they'll put me in Canon City this time."

"What have you been arrested for each time you have been arrested—the same charge?"

"Yep, forgery. Usually don't get caught, but a few times I have," Lucky said, adding, "I'm the best, though. Ask anyone."

Brandon pointed at Preston Millard and said, "Ever meet that man before?"

Lucky said, "Shore did. That's Preston Millard."

"How did you meet Mr. Millard?" Brandon asked.

Carrington stayed seated, but called out, "Objection, Your Honor. No relevance to this case."

Brandon said, "It has great relevance, and I'll show that, Your Honor, if I may proceed."

Offenbacher said, "You may. Objection overruled."

Lucky said, "When I got out of Yuma the last time, I was hunting for a job. Even thought about straightening my life out and repenting for all my sorry ways. A friend who was in the hellhole with me had tole me to look him up when I got out. He was a crooked banker and made him some money in his day, too. Anyhow, he told me about this rich bird up Canon City way he knew who needed a good forger. He sent me up, only Millard had me meet him down at Trinidad. He give me a thousand bucks to fake him a deed for mineral and water rights to a ranch up here. It was called the Coyote Run. Remembered that, 'cause it was such a catchy name."

Preston Millard jumped up and hollered, "That's a lie! I never met this man before. Somebody's bought him off. He's using me to try to save his own neck."

The judge rapped a new gavel and said, "I'll thank you, Mr. Millard, to sit down and keep as quiet as a churchmouse. You also are not to leave this building, or room, for that matter."

Lucky just laughed, saying, "Do I look like someone who's made some kind of deal? I'm headed back to prison stripes."

Brandon said, "Then why did you agree to testify here today?"

"Well," Lucky answered, "I heard you, or someone from your office, sent a wire to Yuma, then to Durango, inquiring about anybody convicted of forgery, and the good folks in both places sang like birds. When I found out about the case, I was glad to testify, for one big reason."

"What's that?" Brandon asked.

Lucky lost his smile and said, "I ain't no good, mister. I am a forger—a damned good one, and I guess proud of it in a queer sort of way, but I ain't no murderer and won't have no truck with murderers. Most of the time I've never even carried a gun. Used my wits to keep me alive all these years."

Brandon showed him the deed to the Coyote Run, saying, "Mr. Silverman, is this the deed you forged?"

Lucky said, "It shore is. That is definitely it, but I don't want to be tied in with no killin's."

Brandon said, "You aren't. Thank you. Your witness," he said to Carrington.

Carrington said, "You're facing another long stretch behind bars, Mr. Silverman, aren't you?"

Silverman said, " 'Fraid so, mister."

"So you would probably say anything to save your neck from the hangman, wouldn't you?"

"I suppose so, but—"

Carrington cut him off. "Thank you. No further questions."

The judge said, "You may step down. Next witness."

Brandon walked up and said, "Your Honor, because I have to make some preparations for the next witness, and there is a man's life at stake here, if it please the court, may I ask for a recess until right after lunch?"

Offenbacher thought for a minute and said, "First, who is your next witness."

Brandon said, "The defense would like to recall Preston Millard to the stand."

The judge said, "All right, Mr. Rudd, you get your wish. The court is in recess until one P.M. sharp. Mr. Millard, in light of what's been said here under oath today, you are to remain in this courtroom during the recess. Do you have any employees here today?"

Millard scowled. "My attorney."

The judge smiled, saying, "Perfect. He can go fetch you lunch and bring it to you." The judge rapped his gavel and walked out.

Walking from the stone courthouse, Elizabeth said, "What preparations do we have to make for Preston Millard?"

Brandon replied, "None, except for a short talk with my friend Colt here. I knew the judge would ask me who my next witness was going to be, and I knew he wouldn't let Millard leave, so this will give him a chance to sweat for a few more hours before I question him. He's used to winning and being on top, but that building back there contains my battlefield."

Colt said, "And you can stand with the best of the generals I've seen, Brandon."

Brandon hadn't eaten lunch and his stomach was grumbling as he paced from the witness stand to the jury box and back.

He walked over to the witness stand and leaned against it, saying, "Mr. Millard, have you ever heard of the Lost Brother Mine?"

Preston Millard had sat through the long lunch

recess and had plenty of time to sweat, but also to think. He knew that Brandon Rudd would try to rattle him, but told himself he mustn't let it happen.

During lunch, when Preston sat there thinking with guards at the doors of the courtroom, he thought back to a time when he was in his early twenties. Because things had gotten a little hot for him around Tombstone, he had moved on to Cheyenne in Wyoming Territory and decided to use a different name for a while.

This was in Preston's early days, before he was a man of substantial assets. He felt it was a good time to acquire them, though. To do so, he was quite prepared to utilize any means possible, and he did.

Preston Millard—or, as he was known at that time, Pete Miller—figured that the best way to fill his coffers would be to empty the coffers of others. He prepared a burlap bag to tie over his head, with just eye holes and a mouth hole cut into it. A kerchief would be tied around his neck to hold the bag tight over his head and keep it in place.

On numerous robberies, Millard not only took the strongbox from the stagecoaches he robbed, but he also lined up the passengers and emptied their pockets, purses, travel bags, and even took jewelry off their bodies. In so doing, Preston Millard went out of his way to be very rough with the passengers. He felt that if he did this, the word would get around and people would be too intimidated to argue with him when he held them up. On top of that, he also had a mean streak and simply enjoyed frightening or hurting people.

On one of his holdups, he made the mistake of robbing a stage carrying one of the deputy marshals from Cheyenne. The man spotted Preston three nights later at a Cheyenne saloon wearing the exact same clothing.

The deputy came up behind Preston and stuck a Russian .44 in the small of his back and said, "Why don'tcha jist reach down and grab thet hogleg a yourn and try to spin roun' an' plug me, boy? I shore would love to put a hole in ya thet a teamster could drive a full load through."

Pete Miller raised his hands and said, "Why, I'm not going to give you any trouble, Deputy. You apparently have mistaken me for someone else, but I will fully cooperate with whatever your investigation."

The deputy said, "I come up behind ya and stuck this iron in yer back, so how did ya know I was a deputy?"

In actuality, Preston spoke at some length with the deputy when he held up the stage, but he spent even more time striking the lawman several times, in several ways, with his pistol. The deputy had a very gravelly voice that one would not forget easily. He had to quickly cover his tracks.

Thinking fast, Millard said, "Why, I saw your reflection on those bottles there on the shelf."

The deputy looked up and did see his reflection, but it was distorted and hard to make out. After that, Preston was let go in court. In fact, the case was thrown out, because he had hired two money-hungry cowboys to testify that he had been playing poker with them when the robbery had taken place. The other reason was because of the mask that completely covered his face.

This episode had two major effects on his life. One was that he developed even less respect for the system of law and the courts. Second, he developed the attitude that he would be virtually invincible as far as breaking the law was concerned if he simply bribed phony witnesses whenever he needed to.

Preston Millard was concerned now but not really worried. He was just too cocky to think that he was going to get beaten by Brandon Rudd and the Colorado legal system. He would just have to be cool and figure out who else he could bribe to help him. Besides, he had already made contingency plans, just in case everything came unraveled in court. Millard really worshiped money and figured that, in the end, money could make one come out on top of any situation.

Brandon said, "Mr. Millard, maybe you didn't hear me. Have you ever heard of the Lost Brother Mine?"

"No, I haven't," Preston Millard said.

Brandon said, "Now, wait. Let me understand this. You own a large successful mining concern, have spent a number of years in the mining business, and almost everyone in the southern Colorado area has heard about the Lost Brother Mine, but you have not heard of it. Is that correct?"

Millard said, "That's correct."

Brandon said, "Have you heard of a local man from Ula, named William Perkins, who goes by the moniker of Moccasin Bill?"

Preston Millard hesitated a little too long then said, "Yeah, I suppose I've seen him around. He wears Injun moccasins all the time and guides hunters up in the Sangre de Cristo Mountains, right?"

Brandon said, "Now, I can bring Moccasin Bill in here to testify, but maybe you can save us some time and trouble."

That statement let Preston Millard know that he better not try to lie out of this answer.

Brandon went on, "Didn't Moccasin Bill tell you that he had discovered the Lost Brother Mine, and it was really on Spread Eagle Peak instead of on Horn Peak like most people thought?"

Millard said, "Yeah, he showed me some nuggets, some large ones, and told me the story. Is there something wrong with being a good businessman?"

"No," Brandon said, "just being a murderer."

Carrington jumped up again. "Objection, Your Honor! Is Mr. Rudd going to be allowed to insinuate that the witness is a murderer?"

"No, he's not," Offenbacher said. "Objection sustained. Mr. Rudd, I believe you owe the witness an apology for that last remark."

Brandon smiled and said, "Mr. Millard, if you are not a murderer, I apologize."

"Mr. Rudd!" Judge Offenbacher fumed. "I'm warning you."

Brandon said, "Yes, Your Honor."

Brandon paced again. He walked back over to Preston Millard and looked at him, shaking his head and smiling.

Brandon stuck one hand in his pocket and stuck the other one forward to offer his hand, saying, "Mr. Millard, I apologize if I offended you with my remark about being a murderer."

Preston Millard was given no choice whatsoever. If he didn't shake hands with Brandon, how would he look to the judge and jury? He stuck out his hand and shook.

Brandon Rudd yelled, "Colt!"

Brandon squeezed Millard's hand and with his other pulled out the knife he had used to slash the

Mona Lisa print. As everyone screamed in shock and disbelief, the blade was quickly shoved straight up the sleeve of Preston Millard, and Brandon ripped it backward, tearing the sleeve from the elbow down.

Millard jumped back and Chris Colt said quietly, "Huh-uh."

Preston Millard looked at Colt's cocked Peacemaker pointed at his face. He froze, and Brandon Rudd removed the derringer from the contraption strapped to Preston's wrist. Colt nodded at the deputy sheriff standing in the corner and holstered his gun, since the deputy had finally gotten his out. The lawman walked forward, holding his gun on Preston Millard. Brandon held the man's arm up, showing the contraption strapped to his forearm.

Brandon said, "Your Honor, when he raises his arm like this, the derringer would slide back into this track, then lowering the arm would drop it right into his hand."

Brandon let go of Preston's arm, and the man sat down glaring at the attorney. The deputy came up to the witness stand and put cuffs on Preston's wrists. He escorted him away from the stand.

"Your Honor, I would like to call Christopher Columbus Colt to the stand."

"Not wearing that arsenal of weapons, he's not," Judge Offenbacher fumed, still upset over what had just happened. "You hear me, Mr. Colt? You're lucky I don't toss you in the hoosegow for bringing a gun into the courtroom."

"Yes, sir," Chris said, grinning as he handed his guns to his wife and walked forward.

Colt was sworn in and then sat down.

Brandon said, "Judge, I want to declare Mr. Colt as an expert witness."

The judge said, "In what field?"

Brandon said, "Guns."

Judge Offenbacher smiled at Carrington and said, "Now, Mr. Prosecutor, considering his last name is Colt, I dare you to jump up and object."

Brandon smiled, then looked at Preston Millard behind held in the corner and sulking. "By the way, Mr. Millard, I was just kidding about offering my apologies for calling you a murderer."

He looked at Colt and went on, handing Chris the gun off the judge's desk, "Mr. Colt, can you identify the caliber of this weapon?"

Colt looked at it and said, "Sure, Brandon. That's a Reid's My Friend .32-caliber Knucklebuster. It is a .32-caliber derringer and you can use it like brass knuckles, too. That's why it's shaped with that handle so you can put your fingers through."

Brandon said, "Thank you, Mr. Colt. Your Honor, I would like to move the court to declare a mistrial and drop all charges against my client."

Carrington jumped up. "Your Honor, what about the charges we also filed about the deputies who were killed in the posse?"

Offenbacher said, "Mr. Carrington, those men were not duly sworn in deputies. They were an armed drunken mob pursuing a very dangerous but innocent man. Those boys knew what they were up against and probably got what was coming to them. Mr. Man Killer, you have been done a great disservice by that sneaky scoundrel over there. Wait, deputy, unlock his cuffs and shackles."

The deputy removed Man Killer's cuffs and shackles.

The judge continued, "Man Killer, there are many of us who are white who look down upon the red man, and there are some who hate the red man, but

I would say by the parade of witnesses of some bearing and stature and the glowing tributes they lavished upon you ... well, I think that indicates you are indeed a very fine citizen no matter what your color. You also are probably just as distinguished in the Indian community as well."

There was a brief noise outside the room, and the doors were kicked open as eight men burst into the courtroom with shotguns and rifles. The lead man was Wolf Keeler, and the first thing he did was shoot the deputy guarding Preston Millard. The man behind him, standing close to seven feet tall, shot the guard who had just unlocked Man Killer's steel bonds.

Women screamed and Wolf yelled, "Shut up!"

One of the men ran over to Preston, fumbled through the dead deputy's pockets, and got the key out for the cuffs and shackles, unlocking his leader. Preston took the man's gun and walked forward, lips curled back over his teeth. He aimed the gun directly at Brandon's head and the lawyer stared at him.

The silence in the courtroom was so thick it could be cut with a knife.

Preston, seething, said, "You cost me a fortune, lawyer, you cursed devil. Well, now you can go to hell."

He stuck the pistol up to Brandon's forehead and Chris Colt started to jump up, but the tall outlaw pointed a rifle at Colt, cocking it. Chris sat back down, a concerned look on his face.

Brandon was sweating, but he said without fear, "Millard, if I go to hell, I'll soon see you there."

Preston stuck the barrel against Brandon's forehead and laughed. "We'll see." Then he squeezed the trigger.

Elizabeth jumped up and screamed, "Brandon!" at the top of her lungs.

The click seemed as loud as a gunshot itself, but the bullet didn't fire.

The tall man said, "At's awright, boss, git outta here. I'll plug 'im. I always wanted to kill me a lawyer."

Preston raced toward the door and said over his shoulder, "The judge carries a sidearm!"

Wolf walked to the judge and removed his gun, tossing it in the corner, while the tall man raised his carbine and aimed it at Brandon's face. This time Colt could move a little. His right arm came up fast and went over his shoulder while he reached down his back between his shoulder blades. His hand whipped forward and a large scalpel-sharp horn-handled bowie knife turned over several times in the air and stuck right in the tall man's breastbone, going halfway to the hilt.

The big man dropped the gun and grabbed the knife handle with both hands, trying to yank it free. In the meantime, Man Killer ran across the room, jumped up, his foot touching the railing separating the gallery of the courtroom from the judicial section. He leaped from the railing and his two feet struck out, the right one hitting the end of the knife blade and driving it all the way to the breastbone. The giant let out a death scream, and Man Killer froze as another outlaw cocked a gun and held it on him. The rest of the gang ran out the door of the courtroom, and they could be heard riding off on their horses. The last one slipped out the door and shoved a large steel pipe through the handles of the double doors. He ran out, jumped on his horse, and took off after the others.

In the courtroom, while several men tried to shove the door open, Chris Colt ran to his wife, who handed him his guns. Man Killer stepped on the dead giant's chest and yanked the knife free. He wiped it on the man's shirt and tossed it to Chris Colt. Man Killer bent over the dead deputy near him and started unbuckling the gun belt.

Judge Offenbacher stood up and yelled, "All charges against Man Killer are dropped. You and Chris Colt are hereby deputized to pursue those men and bring in any or all of them dead or alive."

Chris nodded, as did Man Killer, as he buckled on the dead deputy's six-gun. He nodded at Colt and smiled briefly at Jennifer Banta, whose hand was being held by Shirley Colt. Chris gave Shirley a wink, ran across the courtroom, and, amid screams, dived headfirst through the courthouse window, followed by Man Killer.

Brandon looked at Elizabeth, ran to the judge's gun in the corner, picked it up, and ran to the window, diving out as the judge yelled, "Mr. Rudd!"

Colt had placed War Bonnet in the livery stable, where Hawk was also stabled. When they hit the ground, they both did somersaults, although Chris had suffered a cut along his forearm which was bleeding quite a bit. They immediately jumped on one of the many wagons running along the road and Colt pulled a shiny gold piece out of his pocket.

He said, "Get us to the livery stable! No, wait!"

Brandon had just dived out the window and Man Killer waved him to the wagon. Brandon ran after it, taking Man Killer's hand. The driver put the whip to the horses, and they roared the two blocks to Main Street in Westcliffe, and slid around the corner heading for the livery stable.

This was no easy feat, as the early 1880s were a boom period for Westcliffe, Silver Cliff, Rosita,

Canon City, Florence, and all the other smaller communities around Fremont and Custer counties. Because of the mining boom, people would take wagons up Copper Gulch from Canon City and would have to sit for up to an hour at the end of the road, a few miles north of Westcliffe, waiting for an opportunity to enter the heavy traffic going back and forth on the road. This was the same road, the Texas Creek road, which ran by the entrance to the Coyote Run Ranch.

There was also the road straight down to Wetmore, the oldest white settlement in Colorado, then the Hardscrabble Road to Florence. The other road to Canon City would be the Oak Creek Grade from Rosita down to Canon City. Colt knew that the gang probably would have taken one of these routes, knowing he and Man Killer would be hot on their trial, and he also knew that Preston Millard would not be stupid enough to try to lose them in the mountains.

Brandon rented a horse from the hostler while Colt and Man Killer saddled their horses. Chris was embarrassed, because he had used his fancy black saddle with tapadero stirrup covers and silver conchos all over it. Normally, like Man Killer, he used a U.S. cavalry issue McClellan saddle.

The three rode out of the livery stable and headed out of the town. Chris Colt stopped several incoming wagons and asked them where they came in from and if they saw a gang of mounted men riding away from town. Several saw Preston Millard and his gang headed down the Oak Creek Grade and all made various statements about the speed the gang was employing to make their getaway. One wagon driver saw them ride into some trees just off the grade, but said they reappeared again before he had gotten around the bend. Apparently they were going to try to hide in the mountains along Oak Creek but thought better of it. Colt figured that they would try to board a train at some point and get out of the territory more quickly.

All the wagons traveling up and down Oak Creek Grade wore bells on them. The road was so steep and winding in some places the bells were needed to warn oncoming wagons.

Colt, Brandon, and Man Killer rode their horses at a gallop, alternating with a fast trot. They tore down Oak Creek Grade and finally made it to the high ridge overlooking Canon City and Florence. Far off to the north, they could see the top parts of Pikes Peak and Cheyenne Mountain.

Down below them, Oak Creek Grade wound in a series of tight curves and dropped drastically.

Man Killer pointed and said, "Look!"

The three spotted the gang far below at the base of the curves, where the road straightened out and passed on down to both Canon City and Florence. Instead of taking the road, Colt plunged over the edge of the road, while several wagonloads of people gasped in amazement. Man Killer and Brandon Rudd followed, and the three men went down the mountainside through the oak brush, buckbrush, and scrub oaks which cluttered the mountainside. The drop was so steep that the three horses actually slid on their rumps part of the way down. Their legs were out straight in front of them acting as brakes, while the hind legs were drastically bent. Numerous rocks rolled down the mountainside in front of them, and people below stopped and moved their wagons out of the way.

Finally they reached the bottom, and the three took off after the gang at a fast gallop. Here the mountains rose up on their left and the countryside gave way to gently sloping meadows with occasional patches of scrub oak, cedar, and pĩnon off to their right side. Hawk and War Bonnet were sweating freely, but Brandon's rental horse was heavily lathered by now. They had to catch the fugitives shortly.

The Oak Creek Grade slowly descended, and soon the three men saw that a large rock wall rose up directly to their right while the high mountain ridges were on their left. The road, just two miles outside of the outer southern boundary of Canon City, suddenly took a sharp turn to the right and went through a break in the towering rock wall. It was as they made this right turn that they spotted the last of the gang trotting their horses around the bend just ahead.

With Colt in the lead, the three spurred their tired horses around the bend, pulling out guns, Brandon with the judge's pistol, and the other two hauling out their rifles.

Within minutes, they overtook the trailing members of the gang, and Chris Colt and Man Killer almost simultaneously fired their long guns over the men's heads. The entire gang, as one, slid their horses to a halt, and the three pursuers rode up on either side of the gang. The fugitives all raised their hands in the air and looked at the three with frightened looks on their faces.

Finally one in the group, who were all obviously cowboys, hollered out, "Hey, ain't you Chris Colt?"

Colt said, "Where is Preston Millard?"

Another puncher said, "You mean the fancy-pants with the expensive clothes?"

"Yes."

The puncher said, "Well, hell. We don't know. He give us these horses up at the top of the grade where he had us bring the wagons. He and his boys climbed on the wagons, and we took off to deliver these nags to Canon City as quick as we could, just like we was paid to do."

Brandon said, "Who paid you?"

The first puncher said, "A weasel with crazy eyes named Wolf. Used to be a deputy in Custer County. He told us to pick up these big wagons in Canon City with big wooden covered freight boxes built in. We had to bring them up the grade and pull them into this one grove of trees. Durn purty view of the Sangre de Cristos. We were just supposed to make coffee and smoke or whatever and wait and see if they wanted to change this group of horses for the wagons."

Colt put away his carbine and the other two followed suit. The punchers lowered their hands and relaxed.

The speaker went on, "If they didn't show till dark, we was to leave the wagons and hoof it to Rosita and git. But if they came, which they did, we was to be ready to switch and ride within one minute, or we wouldn't get our money. Got a pair of double eagles per man. That ain't bad, pardner."

Colt said, "You're right. Go on, men. We thought you were them."

Man Killer said, "Did any of them say where they were going?"

The second puncher said, "Hey, you speak good, Injun."

Man Killer said, "Thanks. You do, too."

A number of the men in the group laughed.

One of the other punchers said, "I heard thet Wolf

feller say sumthin' ta one of 'em 'bout how he couldn't wait ta git ta their town. Said sumpin' 'bout a Mexican gal with sweet lips."

"Their town?" Colt asked.

"Thet's what I heard. No doubt about thet."

Brandon, Colt, and Man Killer all gave each other blank looks.

Chris said to the men, "Sorry, boys."

The trio waved and rode on into Canon City, crossing the river at the lynching bridge, so named for obvious reasons.

They went straight to the Western Union office and sent a wire summoning the sheriff along with Shirley Colt. Five minutes later, a wire came in addressed to Chris:

Colt STOP Did u catch PM STOP

Chris wired back and forth several messages with the sheriff and suggested he immediately send out a posse on the road heading south toward Walsenberg and east toward Pueblo. He also sent a message that they would return to the ranch after dark. The train heading up Grape Creek had been a flop, basically, and the one from Hardscrabble as well. Brandon, however, made arrangements for them to board their horses on a freight heading up the Arkansas River Canyon. They could get off at Texas Creek and only have to ride about six or seven miles to the Coyote Run.

The men left their horses at the livery stable to be fed and watered, after Chris and Man Killer walked their mounts down and brushed and curried them. The hostler took care of Brandon's and told him that he would rent the horse out to someone going up to Westcliffe, Silver Cliff, or Rosita, as he and

the livery in Westcliffe had a cooperative agreement.

They went to Brandon Rudd's and got his horse,
guns, saddle, saddlebags, and bedroll. He had picked
up the new lineback buckskin gelding when he first
came to Canon City, and Colt really liked the way
the horse was put together. It stepped out like a real
mover.

When they arrived that night at the Coyote Run,
they were greeted by not only Shirley Colt, but Elizabeth Macon, Jennifer Banta, Sheriff Schoolfield,
and even Judge Offenbacher.

Over coffee and some of Shirley Colt's delicious
apple dumplings, the three men told of their chase,
the run-in with the cowpunchers outside Canon City,
and the details they learned about the escape of the
gang. Colt and the other two had easily deduced that
the entire gang had hidden inside the wooden boxes
built into the wagon beds. The problem was that
there were so many wagons coming and going from
the three towns in the hub of Custer County, it was
almost an impossible job to even spot wagons which
may be involved in suspicious activity. The traffic
was like that on a street of New York City.

Chris had figured that, if the fugitives were smart
enough to plan ahead to fool Man Killer and himself on the trail out of town, they would have had
more of an elaborate escape plan afterward. He and
Man Killer would have to carefully work out this
trail.

The first thing a scout learns is to read sign other
than tracks. An entire story can be worked out by
properly reading a man's trail. A good tracker can
see things that others cannot see.

Working out the trail of Preston Millard and his
gang was on the mind of Chris Colt and Man Killer
while they ate pie and drank coffee.

Man Killer thought back to the big campaign he and Chris Colt had spent so much time on. Chris Colt was the chief of scouts for the Ninth and Tenth cavalries, the buffalo soldiers, in their campaign to capture or kill the renegade Mimbres Apache chief Victorio. The Mexicans, not allowing the Americans to cross their border, finally killed the Apache leader, but Man Killer and Colt had been instrumental in the final accomplishment of the joint military mission. At one point, in Texas, Man Killer had been sent by Colt to be chief scout for the Tenth Cavalry, while Chris remained with the Ninth Cavalry in New Mexico. Man Killer showed the Tenth Cavalry commanding officer, Lieutenant Colonel Grierson, a little bit about reading an entire story on a trail.

The Nez Percé had gotten off his horse and was checking out some rocks. Lieutenant Colonel Grierson looked at Man Killer studying the rocks and tried to figure out how the Nez Percé scout could possibly ascertain anything about the Apaches from them. Man Killer walked over to the colonel and threw himself up into his McClellan saddle without the aid of a saddlehorn. He just leaped onto the tall Appaloosa's back. He was holding something in his left hand and kept looking closely at it.

Grierson said, "Did you learn anything from the rocks, Man Killer?"

The scout said, "Yes, a small group of Apaches came this way not long ago."

"What are you looking at?" Grierson asked.

"Manure," Man Killer said. "The droppings of the Apaches' horses can tell me a story about them."

"Like what?"

Man Killer said, "They can tell me what type of land this band of Apaches likes to stay in. The droppings may have cactus pulp, and I know what type of ground that cactus grows in, or it may have mountain grasses that only grow so high in the mountains, or there may be grain, which tells me that they are getting supplies from a reservation. Do you understand, Colonel?"

Grierson nodded and watched the scout ride ahead, his eyes scouring the ground and horizon.

They rode for another half hour when Man Killer rode back to Grierson.

"Come with me, please," he said.

The commander rode up ahead of the column, a small detail accompanying him. A half mile ahead of the column, Man Killer raised his hand and quickly dismounted. The colonel could see a fresh pile of horse droppings on the trail. He dismounted and joined the scout, kneeling down.

Man Killer said, "We were talking about droppings, Colonel, and I want to show you. See these tracks?"

The CO said, "Yes, I do. They're wearing shoes."

Man Killer said, "Yes, they are military shoes."

The colonel said, "There's no other cavalry unit in this area."

Man Killer said, "These are Mexican cavalry horses."

Grierson was certainly astounded and his face showed it.

"How in tarnation do you know, young man?"

Man Killer held up one of the fresh droppings. He pointed at whole corn kernels in the manure.

"See the maize and hay in the manure, Colonel Grierson?"

Grierson replied, "Yes."

Man Killer said, "Most times, a scout can tell Mexican cavalry shoes from American, but around here, they are much the same. The Mexican cavalry feeds their horses maize and hay, though. Your army feeds their horses barley and hay. That is how we can tell which is Mexican and which is American."

Grierson said, "Amazing. I didn't know that the Nez Percé were such incredible trackers."

"We are not," Man Killer said, "most Indians of most nations are equally as good."

"How did you get so knowledgeable?" Grierson asked.

"Chris Colt," he replied, "the mightiest scout of all."

Man Killer led him several feet farther and showed him a number of boot tracks.

The scout said, "You see, they stopped here, because this horse had a stone in the frog of his hoof. Here is the stone. See where the knife marked it when it was pried out?"

Grierson said, "You not only speak as well as any white man, I have never seen a tracker like you, Man Killer. I wonder why Mexican troops have crossed the border."

"They haven't, Colonel," the Nez Percé warrior said. "these are Apaches. They killed Mexican soldiers and stole their boots and horses and try to fool us."

Speaking to the adjutant, the colonel said, "Have you ever seen such a tracker?"

The lieutenant shook his head, saying with a thick Irish accent, "Never, Colonel Grierson. Never have I seen the likes a the young red lad here. I'd bet a pretty copper or two that the lad could trail a trout upstream and give the fish a one-day head start."

"How far ahead are they and how many?" Grierson had asked.

Man Killer had said, "There are seven of them and they are two hours ahead."

"How do you know how far ahead?"

"By how fresh the droppings are."

But now Chris Colt had to find out more about what the fugitives meant by "their town." Another thing that made a scout a truly good scout was the ability to recognize and use the talents of others who could help work out a trail. Colt thought that Brandon Rudd could probably figure out where this town was and what the name of it was a lot better than Colt himself would be able to do. The chief of scouts felt that Brandon Rudd could look at papers and read a trail in them the way Colt could look at the trail of a wild animal or a man.

A normal tracker, for example, if he was good, might see mountain lion tracks declare the lion to be 150 to 200 pounds in size and seven feet long and the tracks two days old. Chris Colt, however, had learned the ability to tell the difference between a male and female lion by the track. The male generally, as with many species, has larger tracks, but the tom lion's track has more rounded toe pads. A female's toe pads are also round but slightly pointed at the front.

Many trackers would look at deer or elk tracks and declare them to be those of a buck deer or bull elk because of the much larger tracks. Colt knew better. He had learned that many cow elk and many doe deer grew to large size or simply had larger hooves than average. Buck and bull elks, however, Colt had learned years before, had a growth in the rectum which made a slight groove on one side of the animal's pellet-type droppings. The females had perfectly round pellets. Most trackers did not know this, but that was just one of the things that separated Colt from most trackers.

Chapter 7

>>>>>>>>>>>>>>>>>>

The Chase

The men spoke long into the night and were invited to spend the night in the bunkhouse. The women stayed in the main house. Brandon left the next morning, along with the judge, sheriff, the two women, and a young teenage hand Joshua sent. Colt and Man Killer agreed to meet Brandon a little bit later, after he sent some telegraphs and got some answers.

Chris hated to leave Shirley again, but that was something they both expected because of the nature of the work he did. He and the Nez Percé ate some breakfast, then Man Killer went to help a little bit on Joshua's house, which was in the process of being built out beyond the old barn, on the bank of Texas Creek. While he did that, Chris played with Joseph. Shirley watched her husband playing with their little son in the yard and a tear came to her eye. After an hour, she knew it was time for the famous scout to leave, so she put on her best smile.

Shirley would always have to put up with a mistress, as long as she was married to Chris Colt. That mistress was history, and he was helping carve it out in the great American West. She could not deny that or hide from it, but had to learn to live with it in a positive way.

Not long after that, Chris emerged from the barn, looking resplendent on his majestic black and white stallion. Man Killer rode beside him, his black and white Appaloosa gelding prancing as proudly as War Bonnet. The men had full canteens and full saddle-bags and Man Killer led a packhorse, a blood bay about fifteen and a half hands tall, with supplies. All were tied in large bundles with diamond hitches over a wooden pack saddle.

They met Brandon in Westcliffe, just in time to load up on the mining freight and ride down to Canon City. Brandon had contacted several people and Sheriff Shaffer in Fremont County had some information for them.

In Canon City, they had coffee with the sheriff in his office and discovered he had learned that Preston Millard had actually spent much more time away from Fremont and Custer counties than he had spent in the counties. Checking at the railroad, the sheriff spoke with a conductor and the ticket agent, both of whom had remembered Millard making numerous trips to Santa Fe and back. Nobody had any idea why he had made so many trips, but several people remembered him leaving quite often.

Chris and Brandon had a short-lived argument about whether Brandon would accompany the two scouts, but Brandon won when explaining that this case had become personal with him. Brandon also explained that, from a professional point of view, it would not hurt his new reputation if he helped Chris and Man Killer find the wanted men and bring them back.

Colt had developed a tremendous amount of respect for Brandon, so his heart wasn't really in arguing too much. He and Man Killer had also been surprised to find that Brandon had purchased a Colt revolving twelve-gauge shotgun when he arrived in Westcliffe and had the blacksmith cut it down to an eighteen-inch barrel. Brandon explained, while boarding the train, "I have a carbine, but do not have the experience of fighting and shooting with a pistol, so I figured this would give me an additional advantage if we run into shooting trouble."

Colt said, "Well, Brandon, we certainly will have shooting trouble, but if you blast Millard with that, we'll have to carry his body back on several different pack mules."

The one thing Man Killer sometimes had trouble with was understanding jokes told in English, but he got this joke and laughed heartily.

Colt bought them all tickets on the next train south to Santa Fe. He also paid freight charges for the horses. The train would not leave until morning, so he got them rooms in the McClure House and took them both to dinner.

In his shared room with Man Killer, Colt explained, "If it was just you and me, we would ride in the stock car with the horses, but Brandon is an attorney and he is used to finer things."

Man Killer said, "Because of his work, he is treated with respect like a shaman or chief."

Colt said, "By some people—but many hate lawyers, until they need one."

Man Killer said, "I like Brandon Rudd. He would ride in the stock car with us if you asked. He is a good man."

"Yes, he is," Colt agreed. "I consider him a good friend."

Man Killer smiled. "Did you see how he looks at Elizabeth, and how she looks at him?"

Colt laughed and said, "Yes, I did. They look at each other the same way you and Jennifer look at each other."

Man Killer blushed bright red and threw a bar of soap at Colt, who ducked out of the way, laughing. The bar hit the wall with a loud thud. Man Killer laughed and picked up one of Colt's boots and tossed it at the big scout. He ducked and it, too, hit the wall.

They heard the door from the next room slam and footsteps approaching their door. There was a loud knock. Colt, still chuckling, opened the door. A giant of a cowboy stood there in long johns and wearing a holster and .44 revolver. He was furious and had the look of one who has been a bully most of his life.

Colt, smiling broadly, said, "Yes?"

The giant fumed, "Ah'm stayin' in that next room thar, an' I don't wanna heah no mo' noise, or somebody's gonna have some busted ribs and legs! Unnerstan'?"

Man Killer pointed at the man, looked at Chris, and burst out laughing. This made Colt start laughing madly also. The big man's face got even redder.

Chris pointed at the man's dirty long john bottoms and said, "Nice chaps, cowboy."

He and Man Killer laughed even louder, while the brute of a man got even angrier. Man Killer, tears running down both cheeks, pointed at the man's beet-red face. Colt chuckled loudly and slammed the door. He and Man Killer fell on the floor howling, tears streaking down their cheeks. In a mood of hilarity and merriment now, Colt jumped up and opened the door to see the angry bear just ready to knock the door down.

Colt looked at Man Killer and sheepishly, but still laughing, said, "Uh-oh."

The brute swung a ham-sized right fist at the head of the guffawing chief of scouts, but Colt ducked at the last millisecond and the man's fist slammed into the doorframe, splintering it and breaking two of his knuckles. The big man let out a shriek of pain.

Colt grabbed the man's hand and sympathetically said, "Oh, no, are you okay?"

Colt's right foot lashed out, the edge of it catching the man's kneecap, and the brute started jumping up and down, howling in pain. In the meantime, he tucked his injured hand under his armpit, and held his hurt knee up with the other. Chris Colt smiled at Man Killer and winked. He closed the door hard, hitting the bent-over man on the top of his head and hearing him crashing into the wall in the hallway.

The two men fell on the floor again, laughing. They laughed even more as they heard the man return to his room and slam his own door. They heard him apparently trip and fall once he was in his room.

In Santa Fe, the men stabled the horses and got more hotel rooms. Again, Colt insisted on paying.

Brandon said, "Look, Chris, this is costing you a lot of money and I am just fine staying in the mountains or sleeping in the livery stable."

Colt laughed and said, "I wouldn't say this to anyone else, but you are my attorney. I am wealthy. Don't worry about it, Brandon. I'm sure we'll get plenty of nights under the stars before we find Preston Millard."

Brandon had checked at the railroad station when they first arrived but could learn nothing about Preston Millard. Brandon then led the other two straight to the sheriff's office. He identified himself and the others to the sheriff.

The sheriff said, "The federal marshal's waitin' fer ya over ta the Bon Ton Café."

Colt was puzzled but went along and soon found himself in front of a U.S. marshal.

The man introduced himself and pulled out three badges with six-pointed stars. He handed one to each man. The silver-colored badges read, "Deputy U.S. Marshal," with the "U.S." in larger letters in the center.

The marshal said, "Mr. Rudd, the governor of Colorado sure thinks highly of you, but I have never sworn in an Indian as a deputy marshal before. Anyhow, I have a justice of the peace waitin' to swear ya'll in. C'mon. It's right around the corner."

They followed him and were soon standing with their hands on the Bible.

When it was Man Killer's turn, the justice of the peace said, "I have certainly never sworn an Indian in as a peace officer before, especially as a federal one."

Man Killer smiled and shocked the man with his educated tongue, saying, "Do not worry, sir. This is just temporary, until I shoot some white men. Then I'll give the badge back."

Colt and Brandon laughed and the marshal joined in.

The marshal handed Brandon a stack of warrants and said, "The names on these are blank, but the judge signed them all. Just fill in the names of each man you arrest, but the top two have Wolf Keeler's name and Preston Millard's already filled in. I would help you but am on another case right now. Good luck."

He shook hands with each, as did the justice of the peace.

They left, with Colt shaking his head. "The governor of Colorado sure thinks a lot of you. Tell me, Brandon, what kind of power are you going to have when you've lived here a few months?"

Brandon said, "He had told me to wire him if I ever needed anything. Just wanted to see if he was a man of his word. Apparently he is."

Man Killer said, "If I get mad at you now, great scout, can I shoot you and not hang?"

Colt grinned at him and said, "Yes, you can try, but will die from a bullet, not a rope."

That night, the three went to an apparently popular saloon.

Saloons in the Old West were like local news broadcasting locations. They were public meeting places where gossip was readily shared by one and all. Anybody who came into town who was a famous outlaw or well-known gunfighter was always spotted and the word spread like wildfire, which is what started happening within five minutes of Colt's entrance into the Sweet Bird Saloon. Anyone who seemed to be rich or evil was spoken about.

Colt ordered a beer, while Brandon had a glass of port.

The bartender made a face at Man Killer but looked at him for his order.

Man Killer said, "Give me a beer."

Colt said, "Give him a sarsaparilla."

Man Killer waited until the bartender walked away and said sarcastically, "Injun drink firewater. Go crazy, huh, Colt?"

Chris said, "No, not at all, but you are still a teenager, and I think alcohol affects younger people worse than it does full-grown adults."

Man Killer was angry, saying, "I am a man."

Colt smiled. "You sure are, but your body is not fully grown yet. Wait until it is before you put alcohol in it."

Man Killer was still angry. "Then why have you always shared tobacco with me? It makes people cough much."

Colt said, "Because tobacco is part of your spiritual life. It is used in religious ways with all nations. Alcohol is not."

Man Killer said, "I am a man. I can make my own decisions."

"That's right. You can. Go ahead and have a beer, and ride with someone else."

Man Killer stormed outside the bar, while Brandon and Colt watched his back.

Brandon said, "You were tough on him."

Colt said, "Probably, but I want him to wait until he's full-grown before he tries that stuff. I've seen too many people ruined by it, especially red men."

Brandon said, "Well, he was awfully steamed."

Chris said, "Well, he still is a boy in many ways, but he's had to be a man ever since he was about thirteen. We'll see if he handles this like a man or boy. That will tell a lot."

Brandon said, "I'll wager you he handles it like a man."

Man Killer walked in the saloon and returned to his spot next to Colt. He picked up his sarsaparilla and sipped from it.

The bartender said gruffly, "Thought you left, redskin."

Man Killer said, "I had to go outside and get rid of my water. Unless you wanted me to stay here and get rid of it on your bar, whiteskin?"

The bartender's face got bright red, and he walked away. Brandon elbowed Colt, and they both grinned slightly.

Man Killer said softly to Colt, "You have been like my older brother. No one else has. You are also my boss. Wise men seek your counsel, but I wanted to pretend to know more than you. It will not happen again."

Colt said, "Your body is almost a man's but not all the way. Yet in your mind and your heart, you are surely a man."

Man Killer looked over at his mentor, and Colt gave him a smile and a wink.

A gambler sat in the corner dealing poker, his back to the wall. Wearing a striped burgundy ascot, white ruffled shirt, and pin-striped suit, he had gold and diamond cuff links and tie pin, and a handsome gold and ruby ring on his little finger. The man clearly had money, lots of it, and would recognize money.

Colt left Brandon and Man Killer standing at the bar and walked over, taking the seat of a man who got up from the table in disgust, while the gambler raked in a large pot. Colt nodded at the man and pulled out two cigars, lighting one for the man and one for himself.

He said, "Mister, you look like a man who knows what's going on."

With a thick French accent, the man replied, "No, monsieur, I jus know zee cards in zee deck and zee moles on zee ladies from upstairs."

Colt pulled out some money. "What's the ante?"

One of the players, who looked like a well-to-do rancher, "Ten bucks, partner."

Colt anted and the gambler dealt him in, saying, "Seven stud."

Colt looked at his first two hole cards. They were both threes. He had an ace turned up.

The gambler said, "Ace bets, monsieur."

Chris looked at the other players' up cards, a jack, a queen, and another ace. He said, "What's the betting limit?"

The gambler said, "Pot limit, monsieur, weeth three raises per round."

Colt tossed out a double eagle and said, "Twenty bucks."

Everyone called and the gambler dealt more

cards. Colt had a three showing and the others got an eight, a nine, and the dealer got a second ace.

The dealer said, "Ace still bets, monsieur."

Colt bet another twenty and the dealer raised fifty. Chris tossed out fifty and called. The rancher folded.

The Frenchman dealt out the next cards. Colt got a four, the next man got a five, and the dealer a king. Colt bet twenty. The dealer raised fifty and Colt and the other man called.

On the fourth pass, Colt got yet another three, the second man a king, and the dealer another king.

Chris now had four threes and was sure the dealer would not fold, so he raised fifty after the dealer bet fifty on his two kings. The next man raised and again the dealer raised fifty. Colt raised another fifty, and he was called.

The dealer gave everyone the last card down and Chris looked once again at the table. The man next to him had four hearts showing on the table. Chris was glad. A flush would keep the man in the game. If the man only had four to a flush and raised, he might even be trying to bluff his way into the pot, which would be stupid, but it was often done. The dealer had two kings showing, but there was another on the table, and Chris figured him for a third king and maybe another pair with his down cards hiding it. A full house would not beat four of a kind.

The dealer, who still had two kings showing, held the betting. He bet two hundred dollars. Colt raised him two hundred. The man to Colt's left called. Good, Colt thought, he had a flush. The dealer had deduced that, but, seeing Colt's pair of threes, just figured him for a smaller full house than himself, for he had another king turned down plus a pair of aces.

He raised five hundred dollars and the man with the flush folded his cards and slammed them down.

Chris said, "I will call and raise you, pardner, but I have no funds on me. Can I write a promissory note? I can have the funds wired tomorrow."

"Hell, no, stranger. No notes in here," said a man who was obviously the saloon owner, walking over and pushing his way around the assembled crowd around the table.

The gambler said, "*Pardon moi,* Pat, but do you not know who zees man ees? He ees Chrees Colt, famous scout and gunfighter. He ees good for zee money."

A murmur went through the crowd and the owner said, "Oh, well, sure. If you're really Colt. Your word's good anywhere, sir."

Chris said, "Thank you." He raised his beer mug in salute to the gambler, who mirrored him with his little brandy glass.

Colt drew money out of the pile, saying, "I'm drawing light. See your hundred and raise you five hundred. If I win, you tell me whatever I want to know, but if you win, I'll throw another five hundred into the pot."

The gambler said, "I see your five hundred, Monsieur Colt, and agree weez your side deal. I weel also raise you one thousand dollars. Ah, eet ees games like thees that let's you know you are alive, *n'est-ce pas?*"

Colt said, "Naw, breathing generally lets me know that. I'll call." He drew light again as several people chuckled at his joke.

The gambler confidently turned over his hole cards. "Full house, my friend, kings over deuces. Eet beats your full house, *n'est-ce pas?*"

Grinning, Colt said, "It would if I had a full boat, but I just got some little trays."

He turned his cards over saying, "Four of them, in fact."

There were numerous whistles and comments of approval from the assembled onlookers. Colt raked in his money while the gambler smiled and shook his head in amazement.

He yelled to the owner, "Pat, drinks please for my friend Colt and his compadres."

Chris smiled, then leaned across the bar and shook hands, saying, "Quebec?"

The man said, "*Mais non, sacre bleu,* Monsieur Colt. I am from Paris. Why, before being *Canadien,* I would rather be a . . . a—"

Colt interrupted, "American?"

The gambler laughed and said, *"Mais oui."*

Both men chuckled, as Brandon and Man Killer sat down and the crowd went back to its serious drinking and faro games.

Colt introduced his friends, saying, "These are Man Killer and Brandon Rudd, my friends."

The man shook and said, *"Pardon moi,* I am Jacques Lucerne. Your friend here, gentlemen, knows cards the way I have heard he handles a gun or a trail."

Man Killer said, "This is only the second time I have seen him play."

Jacques looked at Chris with his eyebrow cocked. *"Que est ce que c'est?"*

Colt said, "I've sat down at a few tables before. Poker's okay."

The man laughed.

Jacques said, "My friend, weeth your ability at poker, you should play all the time."

Colt said, "No, thanks, I got a wife and kid. I'd lose them. Poker's fun sometimes, but I'd rather be in the saddle smelling the cedars."

"Ooh, sunlight!" Jacques said, screwing up his face. The three other men laughed at this.

Jacques went on, "I owe you answers, monsieur. That was our deal."

Colt said, "A man in his fifties, graying hair, handlebar mustache, name's Preston Millard. Has lots of men working for him, some gunslingers, some miners. Expensive clothes. He rides down here and back a lot from Colorado."

Jacques thought a minute and said, "Bad man, Monsieur Colt. Go north toward Taos. Somewhere around zere, he has a beeg ranch. I zink he owns a town."

Brandon said, "Owns?"

Jacques clarified, "I am not sure. I hear things, you know. I mean he controls a town, maybe. Who knows? Taos will have you close."

Colt tossed two hundred dollars from the pot and said, "Thanks Jacques."

Jacques made a face and pushed the money back. "I cannot take that, monsieur. Eenformation was part of our deal."

Colt stood up and stuffed his winnings into his pockets. He and the other two shook hands with Jacques.

The bartender came over, saying to Colt, "Usually if I have served someone who wins big, I get a big tip."

Colt said, "Tip. After insulting my friend here"— indicating Man Killer—"your damned lucky you didn't get a bullet from me."

Jacques laughed loudly as the bartender turned and fumed away, and the three Coloradans exited the saloon.

Brandon stared in awe out the window of the train as they rounded a bend on the western crest of the hill and overlooked the valley in which Taos lay. They had been traveling along a roadbed track laid along the fast-running Rio Grande. As they rounded the bend, the view opened out into a broad green valley, mountains all around. The sleepy little town of Taos, comprised mainly of adobe buildings, lay nestled against the base of the northern mountain range. The most amazing sight that stirred Brandon's soul, however, was the giant cut in the valley floor. This was where the Rio Grande had carved its way deeper and deeper through the green flat land. Brandon could not see the river, only a giant slice through the earth and the rock walls of the cut going straight down into the bowels of the earth. From that spot, he could only imagine the depth of the Rio Grande Canyon. It was an amazing view that could only really be appreciated by being there, and Brandon felt that this view made the whole trip worthwhile, even if he should be killed. Back in the East and the Midwest, there just were no views like that or like many that he had seen in the West. He knew why people always seemed to stay in the West or return to it. He could never leave, except for briefly. Brandon was now a westerner and always would be.

To add an exclamation point to the awe he was feeling, he saw a flock of buzzards fly off the train-struck carcass of a dead mule deer lying next to the tracks, only to circle with halfhearted effort and land on the feast again. Seconds later, he saw a magnificent bald eagle sweep down out of the heights and snatch up a jackrabbit near the left side of the train. Taking a second and firmer grab with its talons, the mighty bird winged skyward, carrying a nice meal to its young ones, perhaps. It would land on the edge of the aerie, tear shreds off the dead mammal and chew it up, then regurgitate it into the mouths of the young eaglets.

Brandon wiped away a little moistness from the corner of his left eye and turned his attention back to the train. Turning his head, he looked straight into the smiling face of Man Killer seated next to him.

The young scout said, "The rabbit cries out, 'Please do not kill me, Sister Eagle! I am but a rabbit and a tiny meal! The deer is a mighty and great meal.' But the eagle screams back, 'But my job is to kill you and feed you to my young babies, so they will become big and strong.' The rabbit then says, 'So they will kill more of my cousins,' and the eagle says, 'But that is your job, you and your cousins. To feed my children and my cousins.' You white men call this nature, Brandon. It is a good thing, but sometimes it can be hard and tough, but that is all part of it. You see this. I can read it in your heart. This is a good thing, too. It is the way of a warrior."

Brandon looked across at Colt, saying, "Are all Indians poets?"

Man Killer grinned. So did Colt, and he said, "Only the ones who really see with their eyes and hear with their ears. They have some folks who can't toe the scratch, either, just like the white man."

A little towheaded boy walked over to Chris Colt, paper and pencil in his hand. Wide-eyed, he handed them to Colt. "Mister Colt, can I have your auto . . . auto . . ." He turned to a pleasant-looking blond lady in a faded sun bonnet and calico dress.

She smiled at him and whispered, "Autograph."

The boy turned and proudly said, "Autograph?"

Colt smiled down at him and started writing. "I

don't know, pardner. Do you do lots of chores at home?"

The boy said proudly, "Yes, sir."

Colt said, "Well, in that case, it's my pleasure."

The boy looked at the autograph and held it up for his mother to see.

He said to Colt, "Mr. Colt, how can a boy grow up and become a famous scout like you?"

Chris winked at Brandon and said, "Two things you have to do, son. One, you have to study your three Rs every day and do all your chores. The other thing you have to do is just want to be a scout so bad that nobody can ever talk you out of it, no matter what."

The boy said, "That's it?"

Colt said, "That's it."

"Gosh, Mr. Colt, thank you very much."

"No, Sonny, thank *you* very much."

Man Killer and Brandon gave each other grins as they looked at their embarrassed friend looking out the window.

A woman suddenly screamed two seats back and a man rushed to her, carrying a bucket of water. She had dozed off reading a copy of *Blackstone* and a hot ash from the engine's smokestack had blown in the window and caught the pages on fire. The man poured the water on the smoldering book and tipped his hat.

Fanning herself from the fright, she thanked him and tried to catch her breath.

Referring to the constant problem on trains of hot ashes coming in the windows, Man Killer said, "If the white man wants to kill all my people, they should just make us all ride on your trains. We will catch on fire and burn up."

Colt and Brandon chuckled.

In Taos, nobody had ever heard of Preston

Millard, but a Navajo scout who had worked with Colt and Man Killer against Victorio knew something.

Colt, Man Killer, and Brandon sat with the scout, Bird Man, in his hogan and smoked cigarettes furnished by Colt. The scout's grandfather was also there, dark skin wrinkled like a piece of old dried leather. To Brandon the man looked to be 150 years old.

Brandon was learning by observing that Colt would not press this young man for information. When Bird Man was ready to tell what he knew, he would.

The man dug into the tin of peaches that Colt had given him and poured most of it into an earthern bowl for his grandfather, who ate it with relish.

Colt shared more cigarettes with the two Navajos.

Bird Man took a long puff and, pointing west, said, "On the trail the sun takes to sleep, along the top of the big gorge, at the feet of the big mountain, is a new white man's village. One man is chief there and the men who go there are bad white men."

Brandon said, "How do you know?"

Colt shook his head slightly and Brandon knew not to open his mouth again.

Colt said, "What is the name of this village?"

Bird Man said, "This I do not know, but all lodges there are new. None are old."

"Then we will find it easily," Colt said.

Bird Man said, "Yes, you will."

Colt asked, "What is the name of this chief?"

"Prentice Mills," came the reply.

Brandon and Man Killer both gave Colt smiles of satisfaction, of success.

Colt stood and the others followed suit. He

handed a pouch of tobacco to the old man, who did not even look at him.

Colt said, "Your grandson is a mighty scout."

Without looking up or changing expressions, the wrinkled one replied, "If he was not, he would not be my grandson."

Colt handed Bird Man five double eagles and said, "Your information has saved us many hours of work. You have done a good thing, my friend."

They left and, by way of explanation, Colt said to Brandon, "The Indians do not say thank you."

Brandon said, "Really. Why not?"

Man Killer said, "Because that is understood by both people."

Brandon mounted his horse and rode off after the two scouts, thinking about that.

They had to ride back far to the south, near where Brandon had first seen the giant Rio Grande Gorge, to cross. The gorge was so deep and the river so fast, it was not easy to locate a crossing place, but in the eddy at the tail of a section of rapids, someone had constructed a makeshift bridge.

They led the horses across one at a time. Colt offered to lead Brandon's across and let the attorney cross the bridge without a mount, but Brandon refused.

Colt asked, "Why?"

Rudd replied, "I heard Tex say something in Kansas one night that has stuck with me."

"What's that?"

"A cowboy always saddles his own horse."

Colt grinned.

The three men made night camp above the bank of the river in some cottonwoods.

The next day, they departed before daybreak for the new town under construction.

It was midday when they topped out on a little

knoll near the base of the western ridge overlooking the sweeping valley, and they saw below them a small town of new buildings and tents, with a very large mansion overlooking the whole community. A small stream ran down out of the mountains and next to the town.

The three made sure their badges were showing and rode down the knoll. War Bonnet was prancing as if he knew a fight was brewing. Man Killer felt a chill running down his spine.

He said, "Colt, something is wrong."

This alarmed Brandon.

Colt responded, "Yeah, I know. War Bonnet's sensing it, too."

"What should we do?"

Colt pulled out a cigar and lit it. "Well, you could go home and weave blankets."

Laughing, Man Killer made a mock swing with his rifle at Colt, which he now carried across the front of his saddle. Colt chuckled. Brandon Rudd had already seen this with these men and wondered if maybe other men were this way before battle. Humor was probably what they used to hide the extreme tension and pressures. It was probably used as a method to cope with fear as well, he thought.

As they got to the edge of the town, they saw a sign which read MILLSVILLE.

They rode into the town and everyone stopped what they were doing, men and women alike. People even came out of stores to look at the three.

Brandon, to break the tension, whispered, "I guess we are an unusual-looking trio."

Colt seemed not to even hear this remark. "You notice it?"

Man Killer said, "Yes."

"What?" Brandon whispered.

Man Killer said, "Look at all the people. Where

are all the children? Do the ladies not look like the kind of women who stay in the back of saloons?"

Brandon looked all around and realized they were right. This was very queer, he thought.

The three men rode to the town marshal's office, which was halfway down the street between two of the numerous saloons and gambling halls. The men noticed only a livery stable, small mercantile and feed store, and hotel, besides saloons. They saw no school, church, lawyers' offices, doctor's office, assayers, banks, or any of the other numerous businesses that were part of a small town.

They dismounted and walked into the marshal's office and Colt did not like what he saw. The town marshal sat with his boots up in the desk. He did not stand when the men came in the door. Chris did not like the looks of him at all, nor did Man Killer. He wore two six-guns, Colt standard Peacemakers, in tied-down holsters. The black concho-covered holsters were very well worn from hours of practice on quick draw and were tied down over black pin-striped pants. These were tucked into shiny high-top black boots with tall riding heels and large-roweled Mexican spurs similar to Chris and Joshua Colt's. He wore a black western bib shirt and black Stetson and shiny black scarf around his neck.

The young man had a black drooping mustache and a puckered scar that ran under his chin, along his jawline, and up in front of his right ear into the hairline. He smelled of some fancy perfume or cologne. The thing that was most noticeable, though, to both Chris and Man Killer, was the man's powder-blue, steel cold eyes. They had death in them.

This man was a professional gunfighter, and he did it more for fun than money. He had that look. Colt had seen it many times before.

Colt stuck out his hand and said, "Name's Colt. Deputy U.S. marshal, like my friends here. We're here to find a man named—"

The town marshal interrupted, "Nobody in their right mind swore in no red nigger as a deputy U.S. marshal."

Man Killer said, "Why don't you take my badge away from me?"

The town marshal stood up, his hands hovering near his guns. Now he had gotten himself into a situation and didn't know how to get out of it. He was just a small-town constable and these three were federal marshals. He could get himself attached to the wrong end of a rope real easily. He was also nervous about the way the Indian just smiled without even moving his hand close to his six-shooter.

Brandon diffused the situation by saying, "Well, Marshal, you obviously are looking for trouble, while we are looking for troublemakers. Since you don't want to help us, we'll just go find the county sheriff and get his help."

The marshal did not want trouble from the snooping sheriff. He had run the nosy lawman out of the town several times and knew he was suspicious.

The town marshal said, "Sorry, we don't like strangers much around here, and I get touchy at times."

Colt said, "You don't like strangers and you are a booming new town."

The marshal said, "Naw, there's just enough people here now."

Colt gave Man Killer and Brandon a sidelong glance.

The marshal stuck out his hand and shook with Colt, saying, "Sorry, Marshal. Name's Duke. Duke Wayne. Guess I'm edgy. Had a couple hard cases come in here a couple days ago. I had to plant 'em."

The three men shook with him and pulled up chairs. Colt and Man Killer both made mental notes to make sure there was no chair arm in the way in case they had to make a fast draw.

Colt almost laughed out loud, wanting to ask this supposed lawman if he thought that he had just frightened Colt or Man Killer with that phony statement.

Duke Wayne said, "Who you looking for?"

Colt said, "Mills. Prentice Mills."

Brandon added, "Also known as Preston Millard. And another man, named Wolf Keeler."

Wayne said, "Never heard of either of 'em, but you might want to try Sante Fe or Las Vegas."

Brandon said, "But the name of your town, Mr. Wayne, is Millsville."

Duke said, "Aw, it was named for some old miner that started the town. He got killed last year. Drowned crossing the Rio Grande."

Colt knew better but decided to play along. "Thanks, Marshal Wayne, we'll get a hotel room down the street and maybe you can ask around tonight. Maybe somebody will know something."

Duke Wayne said, "Yep, good idea. Livery stable's just past the hotel. See you tomorrow."

Colt and the other two left the office and mounted their horses outside. Man Killer leading the packhorse, they rode down the street toward the livery stable.

Brandon said, "This is a very queer deal."

Colt chuckled. "To say the least." He went on, "We'll get a hotel room temporarily. We'll watch him and see who he reports to as soon as we're out of sight. I'll also want to look inside that big mansion at the end of the street."

They checked their horses into the livery stable, gave them a rubdown and some grain, and hayed them. Water ran through each stall in a continuous spring-fed trough.

They walked out into the blinding sunlight and froze at the sound of at least one hundred guns being cocked. Literally every man in the town was pointing a gun at the trio. Even some of the women were leveling guns, too.

Colt looked at Man Killer and whispered, "On second thought, you and Brandon stay here and investigate Millard. I'll go back to the Rio Grande and go fishing."

Duke Wayne walked down the street, a triumphant smile on his face. He removed the three men's guns and tossed them to the town's men. He even knew about Colt's bowie knife down the back of his shirt.

Drawing his guns, he said, "You three are under arrest. Grab some sky, boys."

Brandon said, "We are deputy U.S. marshals. What are we being charged with?"

Duke laughed. "Hell, I don't know. I'll figure that out later."

Colt said, "Don't even bother trying anything legal, Brandon. We're getting railroaded."

Man Killer said, "All the people here are outlaws."

Hearing this, Duke laughed loudly. "We all work for Prentice Mills. He owns the town. He owns everything in it and all the people in it. You three were going to come in here and arrest him. There's a good one."

He prodded them into the jail, placing each in a separate cell. Duke stood back and chuckled. "Just wait till you go in front a the judge. I'm gonna have fun hanging you."

"What judge?" Brandon said.

"Prentice Mills," Duke answered. "He's the municipal judge and the mayor."

The three men slept most of the rest of that day and that night, each with his mind working on an escape plan. Getting out of the building by cutting, sawing, digging, or burning would be impossible, because the floors and walls were crisscrossed with steel bars.

The prisoners were fed twice each day, and at least the food was good. It was brought over, more often than not, by one of the many prostitutes who worked in the town. Colt, Man Killer, and Brandon each tried to strike up conversations with the women to get more information, but it was obvious that Preston Millard created a lot of fear among his employees. These women were apparently under strict orders not to speak with the prisoners.

One day, however, after a week and a half of internment, a young blond strumpet looked at Man Killer appraisingly and batter her long eyelashes, saying, "Yer cute. I ain't had me no Injun before."

Duke Wayne walked in just then and she quickly turned her head and walked out the door. Duke followed her out to flirt with her.

Colt and Brandon both stood up to the bars of their cells, which bounded Man Killer's

Colt said, "Man Killer, you have to work this woman."

Brandon said, "Yes, she has an interest in you. Keep it going until you can get information from her. Maybe you can get her to help us escape."

Man Killer stood with his arms folded across his chest, saying, "I love one woman. That is Jennifer Banta. I cannot do this thing."

Chris said, "Man Killer, we aren't telling you to fall in love with this woman. Just use her to help us get out of here. She gets paid all the time to be used. You just need to trick her into being used for free."

The Nez Percé said, "No, that would not be loyal to Jennifer."

Colt kicked the bed mattress and said, "Stupid kid."

Man Killer said, "I am a man."

Colt, angry, said, "Not now you're not. You're acting like a kid."

"You have often taught me to be loyal," Man Killer said.

"What about loyalty to your friends?" Brandon countered. "We are all going to be killed, and you might be able to play up to her and get us help. Jennifer would not consider that disloyal."

Man Killer looked out the window for a few minutes, then looked at each man and said, "That makes sense. I will pretend."

Two days later, the same young trollop came back, and the deputy on duty had gone out to the saloon for a beer.

Man Killer looked at the woman and said, "You are a beautiful white woman."

She fluttered her eyes. "Thank you, redskin. What's your name? Mine's Becky."

"I am called Man Killer."

"Ooh, that sounds dangerous," she cooed.

"I am dangerous, but before my name was Man Who Loves Much."

She smiled and said, "How did you get that name?"

Man Killer smiled back. "Come into my cell and I will show you."

Colt almost laughed out loud at the ridiculous, but apparently effective lines this boy was feeding this poor, naive young trollop.

She looked around and said, "I can't get into the cell."

Man Killer said, "Yes, the keys are in that desk."

She quickly ran to the desk and retrieved the keys, looked out the windows, and ran to his cell, unlocking the door.

She said, "I can get killed for this."

Man Killer rushed for the open cell door, but stopped dead in his tracks when Duke Wayne came in the door of the jail and drew both guns. His face turned several shades of red and contorted with rage. Duke walked forward and Becky started whimpering. He yanked her roughly out of the cell, slammed the door shut and locked it, retrieving the keys, and hurled her against the bars of another cell across the way.

Man Killer said, "It is not her fault!"

Duke Wayne dragged her roughly into the other room. He cuffed her to the rifle rack and walked out of the building without saying a word.

Fifteen minutes later, the trio finally got their first glimpse of Preston Millard since the trial. He walked in the building, followed by Wolf Keeler and several other gunslingers. He grabbed the woman by the hair and glared into her face. She sobbed hysterically. He motioned for Duke to uncuff her, and she was brought over in front of the three men.

Man Killer said, "She thought I was sick and dying and just came to check. I screamed in pain and pretended I was dying. Do not blame this girl."

Preston said, "This is my town. I can do whatever I want."

He grabbed the girl roughly by the hair, drew a gun from shoulder holster under his jacket, stuck the barrel up against her temple, and started squeezing the trigger.

Brandon screamed, "No!"

The gun went off, and the girl's dead body flew sideways and hit the floor. The three men stared in horror.

Colt stared at Preston Millard and said, "Millard, Mills, whatever your name is . . . I'm going to kill you."

Preston Millard felt a chill run down his spine. It was as if someone had just stepped on his grave. But he shook it off, laughing. "Do you know how safe and wonderful it is to own your own town, gentlemen? I also provide my men with everything: women, money, liquor. Who says you can't buy happiness? I can buy anything I want to make me happy, even loyalty. Oh, let's see, Mr. Colt, did you threaten me? That isn't very smart. I don't want any of you to die too quickly after we hold court, and I will sentence you to die. Let's see. You threatened a judge. Hmmm. I know, Wolf, cut off the little finger of his left hand and toss it to the curs in the street."

Colt felt the blood drain out of his head, but he mentally prepared himself. He would not let out a peep or whisper. In fact, he would smile and laugh. Preston Millard would not get the satisfaction of watching him be anything other than a man.

Wolf drew his gun and said, "Back up to the bars here and stick your hands through."

Colt sneered. "Go to hell, Keeler."

Duke grinned and drew one gun, sticking the barrel up and pointing it at the head of Brandon Rudd. Colt immediately stuck his hands backward through the bars and Wolf cuffed him that way, drawing his sheath knife.

Preston Millard said, "You see, Colt. Money can buy me anything I want: happiness, freedom, women, liquor, loyalty."

Keeler grabbed Chris's little finger and held it tightly.

The ex-deputy said, "Boss, ya want me ta just whack it off, or can I take my time and saw it off slow-like?"

Preston said, "Oh, help yourself, Wolf. Take your time."

Wolf started sawing on Colt's finger and Colt felt some of the most excruciating pain he had ever experienced. He blocked it out and looked over at Man Killer, smiling. Everyone in the room winced as they heard the bone being sawed through.

Colt said, "Man Killer, that reminds me, pardner. After we clean out this gang and get home to the ranch, we need to cut up some firewood for next winter."

Wolf cut the finger off and held it up in front of Colt's face.

Chris looked over at an ashen-faced Brandon Rudd and said, "That's his lunch. He's having finger food."

Wolf unlocked the cuffs and Colt turned, letting his bloody hand dangle at his side as if there were no injury at all.

He looked at Preston and said, "Is that all you want of us? I need my afternoon nap."

Millard said, "Toss that thing to the dogs. Duke, get that body out of here. Let people know that she did not obey the rules."

"Sure, Mr. Mills," Duke said.

Preston said, "We'll see how brave you are after you are sentenced and I decide how I want you to die. I can only promise this: It will be very slow and painful. Until then, you can just think about it."

He and Wolf started for the door, but then he stopped. "Oh, by the way. In case you think people will look for you, we sent a wire last week to your wife, Colt, saying it was from you. The wire told her that you fell in love with a rich greaser woman and were going to live out your days on her hacienda down in Mexico. The wire said that Rudd and the red nigger were killed in a gun battle."

The two men left the building and Wolf Keeler tossed the amputated finger to three dogs standing near the corner. A little black one grabbed it and ran between two buildings, growling a warning at the other two.

Between the buildings, a man, holding out a piece of antelope jerky, said, "Come, dog."

The dog ran over to him and sniffed the jerky, dropping the finger. The man grabbed it up off the ground and brushed the sand off of it.

Jennifer and Elizabeth both gagged, but Shirley Colt's eyes welled with tears, "That's Chris's finger. They're torturing him. Oh, God."

Then she stopped her crying and steeled herself once more to the task ahead.

Shirley had already decided to leave for New Mexico to save her husband when she got the wire, for she knew he would never leave her like that. If he did fall in love with some woman and want to run off with her, he would come and tell her face to face. She had gotten the other two women together and the three decided they would save the men they loved, because nobody else could. The lawmen they spoke to didn't have authority, jurisdiction, or maybe the gumption. When a Navajo scout rode into the Coyote Run on a lathered pony because he had been given a message by Bird Man that Colt was in trouble, big trouble, the women were on the next train south.

Shirley looked at Bird Man now and said, "We will stay here, but you must get help, Bird Man."

Bird Man said, "First, I see if Colt lives. Go hide in trees. I see. Then tell you. Go get help."

Brandon and Man Killer stared at Colt in worry and sympathy as he wrapped a piece of Brandon's scarf around the stump of his little finger. The two men could hardly believe his courage and stamina, as Colt stood there joking with them and whistling while Duke Wayne struggled with dragging the young woman's body outside. Man Killer felt horrible about her death.

Once they were alone, Colt immediately asked for something to make a bandage. He put a lot of pressure on the finger trying to get the bleeding stopped.

Brandon said, "What about your finger, Chris?"

Colt smiled and said, "God gave me nine spares. I'll get along without it."

Man Killer said, "Millard will pay for your finger and that girl's death with his life, my brother."

Brandon said, "Man Killer, we have warrants for his arrest. We have to try—"

Man Killer interrupted solemnly, "I have spoken."

Colt gave Brandon a little shake of his head, and Brandon didn't speak anymore. He understood. Man Killer had just made a blood oath.

It was an hour later when an Indian walked in with a broom, mop, and bucket of water.

The deputy sat up behind the desk where he had been dozing and said, "What the hell you doing here?"

Bird Man said, "Clean."

The deputy said, "We don't allow no niggers, blanket niggers, or beaners in this town, so how the hell did ya git in here?"

Bird Man struggled to remember the white man's name.

He said, "Mills hire me. Clean buildings. Me good Injun. Work hard."

The deputy leaned back and said, "Hell, you blanket niggers are just good fer scalpin' and collectin the bounty fer Apache hair. Go on, hurry up, and scrub up thet blood back thar by the cells."

Bird Man swept without looking up.

Colt, Brandon, and Man Killer were all excited.

Colt mouthed the words to the other two, *Something to write with*.

Both shook their heads. Colt nodded at Brandon for a piece of the man's white shirt.

Brandon quietly tore off a large piece from the back, handed the piece to Colt, and put the shirt back on, then replaced his jacket.

Colt removed his bandage and gritted his teeth, scraping the stump of his finger on the floor, causing the bleeding to start again.

With his own blood, Colt wrote; "HELP MILLSVILLE, NM JAIL NR TAOS COLT." He blew on the piece of cloth to dry the blood and waited by his bars for Bird Man to reach him as the scout swept and mopped. Bird Man didn't even look like he had noticed Colt or the others, but when he got up to Colt's cell, he reached out with one hand and took the cloth from the chief of scouts.

He finally looked up and Colt whispered, "Buffalo soldiers."

Bird Man nodded quickly and kept mopping.

The deputy called out, "Hey, nigger, yer too slow. Git outta here."

Bird Man shrugged and left the building.

As he walked back between the buildings with the mop and pail, a voice from behind stopped him. "Hey you, red nigger, where ya goin' with that?"

Bird Man did not move as the cowboy approached him from behind. The man pulled out his gun as he got closer. When he was right behind the scout, the Navajo jammed the handle of the mop straight back into the man's ribs. The wind left the cowboy with a rush and Bird Man struck the man's gun hand with the end of the handle.

He then dropped the mop against the building to his right and stepped on the handle, breaking it into two pieces. He grabbed the longest piece and jabbed its jagged end into the cowboy's throat. Eyes open so wide they looked like they would pop out, the cowboy grabbed the mop handle with both hands and Bird Man ran forward pulling the dying man into the trees. The man fell behind a bush, his body convulsed several times, and he died.

Bird Man turned and Shirley Colt stood there refusing to let herself be upset by the sight of the dead man.

She said, "Is my husband alive?"

He showed her the message and said, "Yes. I take to Fort Union."

She said, "No, I will rewrite the message and Elizabeth and Jennifer can escort you to the telegraph office in Taos and wire it."

Jennifer said, "Shirley, I think we all should go. We aren't going to leave you here alone."

Shirley said, "Okay, let's go. If we ride straight through, we can be back here by daybreak."

The three women, guns on their hips and in their rifle scabbards, and the Navajo scout saddled up and rode off for Taos.

The three prisoners were shoved roughly through the doors of the Golden Lizard Saloon and saw a large crowd of drunken outlaws. Preston Millard had gotten a black robe somewhere and sat behind the bar on a barstool.

He said, "Court is now in session. How do you three plead?"

Brandon said, "Not guilty."

Millard laughed and said, "You're liars. Guilty as charged. I sentence you to be hung by your arms tomorrow at sunrise and folks can walk by and whack you one with an ax handle or stab you with a sharp stick. This will go on all day, unless you three die too quick. Court's over. Get them out of here . . . Wait, on second thought, you'll die day after tomorrow. Give them another day to be scared."

They were taken back to their cells. Colt's finger stump throbbed like a toothache, and every once in a while it felt like the finger was still there and itching like the dickens.

In the cell, Colt said, "Well, there it is, boys. We have to figure out some way to escape, but I haven't come up with anything yet."

Brandon said, "Something will work out, somehow."

Colt said, "That is how we always survive, my brother. It is easy to give up and die, but sometimes it is harder for a man to believe he will win when it seems there is no way to win." He winked at Brandon.

That night, the three men lay on their beds staring up at the ceiling. Colt knew that Bird Man could not get to Fort Union with his message and back in time. Maybe, if he and Man Killer and Brandon took a long time to die, soldiers could get there before they were too far gone, he thought.

In Taos, accompanied by a Navajo scout, three lovely women—one a blond, one auburn-haired, and one brunette—rode through the middle of town, wearing blue jeans, shirts, cowboy hats, and six-guns on their hips. Those clothes could not hide their obvious features, though, and their appearance stopped people in the street, especially men, who stared in awe.

They rode up to the Western Union office, and Shirley went inside quickly. She sent a wire to Fort Union and was told the message was received. Shirley walked out, mounted up, and the women and scout turned back the way they had come. They took a couple steps, but reined up as a group of riders approached from the rear.

"Shirley, dagnabbit, hold up!"

The women turned around and saw Joshua Colt, Tex Westchester, Muley Hawkins, and all the new hands from the Coyote Run riding up.

Joshua said, "Why didn't you tell me you were coming after Chris and them, doggone it?"

"Because you have a ranch to run and cannot spare a hand," she said.

"Women," he fumed. "What kind of ranch would it be if Chris and Man Killer were dead?"

The relief seeing those men and hearing those particular words just hit Shirley in the pit of her stomach, and she bent her head over and started sobbing. Joshua rode forward, pulling right up next to her horse, and held her against his chest.

"I'm sorry, Joshua!" she sobbed. "They cut Chris's little finger off, Joshua! We have to save them!"

Jennifer and Elizabeth both came forward to comfort her, but Shirley stiffened up and dried her cheeks.

She said, "I'm sorry. That won't happen again. Thank you for coming, men, but any of you that wants to leave may go now and your job will not be in jeopardy. Mr. Colt, Man Killer, and Mr. Rudd are all being held and tortured in a jail in a town full of outlaws. Bird Man here watched them for days, and they are all bad men, every man in the town, and there are several hundred. If you want to return to the ranch, nobody will say a word."

Tex Westchester said, "Ma'am, they ain't no man from the Coyote Run whose gwine a tuck his tail betwixt his legs and run home. We all ride fer the brand, ma'am. 'Sides, if they was a man ta run, none of us would have nothin' ta do with 'im from now on, so he wouldn't be welcome back ta work. Now we gotta git goin'. We don't care what the odds is. Let's git this here fight over with so's we can git back to our cattle, and in Muley's case, the bunkhouse."

Big Muley Hawkins took a mock swing at Tex with his quirt and said, "Aw, Tex, quit yer shuckin' me all the time."

The group took off out of town at a fast trot.

The day after the sham trial, deputies kept coming in to the jail all day teasing the three men about dying the next morning.

Brandon told his friends, "I guarantee you that Millard told them to harass us today."

"Well, no matter how scared you might get," Colt said, "don't let them see an inch of it."

Man Killer said, "I am not scared."

Colt said, "I am."

"You are scared?" Brandon said.

Colt grinned at Man Killer and said, "Only a fool does not get scared when facing death."

Man Killer said, "I know that. I am not scared, because I do not believe we are facing death."

"Why is that?" Brandon said. "Because of Bird Man getting the message out?"

Man Killer said, "No, it is because of the telegraph Millard sent to Shirley. She will never believe that he would leave her. Shirley has help coming to us from somewhere."

Colt smiled.

It was around ten o'clock when Christina Braverman, a trollop from the saloon directly across from the jail, crossed the street. A pretty woman, she wore a shiny green low-cut dress.

Before she stepped onto the board sidewalk, she was summoned by a low hiss from between the buildings. She saw a woman with auburn hair standing there summoning her with her finger.

Christina walked over and stepped into the shadows. She didn't see Shirley Colt's right fist as it came from Shirley's hip. The punch caught Christina on the point of her jaw and sent her up on her tiptoes. She folded up like an accordion and fell to the ground. Muley Hawkins picked her up and carried her into the darker recesses of the space between the buildings.

Chris Colt, Brandon, and Man Killer all looked over to the door as the prostitute entered. Colt missed Shirley seeing the lady's beautiful long red hair flowing down her back and the gorgeous legs, as shapely as his lovely wife's.

The men stood up and watched as the woman leaned across the marshal's desk and stroked Duke Wayne's cheeks. The could see his chest rising and falling. He looked befuddled, in fact. The woman made him stand up, wrapped both his arms around her waist, and kissed him. She stepped back and unbuckled his gun belt, while he fumbled with the buttons on his shirt. Colt gave Brandon and Man Killer a grin and a look with his eyebrow cocked.

With her back turned to the marshal, she reached

up her long shapely leg and removed a garter. The phony lawman could hardly breathe seeing this; nor could the prisoners. Her hands went up her other leg while he licked his lips. Her hand suddenly whipped out and Colt saw a flash of steel in the lantern light. She had a blade in her hand, and she viciously drove it into Dukes's stomach, twisting the knife while he convulsed in excruciating pain. Finally the pair's bodies turned and the men saw that the temptress was Shirley Colt. Chris grinned broadly.

She grabbed Duke by the hair in the back of his head and said between clenched teeth, "Torture my husband, will you, you son of a—"

The man slid off the knife blade and dropped dead on the floor in a pool of his own blood. Shirley looked down at his body, gave a little whimper sound, then steeled herself again. She went through the drawers and found the keys, then ran to her husband, smiling.

He grinned and said, "How come you never kissed me like that before?"

She opened the cell door and flung herself into his arms, crying and kissing him all over. He held her tight, took the keys, and tossed them to Brandon, who, in turn, released Man Killer. The men ran into the office and retrieved their weapons, strapping them on.

Shirley said, "Follow me."

They followed her out into the night.

The gunman opened the door to the mansion and two harlots walked in.

He said, "What do ya want, ladies?"

The blonde said, "Mr. Mills sent for us."

He pointed up the stairs. They walked up and entered the double carved oak doors of the master bedroom. Preston Millard lay on his bed in silk pajamas and a smoking jacket.

He smiled, saying, "Well, this is a nice surprise. Get undressed and come here, girls."

They both bent over, reached up their skirts, and pulled out six-guns, cocking them. Millard literally wet himself, a large stain appearing on his silk pajamas.

Jennifer smiled at Elizabeth and said, "He's a real hero, isn't he?"

Elizabeth said, "Yeah, a real man. Better change your drawers, Millard. You're coming with us. We want to show you something."

He got some trousers from the maple bureau and looked embarrassingly at his wet pajamas.

Preston said, "Will you turn your heads, please?"

Elizabeth said, "And get shot in the back? Forget it, Millard."

He angrily removed his pajamas and underwear, dried himself, and pulled on his trousers. Then quickly he grabbed a gun from the dresser drawer and swung it toward the women.

"Look out!" Jennifer screamed, and shoved Elizabeth to the side.

At the same time, Jennifer planted her feet, cocked her pistol, and fired, her bullet crossing with Preston Millard's except his missed her head by inches and hers slammed into his breastbone and slammed him into the wall. Face ashen, his gun hand came up slowly and Elizabeth fired from the floor at the same time that Jennifer fired from her stance. Both bullets tore into his stomach and slammed him against the wall again, but this time Preston Millard was dead, very dead.

The women heard shooting downstairs and lots of shouts. Both dived behind the big oak-framed feather bed and aimed their guns at the door. Man

Killer, Brandon, and Muley, guns in hand, ran in the door.

Man Killer shouted, "Jennifer!"

The two women stood up smiling, and both men ran forward and swept them into their arms, kissing them both. They stepped back and looked at the bullet-riddled body of Preston Millard.

Elizabeth said, "Jennifer saved my life. She shoved me out of the way and fired the first shot into him, even though he was firing right at her head. She didn't move, just stood her ground and fired."

Man Killer gave her a squeeze. "Come," he said. "We must join Colt, quickly!"

The saloon doors opened and Chris Colt walked in, while his brother and Tex walked in the back door. Each man was followed by several hands from the Coyote Run and finally Shirley, carrying a greener. The place came to a standstill.

Colt whispered to Shirley, "I told you to wait."

She whispered, "Hush, you need every gun you can get. I want the rest of you back in one piece, even if your finger stays here," She winked at him. Even Shirley Colt could joke to relieve herself of fear and anxiety.

Wolf Keeler stood at the bar and turned around slowly. Colt walked forward.

Chris said, "I am a deputy U.S. marshal and have a signed warrant for your arrest, Keeler. I don't suppose you want to come along peacefully?"

Wolf laughed and Colt said, "Good, because I owe you for sawing off my finger. Grab iron."

Wolf said, "You ain't gonna git outta here alive, Colt."

Colt said, "It won't matter to you. You'll already be in hell, Keeler."

Wolf Keeler's eyes opened wide, and he grabbed for his guns. He heard two quick shots and something slammed hard into his stomach. He fell back against the bar and tried too bring up his gun. Chris Colt was walking forward, fanning his gun, flames coming out of it.

Bees kept stinging him and Wolf was hollering, "Get them off, Ma. Get them off."

Everything was black and something slammed hard into his face. It was the floor.

Wolf Keeler heard a voice say, "He's deader than a doornail."

Wolf felt a horrible surge of panic and wanted to scream *Help me,* but his voice didn't work.

He took one more breath and couldn't draw air into his lungs again. His mind knew this was happening, but he couldn't make himself breathe. He wanted to cry and bawl like a baby, be was so scared. He didn't want to die. But he did die.

Man Killer, Brandon, Muley, and the two women all burst into the saloon, but only to find the patrons all holding their hands in the air. One at a time, they were walking forward dropping their guns into an ice barrel behind the bar.

This was repeated in several other saloons in town, and each place was set afire, as the people were herded into the street. All watched their town burn, along with the big mansion at the end of the street.

One of the outlaws said, "This is like Hades."

Chris Colt said, "Not anymore."

Brandon told the townspeople, "The Ninth Cavalry is on the way and you all will be taken into custody. The three of us are deputized U.S. marshals and you assisted in our abduction and illegal bondage. You are all being charged as accomplices."

One of the outlaws in the street said to his riding partner, "What'd he say?"

"He said, we're in big trouble again, Rube," the partner replied. "Maybe hangin' trouble this time."

Rube said, "Aw, hell."

Standing in front of Judge Offenbacher's bench in the courthouse, Brandon said, "Your Honor, would you do us the honor of marrying us?"

Offenbacher smiled and joked, "I don't know. A good wife should stay home and bake pies and such, not go out and shoot bad men."

Shirley Colt said, "Judge, I would rather stay at home baking pies and such, because that is what I like to do, but make no mistake: If we need to fight for our families, we can and will."

He laughed and said, "I concur totally, Mrs. Colt, and you have earned my deepest respect, ma'am. Say, where is that young Man Killer?"

Colt said, "Oh, he's over at the Banta spread. Jennifer's got a rich uncle who wants her to come back East and go to a finishing school. Man Killer's over there giving her every reason in the world why she shouldn't go."

The judge, still smiling, said, "Now, Mrs. Colt, aren't you worried people will consider you one of those angry suffragettes?"

Shirley said, "If Joseph has a tummyache in the middle of the night, Judge, I awaken, Chris does not; it is instinctive with me. But if a grizzly wanders too close to the house without even making a sound, Chris is out of bed with a gun to protect his family; it is instinctive with him. I can protect my family, too, but I like it this way. There are differences between men and women, and I love them. That's the way it should be. Men are not any tougher than women, but we don't need to hold a contest with them to prove they are not. I love being a woman, period."

Clean bandage on his finger stump, Chris Colt said, "And I love you being a woman, too. Looks like we're all proof that Preston Millard was totally wrong."

"How's that, Mr. Colt?"

Chris said, "Millard thought money was the most powerful thing in the world, but love is more powerful than anything."

A few miles away, Jennifer Banta looked deep into Man Killer's dark eyes and saw nothing but love. Back in the court, the same thing was seen between Brandon Rudd and Elizabeth Macon, and between Chris and Shirley Colt.

High up in the Sangre de Cristos, a magnificent bald eagle swept down from the sky and tried to grab a snowshoe hare in her mighty talons, but missed. Her mate watched from the edge of the big heavy aerie built in the fork of an old gnarled cedar on the edge of a cliff. His wise eyes looked over at their squawking eaglets, then back to his mate thousands of feet below. She missed another pass at the snowshoe, and the big male aimed his white feathered head at the ground below. His powerful wings beat several times, then swept back as he streamlined himself for the powerful dive. As he had done so many times in the past, the male eagle swept past his mate and spread his wings at the last second to brake his dive, his legs stretching out, talons apart. He grabbed the rabbit up in his mighty talons and bit the back of its neck. The death was swift. He swept up, then back down and lit softly on the ground, leaving the prize for his mate to pick up.

The West was still tough and untamed, but was gradually becoming civilized, not so much because of the power of guns, or even the law, but because of the powers of love and survival. Those two powers went hand in hand in the settling of the Old West, the land of the strong.

"Taut, highly literate . . . Barbara Parker is a bright new talent."—Tony Hillerman

"Superb . . . masterful suspense . . . hot, smoldering, and tangy."—Boston Sunday Herald

SUSPICION OF INNOCENCE
by Barbara Parker

This riveting, high-tension legal thriller written by a former prosecutor draws you into hot and dangerous Miami, where Gail Connor is suddenly caught in the closing jaws of the legal system and is about to discover the other side of the law. . . .

"A stunning, page-turner!"—Detroit Free Press

"A fast-moving thriller . . . charged Florida atmosphere, erotic love and convincing portrayals make it worth the trip."—San Francisco Chronicle

Available now from **SIGNET**